MW00584042

THE SON

ELENA WILKES

Storm
PUBLISHING

This is a work of fiction. Names, characters, business, events and incidents are the products of the author's imagination. Any resemblance to actual persons, living or dead, or actual events is purely coincidental.

Copyright © Elena Wilkes, 2023

The moral right of the author has been asserted.

All rights reserved. No part of this book may be reproduced or used in any manner without the prior written permission of the copyright owner.

To request permissions, contact the publisher at rights@stormpublishing.co

Ebook ISBN: 978-1-80508-261-3
Paperback ISBN: 978-1-80508-263-7

Cover design: Emma Graves
Cover images: Arcangel

Published by Storm Publishing.
For further information, visit:
www.stormpublishing.co

ALSO BY ELENA WILKES

The Man I Married

Keep My Secrets

In Memory of Annie

PROLOGUE

She has no idea she's about to be chosen.

She walks down the street, the soles of her boots squealing against the wet pavement. Gusts of noise and laughter ricochet into the darkness and her pace slows. The entrance to the bar up ahead swings open with a bounce of light, squeezing down to a strip of white. There's a guy on the door. He's huge: a craggy head swallowed into the mountain range of his shoulders.

She wants to turn around right now.

No one would care, would they?

She could go home and take off the layers of makeup and too tight clothes and watch some reality dating on TV. It's the horror of that thought that keeps her feet moving forward.

You're not going to meet anyone sitting in your room, are you?

Like Libby said, she has to put herself out there. She has to make the effort.

She reaches the entrance. The huge guy steps back with a slight incline of the head as though he's been expecting her. She

wavers an uncertain smile as she steps past him, aware of his
eyes drinking in her hair, her breasts. She instinctively pulls her
jacket closer as she half-pushes, half-shoulders the saloon door
wide, stepping over the threshold into the heat of people and
noise.

This place is new. A thrum of excitement shivers through
her. *Something's going to happen tonight: something that could
change everything.*

She can feel it.

There's a dance floor off in the distance: the whorl of
coloured lights spins amongst the jostling bodies and waving
hands. The bar is tightly packed with people but she can't
see Lib.

Gusts of laughter, hooting shouts, music blaring, the snug
heat of too many shoulders pressed together. It's difficult to
breathe.

She has no sense of the pair of quiet eyes watching her.

She tries to look around casually, wanting to see someone,
anyone she might know. She sets her mouth in a slight upward
curve to hide her awkward discomfort. Her fevered eyes scan
back and forth.

Something feels off.

You're overthinking things again. Relax.

The eyes hone in.

The whole time her gut jangles, her body knowing instinctively the things her head refuses to accept.

You're overreacting.

You just need to chill.

Some girls look over. Their glances slide across her; they see
someone pretty, dressed in that casual, slightly sexy way: tight
short skirt, Doc Martens, denim jacket, a girl who's easy in her
own skin.

A gang of lads barge her out of the way.

'Oops! Sorry... sorry...' she says to the elbows and backs. No one hears her. No one's looking. Why would they? They sense the girl beneath the clothes and the makeup. *Not a laugh, no game. Dull as dirt.*

She's suddenly aware of a guy's eyes slanting across her as he makes his way past. Her hand instinctively come up to push back her hair that swings to hide her face.

'Sorry...' She tucks a strand behind her ear, but it only falls again.

'No, you first. Please—' He steps back. 'Oh!'

He has barged someone carrying a tray of drinks. They teeter alarmingly, sloshing over the sides. She automatically reaches out and grabs one, saving the whole thing from disaster.

'Wow! That was close!' she says, laughing nervously.

But the guy with the tray only glares. 'Why choose to stand in everyone's way?' He shakes his head. 'Prick.'

'Shall we move?' The guy ignores the comment, unbothered by it. His voice is nice: friendly. 'Over here, maybe?' He's smilingly apologetically.

Attractive, her head says.

She nods quickly, wanting to defuse the situation as he gestures the way through, arm outstretched, to a quiet corner. She slides into it, aware suddenly that her back is against the wall.

'I'm not crazy about clubs and bars, are you?' He has brown straight hair and hazel eyes. They're kind eyes.

'No.' She shakes her head and smiles, unable to think what to say. His attractiveness pushes everything away, making her tongue-tied. All thoughts of what to say next fly out of her head. She hopes her encouraging smile will tell him what her mouth can't.

'Can I get you a drink?'

She looks across at the crush. 'No... No it's fine. I should be meeting my friend here.' She smiles again, wanting to keep the conversation going. 'I don't really know whose party it is. Do you?'

He shakes his head. 'Yeah, I've also got a mate around somewhere, but look like he's bailed on me.' He pulls a comic face. 'Clearly he's found someone else more interesting. Wonder if he's found your friend?' He grins. 'I mean, here we are and we're both stood here like a pair of billy-no-mates. Maybe we both should've stayed home and found something good on Netflix.'

'Yeah, yeah!' She laughs. 'Maybe we should!'

Did that sound rude?

'But now I've met you...'

She can't meet his look.

'I didn't even have anything to eat before I came out,' he tuts.

'Me neither,' she admits.

'You don't want pizza, do you?'

'Pizza?'

'Yeah, would you like to get pizza? We could share.'

'Oh, I don't know.'

'It's okay, I'll split it down the middle like a barrier.' He grins, holding out his hand. 'Your half, my half. All very respectful.' He laughs, his finger making a line down his palm. 'I'm starving. Go on. What d'you say?'

He's jokey and wanting to play. Plus, it's only pizza. Pizza can't be dangerous.

'How about I throw in a can of Fanta? Will that do it?'

She takes a sharp intake of breath. 'Ooh... I think that's just sealed the deal.'

She's playing right back at him. She relaxes a little, laughing; they're matched, equals now. She touches her hair again, but he stops her hand. It feels very intimate.

'I should message my friend.' She reaches for her phone.

'Sure you should.'

She's aware of him glancing over her shoulder as she hastily types, deletes, and types again. Awkward. *What should she say?*

It pings immediately back.

She reads it and laughs. 'She's met a guy.'

'Really?' He cocks an eyebrow.

'He's invited her to an after-party. She's sent me the address. She says I should come.'

'And do you want to?'

The question feels loaded. 'Yes and no.' She's glad it's dark. He can't see she's blushing.

'You could always invite me as your guest.' He's smiling at her. He has dimples. Her stomach somersaults.

'Food first though.' She raises an eyebrow. 'And the Fanta, don't forget.'

'Come on then' – he holds out his hand – 'I don't want to lose you.'

His fingers feel warm and soft as he jostles his way through the sea of people.

He's holding my hand! She keeps giggling. His palm is soft, but his grip is firm; she feels breathless suddenly, as though she might burst into laughter any moment. They clatter through the door and the bouncer turns in surprise. He doesn't look her over now, shifting away disinterested, shucking up his jacket.

It's raining a little. The night air surrounds them; it feels different: fresher, lighter. He hasn't let go of her hand. She's exhilarated. This is funny, daring, sweet – romantic, almost.

'It's this way,' he says.

'But I don't even know—' She wants to question him more, but the moment of asking his name is lost as he glances quickly right and left, leading her across the road towards a side street. A car's yellow immobiliser bleeps, blinking into the darkness. There's a moment. She wavers. She hadn't considered how she'd get to the pizza or to the party.

But I've just invited him. I've agreed to it all. I can't back out now.

He lets go of her hand, pulling the door open. The interior yawns into shadows.

'Ten minutes to the pizza place – five with no traffic. It's not far. You'll have to give me the address of this after-party.'

There's a second's hesitation: the pit of darkness in front of her, the stillness of the street, when a sudden hoot of ill-disciplined laughter explodes into the darkness behind them. There's a scuffle of lads yelping and shouting.

'Looks like the fun's about to start.' The guy tips his chin in their direction. 'Plus we're gonna get soaked if we stand out here much longer.' He runs around, getting in behind the wheel. She's caught, suddenly alone. Every choice feels difficult. Weird.

What would Lib do? She'd say pretend. Fake it till you make it. She imagines Lib's face when she shows up with a guy! It'll be a hoot. A foursome!

Sliding one leg into the footwell, she eases her weight from the world outside to this new exciting one, playfully grinning back at him, jokey, but challenging too: *I'm fun. I'm a laugh. I'm not scared.*

The door closes tight and flush. The side of his face looks strange in the grey light. Her gut antenna flickers a warning, but she turns it off.

Enjoy this moment, for goodness' sake...

'What did you say your name was?' she says, smiling. He turns the engine over and the doors automatically lock.

'I know yours.' He looks across at her. 'You're "Brave".'

She laughs along as he pulls away, uncertain now, glancing out into the road where the white lines on the tarmac are picked out by the headlights. They flit by in a stream, faster and faster beneath the spin of the wheels, her heart rate quickening, the black tunnel of darkness looming up ahead as they plunge towards it.

Nothing bad is going to happen, she tells herself. *Enjoy. Be happy. He could be the one you've been waiting for. What's the matter?*

You should be grateful someone even noticed you at all.

ONE

'Everything okay?'

I glance across the table at Joe. He has his phone in one hand and fork poised in the other. His hair drops annoyingly into his eyes but he leaves it there. He doesn't answer my question. A blob of gravy drips, sliding over the edge of his plate. There was a time when he would have casually shared who he was messaging. But not now.

Drew is busy piling food onto his fork. He darts a look at me and swallows uncomfortably. I know he's doing his best – he's got this stepfather deal sussed far better than I could've hoped and I'm the one who's supposed to know what I'm doing.

Pressing my lips together, I look down at the mound of food on my plate, knowing I'm not going to be able to eat any more. Glancing across again, I itch to point out that Joe's dinner is getting cold.

I pick up my wine glass. Joe's fork drops with a clatter. He frowns at the phone screen, his head dipping, his unwashed hair falling into his eyes again as his thumbs jerk and flick at an impossible speed.

My gut tells me that whoever, *whatever* this is isn't good, but I breathe the anxiety away. He's still my little boy, despite it all. His wrist pokes from the cuff of his sweatshirt. They're still childishly thin for the size of his hands – his man's hands now, no longer small and endlessly grubby-looking no matter how often I washed them.

Look, Mummy! The way he'd bring something in that he'd found in the garden, tiny fingers cupped, caging a thing, no matter what it was: a bug, a dying butterfly, an empty snail shell...

There's a faint squeal as he slews his chair back a little, dinner forgotten – whoever it is, whatever they're saying, taking all his attention. He types frantically in a furrow of concentration.

I've been shut out. I stare at his bowed head, at the tiny point of hair, like an arrowhead in the nape of his neck. A wave of something, absolute love – worry, definitely – squeezes tight. I put my fork down and blink a look at Drew. He picks up on my meaning. There's a moment's pause.

'What you up to tonight?' Drew says brightly.

Joe instantly looks up, eyebrows attentive, open. He half smiles and shrugs. 'Bit of this, bit of that.'

They share a humorous wink. My son visibly thaws. I bite my lip.

'I'm out with Nate later.'

I gaze at the splash of gravy.

'You going to Cahoots again?' Drew is simultaneously questioning and encouraging in a way I wish I was able to be.

'How d'you know about Cahoots?' Joe sounds almost admiring. 'Bit young and hip for you, isn't it?' He drawls the words, taking the mickey.

But Drew adeptly swerves the question. 'Is it the beer or the girls that're the attraction?' He winks.

In these split-seconds I see how quickly their relationship has cemented. There's a pang of jealousy: tiny but it's there. I smile to cover it, picking up my wine glass and taking a sip. It sticks in my throat, making me cough a little.

'Or both?' Drew gives him a sideways glance.

'Nate's worked out how to nick his mum's car so she never notices.'

Joe is being deliberately provocative, checking my reaction at his mention of Sarah. I pick up my plate, pretending I haven't heard.

His gaze follows me upward. 'Bet she hasn't said anything, has she, Beth?'

This new thing of him using my first name rankles.

'Go on. Has she?' he pushes.

I pause. 'Is this a wind-up, Joe? You're not being serious.'

'Deathly.' He googles his eyes at me.

I take a deep breath. 'Honestly, Joe, this is—'

'Oh, you're not gonna drop me in it now and tell her, are you?'

'What I'm saying is, if the car thing is meant to be a joke, it's not funny.'

'It was only the once,' he mumbles.

I can tell by the hitch of his shoulder and the way his eyes shift he's not telling me the truth.

I gather the plates together. 'Right... Well, for now, no one's going to tell anyone anything—'

Drew shoots me a look that I know Joe sees.

'However,' Drew says firmly.

We both look at him.

'However, can I suggest you talk your friend out of being such a twit? The last thing anyone wants is Sarah reporting her car stolen and then you two get pulled over.' Drew's still smiling, but it's clear he means it. 'I mean, can you imagine if I'm the copper who stops you. How would that go down?'

Joe colours. His gaze flits from Drew to me and back again.

'We know you're a clever lad. We know how bright you are,

so there's no need to start doing stupid things like ask me to fish either of you out of a Friday night police cell. If you do, I might be forced to leave you there with the piss-heads and the pukers.'

Despite his embarrassment, Joe flickers a smile as he goes to stand.

'Yeah?' Drew's eyes follow him upward. 'You're not going to do anything bonkers like take someone's car. Do we have a deal?'

I see Joe's neck has prickled into a blotchy red.

I instantly want to rescue him – make excuses – *yet at the same time...*

Joe glances down at me, questioning. I know what he must be thinking: *Drew's not his dad. He can't tell him what to do.* He's embarrassing him, treating him like a kid.

My spine stiffens with dread. *I know what happens next...*

The chair squeals again as Joe knocks against it, making for the door.

'Yeah, we have a deal.' Joe hunches affably. 'I'll sort it with Nate.'

My stomach quails with relief. 'See you later.'

The door slams shut.

I hear the thump on the stairs and then a crash overhead.

I let out an exhale of anxiety. 'Wow!' I slump back in my seat. 'Wow!'

'I shouldn't have said anything, should I? I should have left it to you.'

'No, Drew. You were great.' There's a tiny itch of irritation, but I instantly quash it. I so want him to feel like he's Joe's dad. 'You handled it perfectly.'

I listen for movement overhead, because deep down I'm not so sure this is over.

Joe *is* bright, he's right. Bright and charming enough to say whatever you want to hear.

'Kids, isn't it?' Drew pulls a wry face. 'They say stuff to get a reaction, don't they? Hell, I don't know... I'm new to all this.'

'Well, you're doing a really good job,' I reassure him.

It's the constant eggshell feeling: the tiptoeing around every situation, wanting to know what's really going on.

'He's easy in comparison to the kids I normally have to contend with.' Drew scratches his stomach through his shirt, satisfied. 'Yeah, I get it though. Teenage boys. Tricky age. Me, moving in... It's a lot when you don't know what's going on inside his head.'

Dear, decent Drew. If only you had a clue how true that statement is. I can't describe the fear I have every time Joe's alone in his room: that sick-shiver of creeping up to stand outside his door, listening, wondering what he's thinking... what he's doing...

I shake the thoughts out of my head and attempt to change the subject. 'I know, I know, but—'

'Yeah, I get it. You're scared how these things can escalate.'

'It's not just the thing about Sarah's car.'

'It's the endless texting too?'

I nod. 'I don't want to make a big deal of something if it's nothing. What do you think? He's got it on silent, but it's lighting up constantly, and then he's messaging someone day and night.'

'It's probably a girl he's crazy about.'

Drew means well. I know that, he just doesn't get it.

'It's not. I got Sarah to ask Nate on the quiet and I don't think there's any girl.' I blow out my cheeks, exasperated. 'It's just he's different somehow. Secretive. And it bothers me. Then there's this bar I've never heard him mention before – what is this Cahoots place anyway?'

'It's just a place in the city centre,' Drew explains. 'They have live bands. It's fine. Honestly. I'd say if it wasn't.'

I take a breath. 'He's *seventeen* though, Drew. I mean, I

know we've all done it.' I pick up the rest of the plates and roughly shove the knives and forks together. 'And what about Sarah's car? I don't know if I should say something to her. What do you think?'

'I think you should leave all that.'

I'm suddenly aware of Drew's hands stopping my jerky movements, gently taking the cutlery, gathering the crockery.

I glance at the clock. 'No, Drew, you're on late shift,' I protest. 'You haven't got time to mess about with washing up!'

But he holds the plates away from me defiantly. 'I know all this is upsetting you, Beth. Take your wine and go and sit down in the other room. It won't take me five minutes to load the dishwasher. You've done enough.'

'It's fine.'

Drew takes a breath. 'No, it's not. I get you're upset and me saying "don't worry" is pointless. Of course you worry. It's in your job description.' He smiles.

I watch as he loads the plates into the machine.

'It's just this is a new thing... this secrecy business. He's never been like this before.'

Drew pulls a mock grimace as he straightens. 'You mean before I came on the scene.'

He's joking, but I don't want him to even joke that things aren't perfect; *he's* perfect. Perfect for me. Everyone says so.

'Don't be silly – it's absolutely not you. You're so good with him. He really likes you. I even think he'd open up to you more than he would to me, it's just... Well, something just doesn't feel right.' I know I can't explain it properly. 'I think... I think— Oh, I don't know!'

Drew gently unwraps my fingers from the final knife I'm clutching, dropping it into the cutlery basket as he pulls me to him. I nestle into the warm softness of his chest.

'Well, be concerned by all means, but don't *overthink* the thing.' His voice sounds smiley as it booms into my ear. I know he's trying to nudge me into seeing that I'm overreacting. I bury my face deeper into the comforting darkness of his sweater and breathe him in.

'Let me tell you, lads of seventeen do far worse things than borrow their mum's car and have a sneaky pint of lager.'

He's right. I know he's right.

'Plus, you're carrying on as though you're alone in this. You're not a single parent anymore, Beth. I've told you: I'm here now. Whatever it is, we'll sort it. We can sort anything as long as we're a team.'

I nod without opening my eyes. *I know this. I know I need to chill out a bit.*

'Joe's a kid. Kids push boundaries. I'm a copper, Beth! If there's something going on out there, I'll get to hear about it before anyone else.' His hands wind into my hair, pulling my head back and gazing into my eyes. 'I'll look out for him; I promise you. Will that do for now?' He smiles at me, and I feel myself relax just a little.

'That'll do me.' I smile back. 'And not just for now.'

'Well, I'm not going anywhere.' He tenderly stokes the hair back from my forehead.

'Do you promise?' Wrapping my arms around him, I hold him close.

'I promise.'

You're lucky, my head tells me. *To have met someone who cares. Really cares.*

I'd prayed for someone like Drew. All I'd ever wanted was a real partner, who would love me and love Joe, and be *there* for me in the way that I'd be there for them.

'I'll never set the world alight, I told you that from the off, but if you want loyal, if you want broad shoulders, I'm your man.'

How many times had he said that to me?

That serendipitous barbeque at Sarah's and there he was with his pinny on: beer in one hand, spatula in the other, 'helping out' but actually cremating a ton of sausages in plumes of smoke.

'*Beth, Drew – Drew, Beth.*' Sarah had squinted, coughing, but I saw the smirk as she left the two of us alone. I remember thinking how square and solid he was as he asked all about my life, admiring my four part-time jobs, congratulating me on bringing up a child, nodding at how stressful it must be: the struggles I'd had to face alone.

He was easy to talk to. I found myself opening up: about the never-ending anxiety, money, work, my mother's judgement – as I left a little child all day. Then the pre-teen years, that bewildering time when I never knew whether it would be my sweet boy I'd wake up for school in the morning, or some surly resentful kid I didn't recognise.

I'd stopped talking, looking away for a moment, embarrassed.

'*I don't normally go on about myself so much. I'm so sorry, I must come over as utterly boring.*'

'*So... can we go out sometime? Would that be okay?*' He'd looked at me and smiled at my blushes.

In a matter of weeks, he'd lifted me out of my old life and shown me a new one. Not chaotic – ordered. Not irresponsible – steady. All I had to do was say 'yes'.

'Uh-huh.' I lift my head and gaze up at him now. 'I'm so lucky to have you.'

'So will you think about chilling out a bit?'

I'm aware that my smile feels fixed. 'You think I'm too uptight?'

'I think we're on Joe's case a bit.'

He's said 'we' but now I only hear 'you'.

Drew pulls back a little, scanning my face. 'If I say I'll keep an eye on him, will you let me handle it? The comment about the car was about getting a reaction from you, wasn't it? Let's back off and see how he responds to me, eh?'

I know he's right. I nod, biting my lip in agreement. I should be pleased that Drew is taking control of the situation. I know that Joe respects him. I should be grateful that my seventeen-year-old son has taken so easily to this new man coming into his life and is prepared to listen. *It's because I've been parenting alone for so long,* I tell myself. *To relinquish control now feels so difficult.*

Am I a bit wary of how quickly they've bonded?

No.

Am I, though?

Sarah tells me how lucky I am. I've listened to the horror stories about how some kids make it almost impossible to even go out for a drink with a guy, let alone marry one. I know what Sarah's hinting. The same as my mother's strident declarations: *Drew has sorted my life out.*

'At least you can stop all that running around now.' My mother's voice plays like a record in my head. *'All those jobs, different boyfriends.'* Her disapproval loud and clear. *'Children need routine. They need a mother at home.'*

My indignation smarts, but deep down I know I'm grateful I don't have to live like that anymore. *Drew has given me this new life. Where would I be if he hadn't talked to me at that barbecue, if he'd talked to someone else?*

'Hey. Mrs Douglas!' Drew gives me a little shake. 'I haven't upset you, have I?'

'Of course not.' I proffer a real smile.

'Good.'

The use of my new name still has a hint of unfamiliarity about it.

He lifts my chin. 'Do I get a kiss?'

Our lips touch tenderly. He breathes and I can feel an urgency in his breath. His hand slips down briefly touching my breast, making me shiver. He shifts his weight, the worktop edge digging into my hip. *We could, I know we could, but—*

He glances up at the ceiling with a wry grin. 'I suppose I ought to get going.'

'I suppose you ought.'

'Shame.'

'Yeah, shame.' We laugh.

He glances ruefully at the pile of dirty plates on the table.

'Oh, don't worry. I'll sort all that. The thought was there.'

'I'll call you later if I get a chance, yeah?' He dips his head to kiss me again. 'I can't promise on that score, but I'll try. it depends what delights Friday night in Birmingham has in store for me.'

'Can you please try to be careful?' My eyes search his as he releases me from the hug and hunts around for his bag; his head is already somewhere else.

'There's a reason they call me Teflon you know,' he joshes. 'Trouble just slides off.'

'Yeah, yeah. Good chat, but I'm being serious.'

'So am I.' He unhooks his leather jacket from the back of the chair. 'Now go and put your feet up and download some silly Netflix romance thing.' He heaves his case onto his shoulder. 'Check out the fridge too. You'll see I've left you a present.'

I glance over at the refrigerator. I already know what it will be: a big bar of chocolate.

'Plus, you don't have to share it.' Drew pecks his chin at the ceiling to Joe's room above us as he makes his way to the door. 'I've already made sure he's got his own stash.'

'You spoil him.'

'Now that's on *my* job description.' He catches my chin. 'You have a nice quiet evening.'

'I'm duty manager with Samaritans tonight, remember?'

Drew rolls his eyes. 'Oh yeah. I forgot. Well, you'll probably need the whole bar of chocolate then, but go easy on the rest of that wine.' He winks back at me from the hallway.

'Right. I'm off... Bye, matey!' he calls up the stairs.

There's a vague holler in reply.

'*Be good!*'

Drew blows me a kiss as he pulls open the front door and I follow, watching as he walks down the drive towards the car. I stand with folded arms on the step as he chucks his bag into the back and then drops behind the wheel, reaching around for the seatbelt. His shoulders are broad and move easily, and I feel the usual pang of desire and a slight pull of possessiveness. We haven't been married long enough for me to be totally at ease with who he's around at work. I imagine young female PCs being slightly in awe of having such a jokey, good-looking boss, easy to be around – *maybe even with tiny touches of over-familiarity...*

The car's engine roars into life and Drew lifts a hand to wave as he reverses expertly off the drive.

'*Don't search for problems where there aren't any, Beth,*' Sarah is always saying to me. '*Look at him! Secure job, decent wage, yada yada... I mean, moving in together after six weeks is quite fast but I'm sure you knew what you were doing.*'

Even though we're friends, I often feel like the poor relation to her: someone to be sorted out, questioned. Given advice whether I've asked for it or not.

I watch the red taillights disappearing at the T-junction, and then the street goes quiet.

Stepping back into the hallway, I close the door, aware of the soft settle of the house around me. I glance up at the creak of floorboards. There's the reassuring click of Joe's bedroom door closing as it dawns on me that he, too, was watching Drew drive away. It's funny how in such a short space of time we've both come to rely on him, when once we'd only ever relied on each other.

Sighing, I go into the kitchen, bending at the cupboard to find the dishwasher tablets, when suddenly a memory hits me. I remember when Joe used to saunter in here, hauling himself onto the end of the worktop, legs swinging aimlessly while he watched me clear up. It doesn't seem that long ago. I always knew those were the times he wanted to ask me something, or tell me what was going on with him – and all I'd have to do was wait, busy myself, smiling, until he plucked up the courage.

When did that stop? I pause holding the box. *Has he been confiding in Drew instead?* If he has, Drew would've mentioned it, wouldn't he? I glance upward, one ear listening out. If he knows I'm in here on my own, he might come down now.

I'd love that.

But there's no movement. Just me alone. Again.

Dropping a tablet into the machine, I pick up a cloth to wipe down the oven before running it under the hot water, but turn the tap off, quickly. My ears are anxiously attuned to Joe. I've spent my life listening out for him: his baby cries, his scraped knee wails, the tone of his voice to catch his mood – my absolute visceral need to put right whatever is wrong.

All that was before.

Before that night.

Clicking the door to the dishwasher closed, I press the button. The machine whirrs into life and I listen to the hiss of water rinsing the grease and the horribleness away. I wish it was quieter. I wish I could quieten my heart.

And my guilt.

My compulsion to go up now and check the medicine cabinet. Hide any tablets. Shift all the bottles.

There are things I haven't told anyone. Not my mother. Not Sarah. Not Drew.

I've failed. I'm a failure as a parent.

Completely. Utterly. No argument.

Big ways, small ways, tons of ways really: all those tiny moments that must have added up to make him feel worthless. That's what he told me once: that he's not worth *the air that he breathes*. No one can imagine how that made me feel.

He was sixteen. No Drew on the scene. I walked into his room and he was sitting on the bed with a bottle of vodka in one hand and strips of tablets in the other.

I can see it all now: the look on his face – that look that crushes my heart even now and takes my breath away.

He had immediately stood up, vodka bottle in hand, swaying a little.

'What are you doing?'

I remember the only sound in the room was the rasping of my own lungs.

His sneering face cracked into a leer. 'What's it look like?'

I remember the shock of it as I stared down at those tablets, scared of what they were and where he'd got them.

'Why would you care?' The whisper of his voice. His eyes, accusing.

'Of course I care!... Of course I do!' I closed my eyes, absorbing his pain and wanting to reach out and grab him and hold him so tight that he would feel my love for him in his very bones.

'Oh, it's all about you, you, you! No wonder my dad couldn't stand it!' he'd exploded, the wrecked emotion instantly switching to fury. 'Always about you, Beth, isn't it? Here!' He threw the strips of pills and they rattled in a heap at my feet. 'There you go! Painkillers! You'd love it if I'd taken them all, wouldn't you? Give you something else to rescue!'

His face was brilliant red, but burning with pent-up tears. He'd stood, glaring at me, taking a massive swig from the bottle, his eyes locking on me the whole time. I felt my mouth working, uselessly.

'Just get out!' he'd yelled at the top of his voice.

'Joe!'

'*Go away! Leave me alone! GO. AWAY!*' He was screaming and screaming – my head ringing with the sound of it.

To my shame I backed off, dazed and floundering down the

stairs to dissolve in a crying heap at the bottom. *What's happening? None of that is real...* My brain stumbled and snagged, falling over itself.

He didn't mean it.

He's not used to alcohol.

It was the drink talking.

He's confused. He had to take his anger out on someone and I'm the closest to him.

Was I the closest back then? Well, I'm not that person now.

Upstairs there's a sound. My head snaps up.

I know he's going to come down at any minute. My hand trembles a little as I reach for the door and open it just a crack. Peering into the hallway, I see him trotting down the stairs with his jacket on, and my stomach sinks.

I pretend to almost bump into him. 'Oh! Off out?' I query brightly.

'Yeah.' He goes to walk past me.

'Anywhere nice?'

I sound ridiculous.

'I said before. Out with Nate.'

'Joe—'

He has one hand on the front door.

He sighs exaggeratedly. 'I said— I told you... I'm not doing anything wrong, Beth.'

'It's really late.'

'Yeah? And?'

'So where are you going? You're not really going drinking, are you?'

'I'm eighteen in five months' time.'

'I know you're eighteen in five months' time.'

'So?' He gives me a wide-eyed shake of the head. 'So, I'm almost eighteen. So, I make my own decisions.'

'I'm not trying to tell you what to do, Joe, I'm trying to tell you that I worry about you.'

'Well, you don't need to.' He twists the Yale lock savagely. A blast of cold night air sends a chill whipping around my legs as he slams the door so hard that the windows rattle.

I immediately yank the door open to go after him, catching sight of his hunched shoulders as he strides away from me. I want to call out, but am suddenly aware of a couple walking on the other side of the road. Their curious eyes snatch across, sensing a situation. I can't bear the indignity; I retreat, head down.

He's practically an adult. Do what Drew says: back off a little.

Sarah keeps telling me it's just a phase. That things will settle down once the novelty of having a man in the house full-time has worn off.

But that tiny thrum of disquiet just won't go away.

Closing the door, I go into the lounge. My phone is flashing. I've had two missed calls and two messages. Drew has tried to call me and has left a voicemail. He tells me that there's an incident going on somewhere. The other is from Robyn, the chaplain at the prison I work at, saying she's got the Samaritans rota to sort and she'll call me tomorrow.

I glance at the clock. It's too late for a film, and as I'm on call with Samaritans I might see if I can get some sleep. Going back to the front door, I make sure the snib is off, knowing that whatever time I turn in, I'll only be lying listening for the sound of Joe's key in the lock.

Switching off the hall light, I make my way upstairs to clean my teeth and then go into the bedroom, drawing the curtains and putting on the bedside lamp. It's a ritual, but it doesn't work. I used to like sleeping alone, but since meeting Drew, I find I need his steady, solid form next to me.

Pulling on my nightshirt, I crawl under the duvet. The room doesn't feel right: the square shadow of the wardrobe looks unfriendly and menacing; the light pendant casts weird shapes across the ceiling.

Reaching for my book, I flick to the bookmark. It's not long before I'm back into it. I am right on the edge of a cliff with the woman about to jump, the wind is blowing; there's the waul of gulls and the boom of the waves on the rocks below. Intermittently, I look up, listening for Joe coming home. But no. Pages turn; time passes. I glance once at the clock: already an hour has gone, and then three quarters. From somewhere far away, there's a haunting cry: a sound that goes on and on, drumming its way into my consciousness, over and over, forcing me to—

And my eyes spring open.

I don't know where I am. The shadows on the walls make no sense – *awake, asleep, dreaming?* – and then I'm instantly present; the noise blats on and on, turning into the sound of my phone. My arm reaches out, my fingers grappling, not working as they fumble for the slim rectangle of plastic. I can't see clearly as I jab at the answer button.

'Hello?'

There's a strange kind of silence on the other end that makes no sense. In my befuddled state I think it must be Robyn, or – my jumbled brain tries to figure it out.

'Hello?'

It's as though my dream of the sea has been brought to life. There's a whooshing sound down the line that comes and goes.

A Samaritan volunteer needing help?

My brain attempts to decipher. *But they'd be in the office. I'd recognise the number.*

'*Hello,*' I try again.

'Beth! You have to help me.' It's a girl: a woman. I struggle to sit up.

'Sorry?' My brain can't make sense of it.

'I've been dumped on the side of the road. I'm scared! You have to help me!'

Has a Samaritans caller got my number?

'I tried to get away from him. He says he'll kill me! I didn't know who to call. I'm sorry... I'm so sorry...' She starts to cry.

My scrambled head doesn't work.

'You know what he is, don't you? If he can do this to me, then—'

The whooshing sound booms and falls.

'You don't believe me! I shouldn't have... I shouldn't have called you... I don't know why I did. You can't help me. No one can—' The line breaks up into a hissing crackle of static.

For a moment I think she's gone, and then...

There's a deafening rumble that I realise is the sound of trucks thundering past. How did this woman get my number?

'Who...? Who is this?'

'I'm just so scared! I don't know where I am!' She's breathy and panicked. 'Can you come and get me?'

'Get you?'

She starts to cry again, mumbling something I don't catch.

'Um... Can you tell me where you are? Look around you. Is there anything? A building with a sign? Anything?'

But the mumbling turns to random words. 'Liar!' she suddenly blurts. 'He never told me about you! He's a liar. Everything he says is a lie!' Her voice fades in and out with the roar of the traffic. 'He's a monster! You need to know what he is.'

I find my mouth is opening and closing stupidly.

'I've seen what he does. I've seen what he's capable of – you have no clue.' She dissolves into choking cries, leaving me unable to think or speak.

I stare at the bedroom wall in dumb silence. I'm trying to picture this screaming, sobbing woman on the end of the line. This isn't happening. Any moment now and I am going to find that the book I've been reading has slipped to the floor and I'm going to wake with a start.

'Can you tell me something about yourself?' I say.

'What?' Her crying hiccoughs to a stop.

'Like, what's your name?'

'No! You have to believe me! You can't trust any of them. You have to listen to me!'

She sounds crazy, deranged. Maybe she's out of her head on drugs? My brain whirls. *Yes, she's an addict. That's it. Someone who's chaotic and confused. Somehow she's got hold of my number. But how?*

'It doesn't matter—' Her voice breaks up with the signal. 'It doesn't matter—'

I want to put the phone down. Something inside me is screaming to end the call, but my throat tightens and won't let me.

'You'll find out. Then you'll believe me. He'll do it to you.'

The line goes dead.

I feel as though I'm somewhere very far away. I look down at the mound of duvet: this is me lying here. I'm in a bedroom that looks ordinary; there are my curtains, there is the chest of drawers, these things are mine and real and true. I watch the phone slipping from my ear and I stare down at the lit-up screen as though not quite understanding what I'm looking at. My thumb comes up from the 'end call' button.

I had pressed it. I cut her off.

I'm instantly frightened, as though the thing in my hand is alive. I imagine it bursting into life again, and she'll be here: in my space, demanding something from me all over again.

Toggling the phone to silent, I turn it face down, sliding it onto the bedside table and put a couple of paperback books on top. One flick of the light switch, and the room goes black as my ears prick at a familiar sound: it's the front door opening. There's the creak of the bottom stair and a slight squeal of his hand on the banister, then seconds of quiet before Joe's bedroom handle clicks closed. He's inside; he's safe. We are all okay.

Nothing has happened. Nothing is different.

My heart thuds in my ears.

Nothing has changed.

But it has.

The adrenaline pulses through my veins as the mattress shudders beneath me. Everything I thought was immovable is moving; everything I thought was certain feels unsafe.

Everything's changed.

Is my husband having an affair?

The thought bursts into my head but I squeeze my eyes shut, forcing it away.

What a ridiculous idea. It was clearly a phone call from someone unwell, that's all.

But how does she have my number?

I want to cry.

How does she know my name?

I can't cry. It won't come out. *Drew*, my head says. *An addict?*

No, worse.

A sex worker.

No.

I just feel numb.

Almost immediately the phone flashes into the darkness. My hand jerks out to grab it, knocking it off the table amidst a scuffle of books. I nearly fall out of bed in my rush to find it, scrabbling amongst the pages to snatch it up, but the screen goes black.

There's a message.

I swallow.

It's from Drew.

Caught up in something nasty. Will call later.

I know now he won't be coming home tonight. I press the 'power off' button and wait a second as the spiralling colours whirl in front of me in the darkness and then everything switches off: the phone, the room, me.

TWO

I don't sleep.

As a grey dawn begins to inch around the side of the curtains, I give up, swinging my legs from the side of the bed and going out onto the landing. Joe's door isn't shut right to; a black beading shows around the edge. Treading softly, I nudge it open just a few inches. There is my boy, the bedclothes a massive hump and beneath it, the sound of his breathing: soft and regular. The pull is almost too much to bear.

Moving silently to the side of the bed, I gaze down at his face. Around his cheeks, I can still see the child that he used to be, and, oddly, in the rumple and creases of sleep, the older man he'll become.

He's only been on the planet for seventeen years and I feel I have inflicted a lifetime's worth of pain on him already. I made the choice to have him when I lived in poverty. I left him with kindly neighbours and kid-friendly acquaintances for hours so that I could work. I didn't give him the father he so desperately wanted. I did all that, and they were all my choices. I did the best I could, but was my best good enough?

He sighs in his sleep. I hold my breath as he turns over. A

huge pull of love rides over me, from the adorable shape of his head to that point of hair in the nape of his neck that I long to reach out and touch. It's an exact replica of my father's. Joe never knew his grandfather; he died when I was young. The relief is almost shameful. I would have disappointed him. I disappoint everyone. It seems everyone wants to leave me in the end.

Quietly pulling the door closed behind me, I go back to my room and slide between the sheets, shivering a little with the cold. Arching my neck back in the pillows, I close my eyes, letting the tears leak slowly down my temples and into my ears. The world is muffled.

All I have to do is stop thinking.

Breathe. Count slowly. Breathe.

None of this has to be true; you're making it true.

You know Drew loves you. What if it was a Samaritan caller? Is that beyond the realms of possibility that someone has breached protocol and given out your number?

No, that just wouldn't happen.

What if it's some random woman who Drew has arrested at some point? That could happen, couldn't it? She wants revenge. She's plotted and connived to get his phone.

You don't know anything for a fact.

Stop chasing worries that aren't there. In an hour's time, you'll be laughing about this.

My eyes drop open.

My heart is thudding.

Somewhere behind me there's the check and catch of breathing and I half turn in shock. There is the familiar bulk and heat of Drew. I stiffen in alarm. *What time is it?*

The gauzy beading of light around the curtain edge tells me it's close to morning. Carefully, so as not to wake him, I lever myself up, feeding the duvet behind me as I slip from the side of the mattress. My dressing gown is within easy reach, and I pull it on, warily creeping across the bedroom floor towards the door.

'Where you off to?'

The boom of his voice sends a jolt of shock.

'You're up early. Come and give me a kiss.' Drew pulls the covers away from his face and turns towards me.

'What time did you get in?' I bend. His skin smells rank: of old coffee and stale perfume. I go to straighten, but his fingers close around the front of my gown, pulling me closer.

'No cuddle?'

'Drew—' I go to extricate myself.

'What's the matter?'

'Nothing's the matter.' I smile. 'Did you have an interesting night?' I perch on the side of the bed, taking his hand and threading his fingers through mine. *I want to ask him, but how do I even say it?*

'Don't even mention last night, I wouldn't know where to start. I'm totally exhausted.' He rubs a hand across his face and yawns widely. 'Your evening go okay?'

There's the moment. All I have to do is—

'You didn't touch the chocolate.' He pulls a mock sulky face.

'No, I—'

'Or finish the wine. Why was that then?'

'Umm... no reason. I came up to bed. Read for a while.'

I could ask him now. How could a woman like that get my number?

'What about that tea? Why don't you make me a cup too and come back to bed? It's still early. Joe won't be up for ages.'

The moment passes. *I'll say something in a bit. Right now, I'll sound accusatory. I'll come across like I doubt him.*

'Sure.'

His grasp relents a little, his fingers slipping across my palm.

'Don't be long – I'm falling asleep already. I had a really

tough night.' He yawns widely again. 'There was a big accident on the main road.'

Something inside me drops.

'Go and get your tea if you're going, otherwise I might be asleep by the time you get back.' He drags the pillow under his cheek and half-closes his eyes. I try to haul back the plummeting sensation as my brain fumbles, unable to process.

Coincidence, my head says. *He wouldn't be so casual, would he?*

I make for the door, my feet catching clumsily on the carpet, pulling it closed behind me, slipping quickly down the stairs.

Why am I feeling like this? I have no reason to doubt Drew. *How easy it is to think that all men will do the dirty.* Sarah's words come back to me: '*Don't search for problems where there aren't any, Beth!*'

Switching the kettle on to boil, I wait for its hissing crescendo as I automatically reach for the TV remote and click the 'mute' button so as not to wake Joe. The local news flashes up, and a grainy bit of footage flicks up in front of me. The screen shows chaos as the headline swims across the page. I glance at the tickertape of first few jumbling words that runs across the bottom of the screen:

M6 ROADWAY FORCED TO CLOSE... My hand pauses on the rim of the tea caddy. ... *FOR HOURS AFTER WOMAN WANDERS ALONG HARD SHOULDER.*

My eyes frantically search and I turn up the volume.

'There has been a serious collision on the M6 in Staffordshire. The crash involved three lorries and four cars – two of the vehicles driving through the central reservation. The driver of one of the vehicles involved was pronounced dead at the scene. The incident occurred after a young female was seen walking dangerously close to vehicles on the roadway, one of the busiest in the UK. They are urging her to come forward to help them with their enquiries.'

I hit mute again. I am aware of the steam from the kettle drifting as it clicks off.

I should definitely tell Drew about the phone call.

The presenter is mouthing words on the screen like a ventriloquist's dummy.

There's nothing to say that this woman on the news is anything to do with the woman that phoned me. I could be making connections where there aren't any.

I think about walking upstairs now, tea in hand. I think about what I might say. I imagine the look on Drew's face. I'll have to repeat the things the woman said: *He's a monster. Everything he says is a lie. He'll do the same to you.*

It'll make me look as though I don't trust him.

And do I?

I imagine him laughing it off; hell, he gets this kind of thing all the time! People have grudges against police officers for all sorts of reasons. He'll reassure me, telling me it's all nonsense: the ravings of a madwoman.

I'll believe him. I'll want to believe him.

I glance down. My phone is flashing with a message.

It's the chaplain, Robyn. She wants to talk to me about an idea for the Samaritans Listener Scheme in the prison. I'm about to reply when '*online*' pops up under her name. I check the time.

> What are you doing up at this hour?

> Could ask the same of you

I smile.

> Were you on duty manager call last night?

I have this sudden urge to tell her what's happened.

> You in the prison today?

I sidestep my own thoughts.

> Sure am. Coming in for a cuppa?

Relief runs through me at the thought. Robyn. Steady, no-nonsense, caring Robyn. I don't know what I'd do without her now. She'd rung me out of the blue six months ago, saying she'd heard 'good things' about me and inviting me into the prison. Robyn, the kind of woman I'd like to be: funny, ballsy, unafraid of a challenge. We bonded like co-conspirators with a common goal: trying to prevent young men from killing themselves in an environment that didn't seem to care whether they lived or died.

> Only if you're free.

> For you, anytime.

She adds a smiley face.

> Let me know when you get in.

> Here now. Didn't manage to get home last night. See you soon. X

My head is a mass of whirling contradictions. I think about going back upstairs, of having to talk to Drew, fearful of what I might say, fearful of my own imaginings. I need to get my thoughts straight – and I know it's Robyn who'll help me straighten them.

It's eight minutes past six. Going into the laundry, I drag out the linen basket, pulling out a thick sweater and a pair of jeggings. Rummaging for a half-decent pair of socks, I make my way upstairs, pausing briefly outside our bedroom door to listen. There's silence.

Prodding it open, I see the humped mound of Drew's shoulders turned away and I send up a quiet prayer of thanks. Creeping over to my side of the bed, I ease open the drawer and find a scrap of paper and a pen to hastily scribble a note.

Didn't want to wake you. Robyn called with a couple of emergency issues. Have gone into the nick. Shouldn't be long.
See you l8r. Love you X

So many fears, so many questions come bowling into my head one after the other as I hurry to my car and pull off the drive. My mind spools away with the road in front of me; I'm on autopilot.

Robyn is the one person who knows what happened with Joe. She got it. She understood.

'You seem to really grasp the impact of young men taking their own lives. It's not just management speak with you, is it?'

We had been sitting in her office. She'd paused and tipped her head on one side, regarding me carefully.

'No. It's not.'

Her silence unbuckled me. That sudden space, there, in front of a complete stranger, non-judgemental, kind-faced, gently asking.

It was as though the great dam of things, unspoken words, feelings, emotions, fell from my mouth in one long stream that I couldn't stop even if I'd wanted to. I was saying the unsayable. She gave me the room to explore the guilt rather than telling me I shouldn't feel it. I laid it all out on the table: saw it, heard it, admitted it.

I'm terrified my child wants to die, and it's all my fault.

I suddenly snap up, realising I am nearly at the prison. Scrolling onto Bluetooth, I place the call.

'Call Robyn Goodfellow.'

There's a moment where the line connects. She answers straightaway.

'Hiya! I'll be at the gate in five. Can you come and get me?'

'Yep, sure. I've just got to chat with the governor about my incident report, and then I'll be right down.'

'Incident report?' I shake my head, puzzled. 'What incident?'

Robyn sighs. 'Yeah, I didn't like to tell you over text.'

'Tell me? Tell me what?'

'We had a suicide attempt.'

My gut lurches in alarm.

'Oh my God! I'm just parking now. Who was it?'

'Leo Hargreaves. Don't worry, he's fine. I put one of your Listeners in with him.'

'Which one?'

'Jaime Lee.'

'Okay. Okay. Don't worry. I'll see if one of the gate staff can bring me over.'

Killing the engine, I make my way to the prison gatehouse. The lit plate-glass windows show a fishbowl of busy uniformed staff weaving back and forth. Walking quickly up to the security doors, I feel a sensation of calm come over me. Strangely, this is the place where I feel in control. It's here, behind these blank, grey, barbed wire walls, where the rules are the rules and things make sense. If only the rest of my life felt like that.

'Crumpet?'

The officer escorting me raises an eyebrow. Robyn is standing next to the toaster as a tiny trail of smoke winds its way from the slot.

'You can stay too, if you want?' She glances at him, amused. 'I've just opened the packet so there's plenty.' She gestures with the buttery knife at the spill of pale crumpets across the top of the fridge.

'Err... no. No... you're okay.' The officer looks flustered. 'I'll... err... leave you to it then.' He beats a hasty retreat, pulling the gate closed behind him.

Robyn winks as she stoops to open the fridge door to take out the milk.

'Go on then – make yourself comfortable.' She waves the carton at the tired old chairs.

I love being here. Her office is more akin to a bijou apartment than a place of serious work. The desk and laptop are tucked well out of the way over by the far wall. The main furniture is the sofa and two armchairs adorned with paisley throws, with a coffee table between. The table is laden with a big bowl of fruit and a smaller bowl of chocolates. I sink gratefully into the cushions. My knees are practically up by my chin. I could fight it, but I don't, slipping off my shoes and curling my legs beneath me. I feel more me here than anywhere else.

'Here you go.' Robyn plonks a cup of tea on one arm of the chair, and a plate with a crumpet oozing pools of yellowy butter on the other. 'Breakfast.'

My stomach growls in appreciation.

'How's Leo doing?'

'He's doing okay. Calmer, definitely.' She prods the plate. 'Let's look after you first. Come on.'

'How do you always manage to give people what they want, even when they don't know what it is?'

'Err, people in general?' She smiles.

'Okay, me then.'

She shrugs. 'Because, Beth my lovely, we're two odd-bod women in this odd-bod environment, trying to create a bit of calm out of chaos.'

I smile ruefully. 'Uh-huh, my life is definitely a bit odd at the moment.'

'Oh, is it?' Robyn drops the last of the buttery crumpets onto a piled-high plate. 'Come on then. Spill.' She takes a bite of one, sitting down opposite.

'It's not what you think.'

'What do I think?' She smiles.

I don't know where to start. I pick up my mug in an attempt to hide my face, suddenly realising, to my horror, I might start to cry.

'Is it Joe?'

'No, not just Joe... God, sorry...' I almost manage a half-smile, but then my face suddenly drops and the tears sting.

'Never apologise.' Robyn takes another gargantuan bite and finishes a crumpet off. 'Crying is good. Scream and shout if you want too. I'll tell the staff I'm conducting an exorcism. The terrible thing is, they'll probably believe me.'

I find I'm laughing and crying in equal amounts.

'You'll think I'm crazy. You'll say I'm totally overreacting.' I sniff loudly.

'Try me.' She holds her plate up close to her chin to catch the drips and looks at me with cow-like eyes. 'Give me all of it. The whole ridiculous nine yards.'

And so I tell her about Joe and Sarah's car, and the endless text messages, and then the phone call from the weird woman, and the accident on the motorway, and how I'd put the phone down when she begged me for help.

'Let's put aside the Joe bit for now. I'm guessing you haven't spoken to Drew about the call?'

I shake my head. 'She sounded seriously scared, but then I got to wondering what her angle was... Am I being used as some kind of revenge thing? Is she crazy? Could any of it possibly be true? Oh heck' – I rub my face – 'I don't know, Robyn, I really don't.'

Robyn frowns. 'What does your gut tell you, Beth? I've

never met this husband of yours obviously, but all this is pretty extreme, isn't it?'

I press my fingers into my forehead; there's a rising zigzag of pain beginning. 'Was I in too much of a rush to get married, Robyn? Did I ignore the warning signs? Have I messed up yet again?'

'What the hell, Beth! Give yourself a break! You said Drew was the first man you'd been with in how many years?'

'Seven,' I say miserably. 'But that's because I'm terrible at relationships.'

'You are NOT terrible! Can you hear me?' Robyn interjects hotly. 'If a man behaves like a dick it's on him, it's NOT down to you!'

I lower my hands and nod. The tears well again as Robyn gets up and rustles past me.

'You've let your tea get cold. I'll make you another.'

She busies herself with the kettle. I hear her words, but I don't really believe them; she's just trying to be kind.

'Tell me what you're scared of.'

'Sorry?' I blink tearfully.

'Well, that's what this is about, isn't it? Your fear. Obviously, there's what's happening with Joe's mental health; that's massive, but your response to this completely out-of-left-field phone call... It's just...' She pauses. 'You're not coming across as angry, or shocked. You just look really, really scared.'

I swallow painfully, unable to speak.

She's right.

I nod, thinking. Trying to crawl deeper into how I actually feel. This relationship can't be a failure – not after so short a time; it just can't. I can't walk into my mother's house and tell her that, yet again, I've made a mess of things. I can't see that look in her eyes, that silent turn of the head. I don't think I can bear it.

No money, she'd say. *Losing your home. Your security. You'll have to go back to what you were before.*

What I was. The awfulness of me.

I take a deep breath and release it, slowly. 'This wasn't supposed to be my life, Robyn. I was clever at school, good at passing exams, I had a place at Lancaster University. I was going to do a degree in Psychology.'

If I hadn't walked into that bar that night and met the boy who was to be the father of my child.

If my own father hadn't died a week later.

If, if, if.

'I got pregnant. I spent years alone and struggling. I was with a boy who I should never have stayed with, all because I felt Joe should have a dad.'

'You've said before you think Joe blames you,' she says gently. 'He uses it, you said.'

'Yeah... yes, he does.'

'What exactly does he blame you for?'

I look up quickly.

Joe's words haunt me. *'No wonder my dad couldn't stand you!'*

'It's the guilt of it, Robyn. I chose Simon – Joe's father. I chose to have a relationship with someone I knew was selfish and unreliable, yet all the time I believed that somehow being with me would change him. I could make him happy when he'd never been happy before. Having a child would complete him. We'd be a family. The one he never had. Only it didn't happen that way.'

The look on his face when I told him I was pregnant.

So, I'd sat at that abortion clinic waiting for Simon to show up like he'd promised – watching every swing of the door, waiting for the squeak of footsteps. But he never came and I couldn't go through with it.

I never saw him again. Messages unanswered. Calls never

picked up. Three months later seeing the newspaper report about a boy found in the River Severn. His death on top of my father's, punching me in the gut so fiercely, I found myself bent double, gasping for air. Even before I read his name I knew. I just knew.

'Drew isn't Simon, Beth.' Robyn tips her head on one side. Her eyes are kind. 'Just like Joe is not his father.'

'No.'

'But you don't quite believe that though, do you?' She smiles. 'You know, you can't kid a kidder.' She stirs the milk into the cup. I listen to the sound of metal on china. Round and round, just like me. An endless circle that I can't quite break.

'It keeps happening though. After I had Joe, I even moved away from the area. Got a rented house. Found work. Met a guy.' I pause, remembering.

'You've mentioned that particular guy before. But seriously, you couldn't have predicted that.' Robyn drops the teabags into the wastebin.

'Joe could have *died*, Robyn... Or, or...' I press. 'He could've been taken by someone!'

'But he wasn't.' She puts the cup on the table in front of me. 'He was fine.'

'No thanks to me.'

I close my eyes at the memory: of coming back from a night shift at the factory. Getting off the night bus at the top of the road and being instantly puzzled at the pulsating blue and red lights in the road. It took seconds for me to realise they were outside my house. I remember my feet felt as though they were wading through deep sand as the police officer on the doorstep turned to me, saying, *'Elizabeth Lister?'*

Who? I remember staring at her, not recognising my own name. My mouth refusing to work, my head blank, as she asked to come in. The house was silent as I dumbly pushed open the door. Joe should have been there – ten-year-old Joe, still tucked up in bed under his space-rocket duvet, and Harry, the man I had brought into our lives, the man who I had entrusted my son to, should have been there too, asleep on his side of our bed.

But instead, Harry was at Stoke Newington police station, and my son was in a hospital bed. Harry had taken him to a party – one I was never supposed to find out about. Joe had drunk alcohol while Harry was off with some girl, and a road sweeper had found Joe: my little boy, my child, passed out in the street and covered in vomit, lying in the gutter.

I heard all this from the police officer's mouth – not quite believing, thinking that I only had to call out, and Harry would appear in the kitchen doorway, bleary-eyed and blinking, asking what the hell I was talking about. Only now we were talking about Social Services, and reports, and police charges, and questions over whether I was a good enough parent.

I was forced to return to my mother's house, suitcases and child held tight. I remember the sight of my mother, her pained face, turned slightly away, unable to look – at the mess of me, as the social worker left, satisfied that if my mother was 'supporting' my parenting, then I might be deemed almost 'good enough'.

'Here,' my mother said one day. 'This is what your father would have wanted.'

And she showed me her bank statement, with the transfer amount of hundreds of thousands of pounds into my account so that Joe and I could have a house of our own.

'But no more boyfriends, darling, please,' she said in a disappointed voice. 'If you can't control your life for your own sake, then please, do it for your son.'

And there it was, her view of me: the implied reproach that I'd turned into one of 'those' women. A woman in her eyes with lax morals and poor judgement. Chaotic lifestyle. Flaky. A waste.

I accepted the money. I accepted her view of me. It was my view too.

'So, what do I do, Robyn?' I hold out my palms. 'What do I do? How do I go home to Drew and smile and pretend everything is fine when I feel this way?' My voice trembles. 'But even if he was having an affair, or seeing prostitutes, how would I leave?'

'You can't leave because...?' Robyn softly queries.

I swallow. 'Because of lots of things. Because Drew is the first stable guy I've met. He's dependable. And then there's Joe. He loves Drew. They have this amazing connection. It's like... It's like he's his own blood. I couldn't do that to him. Drew is the first real father he's had.'

'You haven't said you're madly in love and can't live without him.'

I look up quickly; she's smiling gently.

'But when you've been through the mill for years like you have, Beth, maybe you come to think that hearts and flowers aren't the solid rocks you need to build a marriage on, eh?'

'Maybe...' I falter, catching her gaze. 'But that sounds terrible.'

'It makes you sound like a human being who wants to do the best for her child above all else. That's absolutely evident. How could that make you terrible?'

I stare at her for a moment, before sighing and closing my eyes with a quiet nod.

'Sounds to me that Joe is just a teenager doing teenager things right now,' she says. 'It's a big change having a man in the house, particularly at his age. He'll need to try out a whole new way of behaving. Give him time... Give yourself time too, Beth. Don't jump at everything so quickly,' she counsels. 'Give yourself permission and space to think... And most especially, observe. Watch for any developments in Drew or Joe's behaviour.'

She looks at me pointedly. 'Trust your own judgement. If you need to challenge Drew or Joe, do it when the time is right *for you*, not as a knee-jerk reaction. You've had a phone call in the middle of the night from a woman telling you that you can't trust your husband. Most women would think that was strange! You're only human! But it could be nothing but some random, weird happenstance and you're joining the dots where there are no dots to join. Take a breath, Beth. Take your time. And for goodness' sake, stop beating yourself up!'

I give her a watery smile. 'You're so good for me, Robyn, you know that?'

'Am I?' She's watching me closely. 'Maybe we're good for each other. Have you considered that?'

I smile bitterly. 'It's such an irony that the one place I feel most like myself is in this prison, don't you think?'

But she only pulls a face. 'You and me both, love. Why do you think this office looks more like a cheap hotel?' She waves a hand. 'It's because it's better than the alternative of my cheap bedsit. We've all got baggage, you know.' She turns to gaze out of the barred window. 'We're all trying to leave something behind.'

I don't interrupt her. She clearly wants to speak.

'Only in my case I didn't choose to leave, I was asked to. We might all be equal in the sight of God, but I'm not in the sight of God. I'm in the clergy, which makes me just another woman in a man's world. They're always looking for ways you might have "operated inappropriately"' – she makes rabbit ears in the air – 'as leverage to get you out.

'Do you mean where you used to work, before this? What did they say you'd done?'

She turns to look at me and I'm scared that I've overstepped the boundary, but she only smiles, sadly.

'I made some pretty serious allegations against another member of the clergy and his attentions towards a young girl.'

She shakes her head, tutting. 'And as women, we all know we're not allowed to challenge powerful men, don't we?'

'And so they sent you here?'

'And so they sent me here, telling me it was "a great opportunity to really make a difference".' She nods ruefully. 'My old vicarage came with the other job so that went too. But I learned a very valuable lesson.'

'What was that?'

'That the system is male, the rules are for men, the set-up is so that men benefit from it. Even when women are in charge, they have to operate like men to succeed.' She meets my eye. 'So we have to learn to work the system to suit ourselves. Just like I said about Drew. Don't react to his actions. Don't jump to his tune. Bide your time. Work out what you want, and devise your own strategy.'

She leans forward with a wink. 'Which is why us girls need to stick together.'

I sniff again, pulling out a tissue and blowing my nose. 'Wow, when you think about it, we're a right pair of sad old kippers, aren't we?'

'Yep,' she admits. 'Probably the saddest.'

'But I think you're exactly right, and so on that note—'

She queries a look.

'Can I use your landline?'

Her expression doesn't change.

'Drew,' I explain. 'I think I need to call him.'

'It's all yours.' She waves towards the desk. 'I'll disappear for five minutes while you decide on your tactics.'

THREE

'Sorted?'

'Sorted.'

Robyn gives me an encouraging look as we make our way towards the main wing.

'You were right.'

She inclines her head in a bow and we both laugh.

'And what did you deduce and discover?'

'Well, if it tells you anything about him, as soon as he picked the phone up, all he wanted to talk about was his concern for the girl they'd found on the motorway.'

Robyn nods sagely. 'That's positive.'

'So, unless he's playing double and triple bluff, I'd say he was genuine. Like, he asked me if I'd seen the news. He sounded upset that this kid with mental health issues was wandering around out there. I got the impression she's known to them.'

'She's done this kind of thing before?' Robyn looks at me, shocked.

'He said she was fixated on exposing bent police and gets

herself into all kinds of attention-seeking situations. Sad, not bad, was how he put it.'

'So trust your gut instincts, Beth.' I'm aware Robyn is smiling at me. 'You're smart and you've got great intuition... No, seriously, don't pull that face! You always seem to doubt yourself, yet I've watched you take on this Listener Scheme project as though you've worked in prisons for years.'

I fluster an answer. 'Well, I just see the obstacles you face in here, and I think of ways round them.'

'Precisely. You've got a knack for making things happen in a kind of quiet way. I don't think people notice so they don't try and stop you.' She laughs. 'Its success is really all down to you.'

'Us,' I insist. I hate compliments.

'And it's not just me who's flying your flag; the other departments are too: Psychology, Probation. They all think the work you do is brilliant. And then there's the governor.' Robyn gives me a sly sideways glance.

'Yeah, yeah.'

'He doesn't have a clue what we're on about, really. Nor does he actually care to learn, but he loves the fact that we make him look good when the prison inspectorate rock up.' She grins. 'But you've created this great network of people. If you ever wanted to take up that education you feel you missed out on, the help is all there, you know.'

'It was Psychology I should've gone into from the very beginning. I was thinking the work I've done with the Samaritans might help if I wanted to re-train...' I trail off.

'Definitely, I'm sure it would.' She nods emphatically. 'Even better if you put together a few case studies maybe?'

'Case studies?'

I'm puzzled but detect something in her tone.

'Yeah.' Robyn jangles out a bunch of keys. 'There's this prisoner—'

'Uh-huh.' I almost laugh at the outrageous way she's manoeuvred me. 'What kind of prisoner?'

'The kind I'm very eager to work with. Everyone from the governor downwards is against me, but I know you'll be on my side.' She pouts impishly.

'Robyn!' I protest, but she's already corralling me towards a gate.

'His name is Michael Childs. He's been shipped out of every establishment you can think of. He's seen as a nasty piece of work.'

I glance to where we're heading: it's the segregation unit. My heart sinks.

'You're not exactly selling this to me. What am I supposed to do? I know nothing about conducting case studies... I don't even—'

But she cuts across me. 'He's tried to kill several people. He's got a thing about male prison officers, so you and me are okay, I think.' She gestures me to go in front of her.

'What!' I look at her aghast.

But Robyn only laughs, blackly. 'I'm only kidding. He's troubled, there's no doubt about that, but eventually I want to get him onto normal location. I'm thinking that if I can get him to make at least *some* kind of relationship with just one person, it'd be a great starting point. His social skills are really poor.'

'Oh great!'

She pulls the metal gate closed.

'So, you're thinking *I* should talk to him?' A squeeze of nerves slithers and I suddenly wish I'd never mentioned anything to do with psychology.

'Oh no, no, no!' Robyn smiles. 'He needs a fellow prisoner to talk to. So I was thinking of your fella, Jaime.'

I look at her in horror. 'Jaime?'

'You said you're seeing him later?'

'Well yes, but—'

'I mean Samaritans aren't just about people feeling suicidal, are they? You're the one that's always telling me it's not just about being there for someone when they're in crisis; it's about being there for someone to *prevent* the crisis.'

'Yes, I *know* that, but—'

'Well, Michael is a man in chronic crisis: his crisis is every day he draws breath.'

We reach the walkway that leads directly to the Seg and Robyn pauses.

'All I'm asking is that you meet this guy and, if you're happy, sound Jaime out. The governor is against the whole idea, but I'm thinking if you can persuade him it would benefit Michael's mental health, and maybe *prevent* a suicide.'

She lets the idea hang for a moment. 'Plus, I think your Jaime fella will say yes.' She flickers a faint smile. 'I mean, you know Jaime's being considered for a parole hearing soon, don't you? He was charged with drug possession, but from the outset he held his hands up, and applied for every offending behaviour course going. I happened to mention to him that being seen to be helping other prisoners would hugely beneficial on his parole report... That is, I said I *personally* would ensure it was hugely beneficial.'

'What are you like?' I shake my head in wonder.

'I'm like someone whose only joy in life is to spread the seeds of goodness.' She inclines her head mock-theatrically. 'Plus, a bit of leverage here and there never did anyone any harm. What's the point of having power if you can't abuse it?' She unlocks a solid wooden door set into a recess marked *Segregation*. We step over the threshold.

A gust of heat carries the scent of disinfectant and floor polish. A shiny corridor spans away from me, with blank cell doors on either side. It instantly reminds me of a psychiatric ward. That shiver of anxiety picks up a notch.

Our shoes squeal rhythmically as we make our way to the

main office. There's the quiet murmur of voices behind the half-closed door. The voices pause.

'Ah, Chaplain! How's it going?'

An older, grey-haired officer, with the soft lilt of a Geordie accent, looks up. He has a foot resting on the edge of the desk, slowly twirling his key chain around his thumb.

'Very well thank you, Mr Travis.' Robyn smiles back.

'You're wanting to see Childs?' The officer bats a look at me. 'I've already had the governor on the phone this morning.'

I can tell Officer Travis is distinctly unimpressed as he rocks back in his chair.

'You know what Childs is in for, don't you?' He scratches his neck absent-mindedly with the end of his key. I know he's pausing for effect.

Robyn blinks blankly. 'Yes, I do.'

'Does she, though?' Travis flicks a thumb in my direction, unwinding the key chain and holding it in both hands like a garotte. 'Tssschh!' He lets out a whistle. 'I've never understood the attraction of women for violent men.' He puffs out his cheeks, disbelieving. 'What *is* that about?'

'But if we were two men asking to see him, it'd be okay?' Robyn cocks her head challengingly.

The front two legs of the chair crash down onto the floor, making us both jump.

'All this bleeding-heart stuff does my swede, frankly.' Officer Travis looks from me to Robyn and back again. 'You think you can "rescue" the poor sinner, don't you?' Travis leans forward, lowering his voice. 'You're blind to the fact that he's playing you. He makes these feeble attempts at suicide when he can't get what he wants, and you come trotting over all earnest and flapping.'

'Michael Childs' mother was an addict. She sold him to sex offenders for a bag of smack,' Robyn says quietly. 'We have no idea what he's experienced throughout his childhood, but I'm guessing it's not good.'

The officer gives Robyn a withering look. 'What about the families of those poor girls, eh? None of us know what that bastard did with them, 'cos he's not talking. If that monster *does* top himself, he'd be doing the world a favour.'

Robyn doesn't speak. Travis lifts his palms like, *okay, your choice.*

'Right, *ladies!*' He emphasises the word. 'Have it your way.'

Shunting his chair back, he ushers us into the corridor. There's a cell door with the observation flap open. I have a vague sense of unease at what might be behind it.

He dips to peer in as he sorts out the cell key and then glances over his shoulder.

'You ready?'

Robyn nods and the door is shunted wide.

The seated figure is so still for a second, I wonder if it's real. There's a man sitting quietly, his head bowed, legs crossed at the ankle, with his hands folded neatly in his lap.

The high window in the cell is casting a dulled light through the bars so that he is silhouetted, his head no more than a blackened ball, the light shining through the vague wisps of hair creating a kind of halo. There's something about his still-ness that feels alien: wrong.

I'm aware that Robyn is speaking to him, but I can't concentrate on the words. The officer is hovering close to my right shoulder; his tension is palpable. Robyn's voice rises and falls but feels like it's coming from far away – when suddenly there's a slight movement and the figure lifts his head and looks straight at me.

It's like looking at the Devil.

The eyes are dead, sunken back into the sockets. The nose is pinched, like a cadaver, and the mouth forms a strange black space.

I'm gripped by a violent chill. I want to look away. My neck muscles instinctively recoil, but his gaze holds me in a forcefield.

Beth.

The voice is inside my head. The black hole of a mouth hasn't moved. *Beth.*

'Beth?'

I'm jerked into consciousness.

'Are you okay? Can you take her out please? Find her a chair?'

I am aware of a pressure on my arm and then a force, pulling me back into the corridor. Robyn's outline, black against the light, recedes like time-lapse film. The doorway gets smaller and smaller and then I'm suddenly back in the office. There's the hard edge of a chair pressing into the backs of my knees and I'm forced to sit, swaying clumsily.

'I thought you were going to keel over.'

The concerned face of Officer Travis looms in and out of focus.

'Get her a cup of tea and put some sugar in it,' a voice says from somewhere.

'I'm fine, honestly, I'm fine.' My voice is a croak. 'I don't know what happened.'

Robyn's face is a mask of concern. 'Beth! One minute you were there, and the next, I looked round, and I thought you were about to do a dying swan. You scared me – but at least you got Michael Childs talking.' She grins. 'I think you frightened him too!'

'Did I?'

The image of that face comes back to me: one that nightmares are made of.

'Yep, we actually had a conversation – short, but a conversation, nonetheless. He's agreed he'll talk to Jaime if we can organise it. Anyway, how are you feeling?'

'Better,' I admit, picking up the tea. The sweetness is cloying, and the grainy slick of powdered milk forms a coating on my teeth. 'It's very hot in here, that's all.' I am aware of a spring of sweat tingling the nape of my neck. 'I probably just need a bit of air.'

'Maybe we'll order you a cab home. I don't think you should drive.' Robyn eyes me guardedly.

'No honestly, I'm fine.' I lever myself up straight to show just how fine I am.

'Are you sure?'

'Perfectly. And thank you so much for the tea, Mr Travis. I'm sorry for being such a nuisance.'

He nods smartly. ''S'alright, pet, you don't need to apologise. I totally get it.' He doesn't look at Robyn.

'Shall we go?' I get up, smiling at her. 'I was going to see Jaime on A Wing. I'll try not to cause mayhem there too, I promise.'

Robyn closes the gate behind me onto the walkway. 'I shouldn't have done that to you. I should have given you prior warning. I should've been straight about Childs from the off. I'm sorry, that was wrong of me.'

'I've said I want to do this kind of work. I'm going to meet people who aren't sweet and fluffy.'

'Yeah, but there's not sweet and fluffy and then there are offenders like Childs.' Robyn pauses. 'I should have given you a heads up. It's probably too soon for you to be venturing into the deep end.'

'I think I just need to toughen up.'

She pauses, turning to me. 'Look, Beth, I get what Officer Travis is going on about. I totally get what Childs is, but every single prisoner in this place has done something to someone, and I can't, in conscience, make a judgement and say that one offender is better or worse than another because I don't like the nature of his offence. Michael Childs is going to be let out on the streets one day. We can either contain him like an animal while he's here and then let that animal loose, or we can make tiny steps to try and socialise him. All I want to do is get him mixing with other prisoners on the wing – get prisoners like your Jaime Lee chap to befriend him a bit. That's all. I'm not talking about making him a youth leader for goodness' sake!'

I swallow. 'You're right,' I say carefully. 'What you're saying makes complete sense.'

'Of course I'm right; I always am.' Robyn winks. 'Sometimes it just takes other people a while to realise it.'

She lets me onto A Wing, raising a hand to inform the officer I'm there.

I mentally ready myself, walking steadily towards the main body of the wing. A cavernous domed roof carries the thundering voices, cat-calls echoing. The wing office door is slightly ajar. There's an officer at a desk.

He looks up. 'Hell-oh, hell-oh. What can I do you for?'

He has short, grey, spiky hair and dark-rimmed glasses. His mouth is turned up at the corners in a permanent smile.

'I was wondering if Jaime Lee is on the wing? He's one of your Listeners who was called out to an active suicide last night. I'm Beth Douglas. I'm with the Samaritans.'

'Jaime Lee?' He hesitates. 'Ah, yes, yes, sorry... I know the chap you're on about. Just a moment.'

He reaches for a microphone on a stand and is just about to speak when there's a movement behind me. I turn to find Jaime standing there, smiling a little shyly.

'Speak of the devil and he shall appear.' The officer rolls his eyes. 'You can use one of the probation interview offices if you like?'

He gets up, gesturing to a closed door opposite marked *Interview Room*. I catch sight of a group of half-naked prisoners who have appeared out of a shower recess. They have towels slung low around their hips. They pass amused eyes over me, adjusting their towels provocatively.

'And you lot, back to your cells!'

The officer steps forward, shooing them away with a flap of the hand. 'I do apologise, they've forgotten their manners... I *said*, go away!' he yells more forcefully, and they disperse, laughing.

'Sorry about that. Here you go.' He unlocks the door to an office that contains only a grey desk and two office chairs. 'I'll leave you to it.'

'Thanks, Mr Johnson.' Jaime nods.

And suddenly we're alone.

'Wow!' My jollity feels a bit forced. 'You've had quite a night, Jaime, haven't you! So how are you doing?'

'It's nice to see you again.' He runs his fingers through his mop of thick hair. It stands up comically. 'I'm a bit tired, to be honest.' I'm aware of him studying my face.

'So—'

'So—'

We both speak together and then laugh. Jaime gestures for me to speak first.

'Last night then.' I'm still smiling although I can feel the heat in my cheeks. 'I know you can't go into detail, but how was the guy when you left him?'

'Asleep, thank God.' Jaime relaxes back, smiling. 'I think he really meant to do it, y'know?'

'Well, he didn't, Jaime, and that can only be down to you. So how are you feeling now?' I watch him carefully.

'I'm okay.'

'Like, okay, or not really?'

His fingers touch the edge of the desk. I'm surprised to see they're slightly tanned, the fingernails neat and cared-for.

'Oh, I dunno. I don't know what it was about this kid, Leo. Maybe it's because he's so young and they've stuck him in a place like this.' He shakes his head. 'It's like... he's an alright kind of person, y'know? He's just been dealt a crappy hand. He lived with his dad when his dad wasn't inside, and then, a week ago, the old feller goes and kills himself. Leo's too fragile for these kinds of places; it breaks people. That's what last night was all about.'

Jaime's index finger runs back and forth along the edge of the table as echoes of my own life waver in front of me.

'I honestly believe, with a bit of time and patience, he'll confide in me – he'll tell me honestly if he thinks he's getting close to the edge again.' Jaime pauses. 'Does that sound arrogant?'

'Not at all. I think you've got a real skill for getting people to open up.'

He looks away, a little embarrassed at the praise. 'Maybe if he was located on the same wing as me so he didn't feel so isolated? I dunno – that's just me thinking out loud.' Jaime shakes his head as he ponders. 'But it will take more than me, I know that.'

'You've got really good instincts, Jaime.'

He instantly colours.

'You'd be so good at working with vulnerable people on the outside. I was thinking that as you're coming up for parole...'

He gives me a wary glance. 'Uh, hang on a bit... hang on.'

'What?'

'Why am I getting vibes?'

'What kind of vibes?' I laugh.

'Robyn the chaplain ones.'

It's my turn to go red.

'She's already been hinting. She thinks she's being clever

and subtle.' Jaime sighs comically. 'Maybe someone should tell her she'd never make a grifter.'

I wrinkle my nose. 'Grifter?'

'Shady manoeuvring. A con artist. A hustler.' He pouts comically. 'Nope, Robyn couldn't do that to save her life.'

'Err... you know about the guy in Seg, then?'

He gives me a tired look. 'You know the guy's a beast, don't you? He deals in the dark side: the niche market stuff. The rumour is, he's still doing it from in here; that's how he makes his money. If the other cons knew I was talking to him, I wouldn't last on the wing very long.' He smiles grimly.

'I didn't know that.'

'Maybe someone should have a serious convo with Robyn about the kinds of people she's putting her energy into.' He folds his arms across his chest in a comfort gesture. 'The guy needs permanently stopping, not a quiet chat.'

'I'll have a word with her. I'm sorry, Jaime.' I lean back. 'I wouldn't have even mentioned it. Robyn kind of sold it to me saying that if someone, anyone, could make even the minutest connection with this guy, then there's a chance that it'll ignite just a tiny spark of humanity.'

Jaime looks at me askance. 'I'd say I don't think either Robyn or you have a clue what you're dealing with.'

'No, you're probably right.' I sigh. 'Yes, actually, you're totally right. Ignore everything I've just said. I shouldn't have even mentioned your parole. I'm genuinely, truly sorry. You must think me very naive.'

'You're a nice person. Nice people can't imagine what goes on in these people's heads.'

'I feel a bit stupid now. I know Robyn's motivation is to do anything she can think of to stop men like Childs offending again. But you're right – that's not the way to go about it.'

'Well, don't feel stupid. Being a decent human being doesn't make you stupid.'

There's a slightly awkward silence, where neither of us speaks.

'Of course...'

'What?'

'He wouldn't suspect me.'

'What do you mean? Suspect you of what?'

Jaime shuffles closer in his seat. 'I mean, what if he told me stuff... like, even the smallest grain of information about how he operates? That would be worth it then, wouldn't it?' His eyes are almost excited.

'But you said it's dangerous to go anywhere near him!'

'But I'm getting out soon, aren't I?' He pauses, thinking. 'I know this wing, I know the people on it, I know how to work it so that no one sees what I'm doing. If he trusted me...' He looks away, thinking.

'Jaime... you can't.'

His eyes meet mine. They're very blue.

'If it means that Michael Childs has one less victim because of some titbit of information, surely it's worth it?'

'Jaime—'

'Trust me, Beth. I'm not some idiot.'

'I'm sorry, I can't go along with this. I'm not going to get involved in you sitting in with a prisoner who's a physical danger to you. I won't do that.'

Jaime crosses his arms and puts his head on one side. 'And if Childs gets out and you read about something he's done to some girl, what will you think then? Will you think that you could have done some tiny, tiny thing to prevent that from happening?'

I can't think of a reply.

'As they say, all it takes for evil to triumph is for good people to stand by and do nothing.' He sits there for a second, biting his lip, considering, then pushes his chair back quickly. 'Okay. I've told you what I think. The rest, now, is up to you and Robyn.'

He makes a move towards the door.

'Jaime.'

He stops.

'You are one of those decent human beings too, you know that?'

He pauses; his eyes make a hundred-and-eighty-degree sweep but he can't quite meet my gaze.

'Beth, if I'm in any way decent these days, any way at all, it's because of you.'

And with that, he's gone.

FOUR

'Everything okay?' Officer Johnson looks up from the screen in front of him.

'Yes thanks. Although...'

'Hmm?' He glances back at it, distracted.

'I was just wondering about the prisoner from last night, Leo Hargreaves. From what I can gather, he's posing an ongoing risk.'

'Uh-huh, yeah.' He nods at the screen. 'Leo Hargreaves. I'm just doing a report as we speak.'

'Is there any way—' I start.

'Is there any way, what?' Officer Johnson peers at me, amused, through the top of his glasses.

'Umm... he could be moved so that my Listener has easier access to him?'

The officer widens his eyes slightly.

'So that— Well, it would be less hassle for you and your officers to have someone like Jaime Lee keep a close eye on him. I was just thinking how much easier it would be. For you. All round.' I know I need to stop talking.

'Yeah, I can see the sense of that.' He's looking at me patiently.

'Oh! Right! Perfect!... Okay then!'

'Leave it with me.' And he goes back to his screen.

I find myself walking back towards the main gate, but I know, even with the gate block in sight, I'm not going there.

I'm going to the governor's office. If I can manage it with one prisoner, I can manage it with two.

I pause with my knuckles raised at the open door.

'Knock, knock.'

The governor's secretary, Zoe, flickers a glance up from her screen and she pulls an earbud from her ear.

'Hello you!' She smiles broadly. 'Haven't seen you in ages! I wondered where you've been hiding yourself. Managing to keep the naughty chaplain in check I hope?' She raises her eyebrows and then pulls a face. 'No, I don't suppose you are. What can we do for you?'

'I was wondering if the governor was free?'

I glance at the expensive-looking door to my left. It's firmly closed, with his name spelled out in large, black, embossed letters.

'We-ell.' Zoe squints. 'I'm supposed to be telling people that he's out for the day, but that's not exactly true.' She leans forward conspiratorially. 'He's desperately trying to catch up with paperwork.'

'Oh.'

'But I'm guessing he'll make an exception for you.' She winks. 'Hang on.'

She picks up the phone and taps three digits. Her eyes fix on the opposite wall and then her face suddenly animates.

'Geoff?... Now look, before you start, let me just say if I told you this person had come to see you and I sent them away, I know you'd only complain.' She gives me a wry look. 'How do I know that? Because you're always complaining, that's how.' The pout becomes pronounced. 'Oh, okay then, because I know how much you like her.'

I can feel myself going hot.

'Ye-es, it's Beth,' she says patiently as the heat in my face intensifies. 'Okay. Yes, and no, I won't tell her that.'

She ends the call laughing and nods towards his office. 'Just go in.'

Muttering thanks, I take a breath and turn the handle. I've only been in this office a couple of times before. Everything in here feels expensive: the huge wooden desk, the leather chair, the black and chrome furniture, the low, button-back sofa and easy chairs.

Geoff, the governor, looks up from his paperwork, pushing his chair back and gets up from his desk, his hand extended in a waft of aftershave.

'Beth! How lovely to see you!'

His suit says money. The cufflinks too. The shiny shoes. Geoff seems impossibly young to be a prison governor. He can only be, what? Thirty-something? His hand engulfs mine and draws me further into the room, asking me whether I would like tea or coffee, buzzing Zoe even before I get a chance to answer. My eyes take in the new additions of framed certificates and photographs of himself around the walls.

He follows my gaze.

'Oh, I found them in a box at home. That was me receiving some commendation or other from Princess Anne.' He flaps nonchalantly. 'And the one above was me in riot gear. There was a massive protest after two suicides in a secure unit. It escalated into violence and we were brought in.'

'Gosh.'

I pretend to study them, but the type on the newspaper clippings is so small it's impossible to read.

'That was when I introduced a new initiative to tackle the suicide rates in the last prison I was in,' he says, squaring his shoulders a little. 'That's why I'm so focussed on the work you're doing here.'

'Well, there's a fortuitous coincidence then!' I smile. 'That's exactly why I've come to talk to you.'

'Please.' Geoff pulls one of the scatter cushions aside so that I can sit on the sofa. He perches on the edge of a chair opposite, elbows on his knees, his fingers steepled attentively. 'So. How can I help?'

There's a knock on the door and Zoe appears, beaming, carrying a tray with a cafetière and two cups on it, sliding it carefully onto a side table.

'Enjoy!' She smiles and disappears out of the door.

Geoff busies himself pouring the coffee. I glance down and notice he's wearing Mickey Mouse socks. The madness of this place makes me want to laugh out loud.

He proffers a cup. 'I just had a call to say the area manager said he might pop in some time this afternoon.' He drops the teaspoon onto the tray with a clatter. 'So I'm actually glad we're having this chat. Suicide prevention is one of the hot topics that's come down from head office, so if I'm able to pick your brains at all...'

He peers at me over the rim of his cup as he takes a sip. His eyebrows are raised expectantly. He blinks rapidly and I detect the faintest shimmer of how inexperienced he really feels. I bite my lip; he'll want to impress.

'I've been chatting to Robyn the chaplain about Michael Childs.'

'Oh yes, Childs has become a bit of a pet project of hers.' The governor smiles.

I quickly marshal my thoughts. 'Basically, would you consider moving Childs from the Seg to normal location?'

His eyes flicker uncomfortably. 'Childs?'

I swallow.

'Look, I think I understand your reticence. I mean, I know Childs is high profile and is seen as a risk.'

Geoff nods and puts his cup down on the table.

'Yes, yes, he is. I don't think I'm quite understanding what you're thinking here. For him to be relocated I would have to consider the staff, the other prisoners.' He pauses. 'And then if anything happened and the newspapers got hold of it...' He grimaces. 'It doesn't bear thinking about.'

'But what if... What if one of Childs' suicide attempts were to be fatal? I mean, that's the loss of a life and that's a tragedy in itself.'

I'm not sure the governor looks convinced at the notion.

'But also, what would the media make of that? I understand the man has taken young girls that've never been found. Wouldn't the papers say that while he was alive there was a chance of him confessing and the families finally getting closure? Wouldn't they blame the prison though? Wouldn't they hold you responsible for his death and that vital information had been lost?'

I can see the governor's mind ticking over, weighing up the risks. I'm also aware he has the area manager's beady eye on him. The fact is, we've now had this conversation. If questions were ever asked, they'd be difficult ones to answer.

'Robyn believes his isolation in the Seg is adding to the risk,' I add.

The governor nods slowly. 'Yep, I get that.'

'I know it's a fine balance.' I watch his face. 'Him isolated; making him more of a risk; making the necessity to put more staff in to watch him.' I let each point sink in. 'What if...?'

He looks up.

'What if I could find a prisoner who would be willing to buddy up with him?'

Geoff's eyes spring open in surprise. 'You could find a prisoner who would want to talk to him? How likely is that?'

'If I were able to do it, would you allow it on a trial basis?'

The governor pauses and then takes a breath. 'I'll consider it and let you know. Will that do you?'

'Great. Excellent.'

I pick up my coffee cup. Robyn is going to be over the moon if we can pull this off. I know I've now got to break it to Jaime, hoping to God he hasn't changed his mind.

'In fact, I'll mention your input to the area manager; I think he'll be impressed that we're clearly taking the Samaritans' initiative very seriously.' Geoff nods.

'Thank you. That means a lot.' I feel buoyed but nervous. The impact of this decision could be tremendous, but the fallout if it goes wrong could be disaster.

And my name is written all over it.

My head is full of it as I leave the prison and head across the car park.

Something inside me has shifted.

My confidence level has gone up a notch; I'm buoyed and I feel as though I have taken control. There was a difficult situation: I assessed what could and couldn't be done, thought about it, saw an opportunity, and put a plan into action.

Robyn was exactly right.

She's been right about my situation with Drew too. That telephone conversation had shown me what I needed to see. I'd taken my time, stood back, waited, and given myself space to process it all.

And the result?

Drew had talked openly about the incident on the motorway. He had nothing to hide.

Had I reacted straightaway I would have caused a problem

that doesn't exist. I can't quite believe how close I came to messing everything up.

Dropping into the driver's seat, I start the engine and pull away, allowing the memories of last night to flood my brain. I head home.

I can allow myself to be happy; I deserve it.

I can trust that things are good and right and that nothing is going to come along and take it all away. I can trust myself.

Turning into my street, I glance up at the house and the closed curtains of Joe's room. I imagine he's still there, unmoving under the duvet. As I draw closer, a question forms in my head as I realise Drew's car is missing from the drive. I presumed as he worked so late last night, he'd still be here.

Slotting the key gently into the lock, I pause in the hallway and glance up, but startle at the sudden rattle of plates from the kitchen.

There's Joe, standing with his back to me, pouring cereal from a box into a bowl. My heart catches for a moment: the sight of his ragged hair standing up at the back, that boyish flex and curve of the tendons in his neck as he moves. His T-shirt is old and baggy, tenting out at the back. I want to go over to him so badly, grab him into a hug. A spill of flakes has already scattered across the work surface. I shan't ask him to clean them up.

'Hiya!' I say brightly.

He pauses but doesn't answer, moving over to the cutlery drawer to find a spoon, and then to the fridge.

'Did you have a good night?'

He's hidden behind the fridge door and starts rummaging around, ignoring the question. My heartrate intensifies as I feel the conflict that I'm certain is coming my way.

He closes the door with a *whump* and looks shocked to see me.

'Oh! You made me jump!' He clutches the milk carton to

his chest, pulling an earbud from one ear, and going to retrieve his bowl. 'You've been out already?'

'I went to the prison.'

'Right.'

He goes over, pulling out a stool at the breakfast bar, plonking his bowl down and starts to shovel cereal into his mouth. He pulls his phone towards him, tapping the screen and studying the message. I can't read it from here. I squint a little, but don't move closer in case he sees.

'Drew not here?'

He shrugs. 'Dunno.'

'How's Nate?' The question is veiled, yet pointed enough. I brace myself for the response.

'Got a present for you.' He gestures with his milky spoon towards the sink.

I glance over. There's a bundle of something ballooning over the draining board.

'They're to say sorry.'

It takes me a second to register.

Flowers.

The sink is a mass of multi-colours. I look at him, but he dips his head to his cereal again.

'Joe!' I go over and scoop up the bouquet. I can't quite believe it.

'I got them last night. I was going to give them to you then, but you'd gone to bed.'

'They're gorgeous!'

His head lowers, embarrassed.

'Yeah, well...' He twitches awkwardly. 'I know I was being...' He shrugs.

'You've never bought me flowers!'

'I have now.'

'You have.' I can't get over it. 'I need to show them off properly – I've got a vase somewhere.' I kneel at the cupboard, reaching to the back.

'Yeah, I didn't know where,' Joe says around a mouthful of food. 'Otherwise I'd've left them looking a bit better. I thought you'd moan about me leaving a mess in the sink.'

'I'd never moan at you getting me flowers, Joe.' I find the vase and pull it out.

He doesn't contradict me even though I know he'd like to.

I'm wondering if, while I've got him here, and things are good between us, this might be a good time to chat.

I fill the vase with water and set it on the side.

'I was kind of wanting to ask you something.' I search in the drawer for the scissors.

'Oh yeah?' His spoon clatters into the empty bowl and he pushes his stool back.

'I was wondering...'

'Uh-huh.' He takes the bowl to the draining board.

'About this calling me Beth.' Plucking out one of the flowers, I snip off the end and slide it into the vase.

He pauses. 'What's wrong with that?'

My spine stiffens.

'Well, what's wrong with "Mum"?' I slide him a cautious look. I can't gauge the expression on his face.

'"Mum" sounds a bit lame though, doesn't it?'

'Does it?'

'And I call Drew, "Drew".'

'But that's different.'

'Why is it?'

Snip. Snip. Snip-snip.

I try to concentrate on the flower stem in my hand and the feel of the scissor blade biting through it. I so want this to go well.

'You said you always wanted me to have a dad.'

'I did! I mean, I do, but...'

'So, I'm giving you what you want. I can't call Drew "dad", so I'm making you and Drew equal.'

I pause and blink. I can't fault his logic. I almost smile.

'Is it you're a bit jealous, Beth?'

I almost drop the flower I'm holding. 'Jealous?'

'Yeah. Of me and Drew. 'Cos we're close now. I've noticed you don't like it when we spend time together. You go weird.' He frowns. 'Like if you think I've talked to him about more personal stuff... It's like you need me to confide in you like I used to when I was a little kid. Only I'm not a little kid.'

'Why do you think that?' My tone is level: not accusing at all.

'Things that Drew's mentioned.'

I hold my reaction steady.

'I know you're not a child, Joe. You're practically an adult. I just want you to feel you can come to me like you used to. Like, if you're...' I'm wanting to say, *'in trouble in any way'*, but I don't. 'If you're bothered about anything. Or even just want to share something nice that's happened.'

'Is that what you get from them?' He jerks his head towards the door. 'Those guys in that prison? You get from them what you can't get from me?'

'What? No! Why would you say that? You're my son, Joe. It's totally different. I want to help them, but for you it's about giving you that real family to belong to.'

I feel as though I'm suddenly scrambling, unable to get a foothold.

'*You*. Giving. Me...' he repeats slowly. 'How come you've made this all about you?'

'I don't know what you mean!' I turn to face him, shocked.

'How do you know what I want? How do you know what I *need*?' His face crumples into a frown.

I look into my son's face and I see his dad, Simon. Same age. Standing there in front of me.

'You're so needy, Beth! You want so much that I just can't give you! It's some big, black hole that you want me to fill and I can't! You suck the life out of me. All I want to do is get away!'

Joe goes to walk past me, but I move in front of him to stand in his way. He takes a step to the side, but I move too, to block him.

'Don't do this.' His head is lowered while he glowers at me.

'Joe.'

'I said, don't do this. Let me pass.'

'All I want is for you to talk to me.'

'Can you get away from the door please?'

'No, please stop. Could you just—'

'I said *move!*'

He goes to shoulder me out of the way, but I catch the hem of his T-shirt. His arm swings to shake me off but I realise the scissors are still in my hand. The tip of them catches his forearm and there's a swift beading of red on white skin. I am so shocked I don't let go, my mind racing blindly as the material stretches out behind him, still in my grasp. He yanks it forcefully, spinning me round so it tears my fingernail. With a yelp of pain, I stumble back, hitting my head on the doorframe, as a myriad of stars springs violently in front of my eyes.

My hand lurches out to stop myself falling – and I'm grabbing at him, but he punches me off, his hand connecting with my palm and slipping sideways to crack me on the side of the jaw.

I go down, my knees buckling beneath me, the world spiralling from whirling colours to black.

Then there's a voice from somewhere far away. Maybe more than one.

There are swooping colours and a sudden blast of cooling air. I feel hands around my waist, my head being turned, as

Drew's face balloons in front of me, huge, filling my whole vision.

'Beth?'

He sounds echoey and muffled, and then booms right up close.

'Beth... *Beth*! I'm here! Look at me! Come on.'

I hear him saying something else.

'What the hell happened?'

He's asking a question that I can't answer and then talking about getting a tea towel and running it under the water, but I'm not able to connect. I try to do as he says, forcing my stomach muscles to pull me to an upright position. The world comes into focus. There's the click of someone's knees, and I'm aware of Joe crouching beside Drew and passing him the towel. The shock of cold wetness on my cheek and neck makes me jump. A jar of pain instantly slams through my spine.

'Steady... Steady now,' Drew soothes. 'Calm down.'

I try and gesture to the back of my head but I'm aware of him holding my right wrist so that I can't.

'Don't fight me. Do you still feel faint?'

I manage a dull shake of the head. 'No, I must have...' But nothing comes to me. My mouth feels dry and sticky and won't enunciate the words.

The hallway comes back into focus; Drew is there crouching next to me, his face pale and frowning with concern and something else I can't fathom. Joe is hunkered next to him; his chin is lowered, his mouth set in a grim line.

'What happened?' Drew's leather jacket creaks with familiarity as he looks at Joe.

'It was an accident. One minute she was coming down the stairs and the next minute she was falling.'

I stare at him open-mouthed.

'I... I... We were arguing—'

'Beth.' Drew's voice has an edge of caution.

'I grabbed him; the next thing I know is—' I break off, automatically reaching up to the sore bruised place on my scalp where I can feel a lump beginning to swell.

Joe blinks, pausing for a second. He glances at Drew and then back at me. 'I bought you flowers. You went to get a bigger vase. You said the one you'd got was too small.'

I have this sudden memory of the scissors. I glance at Joe's arm.

'Come on, let's get you upstairs,' Drew says. 'Here we go.' He deftly scoops a strong arm across my back and under my arm, hauling me to my feet. My face is immediately brought close into his shirt. The fabric is crisp and clean. He smells comforting: of outside and fresh air.

'Okay there? Right – one step at a time.' Drew is guiding me, half carrying, half levering up the stairs. I feel as weak and woozy as a newborn kitten as he manoeuvres me into our bedroom, holding me steady while he pulls back the covers and plonks me on the mattress. A sudden surge of emotion at his tender kindness sends a hiccough of tears into my throat.

'Hey... Hey, Beth!'

I'm desperately trying to fight it.

'Are you dizzy still? Do you have a headache?' He peers anxiously into my face.

'No, no, I'm fine.' I half sob. 'I just need to lie down.'

He dips to wrestle me out of my leggings, and pulls my sweater over my head.

'We'll see how you go; you've hit your head. I'm not sure I should let you sleep.' He eyes me doubtfully. 'I'm going to keep coming back in and checking on you.' He holds up a warning finger. 'And there's no arguments on that score. If you start getting a headache or your vision goes blurry, I'm taking you to the hospital, yes? Yes?'

I'm forced to acquiesce as he pushes me back into the pillows, swinging my legs up, and pulling the covers over me.

'Thank God Joe was here.' He tucks the covers around my shoulders, patting and smoothing. 'If you'd been alone in the house and slipped on the stairs like that...' He shakes his head, worriedly. 'I'd only been gone two minutes!'

'Where were you?'

'Looking for my phone in the car. If I'd had a call from work, I would've driven off. You'd have been on your own; it might've been for hours.' He's almost gabbling.

'Drew.'

He stops and looks at me.

'I didn't slip.'

'What?' His brow puckers for a moment, then drops into concern. 'You didn't pass out, did you?'

I go to speak, but can't formulate what I need to say. 'Joe and I... We got into an argument.'

The pucker in his brow deepens. 'What kind of argument?' I watch a range of emotions sweep across his face. 'What are you saying, Beth?'

A lurch of anxiety grips me. 'A stupid argument.' I blink, stepping back from the precipice that's opened up in front of me. 'He said things, I said things. It was all in the heat of the moment.'

Drew's face instantly relaxes and he smiles. 'Teenagers. Hot and cold. Pushing your buttons, eh? But I can't believe he bought you flowers. That was so nice of him, wasn't it? Shows you what a decent kid he is, and how much he cares.'

Drew straightens, gazing down at me. 'Fact is, Beth, you're exhausted.' He bends to stroke the hair from my forehead. 'You do too much at that prison – I mean, going into that place at all hours.' He shakes his head. 'Look at you, you can barely keep your eyes open.'

I nod. I'm too tired to explain it all right now.

'I'll run you a bath later. I'll bet you have a few bumps and bruises.'

I watch him walk to the door. He pauses, a hand on the knob, and looks back at me.

'We'll be as quiet as we can – give you a bit of peace.'

The use of the word 'we' jars. I nod dumbly; my brain attempts to process what's just taken place.

Slipped on the stairs? Why would Joe have said that?

And the speed that Joe spiralled; I couldn't control it. That massive vent of pent-up anger. Where had that come from? Something has triggered him. What?

Things aren't right.

Nothing is right.

I lie back in the pillows, closing my eyes and trying to breathe. Breathe and count. Count and breathe – when suddenly my eyes fly open.

'I was looking in the car for my phone.'

Drew had said that, hadn't he?

But Drew's car wasn't here.

A slow drumbeat of something I don't want to think tightens in my chest.

There'll be an explanation. I know that. Drew wouldn't lie.

I stand at the top of the stairs, pausing for a moment with one hand on the banister. The quiet thump and boom from downstairs tells me they're engrossed in some computer game.

Grabbing a fluffy dressing gown, pyjamas, and some comfy socks, I creep along the landing to the bathroom to run a bath. I bend to turn on the taps, breathing in the soothing steam deep into my lungs. Reaching for the bubble bath, I squeeze out the purple glops, sending amoeba-like tendrils into the water. Carefully pinning my hair up, I slide gratefully under the foaming surface, resting my head back. The bright rectangle of frosted window is imprinted into the backs of my eyes. There's a soft zigzagging of colours that I let fizz and trail, shutting everything else out.

'Beth?'

I jerk, eyes wide.

The door handle squeals.

'What are you doing in there?' Drew's voice is querulous on the other side of the door. My heart skips into a higher beat. He tries the door again.

'Can you unlock the door please?'

'I'm fine! Really, I'm fine, Drew! There's no need to worry.'

'But I do.' I can hear him fiddling with the lock. 'You shouldn't be in there if I can't get to you.'

There's a metallic screeching sound and I lever up in a wash of water. The door opens and his head appears in the gap.

'You can turn these from the outside; all you need is a coin.' He holds up the ten pence piece. 'Joe's gone out, so there's only us.'

Lumbering over to the laundry basket, he pulls it out so that he can sit closer. 'There.' He smiles. 'Hey, have a chill; lie back. Let me run you some more hot water.'

He reaches across as a bloom of heat reaches my thighs and back.

'So how are you feeling?'

'Bit confused,' I say. I see a flicker of alarm light his face. 'Not like that.'

'Then like what?'

'Did you find your phone?' I ask.

His brow puckers. 'Had I lost it?'

'You said you had.'

'Did I? Dunno, I'm always losing things.' He chuckles. 'Might've found it and lost it again.'

I grip the bath edge and draw myself up, hugging my knees against my chest.

'Your car wasn't on the drive.'

'Eh?' I can feel Drew's gaze as he watches me very carefully.

'When I came home.'

His neck recoils a little in query. 'Beth, what is this?'

'You tell me.'

He blinks at my tone then purses his lips. 'Okay. Right,' he says patiently, measuring each word. 'I decided there was paperwork in the office I needed. I pulled the car off the drive, realised I didn't have my phone, so came back to look for it.'

'But that isn't what you said.'

'Oh my God, Beth!' He raises his hands. 'I'd just found you collapsed on the stairs! You want me to recount exactly what I said, word for word?'

He's annoyed, but desperately trying not to be. I suddenly feel the heat of his hand on my arm as he unwinds my wrist from around my knees.

There's an insistent pressure.

'So, while we're on the subject of stories changing, let's talk about what happened with Joe.'

'What about?' The water slews a little.

'He's told me what really happened.' His eyes are kind, like he wants to understand. 'He says things spiralled out of control.' He looks away for a moment. I know something not good is coming. 'He says that you went for him.'

'He said that I *what*?!'

'That you were waving the scissors around, getting angrier and angrier. He wasn't even sure you knew you were holding them.' The pressure of Drew's palm on my arm grows. 'Did you lose it with him, Beth? I know you've been struggling recently.' His hand comes up to pacify me. 'And before you say anything, you know you can tell me the truth. I'm going to be on your side no matter what. All I need is for you to be absolutely straight.'

'No,' I say steadily, inching into anger. 'No, Drew, I did *not* lose my mind.'

'I didn't say *"lose your mind"*. I didn't use those words.'

'He's implying it. You're implying it. The facts are, Joe thinks I'm jealous of your relationship. He accused me of caring about the prisoners more than I do about him. He tried to walk away from me and I grabbed his T-shirt. That's all. I have never laid a hand on him in anger, Drew. It's not something, as a parent, I have ever done.' I labour the word 'parent' deliberately, knowing, even as I do, I'm being unfair. Drew's spine instantly stiffens, and he stands.

'I was only giving you the opportunity to open up and talk to me, Beth, that's all. I'm not having a go and accusing you of anything.' His mouth works awkwardly. 'Although you clearly can't say the same.'

He stands, looking down at me. I instinctively huddle my knees closer to my chest, my skin pricking into goosebumps.

'I didn't say you were. I said you implied it. And I wasn't accusing you of anything.'

I feel vulnerable, beaten down, a bit silly.

'Well, it certainly felt like it.' He lifts his chin with a pained expression on his face. 'It's not my fault that your relationship with Joe is...' He waves dismissively, and my hackles bristle instantly.

'Pass me that towel please.' I lean forward, gesticulating angrily to the rail. 'I'm not sitting here listening to this.'

Drew holds it out and I grab it, rising in a great swell of soapy water and wrapping it tightly around me.

'What the hell's got into you?' His eyes follow me as I step out of the bath. 'What's going on?'

That just about does it.

'What's got into *me*?' My head is pounding with tension. 'Are you being serious, Drew? Like, are you *really* asking me that question?'

'Yes, I really am,' he says heatedly. 'First it was all that stuff over dinner. I mean I'm trying to be on your side and present a real team, but seriously? Then there's clearly something going on when I get home this morning and you're all edgy and secretive, and then you run off, leaving me without saying a word. I leave a ton of messages for you which you don't reply to—'

His breathing is laboured. 'And then I walk back into the house to find you involved in some' – he makes an angry throwaway gesture – 'some altercation with Joe! So I think *"what-the-hell-has-got-into-you"* is a reasonable question, actually.'

The pent-up fury in me explodes. 'I'll tell you then, shall I?'

His glaring at me only infuriates me further.

'I got a phone call last night.'

His face collapses in puzzlement. 'From whom?'

'From a woman who says she's been seeing you.'

He stares at me slightly open mouthed for a moment, and then his jaw snaps closed.

'I have absolutely no clue what you're talking about.'

'The woman on the motorway. *That* woman.'

His face pales – *and with it, my heart.*

No, no, no, no, no.

'The woman rang you? The one from the accident?'

I nod quickly.

'You're sure…? How can you be sure though?' I can see he's scrabbling.

'Are we really going to play this game, Drew? Are we really?' I put my head on one side.

'I just can't get my head around it.' He rubs the back of his neck. 'I can't get my head around what you're telling me. How could she have rung you? What did she say? How the hell did she get your number?'

'You tell me.'

'What did she say?' he asks again.

'She told me I needed to be careful of you. That you were a monster. That you were a liar.'

'*What?*'

'She implied you'd been seeing her.'

His head is swinging back and forth like some bull elephant. 'I've not, Beth... I wouldn't... I'm telling you, on... on...' He casts about frantically. 'On Joe's life, I have not been seeing anyone.' He puts his hand on his heart.

I falter, but I'm not letting him off. 'Then who is she, Drew? What would make some woman wandering on a motorway call me, for goodness' sake?'

'How the hell should I know?' Drew holds out his hands. 'She's definitely the woman from that incident?'

'I put two and two together. She said that you had dumped her on the side of the motorway, then I saw the news report. It seems too much of a coincidence, doesn't it? She definitely knew who I was. She knew who you were.'

His jaw sets. 'So you've got the number on your phone, right?'

'It came up as private.'

Drew's eyes dart. 'Okay. Okay,' he breathes. 'Someone clearly phoned you, so let's start at the beginning. Now, can you tell me, as precisely as you remember it, what this person said?'

I can only stare at him for a few moments, my brain in overdrive as I try to gauge if he's telling me the truth.

'The phone rang—'

'Your mobile?'

'Yes, my phone rang.'

'What time was this?'

'Oh, I don't know... Umm... I know, I was in bed not long after ten, but I read and fell asleep. Midnight, maybe? I don't know. I answered the phone, and it was a woman saying—'

But he interrupts. 'Was there anything about her voice that you remember? Age? Accent? Anything like that?'

I bring a hand up and run it through my damp hair. 'No, no, I don't think so. She sounded... oh I dunno... Young. Twenties, thirties, how do you tell? She was crying, angry.

She said no one would believe her. She sounded...' I bite my lip.

'What?'

'Not right.'

'What kind of "not right"?'

'She sounded like she was terrified.'

'Of me?'

I look at him.

'Have I ever given you the impression that I'm the kind of guy that goes around terrifying women?'

'Well...'

'Have I?'

'No.' I keep my face expressionless.

'Have I ever come across as a bit sleazy – making inappropriate comments, jokes, that kind of thing? Go on, you can say it. Just tell me the truth.' He holds out his hands.

'Well, no.'

He lets out a sigh. 'Okay, okay, that's something then.'

There's silence where neither of us speak. He stands there gazing round the room, unseeing, blinking as he tries to process. His eyes suddenly focus and flit to my face.

'Why didn't you say something? Why didn't you phone me straightaway? How come you've left it until now?'

I open my mouth to speak, but then close it again.

'I spoke to Robyn about it. I was so upset I couldn't think properly.'

'And what did Robyn think?'

'She said I needed to take my time and trust my gut.'

'And what's your gut telling you?'

I pause. *What does my gut say?*

'She said that you'd dumped her on the side of the motorway. I could hear traffic in the background. She said I had no idea what kind of person you were or what you were involved with. She begged me—' I blink at the memory. 'She begged me not to tell you. That she'd be in danger if I did.'

'And what did you say to her?'

'I didn't say anything, that's my absolute shame.' My hand comes up to my throat. 'I mean... I think it was the shock of it. I didn't know what to do. All I managed was to put the phone down.' I can feel the burn of guilt under my fingers. 'Then I saw the news. I saw what happened, and that grainy footage of the girl that the police want to contact, and I put it all together.'

Drew hasn't taken his eyes from me. He lets go of my hands. I can feel his gaze: tracking, assessing, gauging to see if I'm keeping anything back.

'Right.' He breathes. 'Right. Okay.'

I wrap the towel tighter around myself, feeling the slight shiver of a chill prickling my skin. He reaches to touch my face, tipping my chin so that I am forced to meet his gaze.

'Are you prepared to listen to what I'm about to say?'

He looks into my eyes. I make a tiny nod.

'I want you to tell me the truth: do you believe me when I say I am not, and never have been, and never will be, unfaithful to you?' He doesn't blink. 'Beth?' He gives my chin a little shake. 'I need to know that you believe me.'

He would not have sworn on Joe's life. He would not have done that.

I look into his eyes. They are the same eyes that made me feel safe, that told me he was different, that he'd love Joe and we'd build a life together and above all, he wouldn't hurt me.

'I believe you,' I say. I mean it.

'And I believe your version of events with Joe.'

Something inside me tightens as though he thinks, deep-down, I could be lying.

'He says he's gone round to Nate's.' He's being non-committal. 'Probably wanted an excuse to get out of the house. I didn't

question it. I thought it best to give him some time and space.'
His face is shadowed.

'Drew?'

He pauses.

'I do believe you – I mean, I really do,' I say.

'Good.' He proffers a tiny smile but I tense.

'Are we okay?'

His face relaxes, and my gut relaxes with it. 'Come here.'

I step into his arms. They wrap around me like a comforting blanket. I can tell by the way he keeps squeezing and releasing that he's reassuring himself as much as me.

He shifts, dropping his cheek next to my ear and kissing my bare shoulder. The tiny kisses become nips, grazing my skin with the edges of his teeth sending shivers of delight through the small of my back.

'I did say Joe's out, didn't I?' he whispers into my neck. The heat and the wet sending a pulse of desire between my legs. I let go of the towel. It's caught between us, my back bare as his fingers trail in ticklish grooves up and over my hips, his arm cupping my waist.

His hand reaches down to the back of my thigh to hoist me hard in a gasp as I find myself lifted against the cold wall. He fumbles at the front of his jeans, the metal chink of his belt unhooking, the soft purr of his zip, and within seconds he's inside me, filling me up, a pressure pain that thrusts and moves, as his palms grapple me higher, lifting me up until I am gazing down at him, his chin jutting and tilted, his eyes closed in the rapture of concentration.

How could I ever doubt you, my heart says, *when you can make me feel this way?*

I wet my fingers, tracing them across his eyes, lilac lidded, the eyelashes, fanned like a girl's against his cheek. The flush through his temples, the slight sheen across his hairline as he pushes into me, the thump of my desire building into a thigh-shaking, spine-tightening ricochet of pleasure.

We open our eyes simultaneously.

He looks dazed as though not knowing where he is. My arms and legs are shaking as he blinks, coming back to me, his arms relaxing, letting me slide to the floor. He pulls the bathrobe from the back of the door and loops it around my shoulders, encouraging my arms into the sleeves before bending to sort his own clothes. My head suddenly throbs, and I raise a tentative hand.

'I didn't hurt you, did I?' He looks at me, horrified.

'No, no!' I laugh a little. 'Took my mind off the bruises though.'

He grins down at me. We're close now. So close. I can't imagine what I was thinking. The sudden embarrassing shame of me, trying to find reasons not to trust him. *Why would I do that? This is Drew*, my head reminds me. *Drew. Not some random guy. You know this man. You know how he operates. Just talk to him. Tell him you're insecure. Explain why you're scared. He'll understand.*

'I'm sorry about what I said before,' I say quietly.

'And I'm sorry too.' He kisses the tip of my nose and then pulls back a little. 'We good?'

'We're perfect.' I smile.

'Oh, really?' He raises an eyebrow in amusement. 'And I thought that was just me.' He winces apologetically.

FIVE

'So, the deal is, we'll leave Joe to me. Is that the plan?' Drew's standing with his hand on the bedroom door. 'I think things just need to calm down a bit.'

I finish pulling a sweater over my head. 'Sure. Sounds good.'

'And you're okay with me disappearing for an hour and doing a bit of digging about all this phone stuff?'

'Absolutely fine.'

'And you promise to call me straightaway if you start feeling ill?'

I laugh at the list, making a criss-cross on my heart with my index finger. 'Promise.'

'So, I'll see you a bit later. If I find out anything, I'll call you.'

'Okay.' I smile.

'Okay. Good.'

He steps forward to kiss me gently on the side of my face. His lips leave a tiny damp moat as he pulls away.

He taps the tip of my nose. 'You're sure?'

'Haven't you gone yet?' I laugh.

He disappears and I hear the padded thump of his feet as he

runs down the stairs. There are seconds, and then I hear the clatter across the tiles and the squeal of the front door.

The room suddenly feels very empty. I sit on the side of the bed.

I am full, though. I feel warm and fuzzy, wrapped in Drew's attention. I don't ever remember feeling like this: this sense of security and love. I need to be good enough for him. Good enough to deserve it.

'I wish your father was still alive. He would've loved Drew.'

I sigh. My mother and my self-doubt always seem to be intertwined.

We were in her kitchen a few weeks ago, watching Drew and Joe in the garden kicking a ball about. Drew was laughing, shouting encouragement. Their two dark heads, hair flopping. My surge of absolute pride.

'Joe's looking very thin, don't you think, darling? But then I don't suppose you've had much time to cook real meals.' She'd smiled back at me. *'But now you've got Drew, that'll all change, won't it?'*

My head snaps back to the present with the sound of my phone. I close my eyes at the name that's flashing on the screen.

There's no such thing as coincidence.

'Hello, Mum, how are you?'

I open them to stare out at the sky. It's blank, as though every living thing has disappeared.

'More to the point, darling, how are you?'

'I'm fine.'

'That's not what Drew's been telling me. He's very worried about you.'

There's a hitch in my stomach. 'Oh? When did you speak to him?'

'So there is something then!'

'No, no... I just wondered what he was referring to.'

'He says you're doing too much. But I'm glad to hear you're

taking some time away from all that Samaritans stuff, darling. I imagine it gets a bit depressing. It'll be good to concentrate full-time on Joe for a while, won't it?'

'I'm not taking time off.' I shake my head, puzzled.

'He told me he's had a chat with your office people,' she says distractedly. 'Anyway, how's Joe? Is he going to come and see me? I hear he's got access to a car! Goodness! He'll be able to take me out for lunch!'

She twitters on, giggling about places she's been and people I don't know. I should be showing interest but all I can think about is Drew phoning her, Drew booking me time off work, Drew having the absolute nerve...

'I've got someone at the door, Mum. Can I call you back?'

'Of course, darling! Of course!'

And she's gone.

I feel like a pressure cooker about to explode in a whistle of steam.

Joe's lying about me, Drew's trying to control me, and my mother, as usual, is criticising me. I don't know how much more I can stand.

Sarah.

The thought of sensible, straight-talking Sarah leaps into my mind.

I know exactly what she'll say: *Don't just take all this, Beth! Call them out and say how you feel! Don't allow the three of them to manoeuvre you all the time!*

'Hiya!' She sounds a little breathless. There's the yell and crash of boys arguing in the background.

'Sorry, you're in the middle of something.' I try to sound casual. She clearly hasn't got time for me right now. 'Can I just have a quick word with Joe?'

'Joe?' She's suddenly distracted. 'Oi... Billy! I *said* not that!... Sorry,' she flusters. 'No, Joe's not here. I haven't seen him. It feels like I haven't seen Nate for days either,' she tuts.

'He turns up to raid the fridge and then disappears... *Billy!*' she shrieks. 'What did I just say?'

I frown, confused, then turn at the slam of the front door downstairs.

'No worries, Sarah, I think he's just turned up!' I try to keep my voice light. I have this sudden queasy feeling at the thought of facing him.

'Okay! Great. Speak later, Beth. Bye!'

Going out onto the landing, I pause anxiously on the top step. Two voices: Joe's, and then a low murmur in reply. There's a guffaw of laughter and a ton of expletives. Joe joins in; the shock and the ferocity in the stream of vitriol makes me take a step back.

Holding on to the banister, I peer down.

I don't recognise the boy with his back to me. It's certainly not Nate. He says something else to Joe as he gazes round and then upward. There's a registered moment of surprise for both of us. The face that's staring at me is more a man than a boy. Thick-necked and rough-looking, he could be anywhere between twenty and thirty.

Joe hasn't realised. He says something inaudible over his shoulder as he grabs the banister and swings up the first couple of steps. He stops dead as he sees me.

'Actually, let's bail,' he says without looking back. 'We can always come back later.'

'Sure. No drama.'

It's as though I'm invisible. Joe leaps from the stair, playfully bumping shoulders with his new friend. There's the squeal of the front door and then a swift slam. I am left with a heavy, suffocating feeling.

I know the type of man this is. The prison is full of them: foul-mouthed and cocky, swaggering around, with an arrogant disregard for any other human being. And there's my son, bringing that into my home.

And not for the first time.

I thought we'd dealt with this. I thought he'd understood. Me being called into the principal's office. Joe had been *'caught up in something very serious'*, he had said. There was talk of carrying knives. *Drugs.* No. No. The accusation made no sense.

Joe had sobbed next to me – my skinny little Joe, who wasn't capable of bullying anyone. He'd been picked on by a gang; they'd robbed him, pushed him about, warned his friends away from him. I'd had no inkling, and then an older boy, a boy he didn't know, had stepped in. Said he'd protect him, beat the gang leader up, he'd never be picked on again. And all that was true. They didn't come near him. His friends came back. But of course there was a price.

The principal had taken pity on him. Given him a warning as there was no direct evidence or link, but someone had mentioned his name. I was appalled, but I didn't want to make him clam up. I'd said I wouldn't be angry if he told me the absolute and complete truth, which he did. I believed him. I moved him to another school. No more problems. That was all in the past.

Or so I thought.

A phone begins to ring somewhere in the house.

My head turns as I try to locate the unfamiliar ringtone. It's not one I recognise. I stand listening to its jolly trill, and then it stops abruptly, before starting up again.

Slowly retracing my steps, I go back up to the landing and pause. I can still hear it, but I'm mystified where the ringing could be coming from. Joe's room seems the most obvious, but it sounds too close. The ringing stops again. I know I shouldn't be doing this as I push open his bedroom door and peer inside.

The dim room reveals his wreck of a bed, the half-drawn curtain, the fug of teenage socks, the dusty spills of Xbox game cartons littering the floor. I gaze around the blank walls, wrinkling my nose. There are so few places he could stash anything:

there are no bookshelves or drawers, and he refused to have a wardrobe, so we compromised on a hanging rail, leaving his T-shirts in heaps on the floor.

Picking my way over them, I struggle over to the window, pulling the curtain back, letting it sweep through the never-disturbed dead flies on the windowsill. There's no evidence of a phone or its tell-tale charger lead. Nothing.

Kneeling, I peer under the bed where the discarded dirty sneakers live and the odd fluff-balled woolly hat. I can see by the rolls of lint and dust that no one has been under here for a very long time. Levering up, I let out a sigh of relief; what was I expecting? Rolls of fifty-pound notes? Baggies of coke?

Carefully retracing my steps over the wreckage, I'm about to pull open the door, when the phone's shrill jangle snatches my hand back. The sound is confusing: so near and yet so...

My eyes halt.

The grubby fingermarks on the wooden frame look fresh. They're on the door edge too. The sight of them forces my brain to ask questions.

The marks are way too high.

I track them, my own fingers tracing their progress as the shrill jangle goes on and on.

Clambering onto the edge of the mattress, I hold on to the door frame and gingerly feel along the top. Grit and splinters gather under my nails, but suddenly there's a dip. My fingers drop into a gap and touch something that feels like plastic. Using all my strength, I pick at it clumsily, hooking its edge to draw it up. The screen pulses with light; my fingers fumble and nearly drop it.

Melanie, the name says. A whole list of missed calls from 'Melanie' one after another.

The girlfriend? my head queries. *The one he's been texting?* I turn the phone over: it's a cheap throwaway one. This isn't Joe's regular phone. *But why would he hide it?*

The answer comes to me all too readily with the image of the rough-looking guy.

The screen goes black. Hands shaking, I frantically press the 'on' button again just as I hear the front door slam downstairs. Hurriedly scrambling back onto the mattress, I push the phone back where I found it, pulling his door closed behind me, and darting into my bedroom.

The stairs creak as I fling open the wardrobe door, panicking as I pull out odd bits of clothing. There's the crack of the floorboard outside the bedroom.

'Hiya! Only me!' Drew sounds cheery. He pokes his head around the door. 'You okay?' He glances from me to the pile of clothes and back again.

I pause with a hanger clutched to my chest. 'Christ, you scared me. I thought you were Joe... You've been into work already?'

'Nah! Never got there!' He rolls his eyes. 'I got waylaid by a whole lot of calls from Stevie Boy, who's managed to mess up a lot of important paperwork... No, the whizz-kid lad who could help me with the mystery caller isn't on till later. He's good with the dark arts – he'll know if your number was accessed from my phone.'

He drops his hand to pat the front pocket of his jeans. 'And I forgot my notebook. I think I left it next to my laptop... Anyway, you just said you were scared I might be Joe; has something happened?'

I open my mouth to tell him, but his phone rings. He holds up a hand as he answers it, retreating out of the doorway.

I hear the word 'kids' and then 'mule'. My stomach flips inside out. I stand there clutching the hanger and a skirt, desperately trying to hear what he's saying. The door eases back open.

'Sorry... what were you saying?'

'I was worried what I should say to him.'

'Yeah, I get that. But it was me he gave a different version of events to; I feel like it should be me who challenges him.'

'Uh-huh. You're right.'

Drew is smiling. 'And we did agree that you leave Joe to me. Remember that conversation?'

'I do. I do.'

'Old habits, eh?' He's still smiling.

'Yeah, old habits. My mother rang.'

I see him query the non-sequitur.

'She said you rang her?'

'Me? No, she rang while you were having a lie-down and I answered it. I told her you had a bit of a headache, which was technically true.' He smiles.

'She also said you'd rung the Samaritans' office and said I was taking time off work.'

He pulls a questioning face and then his expression clears. 'Oh... right! I know what she's talking about. No, she's got the wrong end of the stick! I said I wished you *would* take some time out. I think you're doing too much.' He looks slightly ill at ease. *Do I totally believe him?*

'But still no dizziness?' He deftly switches the subject.

'I'm fine.' I force the corners of my mouth to turn upward.

'I'll leave you in peace then. I'll call if the whizz-kid lad comes up with anything.'

'Okay.'

He puckers his lips to blow me a kiss. 'See you later.'

He pulls the door closed with a click.

I'm aware of a mounting sense of disquiet as I listen to him moving about in the spare bedroom. He gets halfway down the stairs, clearly forgets something, and then comes back up.

'Bye!' he hollers. There's the drum of his feet on the stairs, and then the slam of the front door.

Kids. Mule.

I daren't say anything to Drew. The less he knows the less

he'd have to hide. Joe. My boy. What else can a cheap burner phone mean?

I could break down and weep right now. *Joe, what on earth have you got involved with?*

I have this absolute visceral need to speak to him. Grabbing my phone, my thumb makes the connection with his name, as I hurry to the top of the stairs.

Joe's bedroom door is not as I left it.

Cancelling the call, I climb up to check the door edge again. My fingers frantically skim, finding the dip. Skimming again, probing in there, deeper and deeper, knowing, even as I'm doing it, what I'm going to find... Or indeed, not.

Nothing.

Nothing.

The space is empty.

An anxiety aches through my core, sending me sliding to my knees. My hands drop and I stare down at my palms, seeing and not wanting to see what's right in front of me.

Pretend, a voice inside me says. *Pretend this isn't happening. Think nothing.*

Say nothing.

You don't have to confront Drew. You don't have to confront anyone about anything. Pretend nothing has changed.

But it has.

SIX

The house feels unreal.

I make my way downstairs, letting my hand trail the wall in an attempt to keep myself upright. My legs don't work. My head won't function.

No matter how much I scramble and try to hold on, the world feels like it's falling apart.

I need to phone Robyn.

I try her direct line at the prison, but there's no answer, so I try the prison's switchboard, explaining who I am and that it's urgent. I'm aware my voice is shaking.

'You alright, love?' the operator clucks, making me feel even worse. 'Let's see if I can find her for you. I know she's here somewhere. Don't fret yourself, my lovely. It'll all be fine.'

No it won't, I want to tell her. *Nothing will ever be fine again.*

I wait on the line for what feels like hours, before slamming the phone down in frustration and grabbing my things together. I head for the car.

A large splat of rain hits the windscreen, quickly followed by another. The early afternoon light changes into a menacing grey. As I gaze up into the skyline, the storm clouds bloom into darkness.

A line of cars snakes its way towards me as I head down to the prison. I'm forced to wait, agitatedly, where the road narrows. The car coming towards me slows a little. I glance across. Officer Johnson has an elbow resting on the side door. I glance away into the road, when, to my horror, he lowers his window and is blinking against the gusts of rain.

'You okay?' he hollers.

I'm forced to lower the window, fixing my mouth into a smile and raising a cheery hand, as I silently beg the car in front to move forward.

His gaze scours my face. 'A call came through; you were looking for Robyn? Cheryl on the switchboard said you sounded upset.' He frowns a little. 'You sure you're okay?'

A flash of the brake lights from the car in front of me, and I'm practically tailgating the vehicle in my effort to get away.

'Sorry!' I mouth into the closing window. 'Got to go!'

Pulling into the nearest parking space, I pull my jacket closer and hurry over to the main gate, giving my name to the smiling officer behind the Perspex screen.

'*Charlie...!*' she calls across to an officer carrying a load of files who is just about to go through the door. 'This lady is here to see Robyn. You're going that way; could you take her over?'

Charlie pauses, pecking his chin for me to follow him as he opens the wooden door leading to the inner courtyard.

'Back again?' Robyn is standing grinning on the other side. 'I thought you'd gone home?'

I almost fall through the gap, tongue-tied and flustered, but Robyn is too busy holding the gate for the officer to negotiate his way through.

'We can grab a few of those for you, can't we, Beth?' Robyn grabs a load of the folders and deposits half of them into my hands.

'Ah you're a couple of stars.' Charlie turns to lock the gate behind us. 'I wouldn't mind but they're not even for me. I get to do the donkey work while my boss swans off home.'

The rain is coming down harder now and it's blowing unpleasantly into the covered walkway.

Robyn hefts her bundle awkwardly. 'Who's your boss?'

'Principal Officer Johnson. I don't think he likes me much.' He raises a wry eyebrow. 'Me and Mr Johnson don't really see eye to eye.' He reaches to unlock the first gate.

'I wanted to tell you I've been to see the governor about Michael Childs,' I blurt out of nowhere.

'You could've told me that over the phone.' Robyn rolls her eyes. 'You didn't need to come all this way!'

'Must be more than that, Chaplain,' the officer jokes, winking a smile at me. 'I understand this young lady has been very insistent.'

'It was just, I needed—' I start.

'Nah, you don't have to explain about Robyn's obvious attraction.' He laughs but then stops abruptly. 'Oh, hell, sorry! Are you okay?'

Tears well unbidden into my eyes and spill down my cheeks. All the pent-up emotion bubbles up out of nowhere. I turn my face away, desperate to control myself, appalled that I'm embarrassing everyone.

'Sorry. Sorry,' Charlie repeats, looking utterly bewildered. 'Here, let me grab all those.' He takes the stack from my arms and I'm aware of Robyn's hand in the small of my back, ushering me towards a side door in the walkway.

'Come on. This is a shortcut. Let's get you to my office,' she tuts sympathetically. 'Thanks, Charlie. I'll look after her, don't you worry.'

A spiral concrete staircase winds up.

'I was going to suggest a cup of tea, but I think we'll crack open Father O'Brian's stash of communion wine, don't you?

He's not taking a service in here until Sunday morning. He'll never notice.' She laughs.

We reach the top. The door opens into the main body of the prison, and I realise we're at the chapel entrance.

'Y'know, I *knew* there was something wrong earlier,' she berates herself. 'I should have prodded you a bit more. I'm such a plank. Here—' She pushes a wad of tissues from her pocket into my hand and unlocks the door.

There's a sudden waft of incense and I find myself inside the calming space as the gate clangs behind me. A sudden peace descends. The only sound is the soft patter of rain against the big stained-glass window. The softly muted light shifts, sending out a cycle of diamonds across the floor.

'God, I feel awful.' I scrub at my cheeks. 'I've embarrassed myself. I've embarrassed that poor officer.' I blow my nose in the not-too-clean tissues.

'Oh, don't be so silly!' Robyn puts a hand on my arm. 'Let's sort out some food for you. That'll make you feel better.' She strides into her office and flicks the kettle on. 'It's way past lunchtime. I'm going to do poached eggs on toast. Want some?'

'Do you eat all the time?' I manage a watery smile from behind the bundle of soggy tissue.

She glances back at me with a bag of bread in one hand. 'Stress always makes me hungry, doesn't it you?'

I manage to laugh.

'I can see by the look on your face you're going to tell me you don't want to eat.' She pulls half a dozen eggs from the fridge. 'But I bet you will once it's on the plate.'

I know what she's doing: she's deflecting and distracting, giving me time. I have to say, it's working. I sink into the armchair, resting my chin on my hands as I watch her deftly slicing the bread.

'Joe and I had a fight this morning. Like a real fight.'

Robyn says nothing. She picks up an egg.

'Then I found a phone that proves that Drew is having an affair.'

Robyn pauses mid-stroke with a half-broken egg. 'A phone? You mean a phone you didn't recognise?'

I can only nod and then swallow thickly. 'It was hidden in a gap in the door. The name Melanie came up on the screen. Drew came back to the house with some story about wanting to pick up some papers, and then the phone disappeared.'

'Heck.' Robyn shunts the bread into the toaster slots. 'And you think this is the woman you mentioned before, the one that rang you?'

I close my eyes in assent.

'You haven't said anything to him?'

My head is pounding. 'He did the shocked and horrified routine. He says he's going to get his phone interrogated to see when it was accessed. But that's not the only thing, Robyn. He wasn't in when I got home. Then he told me he'd popped out to his car to find his phone, then the story changed to he'd come back into the house to search for it.'

I press my fingers hard into my forehead.

'So tell me what happened with Joe.'

I actually feel sick at the memory. 'We had a fight.'

'Uh-huh.' She turns away. 'I'm listening.'

For a moment I don't know whether to tell her the whole truth.

'A real physical fight.'

She glances back at me.

I can't bring myself to go into the detail of it; I can feel myself wanting to offer up explanations and excuses – *it was actually my fault; Joe wasn't to blame. It was all the heat of the moment stuff.*

'Anyone get hurt?'

She pauses with a knife in her hand; the blade flickers in the light and I instinctively look away. I can't articulate the words:

that sudden shock of feeling those scissors in my hand and seeing the spring of blood.

I swallow. Somehow lying to Robyn feels much, much worse than lying to anyone else.

'A few scrapes here and there. Nothing major.'

'Hmmm.'

She knows that's not all of it.

'Is that the whole truth and nothing but?'

I glance up to find Robyn staring down at me, knife poised in the tub of butter.

I'm flustered. 'Well, almost, yes. He told Drew that I'd started the fight. That I'd attacked him first.'

'Wow!' Robyn shakes her head slowly. 'And what did Drew say?'

'That he believed me.'

'I should hope so!' The toaster pings, shunting up a slice.

'Then Joe says he's going round to his mate, Nate, but that wasn't true either.' I suddenly feel very old and very tired. 'He turns back up at the house with this dodgy-looking guy, sees me, and legs it.'

'Okay.' She turns to butter the toast but the rasp of the knife pauses. 'So, I'll ask you the same question as last time: what really, really scares you about everything that happened?'

I can feel the sudden burn of tears at the backs of my eyes.

I press my lips together. 'That I've lost my son... That I've lost my husband.'

It's true but it's not all of it.

My heart is hammering beneath my ribs. I am nodding and nodding, with tears beginning to stream down my face and soak into the neck of my T-shirt.

'Let it all out. Let it go.' Robyn comes over, perching on the chair opposite, clutching a roll of kitchen towel. She tears off a couple of sheets and hands them to me. 'Once you articulate it –

no matter how terrifying it might be, once it's out there, then you've shared the burden.'

I'm agreeing and agreeing, but all I can think is that somehow I've done this. Simon warned me. He told me. What was that darkness in him that he was terrified he would pass on? Is that possible? Can you inherit pain?

I remember the day Joe was born: my huge slippery boy, hauled into the world, his dark eyes looking up at me as he lay on my chest, that lightning fork of black hair plastered against his forehead. I remember whispering into his cheek that I would never allow anything bad to happen to him. But what if the badness wasn't on the outside? What if the thing, whatever it was, was on the inside and lying in wait to come out?

I can't say that, even to Robyn. She'd say that's not possible. That I'm wrong. That I'm crazy.

'I just want it all to stop, Robyn. Just stop.' I'm begging.

She cups her hands around mine. 'You can't stop it, Beth.' She reaches for another sheaf of towel. 'It's not in your power. You didn't make any of this happen. Sometimes people do things just because... well, they do them.' She makes a helpless gesture. 'Joe's no different to thousands of other boys wanting to test boundaries.' She gives me an old-fashioned look, cocking an eyebrow. 'And perhaps Drew is the same. Maybe he hasn't quite grown up either. The fact is, Beth, the only person you have control over is yourself. The only advice I can give is get your ducks in a row. Drew has no idea you're on to him, has he?'

I shake my head dully.

'If you decide to separate, then separate with your finances sorted. Don't give him all the power over that too. Think about what *you* want. Think about your future and what that could look like—' The microwave pings again.

She winces apologetically. 'I hope you like hard-boiled eggs. I've been bumping my gums chatting nonsense for so long, I think they might've spoiled. But it's not about the food, it's about the feeding,' she explains. 'And I like feeding people's spirit via their belly. It always seems to make things so much better.'

'And I came so you'd tell me what to do.' I dry my eyes, proffering a shaky smile. 'But you haven't done that; you've made me think instead.'

'And what have you thought so far?' Robyn is smiling at me.

'I'm thinking I should stop crying and get hold of my anger.'

'Well, there you are.' Robyn's smile doesn't falter. 'Anger is your energy and your drive for change. Now all you have to decide is the direction.'

SEVEN

Pushing open the front door, a whole wash of relief runs through me as I see Joe's jacket hanging half on and half off the peg. His discarded muddy sneakers, the size of two huge shoe boxes, lie at right angles, so far apart that I fall over one then trip over the other.

He's home. He's safe.

The release is so massive it makes my knees go weak.

The TV is blaring out from the living room so loudly it's a wonder he's not deafened.

'Hiya!' I shout brightly.

My voice is pitched all wrong. Joe doesn't take his eyes from the screen.

I perch on the arm of the sofa, pretending to watch for a few moments. He's hugging a cushion and has his chin buried on his chest, staring intently ahead.

'Is it good film?' I yell over the din.

There's silence.

'What else has that actor been in?' I try again.

He only shrugs sullenly, scowling and then suddenly prods

the remote onto mute and chucks the cushion to the floor. 'Where've you been?'

The question jolts me. 'At the prison. Why?'

'Are you sure?'

'Of course I'm sure. Where else would I go?'

But he only shakes his head again and goes back to looking sullen.

'I meant to say thank you for the flowers you bought. I don't think I told you how much I appreciated them.' I need to get onto safe ground before I get into the difficult stuff.

His eyes don't move.

'I'm sorry about what happened earlier. The last thing I wanted was to fight.'

'Me neither,' he says gruffly.

My heart lurches with joy. 'You tried to do something nice and I can see it must've felt like I was rejecting you.'

His eyes flit briefly from the muted screen.

'It was an accident, you know,' I press. 'I would never hurt you.'

'Yeah, I know that.' He rubs his arm. It's a self-comforting gesture. I want to reach out and comfort him myself, but force myself to hold back. He's like a little feral animal that's only just about letting me into its space. That's enough for now.

'I don't think I phrased what I was trying to say very well.' I'm watching his face intently to gauge how far I can push this. 'It's just... umm, since that time when...' My whole gut turns over as I articulate the words. 'Like, after that time when... when you—' I can't bring myself to conjure up that moment in his bedroom.

'I told you then, none of that was what you thought it was,' he mutters.

'Maybe.' I collect my courage in both hands. 'Maybe, if I tell you something, something I've never talked about with anyone, then maybe you'll understand a bit better. I'd really like us to try and communicate properly. Rather than fight all the time.'

He pouts defensively. I hold my courage tighter.

'It's about your dad.'

I have his attention now. Joe's eyes slowly drift from the screen.

'Your dad and me. I don't know how much you've picked up over the years. About what happened.'

'I know he wanted to kill himself. I know he tried more than once.' Joe's gaze is steady.

My stomach roils: *how did he know that?*

'I'm guessing you made it worse by putting pressure on him.'

He's so totally calm, so perfectly reasoned, I'm stunned into silence. It takes me a second to think how to respond.

'She didn't say that, by the way. That's me saying that,' he explains equably.

'Who?'

'Grandma.'

'Grandma!'

'Yeah, I saw a photo and I asked who the boy in the background was, and she told me. It's the first time I'd seen him. You said you didn't have any pictures.'

He's so measured, so contained, it unnerves me.

'I – I don't!'

'Well, she has that one. I look just like him, don't I?' He hasn't taken his eyes from my face.

'A little,' I falter.

'A lot.' He looks back at the silent screen again. 'In fact, I think I've inherited more than his looks.'

A chill slides into my hairline; its fingers creep down the back of my neck.

'So I don't think there's anything you can tell me that I don't already know, Beth.'

His head tilts. His eyes regard me. They're suddenly not my son's eyes. They're Simon's.

'*No!*' I say it so forcefully I see a flicker of alarm. 'You're not like him, Joe! You might look a bit like him, but that's all. Your dad was brought up in care. He felt worthless. He ran around with bad people who made him feel better about himself, but of course, everything just spiralled out of control. And yes, you're right. *Yes*. I did put pressure on him, Joe. I could see he wasn't really that person. I wanted to offer him an alternative. A different path out of the nightmare he was living. So yes, you're right... you are.'

I find I'm breathless and my chest is shaking. Joe only blinks quietly back at me.

'Yeah, she said that too.'

'What, Grandma? What did she say?'

'That she was really proud of you, that you'd shown maturity beyond your years.'

That stops me in my tracks. I can't quite take it in. '*Grandma* said that?'

Joe nods. 'She said it took a lot of courage to believe in someone when everyone is telling you you shouldn't. She said my dad never really stood a chance, and you saw that. You wanted to make a difference.'

This feels like I'm sitting in some kind of alternate reality. I'm slightly light-headed; the world tilts a little on its axis. I have this rush of closeness: a sense of connection between us that I haven't felt for a long, long time.

He sighs, picks up the remote and stabs at the 'off' button.

'Anyway, I'll go and watch the rest of this in my room.'

My eyes follow him, bewildered and silent, as he walks away. There's the slam of the bedroom door.

But I thought... I thought...

I find myself levering up from the chair arm, my feet taking me slowly into the hallway and up the stairs, my lungs only letting out tiny puffs of air, my heart hammering wildly behind my ribs.

I need to know what he's thinking; I know instinctively that there's this moment: this window that I need to reach through, otherwise he will drift so far away I will never be able to find him again.

The blank rectangle of his bedroom door stands before me. The solid face of its panels fills me with a dread that I can barely articulate. I raise a hand, my knuckles grazing it oh so gently.

'Yeah?'

Something gets me right in the heart.

Softly, not daring to breathe, I take hold of the handle. The door edge cracks open, and I push it just wide enough. Steadying myself, I take a step into the room, standing with my back to the door, holding on to it for support.

'Joe.'

He doesn't move. I think he's going to ignore me.

'All that.'

'Yeah?'

'All that about your dad.' I force myself to inch forward to perch on the end of the bed. He flickers a look at me from the corner of his eye.

'You're making connections where there aren't any. You're nothing like him. I know you've had your problems: the issues at the school, the things with the tablets, and now the stuff you've told Drew—'

He blinks and the frown deepens. He turns his head to look at me. 'What stuff?'

'That I hit you.'

'I never...! I didn't! Why would I say that?' He pulls his sleeve back. 'Look – it's nothing, why would I even mention it?'

He shakes his head angrily. 'I've got more important things to stress about.' He shoves his hands under his thighs, hunching miserably.

My brain scrambles, looking for something solid to hang on to – *but Drew said... Drew told me...?*

Joe turns away from me, hiding his face.

'What are you stressed about?'

'Nothing. Look, Beth, can we drop this?'

'We've come this far, Joe. We're being straight with each other. Just tell me.'

'You wouldn't get it.'

The silence ticks between us. I feel sick. I know instinctively it'll be something to do with that man who was here.

Joe drops his head. His hands flail uselessly into his lap. He says something that I don't catch.

'Joe?'

'I said *everything's wrong.*'

'Like?'

He takes a big breath. 'Like, I'm totally screwed.'

I sit up straighter. 'Go on.'

His head lifts slowly and he turns to look at me. His jaw is still working angrily, but his face is bright red. I realise he's crying. Every emotion in me floods in a great rush, sending me reaching out to grasp his arm. My hand slips between his shoulders, feeling the scrawny complexity of his skinny frame in my arms as I turn his face to press it against my cheek. I want to haul him onto my lap like I did when he was six and had hurt himself. It feels like forever ago.

Instead, my hand presses against his cheek so he can't turn away. 'Joe...! Joe! What do you mean?' I soothe. 'Talk to me! What's going on?'

He has his forehead buried. All I can hear are the muffled gasps and sobs. My brain is floundering – I don't know what to think or imagine. I see men after him. Gangs. It's drugs. It's—

'I owe money.'

I'm so glad he can't see my reaction.

'I owe money, and if I don't pay it, I'm dead.'

I nod my head so that he can feel it, wondering if he can also feel the thumping of my heart. *Boom. Boom. Boom.* But he can't know the terror that's coursing through my veins.

I'm okay; he needs to know that. I'm not going to explode any second. I'm here and will listen, because he has to trust me. I put my hand firmly on his chin, peeling him away from me so that he can look into my eyes. The six-year-old little boy is there. My heart cleaves wide.

'Tell me the whole story, right from the beginning. Don't leave anything out. That's really important. There's nothing you can say that's going to make me think less of you, and there's nothing you can confess that will shock me. Whatever you're involved with isn't new, so the solutions aren't new either.' I tip his chin higher so that he can't avoid my gaze. 'Everything is solvable, Joe. You just have to give me all the facts.'

'We...' He gulps. 'We stole a van.'

'You and...?'

'Nate.'

I have this terrible sinking feeling that I'm going to have to talk to Sarah. Even the thought of it fills me with horror.

'Okay, so just the two of you then? Go on.'

'It was Nate's idea.'

Oh God, Sarah.

'He'd seen it parked around the back of some warehouses. We thought it'd been dumped. I mean, it was really old, no plates, no nothing. We were just messing. We couldn't believe it when it we found the keys were stashed in the sunblind; we thought that only happens on the TV.'

'So, you took it?' I prompt.

He nods, ashamed. 'Yeah, we took it. Just drove it around a bit; it was only for a laugh.'

'Who did the driving?'

'Nate mostly, but me too. Well, Drew's taken me out a few times, hasn't he?' His eyes are scared in his face. 'So we thought we'd put it somewhere safe, y'know, so we could use it again, only we thought that the back of the same warehouses was a good place – there are tons of empty lockups.'

I don't even want to ask about how they accessed them.

'But after we'd stashed it, we got stopped.'

'By the police?' I immediately think of Drew.

'By these three guys... older guys, who said we'd been seen driving it, and wanted to know where it was. Only Nate said he knew nothing and they started smacking him about. The whole time it's happening, Nate's like, staring and staring at me, willing me not to say anything. And then one of them says a name: "Jaybo", and I suddenly realised who these guys were.'

'Who?' I feel sick suddenly.

'They're part of this local gang. Like, serious, heavy duty, you-don't-mess-with-them kinda people. And we'd been driving round in their van. I thought they were going to kill Nate and then turn on me.'

'So you told them where it was, right? They weren't going to come after you if you'd just come clean, were they?'

'No. No we didn't. We couldn't.'

'Because?'

'We'd torched it.'

The air leaves my lungs.

'We'd torched it. Nate said it wasn't safe to leave it in a lockup, 'cos our fingerprints were all over the place. I don't know why I agreed to go along with such a stupid plan, but I did.'

He drops his head. The tears are coursing down his cheeks; he's breathless with fear.

'Only their gear was in the back, wasn't it? We didn't know. We had no idea; we just thought it was some stupid old van. They let us go but they've said we have to pay for torching their stuff.'

'How much?'

'Ten thousand.'

'What?' I stare at him open-mouthed.

His eyes are bloodshot with misery. 'That's five thousand each. Nate has got money in his account that his grandad opened for him, but I haven't got anything near that! I've only got my birthday and Christmas money, and that won't be enough.'

His shaking fingers drag through his hair. He looks and sounds so much like my tiny son now I could weep.

'And Nate has paid these people?' I can't believe I'm hearing this. 'And Sarah doesn't know a thing?'

Joe shakes his head. 'He's told her he's taking money from the account to pay for driving lessons, so she doesn't know.' He suddenly looks up at me in terror. 'You can't say a word – not a word!'

'Joe.'

'You can't grass me up! You know what Sarah's like! She'll call the police! Drew will find out! Everyone will know and then I'm dead meat! You've seen what they're like!'

'I've seen...?' I stop as it dawns on me. 'That guy who was here? He was one of them?'

I suddenly have this squeeze of terror through my gut at the thought that one of these thugs has been in my house. He knows what I look like; he probably knows Drew's with the police... *Oh my God.*

'I'm dead, Mum.' Joe's bottom lip is trembling. 'You've got to help me. Please! You've got to help me.'

Mum. I take him in my arms again as he collapses, my body responding to him in the way it's always responded: wrapping him into me, keeping him close as he cries. Of course I'll help him; I'd do anything for him. It doesn't matter what he's done, or what he's involved with, or how much trouble he's in, I promised I'd face death if I had to. I'd pay anything just to keep him safe.

EIGHT

Drew comes home just after midnight.

I listen in the dark to him moving about downstairs and then there's the quiet hum of a toothbrush and the splash of running water as he uses the bathroom.

I turn over in bed, staring mutely at the far wall so that he won't see my face. There's the gentle bounce of the mattress as he gets in beside me, and in minutes all I can hear is his quiet breathing.

We are so far apart there could be a brick wall between us. I should be feeling a whole lot of things, but I don't. I don't care what Drew is or isn't doing right now, what lies he is or isn't telling – all I can think about is Joe.

It's three o'clock when I finally give up and slide from the side of the bed. Pulling on a dressing gown, I click open the door and creep softly down the stairs.

I'm aware of a faint muted light in the kitchen, and there's Joe, fully dressed, sitting at the breakfast bar.

'What are you doing here?' I whisper.

'Probably the same as you,' he whispers back. He's trying to be jokey. Gone is the aggression, gone is the sharpness and the truculence. All I have in front of me is a frightened boy who needs me.

I glance up at the ceiling. The house is completely quiet.

'I've been lying awake, thinking. I'll get you the money.'

Joe widens his eyes. 'What? You will?' He gulps. 'But what will you say to Drew?'

'He doesn't need to know,' I say firmly. 'I have an account with a bit of money in it. I'll use that.'

He only stares back in stunned gratitude. We're co-conspirators now, he and I. We're bound in our secret. Right this minute, I'd find a million pounds just to have this feeling for the rest of my life.

I look at the clock. 'Y'know, if we're going to do this, now is probably the best time. We can get there and back and no one needs to be any the wiser.'

He doesn't say anything. Then his eyes drop. 'I really appreciate you doing this. It means a hell of a lot.'

I almost smile. He doesn't sound like my scratchy teenage son anymore. He sounds like a man.

I take a deep breath. 'Let me go and find some clothes. At this time of the morning, we can do it in twenty minutes. You good to go?'

He nods quickly and I make my way back up to the bedroom, dreading each crack and creak of the stairs. I sneak around the bed quickly, rustling up whatever clothes I can find.

Drew doesn't stir. With the bundle under one arm, I go into the downstairs cloakroom to pull on my sweatpants and hoodie. When I appear, I'm surprised to find Joe in the hallway on his phone. He signals for me to be quiet and then ends the call.

'You ready?' he whispers.

I gently click the front door open, and we hurry to my car. It isn't until we're safely inside that I dare ask the question.

'Who were you calling?'

'Who do you think?' He gives me a sideways look. 'I'm

telling them I'm getting their cash, aren't I? I'm arranging when to see them. I just want all this over and done with.'

We drive in silence, turning into the High Street.

'I was thinking about how I can do this.' My eyes burn with tiredness. 'I've brought two bank cards with me, so I should be able to withdraw five hundred from each. I can do the same tomorrow.'

'But that's only two grand!' He looks sharply across at me. 'You know I need five. I *told* you I need five!'

'Banks don't allow you to take out sums like that from the cashpoint,' I explain. 'I can do five hundred from each of my accounts a day, and I can make bigger withdrawals if I give them notice, but right now I can only—'

'But you *promised*!' he explodes. 'You *promised* you'd help me!'

'And I will help you, Joe. This is me helping you,' I insist patiently. 'You can't expect that sum of money all in one go!'

'What about Drew? He's minted.'

'What about Drew?' I look at him in shock. 'You weren't thinking that I'd access his account, were you?'

'I thought you'd do anything to save me,' he says gruffly. '*Anything*. I might've guessed you'd start making excuses.' He stares moodily out of the side window. The toddler is back.

'I get that you're scared, Joe. I totally understand that.'

'You don't know what scared feels like. Scared doesn't even come close. Two thousand pounds?' He lets out a whistle of disgust. 'You have no idea just how shafted I am right now. They're not messing; they know where I live, remember?'

My heart runs, terrified. *I can't get hold of five thousand pounds, not without Drew knowing. It's impossible.* I can feel myself beginning to panic.

'Why don't you go away then?' I pull up close to the cash point and kill the engine.

He turns to look at me, white-faced. 'What d'you mean, go away? Go where?'

'Anywhere. You can't get the money straightaway, so buy yourself some time. Tell them they can have all the money at once, and give them a date when they can have it – that's the truth, isn't it? I'll give you the money to get out of the country for a while.'

'You mean, like a holiday?' His face changes.

'Yes, like a holiday. A *cheap* one.'

'And Nate too?'

'Sorry?' I frown.

'They'll be putting the heat right on him if I disappear. I can't do that to him.' His head shakes in horror. 'I can't!'

I sigh wearily. 'Yes, okay. Nate too. Fine. Whatever.'

'Cool!' he says, smiling, excited now as he nods across to the ATM. 'If we're getting two lots from two different machines, then you'd better hurry up.'

I get out of the car, pulling my card from my wallet. A chill wind glides effortlessly through my thin clothes and my spine prickles as I punch in the numbers into the too-bright screen. I have a terrible feeling of foreboding.

You know this won't be the end of it, my head says. *You don't just pay off people like that. Joe's a kid, he doesn't know what's unfolding, but you do.*

I look back. Joe is sitting with his head dipped to his phone, busily texting. The child in him has moved on: no more frightened crying. I can see by the intent expression on his face, he's moved away from me, too. I have a falling sensation in the depths of my gut. I've stepped into something without even knowing what I'm stepping into. It feels as though I'm on a moving walkway within a tunnel: there's no way off and no way back. The only thing I can do is keep moving forward into whatever lies ahead.

NINE

'Sarah?'

'Oh, hello! Wow! You're up early. How's it going?'

I've waited until I hear Drew get in the shower. As soon as I hear the drum of the water, I make the call. She sounds cheerful and upbeat. *She doesn't know a thing.*

I steel myself. 'Listen, how do you feel about getting your eldest son out of your hair for a week?'

'What, Nate? Why, do you want to do a swap?' She chuckles. 'I'd have yours for mine any day of the week.'

I feel my cheek muscles tightening with the lie. *When this all comes out...*

'My mum has had a win on the Premium Bonds, and she's sent Joe a present. It's a holiday voucher. I think it's also a "well-done-for-getting-through-your-exams" kind of thing. Well, of course, he's been bugging me to find somewhere abroad that's cheap and cheerful, and there's this deal I've found for Spain, and I was wondering if Nate would like to go with him?'

My words come out in a rush as I'm staring at a gouge of paint in the wall as though it might save me.

'Oh cool. Sounds brilliant! Well... yes! Thank you. I'll ask him but I'm sure he'd love to go! When are you thinking?'

I squeeze my eyes tight closed. 'Umm... I was thinking of tonight?'

'Tonight! Gosh! That is soon.' There's a heartbeat. When all this mess comes out, she's going to hate me. Right now, I hate me. 'But then again, he's only lounging around here doing nothing.'

If only you had a clue what he's really been doing.

'So why not? If he wants to go, then great!'

My relief is mixed with pure guilt and absolute dread.

'So, I'll text you later with the details, shall I? I'll just need his passport number.'

'Wait till I tell him!'

She starts to ask about where in Spain and what the temperatures will be like and how much she'll look forward to a bit of peace and quiet, but I'm not listening. I'm aware of my husband in the bathroom, showering, maybe even washing away the traces of *her*. I think about scary men in the street watching this house. I imagine cars driving past waiting to snatch my son. My life, the one I thought I knew, is slipping away from me. I'm deeper and deeper into the mire at every turn.

That guy knows this address. When he doesn't turn up with the money, what's to stop him turning up here? What if he challenges Drew? It'll all come out... I see disused cellars with blood on a concrete floor. I see police officers and courts. I see gang members talking in prison, and me having no clue.

'Are you still there, Beth?'

I jump. 'Yes, yes, sorry, Sarah, I think you broke up for a second... Oh hang on, there's a delivery guy walking up the drive. I'll text you all the details, yeah? Speak soon! Bye!'

I creak open the bedroom door, listening for Drew. I can hear him whistling tunelessly as I make my way to the bathroom.

He's standing in front of the mirror at the basin with a towel slung around his waist, rubbing at his hair. His face is flushed with the heat.

'I didn't hear you get up. Is breakfast ready?' He grins cheekily.

I squeeze the corners of my mouth into a smile. 'You'll be pleased to know that my son has just announced he's off on holiday! How about that?'

'Holiday?' Drew stops rubbing. 'Where? When?'

'Spain. With Nate. Sarah found a cheap last-minute deal for them and Joe's using his birthday money.'

'Brilliant. That's the life, eh?' Drew isn't questioning it. 'Does he need a ride to the airport? I'd take them, but I'm interviewing ne'er-do-wells all day and I have no idea what time I'll finish.'

I watch his face in the misted glass. He's leaning forward, preening himself, running his fingers down his throat, lifting his chin to inspect it. I glance down; there's a shirt I don't recognise lying discarded on the floor. It's the one he was wearing earlier when he carried me up to bed. It's new. I remember the scent of it. Did he buy it to wear for her? *Have her fingers touched those buttons? Undone them one by one...?*

I despise you, my head says. *I despise the lies that slip from your lips so easily. I despise the smug self-satisfaction. How clever you must feel.*

'What's the matter?' Drew is looking at me.

'Nothing.'

'It doesn't look like nothing. Don't shut me out.'

My hackles rise, but I hold on. 'I didn't sleep very well.'

'You got up a few times.'

My heart leaps violently. 'You heard me?'

Drew pulls a face. 'I turned over a couple of times and you weren't there. I thought maybe you'd gone downstairs to make a drink. I was going to come and check, but then I fell asleep again.'

I'm aware of my heart.

'You do too much with these Samaritans people. You're not back at the prison again today, are you?'

'No, I was thinking I might take a break like you said.' If I appease him, he'll get out of the house.

'Oh really? That's great! You promise you will?'

'I promise.'

'That's good then.' He nods, satisfied. 'I need to get going actually.' He checks the time. 'I've got a lot on today.'

'What are you up to?'

He pulls a face. 'This and that. Interviewing grot-bags mainly... Err, Beth?' He follows my gaze.

'Sorry, I'm distracted. There's tons to sort out before Joe goes.' I manage a switched-on smile again. 'I don't even think I know where his passport is. I'm wondering if I've got time to put some washing on – his summer stuff has been in drawers for months.'

'Sure, sure.' Drew waves me away with his razor. 'I'll be out of your way soon. Sorry I'm not much help.'

'It's fine,' I say, pulling the door closed. 'I'll be downstairs.'

I stand for a moment on the landing. The hurt and the humiliation rises. I've shed enough tears; I've worried and fretted and blamed myself and it's got me nowhere. I remember my life before he slid into it: how hard and difficult it was. Yet, looking back, I see the problems were mine to deal with; it was my life, calling my own shots and dancing to my own tune. Now I've swapped being comfortable for being controlled. How simple it was back then, just me and Joe – how ordinary.

Joe's bedroom door is tightly closed. With a tiny knock, I open it and peer inside.

There's the familiar hump of duvet outlined in the semi-darkness. In this room are the tiny moments, the little memories, each one like a flick-book cartoon: a captured image of those precious times.

'Joe?' I whisper. There's no movement. He's sleeping as a young child would, his fingers curled around the duvet, tucked up under his chin. I remember how each night I'd stoop to kiss him, wanting to take that little face and squeeze his cheeks to death.

Where has that boy gone?

A memory.

'I kissed a girl at school.' His tiny face peeping up at me mischievously from around his Rocket Man duvet cover.

'And is she your girlfriend?' I'd been smiling but trying hard to look as though I was taking this seriously.

'No...' His rosebud of a mouth had pouted. *'Benjamin Harris trapped her in the toilet and said we all had to take it in turns to kiss her before we'd let her out.'*

TEN

I watch Joe in the rear-view mirror as he hunches his bag further onto his shoulder and makes his way across the car park to departures. A sudden wave of sadness comes over me; it ricochets painfully through my chest. I saw the look on his face as I handed him the two thousand pounds this morning, before he stuffed it inside his jacket.

'What did they say?'

'Who?'

I gave him a look. 'The people. The people you owe the money to. What did they say?'

'I told them they'd get the whole lot in ten days.'

'And they accepted that?'

He looked at me angrily. 'Yeah. I said, didn't I? Look, they're not going to come round and harass you, if that's what you're worried about.'

The car behind me honks for me to move out of the drop-off zone. I go to pull away, checking to catch sight of Joe again but he's gone.

. . .

The house is quiet as I let myself in. Walking slowly upstairs to Joe's bedroom, I stand in the doorway, feeling his absence like a dark hole. My mind shifts and eddies, dwelling on unthinkable things: thoughts that up until now I haven't allowed air space. There are dark shadows lurking back there – the notion of *losing my child.* It plays out suddenly: these men, these dark threatening figures, who might take my son away from me forever. I imagine it, standing here in this room holding on to that terrible, terrible possibility.

I go to the window and look out. There's a car parked opposite. Two men are sitting inside, and my heart and stomach collide. I slip back, feeling for the wall, and then peer through the edge of the curtain. They're still there, not moving. Were they watching for us to leave? Did they follow us to the airport?

Heart pounding, I go down and re-check the front door, sliding the bolt across the top. Then I go around the house testing the windows and the locks. The glass panes in the kitchen seem so flimsy now. It wouldn't take much; one sharp blow of a metal bar and they'd shatter. The bushes lining the garden wall shiver in the breeze. Someone could easily come around the back of the house and hide there. Are they watching to see when I'm alone?

Creeping into the lounge, I stand with my back against the wall so that I can see out into the street. The car has gone. My breath leaves me in a long shudder and there's a thump of blood. *I'm going crazy,* I tell myself. *I'm seriously going crazy.*

Drawing the air deep into my lungs, I force my shoulders to relax, feeling the solidity of the wall against my spine.

Joe and Nate are at the airport. They'll be getting on a plane in a few hours. No one will know where they're going and they'll be far away from it all. They're safe. They're safe.

I open my eyes.

There's a movement.

I only just catch it. A shift of someone by the front door. I freeze. They're not ringing the bell or knocking. I can tell by the way they're weaving about, they're peering through the glass pane into the hallway. Every instinct is telling me to drop to the floor, but my spine feels like lead, gluing me hard into the wall.

There it is again.

My eyes dart frantically. The movement has become a shadow beyond the edge of the curtain. The terror of it folds and unfolds my insides as the shadow moves, lengthening a little across the floor in front of me, peeling itself out of hiding, moving away from the door towards this window as I hear the slight scrape of feet on the gravel. Whoever it is, is going to look in here any second.

My eyes snap to the back of the house, my ears pricked for sound.

I bet there are two. One of them could be in the garden right now.

My head jerks back. Someone says my name.

I freeze, holding my breath.

There's a faint knock on the door and I hear my name again.

'Beth...? Can I talk to you?'

It's a woman's voice.

Slithering down the wall, I make for the hallway. My hand waves towards the catch but I don't want to turn it.

There's a tiny rap on the door again. I hear feet scuffle, agitated.

'Please!'

I have this thought, this notion. *They've come for me.* My head swings around, listening for them. *In here, they'll have me trapped. Help won't get to me in time. Can I get out?*

There are the sounds of children laughing outside. I peer through the edge of the pane. A whole family: little children, mum, dad, and a couple of uncles, maybe. *If I could just get out now?*

The shadow on the other side of the door becomes hazy,

moving back to check the windows again. My hands feel for the solidity of the metal lock, my fingers groping blindly for the bolt. I reach up, knowing that once I do, they can force their way in. *I'll have seconds to attract attention. Seconds.* I open it just an inch. The person standing there paralyses me.

It's her. The girl from the news. *Drew's mistress?*

She's there, not four feet away.

I don't want to see her. I don't want to speak to her. My hands automatically swing the door closed with a slam. My palms lean into the wood as I stand, breathing hard, listening to her knocking and knocking, feeling the vibration on the other side.

'I just need to talk to you, that's all!' she keeps saying. 'Seriously! I don't mean anything bad!'

'Go away!' I shout. 'Leave me alone!'

I deadlock the door again and run into the living room, ducking down from the window. She's backing away, staring up at the bedrooms, her mouth slightly open in her pale face and her eyes wide. She's young, much younger than I imagined, hair the same colour as mine, cut the same way, only she's very, very pretty.

She glances left and right into the street, pulling out her phone. Within seconds, mine begins to ring. Grabbing it, I switch it off, watching her face as she frowns, then tries again. Pushing her hair out of her eyes in frustration, she takes a couple of steps as though she's going to walk off, changes her mind, and heads in the opposite direction.

I move closer to the curtain, watching her stride away, pushing her hands into her pockets like the kid she is. She doesn't look back.

I'm shaking. I know I should have spoken to her. Why didn't I? I can't find a sensible answer. I could have found out everything: about the affair, why she phoned me, what the warning was about. I could have gathered every bit of ammunition I could have ever wanted – yet something inside wouldn't let me.

The phone in my hand reflects everything back at me that I don't want to see and I don't want to face. The black screen mirrors the worst of my face: the pudgy nose, the shadowy, hollow eye sockets. I don't look like her; I don't have that young, fresh face, that tight body, that sparkle.

Switching my phone back on, I watch the swirling colours gather, knowing that in a few moments, I'll feel that vibration in my palm and she'll have left me a message that tells me the thing I really don't want to fully face.

I dial into the voicemail, readying myself. My mind is deliberately blank.

'Beth. Can you call me?' It's Robyn's voice sounding harassed down the line. 'It's pretty urgent. I'll keep trying. Please call as soon as you get this.'

The message has only just ended when my phone bursts into life.

'Robyn, what—?'

'You might want to come in.'

'Sorry?'

'There's been a big incident that I think you should know about. Jaime's in a bit of a state, and I thought you might want to come in.'

'What is it? What's happened?'

'I can't go into it all. Can you just get here as quick as you can?'

The phone goes down and I'm on autopilot, gathering my things together, putting my shoes on, finding my bag. I'm running to the car and driving off without even thinking about the girl. It's only mid afternoon but already the day is drawing down, the headlights coming on, bouncing out on the road in front of me in stiff, jerky movements.

The darkness is gathering on either side. The sky has

become that strange inky colour where the dying sun edges the clouds into orange. The prison perimeter floodlights, just visible over the wall, ribbon out in front of me. The dead eyes of the uppermost cells beam out in slitted rows.

Robyn is waiting for me at the gate. There's a frazzled-looking officer behind the desk, who only glances at me as I walk over. She reaches across to a radio and holds down the button.

'Golf Two, receiving – over.'

Robyn gives me a look.

'What's happening?'

She raises her eyes and lets out a long breath. 'The police came in this morning – I'm not sure about what. They've gone now, but while they were here, they interviewed Leo Hargreaves, along with a few others. I have no idea what the police said to the kid in that interview; all I know is that while the prisoners were banged up over lunch, he tried to hang himself.'

My hand automatically comes to my mouth. 'And he was doing so well!' I moan. 'God, Jaime's going to be devastated when he hears this!'

'Luckily, he'd got a cellmate with him, who was napping, woke up and rang the alarm bell. Apparently he was grabbing his legs, trying to take the weight off the ligature, but...' Robyn sighs. 'No one answered the bell.'

I can only stare in horror.

'The cons were all shouting and screaming, knowing what was going on, but there weren't enough staff on, and the ones that were, were too inexperienced. I think we were seconds away from tragedy.'

The officer behind the desk looks across at us. Suddenly, somewhere in the depths of the prison, there's the muted shrilling drill of an alarm bell. Doors crash wide in the gatehouse and there's an instant rush of black and white uniforms.

The only sounds are the thunder of running feet and radios chattering excitedly with officers shouting to one another. The metal gates clang back, juddering their housings.

'Sorry about this, people.' The officer behind the desk looks across at us. 'There's another incident on one of the wings. If you two would like to take a seat for a moment, I'm sure we'll have it under control soon.'

It sounds like pandemonium. There's the loud screaming of endless whistles and a cacophony of metallic banging coming from the yards.

'What's happening?' I glance around nervously.

But Robyn's only matter of fact. 'They've got all the prisoners locked away and now they're protesting by smashing anything they can find against their cell doors. They're demonstrating their frustration.'

'Because they failed Leo?'

Robyn presses her lips together. 'That, and because the police were in here this morning.' She pauses. 'Actually, I think it might've been Drew, Beth. I think he was the officer who interviewed Leo. I overheard the name.'

My shock is interrupted by the gate behind us shunting open. Three officers come through looking a bit red-faced, but chatting with relief.

'All sorted.' One of the officers looks at Robyn. 'There's a ton of grumbling still going on, but the ringleaders have called a truce, plus it's not long to teatime and they know they've got burgers and fries. They're not going to want to stay behind their doors when that's on the menu.'

The three officers laugh together and go into the gatehouse.

Robyn gives me a weary look. 'And that's the sum total of their concern over a young man's life,' she mutters. 'Come on. Let's go and see what we can find out.'

We make our way towards the main prison, following a path

I haven't taken before that skirts the chain-link fence of the exercise yard.

'Robyn, I feel terrible.'

'About Drew?' She shakes her head. 'You have absolutely no need to feel anything at all. You can't be guilty by association.'

But I can't get the idea of Drew being here out of my head. 'What the hell can he have said to push Leo to want to kill himself?'

'They always have their agenda.' Robyn looks away.

'What do you mean?'

'I've been piecing a few things together. The facts are, Leo is vulnerable, not that articulate, and poorly educated. I'm betting they're planning to fit him up for some of their other cases. If they can make it stick, they'll hang a load more charges on him. It'll clear the backlog of outstanding files.'

My pace falters. 'You think Drew would do that?'

Robyn laughs sadly. 'It's an easy fix for the police if they can make it stick, but I can't answer for Drew personally.'

We walk. My head is buzzing in an overload of shock and anger.

'Where are we going?'

'I want to get to see Leo if we can.' Robyn unlocks a door in a blank brick wall. 'I know what the narrative from the police will be: they'll be telling the governor that Leo's suicide attempt is an admission of guilt on the new charges, and they'll be putting pressure on prisoners he's associated with, to get information. Particularly prisoners who have a lot to lose – like the ones nearing their parole date.' She gives me a knowing look.

'You mean like Jaime.'

'He's spent time with Leo as a Listener. He'll be one of their prime targets.'

She leads the way past a sign marked *Hospital Wing*, and then towards a gate with a ramp leading upward. There's a waft of disinfectant as she unlocks the final door.

I am struck at how bright and airy this place feels. The immaculately polished cream lino spans away, leading to bed bays on either side, some single, some grouped together. Robyn takes a quick look around.

'There he is,' she whispers. 'Quick! While there aren't any staff about.'

We slip into a side bay, Robyn pulling the curtain partially round to shield us from view.

'Leo?' she says softly. 'Leo?'

There's a boy lying in the bed. I don't recognise him: just a sad-looking kid like so many others here. I know he must be twenty-one, but he appears so much younger. His eyes flicker lightly under sunken lids.

'It's Robyn, the chaplain, Leo.' Robyn glances round to make sure we haven't been spotted. 'Can you open your eyes?'

The lashes flutter, briefly, and then his lids peel painfully back. The boy tries to speak but only manages a croak.

'He's still drugged up.' Robyn looks across. 'Maybe we should come back.'

Leo shifts under the covers, his hand appearing, inching its way towards Robyn.

She chafes his fingers gently. 'You're okay, Leo. You're going to be fine. We're going to get you right.'

'Sssscchh—' The boy's lips struggle to make the sound. His tongue works painfully.

'Don't even try.' She pats the back of his hand. 'I know. I understand. You don't have to worry about anything.'

'Sssscchh... Sss—' He struggles. 'Sssh— cared. What they're going to do to me.'

Robyn darts an angry look, but tries to rein it in. I feel exactly the same.

'We're not going to let them do anything to you, okay, Leo? I'm going to make sure of that. No one is going to do anything. If they try, they're going to have to go through me first.'

My fury is mixed with a terrific rush of pity.

I bend a little towards him; his eyes fix intently on mine.

'I'm Beth. I'm with the Samaritans, so I know Jaime.' The eyes don't leave my face. 'Like Robyn says, we'll do everything we can to get you back to a good place. I know things must feel hopeless now, but I'm going to talk to Jaime and see if I can get him in here to see you, okay?'

But Leo only swallows painfully. A single tear tracks from the corner of his eye and down his temple. My heart aches with compassion. I glance at Robyn.

'Come on.' She nods to the exit. 'We'll let him get some rest.'

We manage to creep out the same way as we came in, walking back towards the chapel, both lost in our own thoughts. I can see just how Robyn's feeling; I know, I'm feeling it too.

'That boy nearly died you know.' She shakes her head in disbelief.

There's an officer walking towards us. I am aware he's staring at me and I realise it's Mr Johnson from Jaime's wing.

Robyn pauses to unlock the chapel gate. 'Are you going to confront Drew about what he said?'

'Yep. That and other things,' I mutter angrily.

I glance up as the officer draws level. 'How you two doing?' He addresses the question to Robyn, but his eyes slide across me.

Robyn's face lights up cheerily. 'Fine, fine, Mr Johnson! And how are you faring?'

No one would have a clue how she's really feeling.

'I've just started a late shift so only another eight hours to go.' He grins. 'I'm glad I've caught you, Beth.'

I wasn't aware he knew my name.

'You seemed a bit upset when I saw you.'

I blink in query.

'In your car? Coming into the prison?'

'Ah... No, no I'm fine.'

'Good. Good.' He rubs his hands together. There are several slightly awkward seconds. 'I wanted to chat with you, actually. Umm, I don't think I really made it clear when you came to the wing office, how much I really admire the work you're doing.'

I don't quite know how to respond. 'Oh. Um... Thank you.'

He shuffles a little awkwardly. 'I know we've just had a near tragedy with Hargreaves, but it was you flagging it up that made us move him into a double cell. If we hadn't done that—' He breaks off.

Robyn nods. 'Mr Johnson works outside with vulnerable kids, Beth. He feels the same way as we do about supporting people who are struggling.'

'Oh, right. I didn't know that!'

'So we're all on the same side, aren't we?' She gives him a small smile. 'Sometimes it feels like it's us against the world, doesn't it, Mr Johnson?'

The officer looks a little abashed. 'Yeah, I feel quite strongly about it actually.' He colours a little. 'I would've taken it personally if we hadn't got to that lad in time.'

There's a moment's pause.

'Anyway! Good to meet you properly.' He extends his hand and I take it. I know, instantly, that he's genuine. His smile broadens and then he suddenly lets go. 'So. Yes... best be off. I've been detailed to relocate Michael Childs up to a normal cell. Let's hope he behaves himself. Anyway, ta-ta.' And with that he strides away down the corridor with me not quite comprehending the news.

'And again your powers of persuasion work their magic!' Robyn gives me a look as she unlocks the chapel door. 'You're obviously very good at convincing people to do things against their own instincts.' She laughs at my expression. 'You know. Geoff? The governor?' She gives me a teasing look as she holds the door open.

'There you are!'

Robyn clutches her chest in shock at the sight of Jaime's face.

'Oh my word, don't do that!' She breathes heavily. 'You'll kill me! What are you doing here?'

Father O'Brian, the Catholic priest, comes out of his office. He's a lovely man; I've met him once before. 'Sorry, Robyn, I should've told you, he's here to see me. I'd got some people in my office from various charity organisations and I thought it would be good if they all met each other.' He beckons us to follow.

'I was just saying to Jaime, he might fancy working in some capacity for one of the charities when you get parole.' Father O'Brian smiles.

'*If* I get it.'

There are two women standing chatting. They both look round as we walk in.

I recognise Madeleine Grainger, a lovely woman who works in child safeguarding.

'Beth! How lovely to see you.' She comes forward, touching my arm. 'Do you know Nadia? She works for a victim support charity.'

We shake hands and I turn to include Jaime. 'It would be great if Jaime here could get involved with you guys when he's released. He's been a brilliant Listener and it would be a shame if all that talent went to waste!' I smile round, seeing he's gone very red.

'Oh, we'd love to chat further, wouldn't we, Maddie? You're in a unique position, Jaime. My clients in crisis often have the prison experience in the mix. That's especially true for children and parents too, isn't it, Mads? Your input would add another really useful dimension.'

Jaime looks tongue-tied and uncomfortable with all the attention.

Madeleine checks her watch. 'I have another appointment

in an hour. Is the incident resolved now? Am I able to get to the gate?'

'What incident?' Jaime looks at Robyn. 'I didn't hear anything?'

'A prisoner on A Wing. He's been transferred to the hospital,' Father O'Brian puts in. My eyes snap to Jaime's face. This isn't the way we wanted to tell him.

Jaime's face falls. 'Who on A wing? What's going on?'

Robyn takes him gently by the arm, leading him to a pew seat. 'It's Leo Hargreaves, Jaime. He's attempted suicide again.' She holds up a quietening hand. 'No, honestly. Don't worry, he's fine, he's fine. We've just been to see him. He's awake and he's talking.'

'But I only just left him this morning! He was okay. We were talking about some girl he's been seeing, he...' Jaime stops abruptly. 'What did I miss?' I can see he's desperate. 'Did I not pick up on something?' His eyes are wide in shock and then they suddenly narrow. 'Actually, now I think back, the cops came in this morning, didn't they? I saw them talking to the PO... Officer Johnson. Did they talk to Leo?'

Madeleine and Nadia share a concerned look. 'We'll leave you to it.' They glance at Father O'Brian.

'Oh yes, no problem. I'll escort you back right now if you're ready?'

'Yep.' Madeleine bends to pick up her bag and Nadia gives me a nod. 'Great to see you, Beth. And wonderful to meet you, Jaime, I really hope we'll meet again in different circumstances.'

There's the sound of the outer gate closing and only a second's pause before Jaime explodes.

'Those pig bastards!'

Robyn is there with a placating hand on his arm.

'We don't know anything for sure, Jaime,' she reassures him. 'Sometimes these things just happen with no rhyme or reason. We don't know for sure about any police involvement.'

'Let's not pretend!' Jaime is shaking. 'We all know it won't be long before they're back again, sniffing around.'

'We have to deal with the situation and keep a cool head,' Robyn says gently. 'The primary aim is to help Leo, and protect people like you, Jaime. You're coming up for release soon. Don't jeopardise that by playing into their hands. Let's think with this.' She taps her temple. 'Don't give them more casualties.'

'You're right, you're right!' Jaime takes a shuddering breath. 'But I know how the pigs operate. I've dealt with their BS and snakey games. I'm all over it.'

I look at Robyn. I'm concerned he's going to go back to the wing angry and there's going to be some kind of situation.

'Anyway, Jaime, I need a favour from you.'

I can see she's trying to defuse the mood. But Jaime's not really listening.

'There's this job on the wing. I need you to rustle up some interest for a Bible group this Friday and try to deter the drug dealers from seeing my groups as a sales opportunity.' She rolls her eyes, attempting a bit of levity. 'I'm not convinced that "jacking up with Jesus" is a great marketing campaign for me to be running with, do you?'

But Jaime is in no mood to be jollied along.

'Yeah. Sure. I just need a word with Beth, if that's okay?' His face is grim and tight.

Robyn looks at me wide-eyed; I signal it's fine.

'I'll just pop to the wing and start the mission then. Back shortly. Help yourselves to whatever.' Robyn waves towards the office.

Jaime follows me, head down, back into the vestry. I gesture over to the comfy chairs and Jaime reluctantly perches stiffly on the arm.

His face is dark with emotion. 'How bad is Leo really? Like, how close did he get to dying?'

'I don't know the answer to that, Jaime.' I drop teabags into two cups and flick on the kettle. 'We saw him and spoke to him. I think with the right support network—'

'But we're *way* beyond all that now, aren't we?' Jaime interrupts. 'The kid has attempted suicide before, and with all the pressure from the cops and no one to protect him...' He balls his fists angrily. 'What will happen if I'm released?'

'We'll do our absolute best.' I stop and clarify, 'Actually, *I'll* do my absolute best.' I meet his eyes with a steady gaze. 'I promise you.'

He shakes his head in frustration. I can see he thinks I'm naive. 'Leo's a kid, Beth. Kids are unpredictable. He's got himself in a situation that he doesn't have the mental resources or stamina to deal with. I've talked to him. His whole life has been a catalogue of wrong choices.' His gaze is clear and unflinching. 'And before you think it, yes, I'm one to talk. But that's exactly why I know. Because he's a kid, and because he's immature, and because he's allowed himself to be manoeuvred and followed dickheads – that's precisely how he's got himself into the position he's in now.'

Leo's white face against that even whiter pillow comes to me. *He's someone's son.* How easily that could be my son lying there.

'He's made one bad choice after another, found himself in one bad situation or another, got himself in it so deep, I don't know how he's going to get out of it. I totally, *totally* get why he'd choose suicide. It's about the only option left to him – that or wait to be killed.'

A cold stone of fear wraps its way around my heart.

It doesn't have to be like that for Joe. He has support: a family that loves him, opportunities to turn his life around, someone that will protect him no matter what. That doesn't have to be Joe's life.

I attempt to drag my thoughts back.

'I know you care, Jaime. I care too. But you can't get embroiled in his situation. You challenging the police won't do him any good, or you either. Don't antagonise the situation. Leave this for me and Robyn to sort.'

Jaime runs his fingers through his hair. 'I get that. No, honestly, I do. You're right. I know I'm too close, it's just—'

The door suddenly opens, and Officer Johnson's face appears with Father O'Brian hovering in the background.

'You okay in here?' The officer's eyes flit over me and then to Jaime.

'Fine, thanks.' I smile back.

'Just to let you know, they're doing a full head count because of the hoo-ha earlier. Jaime will need to go back to the wing. I can give you a few more minutes, but that's all. Sorry.'

Jaime stands. 'No worries, I'm ready now. Will I see you again soon?' He looks at me.

'I can take him back to the wing if you like?' Father O'Brian says. 'I'm supposed to be helping Robyn rally the troops for the group later, so I'm going that way.'

'Suits me.' Officer Johnson stands back to let Jaime pass.

'We ready? Got everything?'

Jaime nods. 'See you later, Beth. Thanks for everything.'

There's a moment, a tiny split second, that I realise that Officer Johnson hasn't moved. I hear the closing of the chapel gate and then it all goes quiet.

Johnson stands in the doorway, arms folded. He doesn't speak. I have this urge to busy myself with paperwork: picking up things that aren't mine, stacking them into bundles as though I'm readying to leave. Out of the corner of my eye, I see he still hasn't moved. I look up expectantly.

'Actually, do you have a couple of minutes?' He glances behind into the chapel space. I'm aware it's empty and silent.

'Sure.' My fingers pause amidst the papers. There's a vague sense of disquiet. I feel for the reassuring solid edge of the desk.

'Your work with the Samaritans...' he starts. 'It's something I'd be interested in exploring.'

'Okay.' The office chair is behind me, but I can't bring myself to sit.

'As Robyn said earlier, I work with vulnerable kids already. Mainly boys, teetering on the brink of ending up in places like this.' He tilts his chin, leaning against the door frame and making himself comfortable. The disquiet climbs up a notch.

'I was thinking about getting more into the supportive, counselling side of things, not just young boys, but girls too. Robyn was telling me that you've got future plans for maybe Psychology or Social Work. Something along that line?'

I had no idea Robyn had discussed me with anyone.

'I probably don't want to be a screw for the rest of my days, so I thought it might be good experience – get my foot in the door, as they say.'

He leans up from the frame and takes a step towards me. I freeze. I'm aware that he's blocking the doorway. His whole demeanour is totally benign and ordinary, and yet there's something about him that puts my every nerve-ending on high alert. I can't get past without touching him, and I know he could easily stop me.

You're being silly. What's the matter with you? There's nothing wrong with this guy. My eye alights on the telephone sitting on the desk. His gaze registers the direction of my glance, but his face gives no indication.

His eyes slide back to my face. 'So, I was wondering... umm... would you like to go for a coffee sometime to discuss it?' He looks at me expectantly.

I pause, flustered. 'I can send you a link if you like, to the Samaritans website. You can find lots of information there.'

He scratches his chin and takes another step forward. 'It's not really that kind of information I'm looking for. It was more to do with your experience of volunteer work that I wanted to chat over, but if you'd rather not...' He colours a little, his hand dropping.

I instantly feel churlish. 'Oh, it's not that! It's—'

'So you will?' His face brightens.

I want to be polite, despite the warning bells. My head tells me I'm overreacting: this man hasn't done a thing. He hasn't been suggestive or inappropriate in any way, he's only been friendly and enquiring, and yet here I am... Here I am, feeling... *Feeling what?*

'Well, it's...' I don't know how to stop this. 'I'm sorry, Mr Johnson—'

'Tom.'

'I'm sorry, *Tom.*' I proffer a tiny smile. 'I've got a lot on my plate at the moment. Actually...' I pick up some random papers from the desk. 'I probably should be heading off.'

'Absolutely.'

I take a step towards him, but he doesn't move. I know, if I don't halt, our bodies will collide.

My hand comes up to gesture my way through. 'Sorry, could I just...'

He stares down at my hand. My face burns fiercely and I find myself licking my lips.

'Um, I'm sorry, I just need to squeeze past.'

I know I sound silly and apologetic. I snatch a glance at him from the corner of my eye. I am so close I can see the pores in his cheek. There are tiny commas of hair where he hasn't shaved properly. I can smell him.

He regards me for a few seconds. 'Do you enjoy coming onto the wing, Beth?'

'Sorry?'

'Do you ever find it intimidating?'

His tone is still conversational. I'm so tense I falter awkwardly, but there's a chair in the way.

'I just wondered. All those desperate men looking at you. Does it make you feel uncomfortable?' He shifts a little closer.

'I don't think I've thought about it.' I try to keep my voice level but I'm aware of the wobble. I find I can't move.

He frowns with a kind of mock-puzzlement. 'That can't be true though, can it, Beth? You must've thought about it. You must've noticed how they look at you. I was wondering if you feel threatened at all?'

I go to step back, but I end up blundering into the chair. It tilts and I stagger, grabbing on to it.

'I think she wants to leave.'

Johnson's head snaps towards the door. Jaime is standing there.

'Everything alright?' Father O'Brian comes up breathlessly behind.

'Beth was just saying how she wasn't feeling well.' Johnson looks at Father O'Brian. 'She was telling me how she fainted at home this morning. Had a blackout or something. Can I leave her with you, Father? The wing will be wondering where I am.' He backs away into the chapel. Jaime glares after him.

I feel my knees crumpling and I grope for the desk behind me.

'Oh dear, oh dear!' Father O'Brian tuts. 'Let's grab that chair! You sit there and I'll go and get you some water, hang on.' He bustles out of the door.

'What did Johnson do? Are you okay?' Jaime is kneeling at my side. I feel slightly sick.

'He...' I want to repeat what he said, how he made me feel, how he intimidated me, but everything feels wrong and jumbled.

'You came back.' I stare at him. 'Why did you come back?'

Jaime gives me a look. 'I've always had a bad vibe about him. I could tell he was hanging back and I didn't like it. I made an excuse to Father O'Brian that I'd forgotten some papers. Thank God I did.' He looks at me, relieved. His face is kind and concerned. 'Johnson messes with your head, doesn't he? He gets you so you can't think straight. That's how he does what he does.'

There's a warm pressure on the back of my hand and I look down and realise his palm is covering my wrist. Father O'Brian appears with a glass of water, and it instantly pulls away.

'There. There you are.' He proffers it, pulling a chair over to perch on the edge. 'Have a few sips of that.' He adjusts his spectacles. 'If you still feel woozy, I'll call the one of the hospital staff. A blackout? Goodness me!'

'I didn't black out.' I take the glass from his hand and cup it in both of mine. 'I don't know where that idea came from.'

'But Mr Johnson said...' Father O'Brian frowns.

'I know what he said.' I bring the glass shakily to my lips. *Drew*, my mind is whirling. *He must have spoken to Drew about what happened this morning.*

'I need to leave. Get a bit of fresh air.' I stand unsteadily, reaching for the back of the chair. 'I'll be fine. Honestly, I'll be fine. Just tell Robyn I'll call her, will you?'

'I do hope you feel better soon.' Father O'Brian gets up, holding out a hand to steady me. I can't look at Jaime. 'But yes, I'll tell her.'

'Tell me what?' Robyn comes in looking anxious. 'My God, what's happened?'

'She fainted,' Father O'Brian says confidently, but I interrupt him.

'Please stop saying that, I really didn't. Would you mind taking me to the gate, Robyn? I think I just want to go home.'

'Of course, of course! Shall I get you a taxi? I'll come with you, shall I? Come on. Oopsy-daisy!' Robyn supports me. 'You can tell me on the way.'

'Honestly, It's nothing. Don't fuss!'

I'm aware that Jaimie is tracking my every move. My gaze almost meets his, but I can't bring myself to look in his direction. I allow Robyn to guide me out onto the concourse.

'Now, are you sure you're okay to walk?'

'For goodness' sake!' I fluster. 'There's no need for any of that. I didn't faint.'

'So, what happened?' She leads the way along the path and I gratefully breathe in sweet, fresh air.

'That officer, the one we saw before, that Tom Johnson, he came into the office. I was on my own. He was insinuating all kinds of things.'

'What things?' She pauses mid-stride. 'What kind of things?'

'Oh, I don't know! It was more like the way he was saying it. Like asking me if I ever felt threatened when I went on the wing.'

'Okay.'

'And did I know that the prisoners looked at me... in that way, you know.'

'Right. Wow.'

We carry on walking. She has her head down and I can't tell what she's thinking.

'He creeped me out. He kept moving closer. He asked me to go out with him for coffee to discuss my voluntary work. I said no. I mean, I thought the guy was okay. You implied he was too, didn't you? But I'm telling you, he's seriously weird.'

I'm aware Robyn's gone very quiet. 'Actually, Beth, the coffee thing might be my fault.' She winces. 'I think I might've said it'd be a good idea.' She glances at me, embarrassed. 'He's been asking me for some time about different ways he could get involved in the more pastoral side. Err – I might've mentioned your name.'

'Oh!'

'Totally my bad. I shouldn't've put your name in the frame.'

'You can't be responsible for how he behaves, Robyn!'

'No, I know, but still.' She shakes her head. 'I do feel awful. Maybe I should have a word with him? I wonder if he's aware how he's coming across? I suspect his tone was a bit too forceful. I know he's got this "thing" about prisoners behaving appropriately on the wing, especially when there are women about. He's clearly getting it totally wrong.'

'More than totally.'

'Really out of character, though. I mean, I wouldn't have asked him to take over from me as the Samaritans' contact in the prison if—'

It's my turn to halt in shock. She sees the expression on my face.

'I thought he'd be a good fit!' she scrabbles to explain. 'He seems such a nice, caring chap. He's chatted to me at length about his voluntary work and he was really excited to get more involved. There was no reason not to ask him; he looked like the perfect candidate. Oh heck! Now what?'

Did I misread what happened?

'Robyn, he's clearly been talking to Drew about me. He told Father O'Brian I fainted at home. That can only have come from Drew. I had no idea they knew each other.'

'Uh-huh...' Robyn nods. 'Well, that's possible – maybe Drew mentioned you in passing this morning.'

But why would he? I can't get my head around this. We step through the metal gate into the gatehouse.

'So, Johnson would be my contact person then,' I say slowly.

Robyn is squirming with embarrassment.

'Thing is, Robyn, I was thinking about putting in a formal complaint.'

She looks at me, aghast.

'What? Come on! This is the twenty-first century, Robyn! Men can't just go around doing this kind of stuff.'

But she only lowers her voice. 'Beth. We know how that would play out. You're going to make a complaint in this kind of environment? It'll be your word against his. I'm on your side, but you know what they're going to say: what did he *actually* do to you? What did he *actually* say?'

I stop, dumbfounded. 'Jaime saw it. Jaime saw what happened. He said that man's got a "bad vibe".'

'A bad what?' She almost laughs. 'Beth, really honestly, I'm with you on this, but a prisoner waiting for the results of his parole hearing?' Robyn looks at me gently. 'Are you really going to put him in that position?'

'But there are female staff here. Senior managers. They'll understand.'

Robyn nods thoughtfully. 'Yeah, of course they will. But these women have careers to think of. You know as well as I do, no one wants staff around who make trouble. They'll put it down to a "misunderstanding"' – she makes rabbit ears in the air – 'about being invited to go for coffee. You can see how it sounds.'

I feel outmanoeuvred, angry and upset.

We reach the main gate. Robyn sees the look on my face.

'Beth.'

'I can't talk,' I say abruptly. 'I've got too much going on right now.' I take a deep breath. 'I was going to tell you about the girl that turned up at my house this morning.'

'Girl? What girl? *The* girl?' Robyn's stunned. 'Oh my God, Beth! How—?'

But I cut her off. 'I'm too tired, too overwhelmed, to be honest. I just need to go home.'

The security doors open and swish closed behind me. I'm aware of Robyn's dumbstruck face staring after me, but I really can't cope. There's a churning sensation in my gut that won't leave me.

Johnson.

I play back the scene again and again.

Is there any chance I'm making too much of this? Am I feeling vulnerable right now and construed a meaning that just wasn't there?

I get to my car, and it isn't until I'm safely inside that I lock the doors, drop my head, and allow myself to cry. I'm crying for all of it: for what's happened with Johnson, for what's happening with Drew, and definitely with Joe. And yet in the middle of all that, there's one person who has remained stead-fast and true. The one person who, as far as everyone is concerned, is bad and untrustworthy, and yet has proved himself more supportive than all of them put together.

Jaime.

My hands lie curled uselessly in my lap. The tears rain down and I bring them to my face. There's a scent, the scent of *him*: Jaime, the place where he rested his palm against my wrist.

My fingers trace the spot. I remember his touch: soft and tender, as though he really meant it.

My heart tells me the thing that my head won't allow. He cares. He cares deeply about many things, but right now he cares very much about me.

ELEVEN

I sit staring out of the windscreen watching as the prison car park barrier arcs and lowers yet again with a judder, its tip wavering against the skyline as a stream of cars slip through.

I dial Joe's number, listening as it diverts to voicemail. I go to WhatsApp, asking him to let me know how he's doing. The message flicks up with two blue ticks, and he responds immediately, telling me they've gone through to boarding, and he'll contact me as soon as they land.

> I'm worried about u. U'll stay in the hotel compound. Yes?

> Already sorted. We've sussed the pad and the town. No need to go anywhere. Beer, beach, and baes on tap.☺

I feel a flood of relief.
My phone pings again.

> Oh and thanks 4 everything. ♥ u. X

The rush of happiness is indescribable. Joe, my Joe, has told me he loves me. I glance up into the mirror, nearly bursting. I see that my face is flushed. I feel like laughing; it bubbles up inside of me until I could almost burst with giggles as my eye catches sight of a car at the barrier.

My laughter instantly dies.

It's Drew.

He drives right past, forcing me to cringe down in the seat, begging that he doesn't look round, but he's too busy concentrating on finding a space. Squeezing round in the seat, I peer under the gap in the headrest. He's alone. I watch carefully as he parks up and kills the engine, knowing, with a dread of certainty, that he'll spot my car. That he'll come over and ask what I'm doing here. I have no idea what I'm going to say.

I shrink lower as numerous taxis turn up, circling the car park, hiding me briefly from view. Twisting around, I take a chance, peering up over the back of the seat, trying to get a glimpse, when a movement from a waiting taxi catches my eye. The sight punches the air from my lungs.

Dark hair. Pretty. It's *her*. That girl.

There she is: brown curls tumbling in a coronet as the wind catches them. She pulls a tendril of hair from her eyes and dips to speak to the driver. She glances right and left as she straightens, and then her eyes meet mine.

Her.

Me.

Caught.

But she only glances away. I find my whole body is trembling. She doesn't look back as she shoves her hands deep into the pockets of her jacket.

The shock of the realisation creeps into my brain.

She knows my name but she has no idea what I look like.

I watch as she walks quickly across the car park, clearly

unaware that Drew is behind her. I crane forward. *Where is he?* My heart thuds in panic.

'*Melanie!*'

I hear him shout, and she turns at the sound. I watch her face fall as she swings away, picking up her pace.

'Melanie!'

He hurries to catch up with her.

I watch the scene unfolding, mesmerised. He goes to grab her arm, but she savagely yanks it away. There is a queue of visitors forming outside the visitors' centre. Some of them look round, curious. Drew glances up at the camera on the pole – he clearly knows they're being observed – and immediately begins to body-block her, walking backwards in front as she desperately tries to outmanoeuvre him. Finally, she stops, lowering her head, hunching her hands in her pockets, and stares down at the ground. He dips, trying to catch her eye, talking incessantly. She briefly glances over her shoulder, sweeping her hair away.

She's weakening; I can tell by her body language he's managing to talk her round. She nods quickly, bites her top lip, then nods again.

I lower the side window, wanting to hear what he's saying. The wind catches his voice, intermittently bringing it to me and then whisking it away again. He takes her by the elbow, turning her towards me. I immediately drop down, listening to the scuff of their feet coming closer.

She clearly wasn't expecting to see him. Was he waiting for her?

There's the sound of a car engine and I peer over the rim of the steering wheel. Drew's car rumbles past, heading for the exit. My hand instinctively reaches for the ignition. What am I thinking? This is ridiculous; I can't follow them, can I?

I force myself to sit and watch as his car pauses at the barrier. The girl's face is set in stony profile as suddenly my phone jangles into life.

Drew.

His red brake lights flash at the top of the road.

'Hiya!' he says cheerily. 'I thought I'd give you a call and find out how you're doing. Heard from Joe yet?'

I don't know how to reply. His car disappears around the corner. I imagine him holding his finger to his lips to keep her silent.

'Where are you?' I close my eyes.

'At work, still. It feels like it's already been a very long day and probably set to get even longer.'

An ache thrums through me. 'Do you think you might be late home then?'

'Could be. It's like a madhouse here. I'm going to try for a flyer, but I'm not holding my breath.'

The backs of my eye sockets thud with an increasing pressure. I'd love to find that the world had disappeared. I'd love to stare into the distance and *just scream.*

'What time is Joe due to land?' The ordinariness of the conversation grinds even deeper.

'I'm just about to call him,' I manage through tightened teeth.

'Okey-dokey. Send me a text when you know, will you? I'll probably be off the grid for a while, but I'd like to keep in the loop.'

'Of course.'

He says something else, but the intermittent signal crackles and then the line goes dead. I stare at the phone in my hand. It rings again instantly. I think about not answering, but another name flashes up: Robyn. I don't really want to talk, but it could be urgent.

I can hear her breathless excitement.

'You're not going to believe this! He's just heard. Jaime's got parole.' She's overjoyed. 'Are you there, Beth? Did you hear what I said? Jaime's got parole!'

'Oh, that's great news!'

I am happy, I want to be happy.

'Where are you?'

'I'm just on my way home. That's brilliant. Really is. Really wonderful news.' I force a smile into my voice.

'Umm... about earlier.' Robyn clears her throat. 'The truth is, I think I handled the whole Tom Johnson thing really badly. I should never have suggested that he come and talk to you. That was very wrong of me.'

'Right.' I blink.

'I see now how it put you in an awkward position. It gave him a way "in" to approach you. I shouldn't've done that either.'

That's not really the point: it wasn't the offer of coffee that's the issue. But I decide to let it go.

'Thank you for saying all that. I appreciate it, Robyn, I really do.'

'We've never had so much as a cross word before, you know that?' I can tell she's desperate to put this right.

'I know. It's crazy.'

'You're having such a tough time at the moment. You need to cut yourself some slack, Beth.'

'Yeah.' I glance at my eyes in the mirror. They're red-rimmed, bruised-looking with tiredness.

'So, you don't hate me?' There's a smile in her voice.

'I don't hate you, Robyn. I could never hate you.'

She breathes out in relief and then stops. 'You might when you hear what I've got to say next.'

'You're on a roll, Robyn. Just spit it out.'

'It's to do with him, though. Johnson.' Her discomfort is palpable.

'Go on.'

'It's just I already told the governor that Johnson will be the new Samaritans co-ordinator...'

'Right.'

I could rest my head on the wheel now and close my eyes and hope that I never had to open them again.

'So now I've got to find an excuse why I've changed my mind.'

I press my fingers into my forehead. 'So don't.'

'What do you mean, don't?'

'I mean, leave it as it is. I might've read the whole thing wrong.'

There's too much spinning through my head. I don't have the energy for any kind of fight. I'm on a sort of numb autopilot.

There's a pause.

'Are you sure, Beth?'

'Perfectly.'

'And you're okay? We're okay? I'm still your best buddy?'

I stare out across the car park, willing my voice to sound like I mean it.

'Yes, yes, I'm good. I'm nearly home actually.' The world feels muted.

'I've got to hear all about this girl that turned up.'

'She came to the house. I didn't let her in. That was about the sum total of it. To be truthful, Robyn, I can't relive it all right now. I've just pulled up outside the house. We'll talk later, yeah?'

'Yes, absolutely.' She hesitates. 'Okay then, Beth, I'll let you go. And, well, I'm sorry again.'

'Me too. Don't worry about it. We're good.' I smile. 'Speak soon.' And I end the call, my smile fading as I look out across the gathering shadows at the perimeter wall. The afternoon sky is shifting, and a chill tightens down the length of my spine. I'm stiff and cold and miserable and very much alone.

Turning the engine on, I force my hands to grip the wheel and pull slowly out of the parking space.

The road from the prison is as familiar as the back of my hand – the hedgerows flicker past; the signs instruct me which way to go; the road markings guide me forward. I don't have to think, just drive as I head towards home, all the while knowing it doesn't feel like my home anymore.

TWELVE

I turn the corner into the street and my stomach instantly clenches at the unexpected sight of Drew's car parked in the driveway. I consider not stopping – just putting my foot down and keep going.

How easy that would be. *Walk away from it all. Sign into a hotel and just disappear.*

But instead, I force myself to park up, walk to the front door and quietly slot my key into the lock. The light in the living room is on and the TV is blaring as usual.

'Hiya!' he calls out.

My hackles bristle.

I stand in the doorway, pulling off my jacket as he grins at me over the back of the sofa.

'As you can see, I managed to get away.' His smile doesn't falter. 'Had a good day?'

'Not really.'

What's he done? Dropped his girl somewhere? Made plans for later?

His gaze is expectant, waiting for the explanation, but I don't offer one. I walk back into the hallway to hang up my coat and then go straight into the kitchen. I see he's started dinner: there's a slew of ingredients across the work surface. I make no comment, not wanting to engage. I don't want to know. I don't want to hear it.

'So, tell me then.'

I hadn't heard him come in. He's leaning on the worktop, a glass of wine in hand.

I go distractedly from the fridge to the sink and back again without knowing what I'm doing or why. My anger boils steadily.

'No, I'm sure your day has been far more interesting.' I bite the words. 'You were in the prison interviewing, weren't you? Tell me all about that then.' I busy myself pointlessly running the water. My tone is clipped and aggressive, but he doesn't seem to notice.

'How d'you know?'

'Word gets around.' I glance at his face.

'Ah. Yeah.' He takes a gulp of wine. 'By the way, I thought we might have pasta.'

I'm giving him nothing.

'Anyway, yeah, mostly I was seeing a selection of the great unwashed.' He waves his glass absent-mindedly. 'I won't go into detail but mainly low-level druggies who've got involved in high-level stuff. Those are the ones we're really interested in.'

I can't tell if he's baiting me. I'm aware of the air filling my lungs, slowly.

'I don't know how you keep going into those places.' He's not even looking at me. 'I had to come home and shower the stink off. Oh, did you manage to speak to Joe? How's he doing?'

Shower? I know why you're showering again. I want to scream the words. *Your hot date, maybe?*

I could literally stand there, right now, in the centre of this kitchen and open my mouth and let it all out in one great bellow of fury.

His phone jangles and he instantly jerks to answer it, disappearing back into the hallway, his voice dying away to a low rumble as he goes into the living room and closes the door.

The ease of his betrayal is breathtaking. The smoothness of the lies... I know it's her.

I am way, way beyond fury and as far from hurt as it's possible to be. I'm not going to pretend anymore; I'm not going to tiptoe around him.

Striding into the hallway, I see that the living room door is only pushed to; Drew's murmuring voice rises and falls a little.

'Yes. Okay. Are you sure?' I hear. 'No, that's... Where are you now?... No. Hang on.' There's a pause. 'Hello...? Are you still there?'

I push the door wide and walk in. He's standing over in the bay window with his back to me, but wheels round in surprise, pushing the phone into his pocket.

He can't meet my eye.

'I have to go out. Look, I'm really sorry.'

I don't say a word as he searches around at the side of the sofa, picking up notebooks and papers.

My laser-like glower follows every bend, every dip he makes. I am beyond speaking; I don't know what might erupt from my mouth.

He reaches for a folder, avoiding my gaze. 'Don't wait for me. Have dinner, won't you? I don't know how long I'll be.'

He picks up his jacket from the back of the chair and tugs an arm into the sleeve. 'I can see by your face you're not best pleased, but I'll try not to be too long, yeah? It's just really difficult at the moment.'

'Oh, I understand,' I say evenly. The sarcasm is clearly lost.

'You'll be okay?' He goes to touch the side of my face, but I flinch away. 'Yeah, I get how pissed off you are, Beth; I'm disappointed too. I shouldn't have bunked off early, should I?' He gives me a sheepish look. 'But I'll get back as soon as I can.

There's a bottle of wine open; have a glass. Relax.' He sees my expression isn't wavering and he wrinkles his nose. 'Look, I really am sorry.'

'Just go.'

I see the hurt look on his face. His expression wavers as he leans in to give me a peck on the cheek, but I turn away, stalking back into the kitchen. I hear him pause momentarily in the hall-way, but then he's gone.

Instinctively reaching to flick off the light, I watch as he strides towards his car, pulling out his phone, and clearly texting as he drops behind the wheel. Just as instinctively, I know exactly what I'm going to do next.

Yanking my jacket off the hook, I grab my car keys, pausing with a hand on the door latch and peering through the glass. I wait as his car headlights illuminate the pane for several seconds, before swinging round as he backs off the drive. My ears strain, listening for the trailing engine sound, as I slip out into the darkness, running to my car and glancing up the street. His rear brake lights flash at the junction as he signals to turn left, and within minutes I am making the same turning, not knowing where I'm going and not caring either. All I know is that Drew is about to get the biggest shock of his life.

It's started to rain. I follow him through the centre of town, darting looks between the windscreen wipers obscuring my view.

He keeps changing lanes as though he's concerned about being followed, but I keep well back, managing to keep track of his numberplate as he makes his turns right and left.

The traffic dies away as he indicates into a side street of Victorian terraced houses. It's pretty narrow with cars parked on either side and only a few of the streetlamps are working.

I watch him slow down, guessing he's looking for a parking

space. I instantly kill my headlights, gliding quietly into a stretch of kerb space as he makes his way further up on the opposite side. Minutes pass. *What is he doing?*

I wait for a few moments. I can't see any movement. Easing the driver's door open, I slip around the back of the car, pulling my jacket closer and sliding into the shadows of the houses. His car is there, silent and still. I instinctively pause to dip and peer closer: *is that him or the shape of the headrest?* I can't tell. Then suddenly, the driver's door opens and I slam back into the cover of darkness. The shape of his head and shoulders appears above the car roof line and then he makes his way across the road. I instantly copy him, skimming the edges of the shadows, hurrying to keep up.

Somewhere ahead is the dull buzz-thump of a party and the occasional shriek of laughter. Whirling lights pulse out onto the pavement. There's the chink of discarded bottles and male voices shouting obscenities. Keeping behind the roofline of parked cars, I quicken my pace as his silhouette hunches purposefully up the street. Then he hesitates, looking up. I pause and look up too.

All the rooms of the party house are ablaze with colour. There are stone steps leading up to a front door lying ajar, spilling a strip of rainy yellow light across a row of over-flowing dustbins. The sash windows are wide open, the music pumping out, as figures appear and disappear in the back-lit frames.

Drew skirts around a huddle of partygoers as the front door is yanked open in a torrent of light and noise. He's caught for a moment: his face illuminated as a gang of squawking girls come tumbling down the steps. In those few moments I realise he's changed his clothes. There's a kind of numb realisation at how calculating he's been: how he's planned and executed this whole deception, this whole betrayal – only now, right this second, I have the power to blast his shabby facade apart.

He flashes the girls his standard easy grin. It's a provocative flirtation; it's just a few fleeting seconds of exchange, but I feel the burn of it as he sidesteps past them, disappearing inside.

The girls' squeals echo into the night as they protect their hair from the rain, staggering in a tipsy gaggle across the road. One of the stragglers at the back looks me up and down; she's all sooty-wet mascara, a mouth widening in a thickened slash of red lipstick.

'Goaan! If ya wanna...! Get in there!' She lifts her chin towards the house. 'Plenny of gear goin'!' She cackles a laugh. 'Prob'ly loosen you up a bit!' The cackle becomes a squawk as she staggers in a waft of cheap perfume.

I've nothing left to lose.

A greasy wall of heat hits me as I step inside. Bodies jostle and push. It's the kind of place I have only seen in nightmares. The deep drumbeat of music thuds its way into my ribcage as I make my way down a narrow corridor. Everywhere is buzzing with sound. Dim yellow bulbs hang in loops from the ceiling and, at the end, a collapsed staircase leads upwards. The bottom steps are crammed with kids about Joe's age and younger, out of their minds on God knows what, lolling heads, eyes glazed. A dead zone.

A room to my left is bathed in a weird green and red subterranean glow. Dark shapes, cut-outs of people, move slowly like shadows, arms aloft, drifting as though underwater, caught on an invisible tide that only they can feel.

Every part of me wants to turn around and get the hell out. There's a sound behind me and my head snaps back. The front door has swung shut; the heat instantly intensifies and so does my fear.

Panic tightens my throat. There's a rapid spring of sweat. I look back. The door recedes, the bodies in front of it, shoving and bumping, pressing me further forward. The music grinds louder, shivering and shaking its way into my head, gouging a pressure until sparks begin to fly.

I can't breathe.

I'm suddenly suffocating; my heart rate thunders hard in my ears as my head snatches back to gulp for the tiniest sip of air. I try to cry out. I go to open my mouth, but it instantly fills with a weird choking smoke. I begin to claw this way and that, a frenzied flailing as I rake at the sea of shoulders that only offload me, leaving me floundering blind...

And suddenly I'm spat out into an open space as the ground beneath me falls away and catches again in a painful slam of concrete.

I'm in a yard desperately dragging cool air into my lungs. My stinging palms pad forward, my knees following, to graze against what feels like a brick wall. My fingers crawl upward and outward, finding rubble and tufts of grass, my eyes widening, as the party noise mutes and the darkness unfolds.

I'm in a kind of covered area. The moonlight picks out a dirty plastic roof that squeals in the breeze. At the far end is a gap where a gate used to be. I scramble to my feet, toeing gingerly forward, hands outstretched, peering out into what seems to be an overgrown garden.

There are sounds of people – sweeping arcs of white torch-lights, intermittently flashing and blinding, briefly lighting up the bower of straggly trees into a canopy of silvered branches.

From deep in the shadows, there's a shout and a gust of bawdy laughter. There are male and female voices, excitedly calling, their words indecipherable.

The tall brittle grass rustles with heavy movement and there's the occasional chink of glass on stone. Finding my phone, I flick on the torch. There's a pathway running right and left, but the beam only illuminates just beyond my feet – past that there's nothing but darkness.

A sudden giggle close to me and I swing round. The shaft picks out a short skirt and pale length of bare leg. The giggle snorts and stops, as I direct the torch upward. A pair of laughing eyes with a man's hand across her mouth glance at me once but then squint away in the glare. The man holding the girl turns his face to bury it in her shoulder.

My heart misses and almost stops.

I know the jacket. I know the shape of the head. It's Drew.

There's a surge of something: *fight, flight...* my rage and fury turning into panic as I stumble forward, desperate to get out of there, ricking my ankles over rubble and tripping through piles of trash. I bolt down the path, the torch bobbing uselessly, the dry sobs aching in the back of my throat.

An echoing volley of shouts rings out behind me as the pathway squeezes narrower into an alley. Up ahead, the dim streetlights of the road show me where safety lies. I plunge forward into the black nothingness, not caring, glancing up briefly, suddenly aware of silhouetted figures blocking the exit.

Men.

Their shadows lengthen and loom larger as they turn in unison to see what's coming towards them.

I falter, my hand reaching out to skim the wall. I don't know if they're a threat. Glancing quickly over my shoulder, I see all that's behind me is darkness and Drew calling my name.

I'm caught.

Taking a hesitant step forward, I can see now that these aren't men, but boys, nothing but kids really, arguing, shoving each other, playful, aggressive. One flicks a cigarette butt out in front of him, the fireflies of sparks exploding into the darkness. My pace quickens and they come into focus. The face of the boy with the cigarette turns to me in query.

It's Joe.

My brain makes the connection before my lips are able to form the name. He spooks, turns on his heels and sprints off. I can only stand, breathing heavily, flummoxed and struggling.

'Beth!'

Drew's voice bellows out behind me, but I'm not going

to wait. Running up the road, I frantically search the line of cars, fumbling the car keys and dragging the driver's door wide. Thighs shaking, I gun the engine, ramming the car into gear just as Drew's palms hit the side window. He's shouting something; I don't want to hear it as I haul the wheel round in a screech of rubber on tarmac, and speed away.

My legs are like jelly as I slew up to the junction, looking this way and that for a glimpse of Joe. He went this way, didn't he? Desperate now, I crash through the gears, agitatedly checking left and right, speeding up then slowing down: thinking which way he might head, trying to second-guess his movements.

What the hell was Joe doing there?

I punch the phone icon on the dashboard, not taking my eyes off the side streets.

'Siri, call Joe!'

The seconds of waiting for a connection feel like dragging through silt.

'I'm sorry, we're unable to connect your call at this time.' I try again... And then again, my heart hammering like some crazy thing, my brain in overdrive.

I leave a garbled message.

'Joe. It's me. Please, can you call me? Was that you...? I'm not mad or angry with you, Joe, but... Anyway, just phone me, would you?'

The Bluetooth flashes into life with Drew's name lighting up the screen. I ignore it. The only space in my head right now is for Joe. Over and over, Drew keeps on calling, leaving messages, blowing up my phone. *Cancel, cancel, cancel.* All I can do is drive on frantically, taking turnings, left, right. Every gang of kids messing about, and my heart leaps; every gaggle of people crossing the road has me peering wildly through the windshield.

I don't really know what I'm doing or where I'm going, but there's no sign of Joe. Not here, not anywhere.

Slowly, I make the decision to give up, turning around, and heading back home. My eyes scour the house as it comes into view, checking and re-checking for any glimpse that he might be home.

Wearily hauling myself from the car, I make my way inside, pulling all the curtains tight closed before I switch on any lights. The answer machine on the landline is flashing. Heart in mouth, I press it.

'Hi, Beth, it's Joanne from the Samaritans' office. Just calling to say I hope you're feeling a bit better.'

I pause, puzzled.

'Drew said you'd be off for a few days. Not to rush you or anything, but if you could just let us know...'

I don't hear the rest of her message. I call Drew.

'Beth... Beth, I—'

'Don't speak,' I command. 'Just listen. You're a liar and a gaslighter, Drew. You've lied to me from the beginning. I don't want you home tonight, or any other night for that matter. I'll pack up your stuff and you can collect it in the morning. Do not harass me or keep attempting to contact me – not unless you want me to make a formal complaint to your boss. Do you understand?'

I don't wait for him to offer excuses, just jab my phone off and chuck it onto the sofa. The house thunders with an oppressive kind of silence. My body feels the weight of it pressing in. The numbness creeps in tighter.

I am like an automaton as I go into the kitchen to the cupboard under the sink, pull off a whole lot of black plastic sacks from the roll and climb the stairs. I find myself standing in front of the wardrobe, dragging Drew's clothes from the hangers, one by one. My arms piston like machines, going into drawers and cupboards, stuffing the whole lot into the bags and tying the necks. When I'm finished, I pile them all in the hallway and close the door, leaning my back against it and allowing myself to breathe.

Thoughts of Joe fill my mind as my hand reaches again for my phone. It goes straight to his voicemail.

I think of Sarah.

She'll know something by now, I'm sure. My heart shivers, quailing at the thought she hasn't contacted me. *Something bad... something so awful she can't bring herself to talk to me.*

My thumb searches for her name on the screen. I steel myself. The phone rings out and I count, knowing how many rings before she'll answer, feeling that massive tightening knot of apprehension slithering and growing cold, lurching sick in my gut.

'Hello, Beth,' she says dully. I can tell by her tone she's been waiting for this call. The knot squeezes tighter.

'Sarah. I...'

She doesn't say a word. The silence says it all.

'It's Joe.'

'Yes, I know it is.'

I don't understand the reply. 'I need to find him, Sarah. Have you heard from Nate?'

There's another few moments of silence.

'I think you and I should talk, don't you?'

The squeeze of anxiety turns to real fear. 'What do you know? What's happened?'

I hear her take a breath. 'I think you're already fully aware of what's happened.'

There's a hard hint of sarcasm. She's never spoken to me like this.

'Sarah! Please! I really, honestly don't know what's going on. Just tell me, is Nate with you? What's going on, Sarah? Did they come back? I thought I saw Joe; I've been out searching. I can't find him anywhere. If you know something.

Anything. I think I'm going out of my mind... Please!' I break off.

'I'm not doing this over the phone, Beth.' She lowers her voice to a steady whisper.

'Sarah. I'm begging you.'

'I've said, I'm not doing this now. It's late.'

'Then when?' I'm beside myself. She knows it. She pauses.

'Tomorrow.'

'When tomorrow?'

I hear another intake of breath. 'At nine. I'll meet you.'

'Where?'

'That café. The one we used to go to.'

'Sarah! Just tell me! Is Joe okay...? Sarah, I'm—'

But I'm left with silence.

A cry leaves my throat – a cry that's barely human: wounded and terrible. My fingers fumble again to make the connection, but it won't go through.

Searching feverishly for Nate's number, I scroll and scroll, but don't have it. I try Sarah again; but it's a constant busy tone. I don't know if she's blocked me, or...

My head scrambles. I find the airport number for Joe's airline, but everything is closed. All I get are automated voices. I'm almost hysterical, pacing around the house like some crazy thing, up the stairs, down the stairs, in and out of every room, pulling at my hair, gulping for air. I don't know what to do; everything is out of my control. I want to throw up; I want to scream. There's even a part of me that wants to call Drew – but I can't bring myself to do that. I just can't.

My arms drop. My neck feels like lead. I suddenly stand stock still on the landing, looking blankly into the bedroom, *our* bedroom, staring at the open wardrobe doors with their empty rails and shelves in bewilderment. That's how easy it is to unpick a marriage. That's what all your hopes and dreams look like when they're smashed to pieces. You're empty. There's just you left. Alone.

But desperate.

Desperate to find your child.

I dissolve, my knees giving way, my heart cracking open in grief as I turn, clawing my way onto Joe's bed, breathing in the scent of him, hauling the duvet into my fists and burying my face in his pillow just to inhale his presence as if I could drag him back inside me.

Where is he?

Why won't Sarah tell me?

I wrap myself in the duvet, staring out into the room that's so much him and yet so far from being the boy I once knew. *Where has he gone? What's happened to us?*

My eyes won't focus. I am aware of the shadow shapes on the walls changing from black to grainy grey. I don't know how long it's been; it could be an hour or five. Nothing feels real as I watch the darkness limping around the room as it changes into dawn, my thumb jerking to press his number every twenty minutes but getting the same response.

Nothing.

Nothing.

Nothing.

THIRTEEN

5:17.

5:33.

6:12.

6:26.

I have walked the house for hours. I am, indeed, 'beside myself'. I have been outside of my own body for hours. I'm not real; I'm functioning, but I'm not here.

I've considered getting back in the car and driving the streets. I've considered sitting outside Sarah's house to force her to talk to me. I've thought about going back to that party house and finding someone, anyone who might know Joe.

But I haven't done any of it.

6:38. The sky is bearing that blue hint of carbon.

6:40.

... 41...

The silence booms in my ears as I watch the clock, wanting to phone Sarah, scared of what she's going to tell me, scared she won't turn up.

I have two hours to wait: two hours of agony.

I think about contacting the airport again.

Joe was at that house last night. He didn't get on a plane. He lied. Sarah is going to tell me something I don't want to hear. The worst thing. *What's the worst?* I can't go there. She knows that I've lied to her too. She will never forgive me if my lies have hurt Nate.

What have I done? What have I got involved in?

I pick up a piece of paper and a pen.

I train Samaritans volunteers. I tell them that the callers need to write down their feelings if they can: that somehow by seeing it all laid in front of them, they can get some clarity. I write,

I don't think I can forgive myself. I've driven everyone away. I can't see any way out of this mess. I'm completely alone.

The clarity is there for me to see: I really *am* alone. No son, and just a pile of black plastic sacks for a marriage.

I've run out of options.

I'm right: I have.

If Sarah tells me that somehow I've aided and funded my kid getting hurt – *her* kid getting hurt, I don't know how I'll cope.

Chucking the pen and the paper onto the table, I glance again at the clock. It's too early but I can't sit here any longer. Grabbing up the bags of Drew's clothes, I haul them out of the front door and onto the doorstep, then get in the car and pull off the driveway.

The familiar road feels unreal. The streetlights bear down on either side like tall ghosts. A lorry thunders past in a blare of fairground lights and then disappears into the road ahead. I'm emptier and more alone than ever. That wash of fear in my stomach keeps my adrenaline buzzing; nausea is my constant partner. 7:30 and the traffic is picking up. Two more hours. Two more hours and I'll know the worst.

I park up on the street outside the café. The shops in the High Street have a desultory air. Many are boarded up; some have their windows smeared with whitewash. I glance at myself in the mirror. The face that looks back has a white and pinched look of a long-haul flight: the pores on my nose show up big and greasy, my eyes look squeezed in, lips, lying parted a little, are cracked and dry.

Resting my head back, I close my eyes as the wave of dizziness ramps up into a weird vertigo. There's an inexorable slide: an undulation of everything solid that sends my hand reaching to hold on to the door. No matter how much I try to keep a grip, it's like I'm being sucked into a vortex...

My eyes jerk awake.

A recycling truck trundles past alongside a guy clattering a pair of bins. He dips his head leeringly through the side window and I snatch up to glance at the clock: it's twenty past eight. The workers in the café window are shifting the chairs from the tables and a girl comes out to prop open a blackboard on the pavement.

Pulling down the visor mirror, I realise what a sight I am as I attempt to scrub away the sags of eyeliner, pinching my cheeks into some semblance of colour.

The girl behind the counter looks up as I walk in.

'Sorry,' I fluster. 'Am I too early?'

'You're alright,' she says a little grudgingly. 'But I've only just switched on the coffee machine.'

I order tea so I won't annoy her further. She brings over a small pot but made so strong, it pours out thick and orange. I take out my phone and pretend to read the screen. Every time the door gusts open, my heart opens with it. There's an early morning trickle of people ordering take-away coffee and muffins. I try hard not to stare, knowing I must appear anxious and on edge. I've deliberately chosen a seat where I'll see Sarah before she sees me.

My eyes keep flitting to the steamed windowpane, dying a little inside every time I see a car of the right shape and colour driving past. Fiddling with my saucer, I pick up the teaspoon, ripping the corner of a sachet of sugar that I don't take, spilling half of it on the table.

'You're early.'

I nearly drop the spoon. Sarah is pulling the strap of her handbag over her head and unbuttoning her coat. I can't speak. I watch as she drapes her coat over the back of a spare chair and sits down opposite. Her face is set in a mask of barely contained anger, but she manages a smile at the waitress who comes over to take her order.

'I've been going out of my mind,' I whisper, cupping my cheeks. 'Please, Sarah. Tell me, please.'

'What, like you told *me*, you mean?'

Her coffee arrives and she's forced to drop her glare. She leans back in her seat, smiling appreciatively, but the smile disappears as the waitress moves away.

'I know, I know...' My hand reaches across to her. 'But I'm begging you, Sarah! You have to tell me where Joe is!'

She jerks so suddenly across the table I think she's about to strike me. 'Who knows, Beth? And frankly, who cares?'

I realise I'm tilting on the back legs of the chair in shock.

'Your son...' she hisses. 'Your son.' Her eyes are a savage steely grey. 'What the hell do you think you're playing at? Calling me up, talking about holidays! What the—?' Her mouth trembles with fury. 'Are you involved in this filthy charade? Is that what this is?'

My head swings dumbly from side to side. 'Filthy...? Sarah... what? All I know is—'

'Don't you dare lie to me!' she spits viciously. 'Don't you dare! I'm talking about you covering for him! I'm talking about you bailing him out and then dragging Nate into it! I'm talking about openly deceiving me, Beth. Colluding with your son by using my Nate as a cover. *That's* what I'm talking about.'

My head hasn't stopped shaking. 'No, Sarah, I wouldn't! I—'

'Ohhh, come on, please! Grant me with a bit of intelligence!' She raises her voice in exasperation and two women at the counter look over. 'If you're going to pull this "it's-not-like-that" stunt, there's no point in me being here.' She pushes her chair back and goes to stand, but my hands come up to stop her.

'Sarah, sit! Sit down...!' I snatch a look at the waitresses. 'I'll tell you the truth, I promise. I'll tell you everything!'

She pauses and then sits heavily. She stares, unblinking. 'Go on then.'

I swallow, hard. 'He... They... Joe and Nate... got themselves into trouble. They were messing about and stole an old van. They had no idea who it belonged to. But it belonged to these guys – dealers, I think. They told the boys their gear was in the back of it. But it was all too late: Nate and Joe had already torched the van.'

She is sitting there like stone.

'You're right, Sarah! It was my idea for Joe and Nate to disappear. I couldn't get him the money soon enough. I thought he'd be safer out of the country somewhere. I dropped him off at the airport to meet Nate. Joe told me he would message as soon as they landed.'

She hasn't moved.

'Please, that's the whole truth! I just need to know where he is.'

Her gaze falters a little and then she starts to speak, very slowly.

'I can't believe you're for real, Beth. You honestly thought that giving Joe money to score drugs and then roping my son into it was some kind of solution?'

'Doing *what?* No...! I didn't! That's not what happened!'

'Thank God Nate has more sense. Thank *God* he had the strength of character to say he was having nothing to do with any of it. Christ alone knows what Joe would have dragged him into. I don't even think I've heard the whole story, but at least what Nate's told me isn't some fantastic fiction!'

'But the gang beat Nate up!' I insist. 'You must have seen the cuts and bruises, Sarah. I gave Joe the money because he was scared the same would happen to him!'

Sarah frowns, wrinkling her nose. 'Beat *who* up? Nate? Is this another fairy tale story from your off-the-rails son? I've just told you, Nate has more sense! He hasn't been beaten up. I don't know what you're talking about.'

My skin has gone cold.

'That's what Joe told me, Sarah.' I rake my fingers across my scalp. 'Look, okay, okay, cards on the table, Sarah. I don't think you've got the whole picture.' I swallow as my mind scrambles back. 'You know Nate took your car the other night, don't you? I was going to tell you. I really wish I had.'

'Nate took my car? When? Who told you that?'

'Joe said. He made a joke of it. He said—'

But she cuts across me. 'So they had a car each?' She blinks at the table, frowning.

My brain can't compute. 'Each?'

'Joe rocked up in a car to pick Nate up the other night. Said you'd let him spend his birthday money on it. He said he'd passed his test the day before, but he'd been keeping it quiet in case he failed.'

I have no words. My shoulders find the back of the chair as I dumbly stare at her.

'But... he cried in my arms, Sarah. He begged me. If you'd seen the state of him.'

'If I'd seen him, I'd have called him out as a total liar.' Her face doesn't change. 'You've given him money to go and score drugs, and when the heat got turned up, you helped him get away on a nice holiday.' She's bitter and angry. 'For goodness' sake, Beth! Do you just take everything he tells you at face value? Are you really that gullible?'

My face burns with indignation but also with fear.

'No, I'm not!' I retort hotly. 'You don't get it, Sarah. You don't understand how he feels. He's pretty vulnerable. You don't know what's in his head.'

'Really?' she snorts. 'I can guess... Let me put it this way, Beth. He's as nice as pie with me. Never puts a foot wrong. A real charmer, yet the incidents you've told me about tell me the lad's abusive and manipulative. He's a real Jekyll and Hyde, yet you keep letting it go and letting it go, making excuses. Anything that means you can brush it under the carpet.'

'But you've always said—' I protest.

'I've always said what?'

'That I shouldn't make such a big thing about bad behaviour, and it'll pass.'

'Beth' – she purses her lips – 'let me give you a home truth, as bald and black-and-white as I can... The fact is, you only hear what you want to hear. I've said to you time and time again. If Joe was a forty-year-old man, I'd say you were in an abusive relationship. But because he's your son, you've backed down and backed down and made excuses for him, and now you've got a tyrant on your hands and you're *still* closing your eyes to what's right in front of you.'

I stare at her blankly, realising I'm trembling. Not just trembling, shaking: with shock, with anger.

'So it's drugs...' I repeat carefully. 'He used the money to buy drugs?'

'Nate told me the whole story: that Joe showed him the money he'd got out of you. He said they could buy gear and meet some girls. That it would be *"hilarious".'* She sneers the words.

'And there was never any intention of getting on the plane?'

She shakes her head. 'Joe had been texting Nate telling him to go along with the holiday idea. I don't think Nate really believed him until he saw the cash. He said he was just in it for the ride. He thought it was all a joke, but then he realised that the whole thing was really messed up. He freaked. He told Joe he'd forgotten his phone charger and needed to buy one. He managed to find a cab outside and came straight home.' She pauses. 'Nate is *scared* of Joe, Beth.'

I don't believe her.

'He's now scared that Joe will come after him. He won't leave the house. He hasn't made any calls or messaged anyone in case Joe finds out. He says he's been frightened of him for months.'

I drop my gaze, staring at the table. None of this can possibly be true. Nate has made this up to save his own skin. But Sarah's absolutely right about one thing: I've played my part in all this.

'I'm so sorry, Sarah. I'm so, so sorry. I never dreamt— I would never have believed...'

'I know you wouldn't.'

Sarah's voice doesn't have the same bitter and angry edge as before. I venture a look up.

'I know that no matter how furious I might be with you, you've done all of this with the very best intentions.'

I stood at an ATM in the small hours of the morning to get money for my son to do God knows what with.

'I just feel very stupid now.'

'Don't do that.' She shakes her head vehemently. 'You're not a victim, Beth.'

Her words sting.

'But maybe you're finally recognising something. Perhaps you have to take a good, hard look at what's really going on.'

'I have. I've just thrown Drew out. He's been seeing someone.'

'Wow. Drew, eh? The man we thought was straight as a die.' She sits back, thoughtful. I think she's about to start asking questions, but she doesn't. The enormity of what I've just divulged hangs between us; she wants to be 'the old Sarah', but I can tell she's still angry.

'I'm going to be late.' She looks at me, flustered. 'I should be at work. I'd better go.' She pushes her chair back and pauses. 'I don't want to be hard on you, Beth. I know you're sorry. And despite everything that's gone on, I'm here for you, whatever happens. You'll find Joe. Then comes the difficult bit. Do what you know is right. Tell someone what's going on. Tell the police. Tell Drew, for goodness' sake! He's going to know soon enough anyway. And don't forget the most important thing.'

I find I can't look up at her.

'I'm your friend; I'll be there for you, yeah?'

'Thank you.' I stare at the table, hearing the croak in my voice as it betrays me. I would like to break down and weep right here, right now. It's only the inquisitive eyes that stops me making a fool of myself.

She goes to walk away, but then pauses, dipping to kiss my cheek. I feel the warmth of her skin against mine, and the tears immediately spill.

I catch her hand. 'You're a good friend, Sarah. I appreciate you coming. You didn't have to.'

She gives me a little smile and then I watch as she leaves, pulling her coat closer as she walks past the window.

Leaving far too much money on the table, I get in the car, retracing the route back to that party house. Every street holds the potential he could be here; every corner I turn, every dark-haired boy walking by, sends my heart leaping. But each time, I'm faced with the drag of disappointment and queasy desperation – but I'm compelled, *compelled* to keep going.

An exhausting two hours of searching and I finally pull over. Switching off the engine, I sit, dull and empty, staring out across the iron railings to the park. I can't carry on like this. Staring out, I try Joe's phone for the thousandth time and for the thousandth time, I get the same answer.

There are children playing on the swings, their squeals echoing out across the grass. The mothers stand watching, arms folded, amiably chatting. That was me: grateful for half a day off, wanting to meet people, being a bit shy and using the kids playing as an excuse... That's how I met Sarah, Sarah with her makeup done just right, hair in a messy up-do, who always managed to look put-together, making jeans and sneakers look on trend. I was amazed when she spoke to me, invited me for coffee, told me she'd got a couple of freebies from her coffee card, and I'd be doing her a favour rather than sitting drinking alone. None of that was true, of course; I smile faintly to myself at the memory: she'd sneakily paid.

The smile falls. Where are those two people now? Where are the little boys and all those childhood years?

I need to get air. Opening the car door, I lever myself out. The shrill cries of the children carry amidst the trees, their joy and my sadness intertwining as I walk slowly through the gates. A dog walker passes me, glancing at my face. I have this sudden fuzzy sway of light-headedness. There's a bench sitting ten feet away, and I head for it, my ears pounding mutely with each step, the blood roaring numbly as though I'm underwater. I sink onto it gratefully, closing my eyes, and let the zigzags of light pattern the inside of my lids. My cheeks warm with the vague heat from the sun. The children sound very far away. My world collapses inward.

'Hey, are you okay?'

There's a shudder as someone sits heavily next to me. My eyes snap open. I try to focus.

'Jaime...?' For a second I think I'm mistaken. 'Jaime?'

He's turned towards me, leaning forward, concerned.

'Beth? Are you okay? I couldn't quite believe it was you. Jeez! You look as though you're about to pass out. Should I call someone?' He glances round.

I lick my cracked lips and swallow.

'What on earth are you doing here?' I attempt a smile but barely manage it.

'My new place is over there.' He nods across to the other side of the park. 'I only moved in last night. I thought I'd have a look around. I never dreamt I'd see you here.' He smiles, but I can see it's full of worry. 'Look, let me go and get you some water or something. There's a café kiosk over there. Now don't move!'

He gets up. The instruction was unnecessary; I really don't think I'm going anywhere. Within minutes, he's back with a bottle of water, twisting the top off and handing it over.

I sip gratefully. 'I didn't know you'd be released so quickly.' The water is refreshingly soothing. 'I'm so sorry.'

But he only shrugs. 'No one knew. I wanted to keep the whole parole thing quiet until the last minute, mainly because of Leo.' He looks away.

I don't know where the tears suddenly appear from, but no matter how much I try to control myself, it just gets worse.

'Hey...! Hey, Beth... Wow! Please don't cry! Hang on—' He's reaching in his pocket and bringing out a whole wad of folded tissues that he hands to me to mop the unstoppable flood that's coursing down my face. The woman with the dog walks past again. She glances, concerned, but Jaime gives her a smile as I turn away, blowing my nose.

'I'm so... so sorry... P-please don't think it— it's anything you said.' My crying has turned into those hiccoughing sobs that just won't calm down. 'It's oth-other things.'

'Would you like to talk about it?' he suggests gently. 'But only if you think it'd help. Not if you don't want to.' He gives me a hapless smile. 'I mean, this is a bit of a role reversal, isn't it?' He laughs lamely. 'But I am just a human being, offering help. I probably won't have any solutions, but I am here to listen.'

We catch each other's eye and both nearly burst out laughing at this bizarre situation we find ourselves in: him, an ex-prisoner, sitting on a park bench, and me, a Samaritan, sobbing my heart out.

'Well, at least you haven't said no.' He glances over to the kiosk. 'Why don't we grab one of those tables where we can sit and talk properly? Or, at the very least, we could just have a coffee and a sandwich or something? I know it's Robyn's answer to everything, but it seems to work.' He shrugs. 'Even if you don't want to talk, it'll make you feel better.'

'Thank you, Jaime.' I manage a weak smile back. 'That would be really nice.'

He settles me at a table before going over to the hatch to order the food. I watch him standing at the counter a little awkwardly, loading and unloading the weight from leg to leg. I suddenly realise he's no longer used to ordering anything, and my gratitude comes over me in waves. The tight band of tension that's been gripping my neck relaxes a little.

He walks over, carrying cups on a tray. I automatically reach for my purse.

'Beth. Please.'

There's a moment of embarrassment and I kick myself. 'Next time, then,' I say and I see his face soften.

A gang of sparrows immediately gathers. We smile together as a cheeky one perches right on the edge of the table, eyeing us up. Neither of us speak for a moment.

'There was something about me mentioning Leo that really upset you, wasn't there?' He's watching me carefully. 'What did that trigger?'

I concentrate hard on watching the fluttering sparrow pecking furiously at a crumb.

'It's not only Leo...' I say slowly. 'It's my son. Joe. He's in trouble. He's a mixed-up kid and I'm to blame, I think.' A tear leaks down my face and I bring a hand up to brush it away.

'And then there's my husband. He's been seeing someone. We've separated.' I stop to gather myself. 'So, I've got quite a bit on my plate.' Another tear manages to escape.

Jaime sits studying me for a moment.

'Wow. You certainly have. How old is Joe?'

'Seventeen. He's...'

'Go on.'

'Complicated.'

'Aren't we all?' His eyes are kind.

I take a deep breath and begin to tell him, haltingly at first, about Joe, and then I find myself talking about Joe's father, Simon.

'Simon was brought up in care. I thought if I loved him enough...'

'You could make up for what he'd missed?' he says gently.

I nod. 'But I couldn't. He killed himself.'

'That wasn't your fault.'

'No.'

'But?'

My spine prickles. 'He made me feel like it was.'

'I see.' We both look up as some toasted sandwiches arrive. 'Y'know sometimes people use your love against you. They use your care as a form of control.'

How does this man get to be so astute?

'I think you're right.' I wince uncomfortably. 'I've never told anyone that before, not even Drew... God, Drew,' I sigh. 'The added complication: he and Joe are so tight. There's no way I can tell Drew the whole truth about Simon... about how the relationship was. Honestly! I must sound like my life is so chaotic!'

'You sound like someone who has been forced to deal with situations outside of your making.'

'Yeah, things have definitely got weird.' I sigh again and slowly tell him about the night the girl called me, and then how I discovered the hidden phone. I'm embarrassed even recounting it.

'And then there's Leo.' Jaime's eyes skim my face. He pushes a plate across the table towards me. 'Cheese and ham.' He picks one up.

'It was Drew who came into the prison to interview him.' I stare at the sandwich. 'I was so, so furious.'

'He was the one who did that to Leo?' He pauses, mid-bite, letting the information sink in.

'And on top of all that, Joe has gone missing. He told me he was in debt to some shady people, but that was a lie. He asked me for money to pay them off, but now he's disappeared.' I can't face eating anything.

'Shady, as in...?'

I'm about to side-step the question, but then something inside stops me.

'I think it's drugs.'

Jaime nods. 'Right.'

I feel appalled and ashamed. I can't look at him.

'Hey, hey, don't! I'll help you. I don't know if I can, but I'll try.'

'You can help?' My eyes dart to his face.

'I've been inside. I know things and I've met people, which means I have contacts. Tell me the area you live, and I'll ask people I know if they've seen him. I suspect the kid will stand out a bit.' He cocks an eyebrow.

A great surge of warmth rolls over me in one enormous rush.

'I live in the Scaresbrook area, in Beecham Road. Do you know it?'

'I know people who will.'

The very thought makes my insides curl, but this is an offer I have to take.

'Thank you, Jaime. I really appreciate it. You can't imagine how much this means to me.'

'What is it you always say to the guys in prison? "You're not on your own." Well, now you're not on your own either.'

I can feel my eyes smarting. I blink fiercely.

'But there's a condition.'

I gulp and look up to find him nodding down at my uneaten sandwich.

'All that has to disappear, alongside the coffee, and I might have to force you into a slice of that very nice-looking cake that I spied on the counter.'

'Oh Jaime, I don't think I—'

But he only purses his lips comically and shakes his head. 'I'm afraid that's the deal.' He holds out his hand.

I almost laugh at the irony, but my laughter and hope are real enough. My hand tentatively stretches across the table, and he takes it. We shake: his palm against mine, his fingers curling round to hold me fast. I'm aware of a slight pull as he looks straight at me; his gaze is calm and steady.

'Thank you,' I manage. 'I really appreciate this.'

'You've done far more for me.'

I smile, lowering my gaze and going to pull my hand away but his grip tightens ever so slightly.

'I mean it,' he says. 'I don't think you understand what a beacon of sanity and hope you were to me. Without you, I don't think I would've survived that place.'

I chance a look into his eyes, and I see, in those seconds, a whole lot of emotion that he's not articulating. I feel the same way, but know I shouldn't.

I'm in a mess, I'm vulnerable, I'm grateful, I'm terrified... even though there's a tiny, tiny part of me...

No, I can't even go there.

Still, there's a tiny, tiny part of me that would really like to.

FOURTEEN

'Do you want to walk for a while, or do you need to get back?'
Jaime gestures across to where the park turns into a wild mass of
botanical garden. 'If you need to get back, I can call you with
anything I manage to find out. If I have your number, that is.'
He smiles, holding out his phone.

I take it, hesitantly.

'Don't worry. I understand. I know how it is, Beth. I won't
tell anyone we met. The last thing I would want to do is jeopardise your prison work.'

I feel instantly shamed. Here's a man trying to help me,
and... I take the phone, plugging my details in.

'Don't share them if it makes you uncomfortable.'

I snap a glance at his face. 'I'm not uncomfortable.'

'Don't feel bad. I'm really used to it.' His smile is small and
sad. He thinks I'm judging him. He thinks I'm judging him the
way the world does.

'You're the one person, Jaime – the *one* person who's been
totally and unconditionally on my side in all this,' I say firmly.
'Please forgive me.'

'There's nothing to forgive.' He smiles. 'Shall we walk?

You're sure you're happy for me to make a few calls? You don't want to contact your husband and ask him what he thinks? I mean, you know the kinds of people I'm going to have to talk to.'

He's warning me that I'm about to step over a line, and once I make that decision there's no way back. Drew can't know I'm doing this. He can't be compromised.

'Joe's *my* son. Drew doesn't need to be involved, Jaime. I don't care what methods you have to use to find him, I just want him home.'

He nods and we walk on. His head dips to his phone. I hear the tinny voice of someone answering. He slows his pace, waving for me to carry on ahead as he turns away.

The glinting weak sunlight patters through the branches. The only sound is the soft crunch of our feet on the gravel. I push my hands into my pockets as the wind picks up, sending a soughing rustle into the arched canopy overhead. Scudding clouds reveal patches of brilliant blue sky.

I have someone by my side. Jaime has no idea what that means to me. Right now, I can actually breathe.

The warm, mushroomy smell of damp blooms up as the ferns and rhododendrons lean in around me, narrowing the gritted pathway to a track. The bird call is suddenly silent. I look back. Jaime has disappeared from view. I retrace my steps. He's not here. I turn a corner, but I still can't see him. There's a scuff behind me and I wheel round; my heart makes a leap.

'You've found him?' I resist the urge to clutch at his jacket.

He holds up a hand. 'Not exactly, but I've asked someone who's asked someone, who knows someone else. I understand there's a new face on the street who's been flashing around a lot of cash.'

Oh God, Joe! What are you thinking?

'Can we go to where he is? I mean, right now?'

Jaime looks unsure.

'We could just drive round. I just need to lay eyes on him.'

'We will, we will, don't worry, but not right now. Don't worry, I'm working a few things out first.'

We will. I could hug him.

'Okay.' I can barely keep it together. 'So when?'

'Beth...' He's looking at me.

'What?'

'Look, I know your instinct is to rush out there and scour the streets, but the fact is, the kid's trying hard not to be found.' Jaime holds my gaze. 'If you go barging in, you'll only spook him. We need to do this thing properly.'

I nod, dumbly.

'You're stepping into dangerous waters, Beth. There's a darkness out there. You don't want to get too close.'

I imagine Joe, alone, thinking he's a grown man but not knowing what's lurking in the shadows: things, unimaginable things. Something slides around the back of my neck.

'So will you trust me?' Jaime's standing close, stooping a little to catch my eye. 'Will you trust me to handle this? Will you let me do this my way?'

There's a moment, only a tiny second, when suddenly I'm aware of the proximity of him. I can feel the warmth of his breath. I am more acutely conscious of him than ever before.

He checks his watch. 'There must be somewhere nearby we could go for a drink for a couple of hours? Are you okay with being seen with me in the real world?' His look is playful, but I get his meaning.

'More than okay,' I say, lifting my chin. 'You've done more for me in the last few hours than anyone else has done for me in months.'

He smiles then. 'I told you, it's payback. That's all.'

FIFTEEN

I choose an Italian café-bar that's not too far from the Samaritans' office. There are stools in the window bench where we perch as Jaime peruses the wine list.

'I can't tell you what this feels like.' He looks at me over the edge of the menu. 'Can you imagine not being able to go out and have the simple pleasure of drinking a glass of wine for years? It's that small, y'know? These are the things that make the big difference.'

'But you're here now. That's all in the past.' I glance down at his phone. I'm trying to remain calm, but my stomach is churning with anxiety. All I can think of is getting through the next few hours.

'You're going to have to chill.' His eye catches mine. 'That's the fifth time you've looked in the last three minutes.'

I blush. 'I'm sorry.'

'No need, I get it. What are you having?'

I can barely concentrate.

'How about I order for both of us? That'd be novel, wouldn't it?'

I manage a smile. 'Go on then.'

He catches the waitress as she passes. 'Oh, yes, hi – could we have this, and two glasses please?' He points to the page.

'Was that champagne?' I say as she walks away.

He smirks and shrugs. 'Why not? It's a celebration of sorts, isn't it?'

'Is it?'

'My freedom, you finding your son – that's two things for starters.'

I thrill at his confidence, but the thrill soon turns to cold reality. 'Look, Jaime, I'm fully aware that finding him will only be the start of it. I have no idea what he's got himself tangled up in, and even less of a clue how to get him out of it.'

'We'll find a way.'

The waitress comes over with a half-bottle and two glasses. I try to concentrate on the performance of her opening it: the ritual of popping the cork and watching the fizz die down before she tops the glasses up again. But I feel so awkward.

'There...' He's smiling. 'Let's raise a toast—' He stops. 'What's wrong?'

'Jaime... Look, I'm so sorry.' I twist the stem of the glass round, watching the bubbles prinking on the surface. 'This sounds awful, but why are you doing all this?'

The words come out sounding strident and rude. I'm instantly embarrassed.

'God! I didn't mean it that way! What I meant was...'

'No, you're right, you're absolutely right.' He takes another sip, nodding. 'I would be asking exactly the same question. I told you; you helped me more than you know. Helping you is payback.'

'I know, I know, you said that, but you're on licence. This is risky for you. The kinds of people you're having to talk to. It's too much, really it is!'

'It's not too much. It could never be too much, not for you.'

I colour.

'Plus...' He hesitates.

I manage to look up. His jaw works awkwardly, clenching and unclenching.

'I was seventeen when I got arrested,' he starts. 'Never been anywhere near a police station, let alone charged with murder.'

The baldness of the statement stuns me. I realise suddenly that I don't really know anything about Jaime: about who he was before he got there.

'I thought... I thought you were in on a drugs charge?'

He shakes his head and takes a sip from his glass. 'No, manslaughter. I don't know, there was something about the way you described Joe... Maybe I saw myself in the things you said about him? Like, if I could go back and talk to my younger self. If there'd been someone there to rescue me at that point I needed rescuing, maybe things would have turned out very differently.'

He catches my eye and then looks away, touching the stem of his glass with one finger, tracing the line of cold condensation.

'I was brought up in the south of England, but we lived all over the place because Dad was in the army. I have an elder brother I no longer see.' His finger flinches a little. 'Or who no longer wants to see me. He left home when he was fifteen – actually, more "chucked out" than left. My dad was violent.' His finger stops, slowly curling into a fist.

'He was violent towards my mum. He always had been. My brother tried to defend her, but—' He blinks at the memory. 'But it was a man against a boy. He was never going to win.'

'That must've been awful to have to watch that.' I study his face.

'It was. It really was.' He pauses. 'I remember the rage I felt. The absolute white-hot rage.' He stops himself. 'Thinking about it, prison saved me. Weird, isn't it? That being locked up saved my life.' He picks up his glass. 'So...' He swallows. 'There I was.

Seventeen. Doing A levels. It was just before the last exam. For some reason I came home one lunchtime.' He halts, steadying himself. 'I went round to the back door and I could hear Mum screaming...'

I go very still.

'And there was my dad in the hallway. He was roaring like some crazy thing. Totally out of control. She was covered in blood. Her hair' – he lifts his fingers to touch the side of his head – 'it was matted, but hanging down where he'd ripped her scalp. I couldn't see her face, there was so much blood. She kept bringing her hand up to wipe it away and then I saw she had a knife. She was shaking, like full-on uncontrollable shaking. All I could hear was him shouting – hunched over her, crouching with his arms outstretched, goading and jeering that she was too scared to do it. Only then she saw me in the doorway. My dad turned round...' His eyes widen at the memory. 'She lunged.'

'Oh my God, Jaime!'

'She lunged at him with the knife and got him, here—' He presses his hand to his side. 'I remember the look on his face: the absolute disbelief. He staggered.' Jaime lifts his hands in surrender.

'I thought he was going to attack me, but he was actually trying to stop himself falling. He came down onto my shoulders so hard that the sheer weight of him knocked me off balance. I went down and I just remember being frantic that I couldn't breathe. I managed to push him off and I must've grabbed the knife. I have no memory after that. The next thing I knew, there were the police swarming everywhere. They were shouting, and dragging me, turning me face-down and yanking my arms behind my back. And all I could see was my mother cowering in a corner like a little child, shaking and shaking, and an officer kneeling and putting the knife in an evidence bag – the one that had my fingerprints on it.'

'And you were seventeen?'

He nods. 'Everything from that point on felt like a dream.' He looks up and away out of the window. People walk past and glance in. We must look so ordinary, sitting here.

'I was taken into custody; my mother was admitted to a psychiatric unit. I was totally alone. They presented me with evidence that I was in no state to argue with, and they gave me ten years for a crime of manslaughter that I didn't commit.'

'But you served more than that?'

'Getting on for fifteen.' He gives me a weak smile. 'I was angry. I bucked the system. It's not difficult to find yourself in trouble. You're immature, you're mixing with all sorts, you're kicking against the unfairness of it all. Prison... it becomes the constant in your life. It's the only secure thing you have left.'

The sadness of it – the real shame of a life so squandered.

'I had no idea.'

He takes a deep breath. 'No. There was no need for you to know. I think also maybe part of me wanted someone to see me for me, not just someone with a criminal record. That's *massive* actually: to be seen as a person and not just a number.'

'I never saw you as that.'

He smiles a little. 'No. And I'm not that anymore. I don't want a repeat of the past for my future. I have focus now. I can see there are opportunities out there and I want to do something with my life, not spend it rotting in a prison cell.'

He looks out of the window again, narrowing his eyes in the dying afternoon sunlight.

'I think what I said about your son is so real for me. I know you feel bad that Joe couldn't come to you when things started to go wrong for him, but you shouldn't blame yourself. I'm guessing Joe was protecting you, just like I did with my mother. He's got himself into a situation that he thought he could handle. When you're that age, you want to be a man, but you're really still just a kid putting on a brave face.'

I find myself nodding and nodding in agreement – the relief

of how much he understands. 'My friend Sarah doesn't get it. She thinks I'm not aware of Joe's bad behaviour, but I absolutely am! I've seen the frightened child he really is. What you're saying makes total sense.'

'And so that's the field I'd like to get involved in.' Jaime hunches forward. 'I want to help kids who've got themselves into a mess. Runaways, kids with mental health problems, kids coming out of Young Offenders. I get how they feel. I've been there; I've seen it. I know the ways out.'

'You'd be brilliant, you really would.' I relax enough to pick up my glass. For the first time since we've sat down, I can feel the tension slide. The sparkling wine pops on my tongue. 'Thank you for sharing that with me, Jaime, it's—'

His phone flashes and my wine slops with a jerk. He answers it, slipping off the stool and turning away. My anxiety ratchets sky-high. I'm acutely aware of the set of his shoulders. *Do they spell something bad?* He's blinking rapidly and his jaw pulses and tightens.

The phone drops.

'They think they know where he is.'

I am half-off the stool, but Jaime puts a restraining hand on my arm. 'That is, they know where he's going to be.'

'Where?'

'Just give me a minute, Beth. Wait. Someone's going to tell me. Come on, sit back down.'

'What did they say?' The dread shivers in my bones, begging this to be over, when suddenly his phone buzzes again, sending my heart racing.

He frowns in concentration, reading the message. His eyes meet mine and he gives an imperceptible nod. My stomach lurches, a sour squall of anxiety turning my gut inside out as we scramble from the stools and head for the door.

'So? Talk to me. Tell me.' My words won't come out, but Jaime is already heading for the car. He drops into the passenger seat as I fuss with the safety belt: my fingers won't work properly. He catches my hand, a shock there at his touch.

'It's okay, Beth,' he says. 'It's going to be okay, I promise.'

I believe him; I so want to believe him.

'So where are we going?' I reach for the ignition.

'Just drive out of town and head north.' He gestures to the street in front of us. 'I'll give you directions as we go.'

My stomach tightens. 'What happens when we find him? What then? Do I approach him? Do I try to talk to him? What?'

The courtesy light between us fades to black as the engine roars into life. I realise I'm frightened to see my own son.

'We know where he is.' Jaime's eyes are just dark sockets. 'He's with some people at a house.'

My heart is thudding. 'People? What kind of people?'

'The kind of people that you don't just walk in on. What I'm saying is, we might be sitting outside for hours waiting for him to leave. I can't guarantee anything, and I can't control it. This is all the information I have right now. I'm just pre-warning you so you don't get your hopes up.'

We pull out onto the main road. It's started to rain. The windscreen wipers squeal back and forth as every possible emotion inside me squeals back and forth with them.

My brain is a mess of emotion and terror.

Where's that child who was sobbing in my arms just a couple of days ago? Where is that vulnerable boy now?

Jaime has his phone cupped in his hands and is texting furiously. The phone keeps pinging and I glance across.

'Has something happened?'

'No, nothing's happened. Don't worry. Turn left at this roundabout and then take your first right.'

'I just can't believe this is who my son has become, Jaime.' The roundabout exit comes up. 'How can this be possible? Two days ago, he was terrified of what he'd done when he stole a van, and now it's turned into this!'

'The van? What van?'

'That's what he told me. He said that he, and my friend Sarah's son, Nate, had stolen a van that belonged to some heavy people. Sarah says that's all lies.'

Jaime gives me a look I can't decipher. 'And where's this Nate now?'

'Hiding at Sarah's. She says he's too scared to go out, because he gave Joe up.'

Jaime shakes his head.

'What—? Do you know something... Jaime? Was Joe telling the truth?'

He doesn't answer. 'Turn here—' He points to the right and I swing the car into an unlit street. A long chain fence borders one side, with what looks like a building site beyond. An expanse of scrubby grass is pockmarked with craters where the bulldozers have cleaved away great bowls of earth.

'Are these the same people, Jaime?'

'You need to slow down and just use your sidelights.' He's peering out, left and right into the darkness.

'Do you think they are?'

He doesn't answer. My gut knots in a silent scream.

The tattered remnants of a row of Victorian terraces appears, some with half their roofs missing; some are boarded up. The red brick houses on either side are poor-looking and scruffy. Many of the windows are boarded; some contain rags of net curtains, the panes so grimed it's difficult to see if anyone lives there. The tumbledown outline sits bleak against the darkening sky. The streetlights stand up on either side like dead-eyed sentinels.

'Can you pull off this road? Maybe just here?' He points over to the patch of derelict wasteland.

'What, there?'

'Trust me, we don't want to be seen. Park up where the shadows are darkest. Kill the engine as soon as you can.'

The car tyres pop and crack over rubble and broken glass as I ease into the darkness and come to a halt. We sit in silence as the engine ticks as it cools. I look around anxiously. A slow, creeping dread comes over me.

'Okay?' Jaime whispers.

I look across at his face caught in the strange light. His eyes glint as he smiles and there's a sudden warmth as I feel the squeeze of his hand on my knuckles.

'Yep, I'm holding it together – just about,' I whisper back.

I peer at the houses. 'Do we know which one?'

'See that nearest alleyway? Well, count three doors away, and it's the fourth. You can see there's a dim light inside.'

I dread to think what might be going on in there behind those filthy yellow curtains.

'I can't bear this, Jaime. Are they dealers? Users? What?'

'Both.'

My hands cup my mouth as I look back at that window.

'Everything I know, you know, Beth. All they've said is they've heard there's a new face. It's me who's thinking it has to be Joe.'

That twisting knot in my stomach grows even tighter. Joe isn't streetwise; he's totally unable to defend himself. He wouldn't see danger if he walked slap into it.

'I can't just sit here. I have to do something!' My hands are shaking.

'I did warn you. I did tell you how it would be, Beth.'

'Anything could happen! He could be attacked... He could try something and— God! What if he overdoses?' The anxiety rises up. 'We need to force him out of there! We could make it happen... Like, oh I don't know! Call the police? It'd make them run, wouldn't it? – We could get to him that way!'

Jaime looks at me quietly for a moment.

'Beth, this is a different world we're in now. Even if you rang the police they wouldn't turn up.'

'They would. Of course they would!'

'The police have been paid off. That's how these things work.'

I stare at him in disbelief.

'You think that only happens in TV dramas?' He sighs sadly. 'The rules are different out here, Beth. You have to learn to play by them.'

I look back at the hazy window. He's right, I am totally out of my depth. I'm ricocheting wildly between waves of paralysing fear and the absolute compulsion to break down the door. My hands clasp and unclasp, palms itching and stuttering as I rub them together. I can't sit still. My hand reaches for the door lever.

'What are you doing?'

I hear Jaime's horror as the night air stings my face.

'Beth!'

But I'm out, dropping into a crouch and scuttling into the shadows where the wrecked walls of a half-demolished house lean in together to hide me. I hear the car door behind slamming shut, as I slip into the remains of an old kitchen. I'm in what looks like a scullery with an old butler sink hanging off the wall. I can hear Jaime's feet scuffing through the rubble.

'*Beth!*' His whisper is so close I think he must be able to see me.

Squeezing my eyes tight shut, I hunker down, as Jaime's feet scutter and stumble over bricks and broken glass.

Minutes pass. My ears strain into the darkness. I can't hear him anymore. I tentatively lift my head to where the rectangle of a doorway is silvered with moonlight. The quiet street lies empty.

I'm alone. There's no movement in any of the windows. I have no idea where Jaime is. Dead, blank eyes of doorways and alleyways stand silent on either side. I creep quietly along the pavement to where the lit window of the house sits, yellowed and blind, concealing all kinds of horrors.

I scuttle past once, frantic to see a chink in the curtains, but they're tightly drawn. Swearing softly, I turn back, suddenly realising that the layout of the street is familiar. It's the same layout as the party street. I check the houses: I'm right. Every eight, there's a passageway. I can get round the back.

Glancing quickly over my shoulder, I slide into the nearest alley, hurrying through the darkness to reach the end, where the moon lights up a clear path in front of me.

I count the backyards, find the house, and then make my way cautiously along to where a broken wooden fence separates one from the next. There's a brick-built outhouse with a back door sitting squarely next to it. I hesitate. Once I open that door, there's no going back.

I step into the small, paved yard. The outhouse door is partly missing, showing a deep, yawning gap half-full of torn planks and metal oil drums. Fighting my fear, I position myself next to the closed door and slowly reach out for the handle when suddenly a beading of light flashes around the edge and the door is snatched open. I stumble back. Voices echo into the yard as I lurch backwards into the outhouse doorway, shuffling down to squeeze myself amongst the rubble. I hold my breath. A dirty arc of light spreads right into my hiding place, illuminating my feet and knees in a wide pool right before my eyes.

If someone turns their head this way, I'm dead.

I freeze; there's nothing between me and them. Gingerly, I allow one tiny eye movement in their direction. The back doorway holds two swaying figures. Their mumbling chatter rises and falls, laughter hissing into the night; their shapes bob and weave drunkenly.

'Bitch!' one spits. 'What a bitch! I'll give her another go. She's not gonna get away with that.'

The darkness of them twists and plaits before peeling away

as one goes back inside. There's a slam of the door. The other figure staggers forward uncertainly in a wheeze of breath.

It's a gargoyle of a human being. I wouldn't know what gender or age. Skeletally thin, tottering past on tiptoes, neck reflexing, fingers fluttering. I shrink back, and as I do, there's a metallic clatter under my feet. The figure stops abruptly, head cocked, scenting the air. My ears thud; my heartbeat hammers into my throat.

A pair of rheumy eyes pass over the doorway once and then twice, and then finally land, locking onto my own; the gums bump together, mouthing something. Terror grips me: any moment now and the rotten wood will be pulled from its hinges and I'll be dragged out of here on my knees… There'll be shouts, more of them will come—

My legs won't work, refusing to lift me. I shrink back, my fingers scrabbling for purchase, my toes slipping out from under me as the figure comes closer, its rank breath pluming into the night as its fingers close around the piece of wood that separates us.

'Are you lookin' f'r a friend?' The plank shifts. The voice is a husk of something not human. I am staring into the horror. I catch a tiny glimpse of a chin and nose working together to make a mouth, the flexing heart-shape of a blackened gap.

'Are you lookin' f'rsumone?'

I think it's a man. His hand reaches out to grab my arm. I instinctively flinch – there's the slow hiss of phlegm and air and I realise with shock that he's laughing.

I glance over at the pathway – I could make it from here; I could barge this thing out of the way. My spine digs into the wall behind, and I lever myself upright, but he counters, enjoying the dance, blocking my sightline, the dirtiness of him moving closer, pushing me further and further back.

I have one chance.

In a split second, I bring my hands up and shove as hard as I can. He makes a grab that misses and sends him reeling. The smashed door splinters sideways and I find myself floundering forward, my fingertips skimming the ground as another figure steps out in front of me.

'Joe?'

My knees won't hold me as my heart leaps into my mouth, his name choking my throat as he disappears inside. My body responds before my head does, my instinct taking over. I storm through the doorway, tripping and skidding over mounds of trash under my feet. I'm aware of people, lots of people, bodies swarming as I barge past them all into a hallway.

'Joe!' I yell. 'Joe? Where are you?'

I see the front door is wide open. I'm screaming his name over and over – not caring as I thunder towards the door, desperate to get to him, only aware in those last few seconds that an arm has descended from above my head, looping around my neck and chest, taking my feet from under me and sending me crashing to the floor. My shoulder hits the wooden staircase and I yelp in agony.

There's a man standing in the shadows; he has one hand on the newel post, barring my way. I scrabble frantically, my heels skidding against the tiled floor, fear jerking me up, as I lever myself against the stair treads.

'Well, well, well,' says the man. 'What brings you here?'

I know that voice. I know it.

The front door is still open; the night air is cool and fresh. *Jaime,* I think. *Jaime is out there. He'll come.*

'I'm not on my own!' I blurt.

The man starts to laugh. 'You look very alone to me.'

He doesn't move, but I know, any minute now, he's going to trap me here. I instinctively search for ways out, my eyes hunting this way and that. There's a room on my right. A sickly light burns dim. On the floor all around the walls are mattresses: dirty looking, mounded deep with blankets. A blanket moves, unfolding itself, becoming something other. My mouth opens in horror: it's a girl. And another girl. And another. Young. No more than teenagers. Dressed skimpily, knees hugged under their chins, eyes bright and wide at the sight of me.

I drag my gaze to the shape of the figure bearing down.

I know the voice. I know the man.

'Johnson,' I say. 'You…! What the hell is this? What are you doing?'

He moves his hand from the stair post and gestures into the open space. 'There. Just for you. You're free to go… Ta-ta!' He twinkles his fingers. My foot feels for the bottom step of the stair.

I go to get up – the door is there – but I glance at the girls.

'Oh, you've come to join us, then?' He wiggles the door, smiling. 'You're very welcome. You have a great skill-set that I'm sure would come in useful. You could be like a mother-figure, guiding and advising all our young ladies here.' He chuckles heartily at his own joke. He teases the door a little wider.

'Wotcha think?' He smiles, bending in towards my face. The smell of him makes me want to retch.

I see the pavement out there – so close, the smell of the night air… All I want to do is to crawl across that floor and run. Every fibre and nerve-ending is screaming.

His breath slicks against my cheek. My skin roils. I can almost taste it.

'*Boo!*' he shouts and I leap past him, falling down the front step, my hands hitting the concrete as shockwaves of pain cannon through me. I hurl myself forward, the door slamming in my wake, the darkness stretching out in front of my flailing fingers as I try to run. Voices and shouts echo all around, my legs scrambling, heartrate crashing as a figure looms out of the shadows. It's the gargoyle man and he comes at me, arms outstretched and laughing as he lunges, his nails just skimming my arm, the snatch of his touch against my sleeve as I sprint through the pain, the sear of it crippling as I dodge him, only pausing to glance back.

Hands grab me.

I start to scream.

'*Beth!*... Beth!... It's *me*... it's me! What the hell?'

Jaime has hold of my shoulders, his arms encircling, his warmth pulling me to him and I'm collapsing. I can't stop crying and crying, grasping and clawing at him, desperate to get away.

'We need to get out of here! Please, Jaime! Please...!' I'm dragging at his arms, tugging and tugging.

'Beth! You didn't go in there? Don't tell me you did!' He's clutching me to him, tighter and tighter, but he's scared, really scared, looping his arm around me, trying to get me to walk.

'Where are the keys? God, Beth! What were you thinking?'

But I'm limping too badly, and he's forced to scoop me up, carrying me to the car, opening the door and gently putting me in the passenger seat. He pushes the hair from my face, cupping my cheek, and trying to calm my terrified sobbing.

'But you can't!' I'm going to say, 'drive', but he only gets behind the wheel and quickly starts the engine.

'I saw Joe!' I splutter. 'I saw him. They've got girls there... We need to call someone... the police... Social Services.' I run shaking hands through my hair. 'Where's the nearest police station? We need—' But he cuts me off.

'What we need to do is get out of here, and fast.' He glances over his shoulder, the engine roaring. 'Let's get you safe; that's all I care about right now.'

'But Joe was there! I saw him—' I start, but I'm immediately silenced by the severity of his look.

'I said that's *all* I care about right now.' He's angry and it scares me. 'You need to stop all this, Beth.'

I glance across. His jaw is set and jutting as he stares, mute with fury, at the road ahead. 'I just can't believe you did that.'

He bites his bottom lip, shaking his head slowly. 'I told you how dangerous it was. I *told* you.'

We're driving far too fast; the car bucks and sways.

'I know, I know... *I* know!' I start to cry again. 'It was when I saw Joe. I couldn't stop myself.'

'You spoke to him?' He looks quickly.

'Not spoke to, no... but I heard one of them say his name and then he ran.'

'Wow! Honestly, Beth.'

'But they have girls there, Jaime. Young girls. Tom Johnson's part of it.' I can't get my words out. 'Please slow down, Jaime. Please.'

'Tom Johnson?' He glances across, horrified. 'Officer Johnson?'

'Yes. Him. He's got girls in that house. He's got them kept like animals. It was like some nightmare. We have to do something!'

'Oh my God...' he says suddenly. He won't look at me.

'What?' I'm staring at the side of his face that looks like stone. Something inside me goes cold. 'What is it, Jaime? Tell me!'

But he refuses to answer. He shakes his head vehemently.

'What? Jaime! What?'

'Him. Tom Johnson. Christ! It all makes sense now.'

'What does? What makes sense?' I'm almost beyond frustration.

'What did you see there? Tell me everything, every detail. I have to know.' He stares rigidly out into the road. But I can tell from his tone he already knows the answers.

'Girls. I don't know how many – six, maybe more? They were just kids. Fourteen, fifteen years old. Dressed up to look—' I can't finish the sentence. I blink back tears, swallowing again and again. 'It's a horror. Absolute horror. What is it, Jaime? What aren't you telling me?'

'You're right, we need to get you home,' he says stubbornly. 'Which way?'

'Here—' I shakily point. 'Go left here. But—'

'Don't ask me anything else right now, Beth. I'm being serious. I've asked you to trust me, and I'm asking that again right now. Will you do that?'

His eyes are hard. He's deathly earnest. I nod and we drive in silence, me holding on to the seat to try and stop my legs from shaking. I don't really want to hear it. I don't want to imagine. I close my eyes.

We pull up onto the drive. Jaime kills the engine and slumps back in his seat.

'You okay?' He looks over.

'Not really.'

'Do you want me to come in with you?'

'I don't know...' My head feels fuzzy and I can't think straight.

'Come on, let's get you inside.'

I watch him as though in some kind of dream as he comes round to help me out, opening the door, talking to me all the time, half-carrying me up the steps. I see that the black sacks I left have disappeared. Jaime hangs back as I open the door. Drew's keys are there. I pick them up. Attached is a note.

I know you're angry and you have every right to be.
If you would just let me explain. You owe me that. Please.
X

I immediately crumple it up, going to the bin and throwing it away. I look up to find Jaime watching me.

'Your husband?'

'I don't want to talk about him.'

He hesitates. 'Okay then. So, let's take care of you.'

I watch as he fusses round. 'Have you seen the state of your ankle? Do you have ice or something? You'll need to rest it.' He gathers cushions up, dragging a throw from the back of the sofa and tucking me in.

I take a breath. He knows what's coming, but silences me with a hand on my forearm.

'I'm going to tell you everything, Beth, and then you'll understand why we can't go to the police.'

'We can't? Why?'

'Because if you think Joe is in danger now, that's nothing compared to what will happen if you try to take this further.'

'But—'

'No.' He holds up a warning finger. 'Let me do what I need to do.'

I sit back, stunned.

Jaime goes into the kitchen. The freezer door squeals and he comes back, wrapping a bag of peas in a tea towel. Gently, but firmly, he unlaces my sneaker, easing it off and slipping my sock over my heel. I wince.

'You just need to lie back and close your eyes for a minute. You've done all you're going to do for tonight. Now put your head back while I go and get you something to drink.' He pulls a cushion up behind me. 'There.'

I am exhausted beyond exhaustion. The warmth of the blanket seeps into me, drawing me down. My neck muscles unkink one by one, as Jaime clatters about in the kitchen. I feel myself drift and then startle awake. There's the whump of the fridge and freezer door and the ping of the microwave. I can't imagine ever sleeping again. All I can see in front of me is Joe in that doorway. *Joe was there. I could have touched him.* And then I see Johnson and the dead-eyed expression of those girls. I feel sick to my stomach; I could break down right now and weep. Weep and never stop.

'Here we are.'

Jaime is standing in front of me holding a tray. A massive

cloud of steam rises up from whatever it is in the bowl. I struggle upright; my head is swimming. I can barely see straight.

The tray descends to my lap, and he hands me a fork. I look down and realise it's the casserole I made for Drew and Joe.

'It smells delicious.' Jaime has perched on the edge of the armchair. He is looking at me encouragingly. 'Come on. Eat.'

I pick up the fork but my stomach objects to the thought.

'I won't talk about going to the police. I won't ask what's going to happen next.' I put the fork down. 'But Tom Johnson,' I say firmly. 'I want to know everything you know.'

Jaime sighs and takes a breath. 'Tom Johnson isn't even human. Tom Johnson is one of the worst examples of what men are capable of when they're given power, control, and opportunity.' He presses his lips together. 'Every prisoner was afraid of him. Everyone knew what he was capable of, and yet "everyone" never included the governors. They saw him as a very capable, compassionate officer, who runs a great team on the wing and gets things done.'

'Robyn likes him.'

'Yeah, who else to get friendly with but the prison chaplain to hide what you're really doing?' he says grimly.

'And what's he really doing?'

'He's grooming the whole prison system... governors, other staff, but particularly the cons who are vulnerable, putting pressure on them to give him what he wants.'

'Which is?'

'Prisoners go outside – to hospital, to court, to family funerals. Anytime they have access to the outside world it's an opportunity for Tom Johnson to get them to bring a little something back. It's a win-win situation for him: he doesn't run the risk, they do. In return, they get a cushy job, tobacco, nicer food, some perk or other – but that's not the point of it. The drugs are just a means to an end.'

I frown, not understanding.

'Insurance. Once they're hooked into working for him, Johnson has all the leverage he wants.'

There's a slow burn of realisation. 'Is that what happened with Leo?'

Jaime looks at me steadily. 'That's what the first suicide attempt was about. He was supposed to get to an outside hospital – only, he failed.'

I stare at him, disbelieving. 'He was *told* to attempt suicide?'

'Uh-huh.'

My brain won't grip into gear. 'Why... why didn't you say? I could've—'

'You could have what, Beth? Can you imagine the danger you would've been in. No. Absolutely not.' He shakes his head vehemently. 'That's how it all works. There's a system. Johnson is the puppet master. The right strings are pulled, and the right people jump to get prisoners to where Tom Johnson wants them to be. All kinds of people: hospital staff, Listeners, screws on the wing. People who have influence. People who have no idea they're involved. To him they're merely chess pieces.'

He pauses. I look at him.

'What aren't you saying?'

'Think about it.'

'You're saying *me*...? You're saying he's used *me*?' My mouth drops, incredulous. 'How? How would he do that?'

'You make it valid. You give it credibility. You're the in-house professional helping the vulnerable. No one suspects the suicide attempts are strategically being managed. You're their cover.'

I can't find the words.

'Tom Johnson saw an opportunity with prisoners who were struggling and he exploited it, that's all.' He shrugs. 'He works the same way as any other groomer: he sees a weakness, he makes people like him, they do stuff. They unwittingly oil the wheels.'

'I've helped him do that.' I stare in shock, unblinking. 'I've done that.'

'Without having any clue, which of course is the ideal scheme. You can't imagine it happening, so you question nothing. You take it all on face value. It's perfect when you think about it.' Jaime looks at me sadly. 'No one would believe you, even if you told them. And if they did believe you, what do you think would happen? The only people who could testify against him are suicide risks who are classified as having mental health issues.' His shoulders rise. 'Who's going to take them seriously? And if they were to speak up, how long do you think they'd last? If they're found dead, no one's going to look too closely. So no one says a word.' He bites his lip. 'Only, Leo's different.'

'What do you mean?'

'He came to me a week ago. Leo told me he was prepared to take all the risks to gather the evidence against Johnson and to testify. He knew I was getting out; he wants me to help him. I'm the only person he's confided in.'

My hands fly to my mouth.

'So you have to look after him for me, Beth. You and Robyn. You have to watch him. Keep him safe by trusting no one in that place. You never know if they've been bought by Johnson. You're it, Beth: you and Robyn. There's no one else.' He looks at me steadily. 'Leo and I worked it all out between us. We had an inkling that Johnson had expanded his business; we just couldn't work out precisely what and how.' He looks away. 'And then we did.'

His eyes meet mine.

'Which is why I agreed to talk to Michael Childs.'

I stare at him.

'I knew that Johnson had been visiting him in the Seg. I think he and Childs concocted some kind of story to manoeuvre Robyn into getting him put in a normal wing.'

A wash of cold horror courses through my veins.

'Childs? But I did it – I did it, Jaime! It was me who got him moved!'

'You couldn't've known, Beth. No one could've known. Yeah, Childs – trafficker, sex-offender. Big business. Just the kind of individual that Johnson would team up with.'

'And Joe? What about Joe? He wouldn't be involved in that kind of stuff! There's no way!'

Jaime leans forward insistently. 'No, no... I'm not suggesting anything about Joe. I think that's just pure coincidence. Joe had stumbled into that world by absolute chance, I'm sure of it. If anyone had even mentioned Tom Johnson's name to me in relation to your son before this – God! If they had even *whispered* it, I would've said. I would've told you.'

My head is thudding. *What has Joe got mixed up in? How can this be happening?*

'Hey! You okay, Beth? You've gone very white.' Jaime's looking at me; his face is etched with concern. 'I don't think I should leave you. Is there someone I can call?'

'I can manage, honestly.' I shift on the sofa and instantly squeal.

Jaime shakes his head. 'I really don't think you should be on your own. There must be someone?'

I immediately think of Sarah. *But how do I tell her all this?*

'There's no one,' I say croakily. 'There's too much I'd have to explain. All the lies I'd have to tell – I just can't, Jaime! I can't!' The realisation of what I'm dealing with hits me hard.

There's a pause.

'Then I'll stay.'

Hot tears instantly spring to my eyes.

He kneels by the side of the sofa and takes my hand in his. His fingers are warm and soft.

'You're not alone with all this, Beth.' He chafes my knuckles. 'You're not on your own. Stop trying to be strong. Lean on me. That's what I'm here for – right?'

I can't bring myself to meet his gaze.

He shakes my hand a little. 'Right?'

'Right,' I whisper.

He reaches up, tucking a strand of my hair back. It's an intimate gesture. His fingers linger for a second on my cheek and I close my eyes. For those few moments the room and my heart slip a little – and for one split moment of that tiny infinitesimal second, his touch shuts everything out.

SIXTEEN

There's a heartbeat between sleep and waking when the world feels right – and then it all turns wrong.

I open my eyes with a gasp.

Wrong, wrong, to the very pit of my stomach, *wrong*.

The sofa has cricked my neck and I ease my head round, painfully. There's a rumpled blanket and a cushion on the floor, but the house is quiet. I struggle up.

'Jaime?'

There's no reply.

Shuffling my bottom to the edge of the sofa, I tentatively try my foot on the floor. It aches, but it's okay. Testing my full weight, I manage a hobble into the hallway and make my way into the kitchen. No sign of him. I go in search of my phone and find it in my jacket on the arm of the sofa. It's then I see the note on the coffee table.

Gone to sort some things.
I'll bring breakfast.
J X

I stand for a moment, easing my sore ankle, staring out of the bay window into the street.

Joe, my head says. I close my eyes as it all comes flooding painfully back.

My phone screen is blank. My thumb scrolls to his name, and then hovers, uncertain. *What if what Jaime said is right?* If I contact him, might it drive him further into the darkness?

It instantly buzzes, jerking me into life.

'Joe?'

'I've been trying you forever!' Robyn's voice booms down the line. 'If I lose you, it's because I'm in Sainsbury's and they seem to have better ways of blocking a phone signal than any prison I've ever been in.'

'Robyn, I—'

I desperately want to tell her what's happened.

'Beth...? Hello? Are you still there?'

The signal fluctuates, dropping in and out.

'Beth? You keep breaking up—'

'I think I'm in trouble, Robyn. I think I'm in real, real trouble.' My voice breaks.

'Eh?... What's happened?'

'I have to tell someone. I don't know what to do.' My voice shivers.

'Beth, what is it? Where are you? Are you at home? I'll come to you. Ten minutes, yes?'

'No!... No, don't come here!' I can't have Robyn seeing Jaime. 'No... Look, I'll meet you.'

'Right. How about the café here?'

'Sounds good.'

'Text me when you're close. You feel alright to drive?'

'I'm fine. Yes, I'll be fine...' I suddenly wonder if I'll be able to. 'I'll see you then.'

I end the call realising I've agreed to go out and I don't have Jaime's number. Picking up his note, I find a pen, scrawling, *I won't be long. Wait for me.* on the back, wedging it into the letterbox on my way out.

Robyn is already sitting in the supermarket café surrounded by bags of shopping, her expression changing from pleasure to shock as I limp over.

'What on earth have you done?' She half gets up, grabbing my arm and checking me up and down as I ease myself into the seat.

'Nothing much, just twisted it.' I grimace a grin.

'How the hell did you manage that?'

A whole range of possible excuses opens up in front of me.

'Uh-oh...' She slides a mug in my direction. 'This coffee should still be okay, but I can tell you're not.'

I take a sip to buy myself some.

'Out with it.' She's regarding me steadily.

'It's Joe,' I begin carefully. 'He went missing. I know where he is, but I've discovered he's involved in... well, stuff.'

'What kind of stuff?'

'Drugs.'

Robyn puts her cup down slowly onto the table. 'I see.'

'If only it was just that.'

She's watching me.

'I found where he's been hiding, and I tracked him down to a house.'

'What kind of state was he in?' She picks up a spoon.

'I didn't get to talk to him; he ran off. But I saw what was going on there, Robyn. I saw young girls. Teenagers. And guess who else was there?'

She queries a look.

'Tom Johnson.'

'*What?*' The spoon stops in mid-air.

'Principal Officer Tom Johnson.'

She doesn't move.

'He tried to stop me leaving. I was scared out of my mind. I mean, he's clearly involved in something really bad. And I think it's to do with Michael Childs.'

'*Say that again?*'

'I need to talk to someone, Robyn. This is huge, isn't it? Massive. I don't know what to do.' I run a shaking hand around the back of my neck. 'Jaime says we can't call the police. He says they're paid off by these people.'

'Jaime?'

'Oh...' I press my fingers into my forehead. 'I ran into him. He helped me. That's how I found Joe.'

Robyn's expression slips into something I can't read.

'Johnson was in a house where they were dealing?'

'I didn't see them dealing, no, but that was the information from Jaime's contact.'

'And did Johnson see you?'

The memory of him in that hallway runs at me in a tide of terror.

I nod. 'He spoke to me. He was sneering – laughing. Asking me if I wanted to get involved with those girls.'

'Involved?'

'Like some kind of grotesque house-mother.' I rub my hands across my face. 'Can you imagine what those girls are being used for? It makes me sick to even think about it.' I drop my hands. Robyn has an odd look on her face.

'This sounds *way, waay* off beat, Beth. I mean, wow, seriously!'

'It's true, Robyn. All of this is true. It happened.'

She stares down into her coffee. 'Right. Let's think. You know I mentioned Tom Johnson does voluntary work with vulnerable kids on the street, don't you?' She looks up, tips her head quizzically. 'Are you sure this wasn't one of those places?'

I can't believe this.

'Robyn, no! For goodness' sake! Listen to me!'

'He's been along to quite a few sessions in the chapel.' Her palms open on the table. 'He's met Madeleine and Nadia. He's been talking about doing talks on prisoners getting involved with voluntary work with at-risk teens. Are you sure these weren't those kinds of teenagers?'

I look at her open-mouthed. 'It was a derelict house, Robyn. The girls were being kept in filth!'

She bites her lip. 'I thought you were going to tell me Tom had rung you to apologise. Did I mention I'd had a chat with him? He was *mortified* he'd made you feel uncomfortable. He said he was trying to empathise with how difficult it is for a woman to walk onto a wing full of men.' She picks up her mug and blows across the rim. She regards me steadily.

It's as though I'm speaking another language.

'He's told me before that he does work at halfway hostels for addicts and the homeless. Could it have been of those places? Has Joe been sleeping rough, do you know?'

I'm dumbfounded.

'He *threatened* me, Robyn! Can you hear me? He cornered me in that house. I was trapped! He trapped me. I... I thought something awful was going to happen.'

'So how did you manage to get out of there?'

I am about to say, 'he opened the front door', but then I stop. This is pointless.

I slump back in my seat, regarding Robyn stonily.

'You're not going to believe me, whatever I say, are you? I guess you think I'm overreacting – just like that incident in the chapel. You're going to explain how I've got this all wrong and that Tom Johnson is a thoroughly decent chap.'

'But I was on your side!' she splutters. 'I'm always on your side, whatever the situation is!'

'You mean whether you believe I'm telling the truth or not?'

Robyn's face blanches. 'That feels a bit unfair, actually.' She looks terribly hurt. 'I'm really upset you think that, Beth. I hope I've never given you cause to think I've been anything but a good friend. I've always had your back – like you've always had mine.'

I pause, and in that instant my phone jars into life. I snatch it out of my pocket, not recognising the number.

'It's me. Where the hell are you?' Jaime sounds angry.

Robyn's eyes flicker across my face and I wonder how much of this she can hear.

'I had to go out.'

'Out? Why would you have to go out? How can you even drive? I told you I was going to get breakfast! What are you thinking disappearing like that? Do you know the risks you're running?'

Robyn makes a little embarrassed glance away. Her face is blotched red. I can see how upset she is.

I bring the phone closer to my ear and shift away in my seat. 'I won't be long. I'm sorry, yeah? I'll be back really soon. I'll explain everything. Just wait, yeah?'

The call ends abruptly, and Robyn gives me a look. 'Drew?'

I can't tell if she's being sarcastic. I colour. 'No, no, it wasn't.'

'Oh, I see.'

A crawl of shame slides down my neck but I'm still smarting from the argument.

'You clearly need to go,' Robyn says a little stiffly. 'It looks as though you've got a lot on your plate.'

I push my chair back. She watches me steadily as I stand, my anger deflating like some tired old balloon. The pain inside tightens, mixing itself now with indignity, and withering pride – all the exasperation, and fear, and frustration, seeping out of me.

Her phone on the table lights up. We both stare down at it.

'It's the prison.' She picks it up. I watch her face. It changes from inquiry to alarm. 'It's Leo.'

A plunging feeling grips me.

'He's been rushed to hospital.'

I open my mouth, but no sound comes out. 'What's happened?'

'I need to get to the Royal General now.'

'Then I'll drive us.'

There's a second's pause, then she picks up her shopping. 'I'll chuck this in my car.'

We hurry out of the café together. I know she's watching me as I frantically text Jaime. I'm guessing she knows who it is; I know what she must be thinking. I'm aware of the tiniest grain of judgement, but I push it from my mind. I really don't care.

The A & E doors swing open. There's a woman at Reception who glances up as I rush over.

'There's someone... A boy who's been brought in from HMP Crowden Heath not long ago. I think he's a suicide attempt. Where would we find him?'

She taps on the keyboard, me on tenterhooks as she inter-mittently looks at the screen through her bifocals, her head tipping up, then down. It makes me want to scream.

'Name?'

'Leo. Leo Hargreaves.' I clutch on to the edge of the counter.

A woman carrying a load of files comes in through a side door and asks a question about Sellotape. The receptionist stops what she's doing, opens a drawer and starts sorting through it. I don't think I can stand this a moment more. I look around at Robyn, but she's not there.

'Leo Hargreaves,' I repeat loudly, wanting to reach through and grab her. 'I don't think you appreciate how serious this is.'

She stops searching in the drawer and looks at me.

'If you'd like to take a seat, I'll check his whereabouts.'

My stomach squeezes into a hard ball. 'Please – all I need to do is find him.' I glance around for Robyn again. *Where has she gone?*

There's a whoosh of a door behind me and I turn my head. The receptionist looks up.

'We're police, we rang earl—' Drew falters the moment he sees me. He and his mate stand there awkwardly, holding out their ID cards.

'Leo Hargreaves?' the woman says pleasantly. 'Of course. I'll just check and then get someone to escort you through.' She trundles her chair back with an imperious glance at me, before stalking off.

He wheels round. 'What on earth are you doing here?'

His buddy turns his back, pretending there's something outside that's caught his attention.

'Well, I'm not here wanting to harass and bully some kid into wanting to die, that's for sure.'

Drew glowers, but I see I have him on the back foot.

'And how's your friend Tom Johnson, Drew? Oh yes – I know you and he are best buddies these days. Is that how you get to be shagging young girls?' I say it loud enough for the room to hear. 'But then, teenagers are easily impressed. A grown woman would tell you to go to hell – and I happen to be a grown woman.'

I realise, with a burn of embarrassment, that the receptionist has returned. She tries to keep her face expressionless.

'Yes, the patient is in A & E. My colleague Cheryl will take you through now, if that's convenient.' She's trying to pretend I'm not there as the other woman comes out of a side door, sweeping past me, smiling at Drew engagingly.

'If you'd like to come with me?' She extends an arm but gives me another kind of look entirely. 'I'm afraid I can't allow you through.'

'But I'm a Samaritan.'

'Look, I'm very sorry.'

And I'm left standing there, bruised and impotent. I look around. *Where is Robyn?* When a loud bleeping of pagers and a man in a white coat barges past me and disappears through a side door of vertical rubber strips, I get a glimpse of blue scrub uniforms. A nurse goes to bustle past.

'Sorry! Excuse me. I can see you're busy, but there's a patient – Leo Hargreaves. I believe he's here and I'm really concerned.'

'I'm afraid I can't tell you anything. If you'd like to take a seat in the visitors' area.' She goes to move away but I catch her arm.

'He's vulnerable and has no one – I was wondering...?'

'Are you family?'

'No, I'm not family, but—'

'His brother was with him.' The sudden change of tense registers with me and I'm aware of her hand briefly touching my arm.

'I'm sorry. I'm really not the person you need to speak to. Hang on, I'll find someone. Wait there.'

My feet move as if to go after her, but instead, I find myself turning away as I blunder through the main doors. There are ambulances, people, lines of cars toiling around the car park, but they all blur into a kaleidoscope of colours. My ankle cramps, sending a jagging pulse of pain as I lurch across the car park. *Leo, poor, poor Leo.* My heart is heavy and I feel so alone. I wish to God I hadn't fought with Robyn. My eyes blur with tears as I pull out my phone but a movement on the path in front makes me look up.

There's a figure hesitating uncertainly. I have a sudden thump of recognition.

It's *Melanie.*

She is standing, clearly waiting, pacing back and forth, pausing to toe the gravel with the tip of her sneaker as she nervously flicks the hair from her eyes. I falter, slowing my pace.

What the hell is she doing here? And then I remember Drew. Of course! The audacity of it: so blatant, so casual, as if she can just slide in here, in full public view.

My anger boils.

'Are you happy now?'

Her head snaps up and she looks at me in shock.

I gesture to the hospital entrance. 'Desperate to see him, are you? Don't you see how pitiful it is, you having to trail after him like some sick puppy?'

She stands, her eyes frozen on my face. A shiver of satisfaction thrums. I want her to feel the humiliation and pain she's caused me. I want to grind her face in my suffering.

'There's no point coming to my house and banging on the door' – I wave a hand – 'I wouldn't take him back if he begged me. You can have him, you're totally welcome.'

I take a step towards her. She glances anxiously over my shoulder and I look around, suddenly finding myself talking to a flying mane of hair as she turns and begins to run. Drew has just walked out. I don't think he's seen her: he and his colleague are talking, heads bowed, as they walk towards his car. I hear Drew laugh at some joke or other, and my pounding heart breaks in two. I think of Leo on a slab somewhere in that hospital. He was the kid I was supposed to protect.

A giant wave of exhaustion washes over me. I'm worn out: with Drew, with Joe, Johnson, Robyn, that girl – the whole lot. I've been used: played and manoeuvred, just like the boy I've failed. How I'd love to tell him how sorry I am. That I can't bear to think that I've had a hand in something that led him to want to die.

It's on me. I know this is on me. *I hate myself.*

'Beth.'

I lift my head and my thudding heart crashes.

'Joe...?'

He's a lone figure partially hidden by the car park wall.

'Joe! My God, Joe!'

I take a faltering step. My whole being wants to rush over and grab him, but the snatched wariness of his shoulders tells me to keep my distance. I hesitate, my hands desperate, twitching towards him like he's a scared animal that's about to bolt.

He lifts his head cautiously, checking right and left. I see the side of his face is swollen into a mesh of cuts and bruises.

'What's happened to you, Joe? My God, your face!'

He lets me take a couple of paces, but he feels for the wall behind him.

'I'm alright,' he says gruffly, licking his lips. I think he's about to say something more, but he only shakes his head.

'Alright? You don't look alright! Please – let me...' I take a step, but he immediately backs off.

'Look, Joe, I don't care about what's gone on. You're my son, and I love you. All I want is for you to be safe. I can see you're scared and you think you're alone, but you're not. I'm with you, no matter what you're involved in. Trust me, Joe. Let me help you.'

The scowl of his lowered brow softens a little. His feet scuff uncertainly, unsure whether to believe me.

I pause for a second. 'Joe, how did you know I was here?'

His top lip disappears as he chews it.

'I... I put a tracker app on your phone,' he mumbles. His puffy eyes twitch nervously. For a second, I'm speechless then ridiculously happy: he always knew where to find me even when I thought he was totally lost.

He looks away, ashamed, but all I want to do is bearhug him all the more.

'Joe, listen to me,' I try tentatively. 'Will you come home? Please. Let me look after you.'

But his head swings vehemently. 'No way. That's not even

remotely possible.' He shrinks at the very thought. 'No way.' He glances fearfully to where Drew's car was parked.

'Drew doesn't live at home anymore,' I say gently. 'You don't need to be worried about him or the police or anything like that. Our house is a safe space.' I say 'our' so he hears it, but his face only sets more determinedly.

'No. I can't – I can't!'

'Who are you afraid of, Joe? Who's hurt you?'

'You don't get it. You don't understand.'

'Then tell me, Joe. Help me understand. If it's about Tom Johnson—'

His head snaps up. 'What?'

'I saw him at that house. I saw what he's involved with. Did he do that to you, Joe? Was that him?' I can feel my anger gaining momentum. 'We can stop him – us two, together. If you'll tell the truth, then we can go to the police. We could make them listen. You can give them invaluable inside information. You can help stop these people. I know you, Joe; you have the strength and the courage to make that happen.'

'You don't know what you're talking about, Beth. You have no idea what they'd do to me.' His face is pale with fear. He wipes his top lip and winces. 'This is just for starters. I've seen what they're capable of. You end up where you're begging to die.'

The horror, the horror. I see the faces of those girls in front of me.

His eyes are scared. 'They've got CCTV footage of the vehicle. The police. They'll examine the footage, and they'll find out it was me. You don't know these people; they've got informants everywhere: in the police, in the courts. Everyone is being paid. Everyone.'

I frown. 'CCTV footage, of what? What vehicle?'

Joe exhales in exasperation. His palms shake as he wrings his hands. 'The one I told you about! The one Nate and I torched! That's why we torched it! We knew we were on the footage. You didn't see what they did to Nate!'

And I realise that Joe doesn't know I've spoken to Sarah.

'Joe.'

'What?'

'Nate has told Sarah everything.'

He stares back at me wide-eyed.

'Nate wasn't beaten up, you told Sarah you'd bought a car, and there was no van really, was there? You can say all of it, Joe. You can tell me. It makes no difference. All I need is the truth.'

'What the hell?' He takes a step back.

'There was no you and Nate joyriding, and there was no angry gang. I know about the money and why you wanted it.' I keep my voice low and unthreatening. 'What you don't realise, Joe, is that I'm not going to judge you.' I half smile. 'I can imagine how you've got drawn into this, and I don't care, do you hear that? All I need is that you're straight with me. If you're straight with me, we can get through this.'

But Joe is only standing there, shaking his head. 'No, no, no, no, no! For Christ's sake, Beth! I told you the truth. I saw one of them! One of the gang at the airport! Nate, the bastard, set me up! He told them where I was going, and put it all on me. He could've got me killed! Don't trust a word he says, or anything he tells Sarah. It's all lies! You can't trust anyone – if you don't get your head around that, you're dead too!'

His face is contorted with terror. *He's telling you the truth*, my head says. *Does he look as though he's lying? Believe him! Believe him!*

I don't know what to think; I don't know what to say. The only thing I know is that all the time he's here with me, I can protect hm.

'Joe, come on! Think about this! If they're as dangerous as you say they are, it'll only be a matter of time before—'

I break off as his face changes into something beyond

horror. I realise, with a terrible premonition, that I've just artic-ulated his worst nightmare into something real.

He begins to back away, breathing hard.

'Joe – I didn't mean... Look! I'm saying we can fix this! Don't run away! I can stop this terrible thing from happening!'

But it's too late. He darts away, me going after him, but he's too fast, putting feet between us in seconds and I'm forced to stutter to a panting halt as I watch him disappear.

My hands drop to my sides. I'm truly defeated. I can't keep going. I slide wearily behind the wheel of my car, allowing the retch of sobs takes over. There are no tears: just deep aching slabs of pain that I can't choke up. They're too huge; the stones of guilt are too solid to shift.

And then I feel nothing; there's nothing left. My sobs quieten. I'm utterly empty. I rest my head back. The warmth of sunlight soothes my brow. I'm spent – devoid of everything. If I never had to open my eyes again, it would be a relief. The heat moves a little, dims and brightens again. I open my eyes. Through my web of lashes I know there's a shape, blocking out the sun.

It doesn't move.

The web of lashes clears. It's Drew's girl. She's standing between my car and the next, staring down at me. I have no fight left in me. I reach out and open the window.

My voice feels cracked and hoarse.

'What do you want?'

She stands there, mute and unmoving.

'You've got everything, so what do you want now?'

She looks at me sullenly. 'You need to keep away from him.'

'What?'

'I said, you need to keep away from him.'

My head feels thick with pain but there's a dull outrage that I can just about muster.

'*What?* Seriously?' I almost want to laugh out loud. '*You* are warning *me* off? You're kidding, right?'

She glances across the roof of my car and then dips a little, her head levelling with mine. 'No, listen, I'm telling you—'

'No, *you're* not telling *me* anything, *Melanie*.'

Her eyes widen nervously at my use of her name.

'Oh yes, don't worry, I know. And you need to learn something about self-respect.' I look her up and down. 'Trust me, it won't be long before he's coming back to *you* stinking of other women.' I press the button and the window begins to ascend. 'The truth is, you two deserve each other.'

She claws at the closing window but it's too late. My hands tremble as I reach forward to start the car. Her palms hit the glass. Her voice is muffled as I jab on the radio to drown her out.

'I'm not listening!' I shout. 'I can't hear a word you're saying, sorry!' I shake my head, cupping my hand to my ear. I force a steely grin as her hands thump against the window, her mouth contorting, as she carries on yelling at me, grabbing at the windscreen wipers so violently I'm scared she'll yank them off.

Heart in my throat, I manage to manoeuvre out of the parking bay as she runs around the front, banging her fists down, her face a mass of fury. Although I'm still grinning insanely, I'm completely rattled, my thighs quivering like jelly on the accelerator, making the car jump and nearly stall, but I dare not slow down, terrified she'll snatch the door open.

Aiming a final kick to the rear bumper, she whirls away, defeated. I glance in the mirror. She's standing there, her arms held high in frustration, but as I watch, they drop in surrender.

Oh my God! What just happened? I glance quickly at the phone on the passenger seat, desperately needing to talk to Jaime. Giving the voice command, I wait anxiously for him to pick up, but the calls go straight to voicemail.

'I'm coming straight home,' I say at the tone. 'I've got some awful news about Leo.' I pause. 'So many things have happened. I'll tell you everything when I get back.'

I can barely think as I turn the corner into my street and pull up into the drive. My hands fumble with the door key.

'I was wondering where you'd gone.'

The voice startles me. Jaime is standing in the hallway.

'I've been calling you.' He leans against the wall, resting his head against it wearily. He holds up the bunch of keys that Drew left behind. 'I picked these up earlier. I hope you don't mind.'

'Not at all,' I say automatically. 'It's fine.'

'By the way, I know about Leo. I grabbed a cab.'

'You saw him? You saw Leo?'

He nods, sighing angrily. 'I knew they would eventually. They've got what they wanted. He never even regained consciousness.'

He closes his eyes and his mouth tightens into a grimace. 'They told me he'd cut himself, but it was far more than that: he'd taken pills too.' The trauma shadows his face. 'By the time I got there, really it was already too late. God alone knows what they did to him.' He raises his hands in defeat. 'I told them I was his brother. They said they'd tried to do their best, but...' He trails off. 'He went into cardiac arrest in the hospital. All I could do was stand and watch, helpless.' His palm comes up to his chest. 'There was blood on the floor.' His mouth hangs open a little at the memory. 'That moment... going in there, reminded me of...' His breathing becomes ragged and he begins to pace. 'It brought it all back.'

'Jaime...' I go towards him, putting my hand on his shoulder.

He's trembling. 'I tried to find you, but there was so much going on. All that panic. The total powerlessness of it – that somehow, I should have stopped it, Beth! I could have prevented it. I should have seen what was happening and... and—'

He breaks off; his hands hit the wall, his mouth twisting in agony. The only thing I can do is take him in my arms and hold him while he cries: great juddering convulsions jarring his body.

'Shh. Shh,' I say tenderly. 'I've got you; you're not falling. You can hold on to me. I'm strong. I won't let you go... Shh.'

He turns his face into my neck, and into my hair. I can feel the heat of his gasping breath as his fingers come up to wind themselves into the nape of my neck. He holds on tight, pulling me into him, easing my face and lips down – and then we're breathing in each other's breath, not kissing, something more, that takes the air from my lungs and makes my head spin with its intensity. There's this urgency, a massive surge of electricity that grips me right to my core: a huge magnetic pull. I want him. I want him more than I've ever wanted anyone before.

My palms cup his face, my cheeks soaking up his tears. I lick my lips, tasting the salt. Nothing else exists; there's just me and him, him and me – no bodies, no room, no nothing – suspended in that moment.

'Hello?'

The ground catches up, slamming us to earth. I'm aware of a distant knocking.

'Hello? Is there—?'

I turn towards the sound. The front door is ajar with Robyn standing in the gap. Her face contorts in shock for a second, and then disappears. Jaime and I both fall away from each other. I'm confused and dizzy. My brain isn't functioning.

I run into the living room to peer through the front window, to see Robyn's car parked right outside. She's got someone in the passenger seat.

'Is she still there?' Jaime hasn't moved from the doorway.

'Yes, she's there.' I glance back.

'Did you know she was coming?'

'Of course not! It'll be about Leo. I'll go and talk to her.'

Mustering as much dignity as I can, I walk down the drive,

trying not to catch Robyn's eye. She immediately gets out of the driver's side to greet me.

'Robyn! You disappeared! And look, before you say anything—'

But she only reaches for the rear door handle. 'Get in.'

'Sorry?'

'Get in the car, Beth. I need to talk to you.'

'But...!' I glance back at the house.

'There's someone I want you to have a conversation with. Call Jaime. Text him, whatever, and tell him you're going to be half an hour.'

'Robyn, I really don't—'

She doesn't move. I glance back at the bay window.

'Beth. This is important. Believe me. You'll want to hear this.'

'Okay, okay.' I slide in and the door slams. The person in the passenger seat turns to look at me. It's Melanie.

'What the hell is she doing here?' My hand reaches for the door, but Robyn has flicked the child-lock.

'I'm going to drive us somewhere, Beth. Send Jaime a message, then I want you to listen to what Melanie has to say.'

My fingers grip the handle.

'Just open this now, please! You know who she is, don't you? You know what she's done? So there's absolutely no way I'm interested in any crap that's likely to come out of her mouth. I've heard and seen enough of *Melanie* for a lifetime, thank you.'

'I don't think you fully get the picture.' Robyn starts the car. Melanie hasn't taken her eyes off me. Close up, I can see that she's really, really young.

'Oh, I think I do, Robyn!' I yank pointlessly.

'No you don't! Listen, it's not Drew.' Robyn glances in the rear-view mirror and then attempts to pull away.

'Robyn! I mean it!'

'She's nothing to do with Drew, Beth. It's Joe.'

My hand stalls. The girl's eyes haven't left my face.

'What do you mean *"it's Joe"*? What's Joe?' A panic begins to flutter around my heart.

There's silence as the car begins to move off.

I can hear myself gabbling. *'Robyn! Robyn!* Will you stop all this?... In fact, stop this car!' I grab at the back of the seat, pulling at her shoulder and for one second, I actually start feeling scared. We're now heading towards the main road as the car picks up speed.

'Robyn!' I'm fumbling for my phone, dropping it into the footwell where it disappears beneath the seat. I go to snatch it up, but the car goes round a bend, and I slew violently. 'What the hell is going on? What are you doing? Pull over now! Stop this, NOW!'

We take a corner far too quickly, and I lurch, grabbing for the seatbelt strap as we swerve off the main road and down some kind of dirt track. We jolt and bump along a rutted road before shuddering to a stop. Robyn twists round in her seat.

'Sorry about that.'

'What the hell are you doing?'

'I was making sure we weren't being followed.' She looks at me, deadly serious, then turns to Melanie. 'Tell her what you told me.'

The girl pushes the hair from her eyes in a nervous, child-like gesture. She's been crying: her eyes are swollen, and cheeks are streaked with eyeliner. She glances around, unsure.

'No one followed us. I made sure of it. There's no one else here. Look—' Robyn gestures to the blank fields on either side. 'That's why I came here: we're up higher so we'd spot any car from a mile off.'

'I don't know how to tell her.' Melanie's voice crumbles. She won't look at me. 'I didn't know she was his mum.'

I can only stare at Robyn. 'What is this? What's going on?'

Robyn puts a comforting hand on her arm and then turns to me.

'She saw you talking to Joe in the hospital car park just now. She couldn't hear what you were talking about, but she thought you were another woman he's got working for him.'

I blink, not comprehending. 'Working for him? For whom? What are you talking about?'

'I found her crying in the car park. I joined the dots. She didn't know about Leo.' Robyn rubs the back of her neck tiredly. 'What a waste, what a waste.'

I look at Melanie. She starts to cry again: terrified sobbing hiccoughs.

'You're not going to believe what I'm going to tell you, Beth.' Robyn shakes her head. 'Leo was supposed to attempt suicide, get to outside hospital, and then Melanie here was supposed to deliver drugs to him to bring back into the prison.'

'I know.'

'What?' Robyn's face drops in shock.

'It's what I was telling you, Robyn! About Johnson. I know!' I turn to Melanie. 'So, you're a drugs mule, yes?'

She nods quickly; her face distorts and crumples. 'At first it was only for Leo – we knew it was a risk, but it worked at first. But then they got me.'

'*They* got you?' I watch mutely.

'Leo couldn't carry on, y'see.' Her ruined, swollen eyes look into mine. 'He couldn't carry on, knowing what they were going to make me do.' Her face collapses again. 'I got searched coming in to see him in prison, y'see? I'd got gear on me. So, then when they found it they'd got both of us. We had to do whatever they wanted.'

I am aware of Robyn's eyes on me. There's a weird sensation high up in my throat.

'*They?*' My voice is a husky whisper. 'You mean Johnson. What's this got to do with Joe?'

Melanie is a mess of shaking fear. Her hands wrestle and wring. Her eyes are puffed red. She swipes at them angrily.

'I just thought Joe was nice. He seemed like a laugh. I wouldn't... I wouldn't have gone anywhere with him, I wouldn't...' she keeps repeating.

I look at her and then at Robyn, hearing the saliva gulp in my throat. 'You're saying you went somewhere with Joe?' I'm aware of the breath wheezing and catching at the back of my throat.

'I had no idea. How was I to know?' Melanie protests, crying. 'Leo was struggling to cope in prison. He was asking me to bring in gear to take the edge off, but I was too scared and they knew me now. That's when he tried to hurt himself the first time and ended up in hospital.' Her huge eyes meet mine. 'I couldn't say no to him then, could I?'

She shakes her head tiredly. 'I had to do it, but it cost me. The gear for Leo, my rent, my bills. I didn't have the cash.' She holds out her hands. 'Then my best mate said she wanted to cheer me up. She told me to meet her at this new bar. I don't know why I went. Anyway, then this guy... Joe... comes over. He was nice. Funny... There was no pressure. He made me laugh. He wasn't like the other guys. He wasn't pushy or loud... I wouldn't have done it otherwise.'

'You wouldn't have done what?'

Her nose is running; her cheeks are scrubbed raw. Robyn searches for a tissue and hands it to her.

'He said I was too young not to be out having fun. He said him and his mate, Nate, were the organisers for music events, like big after-parties. He bragged he could get VIP passes, but he needed to get enough people together to get the best lounges, like, private ones, y'know? And that if I found other girls, friends of friends, then I'd get a commission. Money... I-I...'

Her palms shrug. 'I couldn't see anything wrong with it: have a good time and make a ton of money on the side, that's what I thought. He said if I was good at getting girls, we could be like business partners, me, him, and Nate. It was just like starting our own club scene, only we had the edge, being young – we knew what was what.'

My child. My son. Joe.

Melanie shakes her head as though she can't believe what she's saying. 'It sounded like a brilliant idea, but then the club parties never happened. Not like he said they would. Instead, we ended up at this place, like a warehouse. Joe called it Casa Amor as a joke, like on *Love Island*. He got a DJ and lights an' stuff, and when me and the other girls went there, we all got dressed up... There were boys there too: friends of Joe and Nate's. It was okay' –she hesitates – 'it was all okay, until...'

I don't know if I can bear this. I want to cover my ears. I want to scream.

'Some older guys turned up. They seemed alright at first; it was like they'd just come to have a bit of a laugh.' Her eyes slide away. She can't look at me.

'And Joe said... Joe said...'

No. No, he didn't... Joe didn't say, he wouldn't...

'We should play games. Like they do on *Love Island*? Just boys and girls messing about... And then one of the girls went out on a date with one of the older guys. He told her she looked sexy and bought her things. She bragged she could get us all boyfriends just the same.' She looks at me. 'What was the harm? Joe said it was just a laugh. The girls started asking me to do their hair and makeup 'cos I'd done beauty therapy. It was a bit of fun, that was all.' Her hands fiddle and clench. 'Until one of my mates, Abby, disappeared, like... completely.'

It's as though there's a cold hand on my spine.

'A few of us went looking for her.' She stops, her eyes big and scared. 'But then we found her. Her guy had said he wanted to "try something new". He'd put a cord round her neck and tried to strangle her.' Her fingers come up to her throat.

'She was in a right state, talking about going to the police, so I went to Joe and told him, but he just gave me a shedload of money and said half of it was for her, only she had to keep her mouth shut.'

'How much did he give you?'

Her eyes flit in surprise at the question. 'A thousand. Why?'

'It doesn't matter,' I say dully. 'Go on.'

'So I told him I didn't like that vibe and that I wouldn't be chatting any more girls into coming to his gigs...' She's getting fretful at the memory. 'But he said I had to remember Leo: that bad things happened to people in prison, and Leo was being protected, but if that protection went away—' Her voice cracks. 'Course I told Leo. I was scared what might happen – to him, to me, to all of us. But now we were right in it up to our necks.' Her eyes meet mine. 'None of us could get out. The only way' – she hesitates – 'was the way Leo did it.'

My fury and desperation gather momentum.

'Did Leo ever say who this contact was in the prison? Did he mention a name?'

But Melanie shakes her head. 'I knew it was a screw, though. I knew it was someone who was coming to his cell at night to keep putting the pressure on him.'

My head is scrambling. Johnson will have needed a sweet kid like Joe to lure the girls in – what a prize to have my son working for him! The absolute bastard. How pleased he would have been with himself when he made that connection.

I glare at Robyn. 'See? Now do you believe me?' I can't help myself. 'Drugs, grooming young girls – and all because of Tom Johnson. I *told* you. I *warned* you. Why wouldn't you listen to me?'

Robyn's face is pale and tight. 'I'm so sorry, Beth. I couldn't get my head around it! I wanted to believe you, I really did!'

I can't bear to listen. I want to punch. I want to lash out.

'My phone...' I scramble desperately, clawing in the footwell. 'I have to get hold of Joe.'

'But there's more,' Melanie whispers.

My hand stalls. Robyn's stare freezes.

'I haven't told you all of it.' She's shaking. Her lips wobble as she glances back into the dirt road behind us. 'Only if I do, I need you to promise me you won't go to the cops. They'll say I'm part of it. I went along with it. I'll do time.'

'I promise, Melanie. Just tell me.'

She pulls her thin coat further around her shoulders as if looking for comfort. 'You have to understand – that's why I rang you that night. I saw your number on Joe's phone. it said *Beth* with loads of calls to you. I didn't know who you were. I thought he was bringing some other girl in. I got scared he was replacing me 'cos I was a problem... And I know how they get rid of problems.' Her eyes flicker nervously. 'I thought if I warned you off, he might have to keep me working for him. Buy myself some time... But time's running out now, isn't it? 'Specially now, with what they've done to Leo!' She starts to cry.

'Shh. You're okay, Melanie. We're here now,' I soothe.

But she's blind with fear. 'I begged him. I'm ashamed, but I begged him and said I'd do whatever he wanted.' Her eyes startle with tears and shock. 'He told me he'd got the names and contact details of the girls he needed. All I had to do was go and get them.' She rubs her nose and swallows. 'Everything was laid on for them: drinks, a DJ, transport—'

'What kind of transport?' My stomach twists.

'A van. Joe had thought of everything. So that's what we did. Joe went round to pick them all up. We had to stop off to get petrol, but when he got out, that's when I saw he'd left his phone.' She looks at me. 'And then I saw the other stuff rammed under the seat. The files.'

I think my heart has stopped.

'Big wads of cardboard folders. They had HMP on the

front. I pulled some of them out. Names were highlighted.
Then I saw what they were.'

No...

'They were prisoner records... Like, sex offender files. I kept
seeing the names of the same girls over and over – but then I
worked it out.'

I can't speak.

'The sex offenders, they'd exchanged the girls' names, that's
what they'd done. Swapped their victims. Passed their contact
details around from one to the other. These poor girls who'd
already been abused were being targeted again by these dirty
bastards who were getting the information from the files.' Her
hands come up. 'And I was the one being used to reel them in.

'I could've puked there and then. When Joe got back in the
van, I chucked the papers in his face. I screamed at him that
these men were sick, but that he was even sicker... But the girls
in the back started yelling and he grabbed me by the neck,
slammed me up against the side door and told me that if I
breathed a word to anyone, I was dead meat. The girls were
going nuts, trying to get out, but he drove off. Joe was crazy –
mental. I thought he was going to kill all of us. He was all over
the road. We ended up on the motorway, dodging in and out of
cars – I thought we were all going to die. I did something really,
really stupid.' She winds her hair into her hands at the memory.
'I grabbed the handbrake. We slewed and skidded, and I heard a
car behind us smashing into the barrier. Everyone was
screaming at him. God knows how he kept control, but he did,
swerving into the hard shoulder. There were lights, horns,
people shouting – I managed to get the door open and I ran, but
Joe came after me, dragging me up the bank amongst the
bushes. He had his hands around my throat.'

Her hands come up to protect herself from the memory. 'He
didn't say a word; his face went dead.' She shudders. 'Then he
started to squeeze. Things went dark: like I was going under...'

Her fingertips hover at her neck. 'I couldn't hear or see anything – just these flashes of light that got dimmer and dimmer. Then he suddenly let go – I dunno what made him. I was gasping for air and the world came roaring back. He could've done it... he could've done it there and then, but all he did was lean right into me and whisper, *"you're ours. Don't you forget that. You're always just seconds away from me ending you for good."* And then he got back in the van and drove off.'

She hugs her arms around her thin body, pulling her coat around her and burying her chin into the collar. 'I dunno what made me call you that night.' Her head shivers in incomprehension. 'I felt like I had to tell someone, anyone.' She gazes at me through wet sooty lashes.

'So, Drew...?' my voice croaks huskily. 'What's Drew's involvement?'

I glance at Robyn's face. It's blank with disbelief.

'You really don't know, do you?' Melanie looks at me, slowly shaking her head. 'You really, really don't know?'

Pins and needles slide into my hairline.

'I got sold.' She meets my look and sniffs miserably.

'Sold?' I can't take my eyes off her.

'The punters get a choice of what's on offer. One of them chose me.'

I know the words make sense, but I can't understand them.

I look at Robyn. By the expression on her face, she clearly does.

'I'll say it plain. I'll say it clear,' Melanie says slowly. 'Your son sold me like a piece of meat.' She enunciates the words slowly to make sure they sink in. 'I was sold for sex to your husband.'

SEVENTEEN

I'd like to laugh out loud right this moment. I'd actually like to start screaming, and crying, and bawling and never stop.

I actually think I might throw up.

'Don't trust anyone.'

I hear her words but it's as though they're coming from a long way away.

'Do you hear me?'

I shake back to the present.

'Don't trust any of them. They've all got their snouts in one trough or another.' Melanie buries her face deeper into the collar of her jacket as though it will protect her.

I swallow thickly, closing my eyes. The horror just spirals: my son, now my husband.

'You lot think it's all black and white, don't you? Right and wrong. Fact is, they're all scrabbling after power: Joe, the cops, all of them. One side wants money, the other side wants promotion for getting some big criminal bust, but who am I, eh? Just some pawn in the middle having to play both sides. And the ones at the bottom? Those poor girls in the back of that van? They're the real victims. They're the ones who bought the idea that "it's all just a laugh" without knowing that the joke's on them.'

I open my eyes as her words sink in.

'You're playing both sides?'

'Joe wanted intel on what the cops are doing. He thinks Drew's a dumb plum – a dirty cop. Sell him a bit of pussy and he'll sing like a canary to me. All too easy.'

I hold myself tight. 'And has he?' I prevent my voice from wavering.

Melanie licks her lips nervously. 'This is why I'm dead.'

I wait.

'He's undercover. Drew is. He's not bent at all.'

'I stare at her.

'I worked it out. He doesn't know I'm on to him. He still thinks he's playing me, but I've sussed him. Only now I realise I'm the one who's caught in the middle of it all. I can't keep out of it; I have to lie to both sides. Joe has to keep thinking I'm giving him intel on the police and Drew has to keep believing whatever I tell him is kosher. Whichever way this goes down, I'm the one who's gonna pay.'

'So what do we do, Beth?' Robyn has been silent this whole time. 'How are we going to help her?'

I jump as my phone flashes into life from beneath the seat. I scrabble to find it. It's Jaime. I can't answer the call; I jab at the button angrily.

'See?' I wave the phone. 'See this guy here? He's the one who gets it. He was the one who warned me. He told me what was going on and has been proved right every time.'

Robyn shifts uncomfortably. 'I know, I know, I should've—' But I shut her up with an irritated wave. 'Melanie, I cannot imagine what you've been through. I don't think I would be brave enough to do what you're doing.'

But she only laughs sadly. 'I'm not brave.' She shakes her head. 'Fact is, you're my last hope... I've got nowhere left to go.

Leo's dead and Joe was right: I belong to them now. Doesn't matter if I give them up or not – I know too much. And the truth is, I'm as guilty as they are – no, I am... I am...' she protests.

'I helped Joe. I helped him take those girls. I *did* that.' Her fists clench in her lap. 'And Drew? He'll throw me in the trash with the rest. All they want is the names at the top, the ones that make the headlines, the ones that get him promotion. So, I might as well do the right thing for once in my miserable life. That's why I'm telling you all this now: I might not be able to stop them, but you can.'

I'm going to get that bastard of a husband of mine. I'm going to get them all.

I'm aware of Robyn's eyes regarding me fearfully. *I should've done something in the first place. I've given birth to a monster and I've nurtured it, and let it grow, stood back as it broke out and pretended I didn't know what was going on as it smashed people's lives.*

I lift my gaze. 'I'm not abandoning you, Melanie – and I'm not abandoning those girls.' My voice sounds stronger than I feel. I put a hand on her shoulder, hoping she can't feel the tremor. 'You've taken such a massive risk, but what if someone's seen you? How can you go back now?'

'I'm a dead girl walking. They know it, I know it, and I think, deep-down, you know it too.' Melanie's sad eyes search mine. 'I've still got the drugs I was supposed to give to Leo.' She puts a hand on the pocket of her jacket. 'They'll know I dare not run.' She drops her gaze. 'They can have me picked up by the police at any time and have me put inside; they can put me to work; they can kill me knowing that no one will care. They can do whatever they want. For them it's always a win-win.'

'But we're not going to let any of that happen, Melanie,' Robyn reassures her. 'You're with us now. We can whisk you away where no one will ever find you.'

But Melanie only gazes sadly. 'They always find you; you

should know that.' She gives Robyn a pointed look as she reaches to open the door, clambering out and casting a furtive glance around.

'Bye then.' She raises a shaky hand to wave. 'And... and... umm. Thanks.'

We sit watching in silence as she makes her way down the path in the field and towards a copse of trees at the back of a housing estate. I let the air escape slowly from my lungs.

'Not great, is it?' Robyn says quietly. 'I'm so sorry about Joe. The last thing I wanted to do is tell you. Need I ask how you're feeling?'

'About as terrified and disgusted as you.'

'But seriously, what are we going to do – I mean, really do?' Robyn stares straight ahead.

'Melanie's in trouble, Robyn. Those girls are in trouble. We have no choice. We can't just do nothing.' I don't think I'll ever calm my heart again. 'Get me home, would you?'

Wordlessly, Robyn starts the car and we begin to trundle back down the path.

'Joe's also in trouble. I've failed my son,' I say into the car's quiet interior. 'I just wasn't paying enough attention to see what was going on right under my nose. I've bought right into it: not asked the right questions, been too easily convinced and manoeuvred by both him and Drew – and now I'm paying the price.'

I cannot, cannot, cannot believe...

'You had faith in them. You believed in them.' Robyn swerves around a pothole. 'Those are good traits, Beth. The best. Don't beat yourself up for being a decent human being. Faith and belief, they'll get you through most things. That's what the teachings tell us, anyway.' She glances dubiously at me with a wry smile.

I hate Drew. I hate him with every fibre of my being.

'Do you believe all that?' I look across at her. 'Even now?

Will those beliefs save Melanie? How do they make Joe accountable?'

She doesn't speak for a second. 'Actually, yeah, they will. Belief that people can change – faith that they will.'

'Really?'

'Yeah, plus a bit of good old-fashioned confrontation and coercion. You know: faith, belief, stealth, lies, and strategy – the way all successful plans work.'

'I don't think your good Lord promoted those kinds of tactics though, did he?'

We bump down the last of the track to the main road. Her face looks pale and drawn. I can tell she's anxious but trying to buoy me up.

'No, he didn't.' She manages a smile at me over her shoulder. 'And look what happened to him.'

EIGHTEEN

She pulls up outside my house.

'Beth.'

I can barely function. I turn painful eyes to look at her.

'Can I ask...?' She nods towards my house.

'Nothing. Jaime helped me find Joe. That's all.' I don't have the energy.

'You're sure nothing—'

'Absolutely.'

Her face softens. 'So, what will you tell him?'

'All of it.'

'All of it?'

'I need him to know everything, Robyn. You asked me to trust you about Melanie; now you need to trust me.'

'Okay.' She glances up. Jaime is walking down the driveway as I get out of the car.

'God, I was so worried! You just drove off and then didn't answer the phone! What's going on?'

'Do you need me here?' Robyn flits a look from me to Jaime.

'No, it's fine. Can we go inside?'

Robyn nods, slipping the car into first. 'I'm going to the prison to do a bit of digging of my own.'

I see Jaime's reaction.

'I'll explain all when we get inside.'

I'm so tired I could lie down here on the drive. I put a hand on his arm that I know Robyn sees but I really don't care. I haven't even got over the threshold before the barrage of questions starts.

'Please, Jaime. I can barely think myself.' My head thuds. 'I met Melanie. Melanie is the girl I thought Drew was seeing.'

'Thought...? You mean, he's not?' Jaime closes the door behind us.

I almost can't believe the words I'm about to utter.

'Drew has been acting as an undercover cop trying to infiltrate that circle of traffickers – the ones at the house. He's using Melanie on the inside to keep tabs on what the traffickers are up to.'

Jaime blinks.

I press my eyes until the pain subsides. 'The traffickers got hold of Melanie through Leo. Melanie was Leo's girlfriend,' I explain, walking into the kitchen. 'And a drugs mule. As soon as she walked into the prison with the drugs, that gave them all the leverage they needed. Then my son "bumps" into her in a bar. He sells her some story about being a club organiser and got her to invite other young girls. Only, I think she was targeted. I think it was all a set-up. I think you're right: Tom Johnson and Michael Childs are in business together so that Childs can continue running his operation from inside prison. They've got Joe in as the young, fresh-faced recruiter to lure these girls into what they believe is a party scene. Leo was effectively murdered to prevent him from talking. They think his death will silence Melanie. It won't; it's made her bolder. She has more guts than anyone I've ever seen.'

Jaime is standing there, silent. Then he slowly pulls out a stool.

'My God.' He sits, resting his head against his fingertips. 'Your husband *knew*? Drew knew?'

I slump onto a stool opposite. '*Drew...*' Bile sits on my tongue and I swallow. '*Bought* Melanie from my son.'

'Bought?' He looks at me, horrified.

'Bought. As she said, *"like meat".*'

'But Joe will have been coerced. It's not like he's got involved of his own free will. This is Tom Johnson's doing,' Jaime says definitely. 'They're all kids, Beth. Johnson will have packaged it as something exciting and fun, and then slowly drawn them further and further in.' He nods sadly. 'That's how grooming works. An infinitesimal wearing away of boundaries. That's how sex offenders operate. Tom Johnson's no different.'

I raise my head. It feels like lead.

'Jaime, that's excusing my son.' I regard him levelly. 'He knows the difference between right and wrong. There was a line and he's chosen to cross it. Even if you're right, at some point he's gone from abused to abuser. He can't play the victim on that. He's going to have to be held accountable... But the problem is, Johnson is so credible. No one will believe my story. People *like* him, they trust him. He's got himself a niche where he's almost untouchable. With Drew involved, I'll never be able to prove it.'

'Yeah, yeah, I know,' Jaime sighs, rubbing his face wearily. 'All I know is, the most successful con artists are the ones you least suspect.'

'You suspected him.'

He half shrugs and then suddenly stops. 'You don't think—?'

'What?'

'No, no. It's too far-fetched.'

'What is?'

'I mean, doesn't all this feel like a bit of a coincidence to you?'

'Sorry, I'm not following.'

'Drew... I'm probably being a conspiracist here, but where are the police in all this? If Drew is part of some sting...' He hesitates, his finger drawing lines on the workbench. 'Melanie gets sold to Drew by Joe. Joe knew that Drew is a cop. Think about it.'

I blink. 'I don't get what you're saying.'

Jaime picks through his words carefully. 'Was Joe deliberately *recruited* by Drew?'

Whatever sickness was there before rises up in a great swell. I am up and out of the door, hands clutched to my mouth as I pound up the stairs. I only just make it to the bathroom where I hang over the toilet bowl heaving and heaving until there's nothing left but a bruised, dry ache.

I'm aware of the warmth of Jaime's hand between my shoulder blades. I sit back on my heels.

'Hell, you're as white as a sheet! You're in no fit state for any of this.' He winds off a roll of toilet paper and I blow my nose.

'You're saying that Drew...?' I'm unable to finish the sentence. 'Drew has specifically used Joe? That it's not Johnson who recruited him, but Drew?'

'Beth, I'm sorry, I shouldn't have spoken that out loud – it was thoughtless and unkind of me... Jeez! What was I thinking?'

'No, you were right to. You're saying Drew would use my son – expose him to all that danger and risk, so he could be the kingpin and set up a *sting*?'

'I'm talking crap. Ignore me. Honestly.'

But my head is buzzing with it now. I find my knees jacking unsteadily.

'Beth?'

I'm running the cold water, splashing my face, smoothing my hair back, reaching for my blusher and lipstick.

'What are you doing?'

'I'm going to do exactly what I said I was going to do – only I'm going to test my new theory.'

'What?' Jaime looks at me in the mirror, mortified. 'No, Beth, stop! What does that even mean?'

'I'm going to ask Drew to meet me.'

Jaime's whole face drops. 'Are you crazy?'

'Probably.'

'You can't! No... no, no, no!' Jaime half gets up with his hands raised. 'Seriously no. You can't. It's a crazy idea! What will you even say to him?'

'I'm going to ask him for the truth.' I set my jaw. 'Let's put him to the test. Let's confront him and see what comes out of the woodwork.'

'You're not thinking straight, Beth,' Jaime says calmly. 'This isn't a game; this isn't a joke! Sit down. Please!'

'Jaime' – I pause with the heels of my hands on the basin – 'listen to me. If you're right and Drew has deliberately involved Joe, then in my eyes he's worse than Tom Johnson, he's actually beyond a monster.' I feel the passion rise. 'He's taken my trust, my belief in him, and twisted it. Drew is acutely aware that I would never expose him if it meant hurting my own son. It's brilliantly manipulative. I'm tied into silence through fear – and fear forces us into colluding with the worst things imaginable.'

My head is pounding. *Drew, Drew, Drew.* 'If it's true, then he's been controlling me from the very beginning.'

Jaime's quiet for a moment. 'Okay, let me ask you something then.'

'Go on.'

'In your heart of hearts, do you think that's possible?'

My mind whirls back to Drew playing football with Joe in the yard, the pleasure on my mother's face; Drew and Joe hooting jokes across the dinner table, gaming together. *Was it all too good to be true?*

And was it ever the three of us? a voice in my head says. *Where were you in all this, Beth? You saw the private looks they shared across that same dinner table. Were those looks more meaningful than you thought?*

'Yes, it's possible, Jaime. In fact, looking back, it's much more than possible.'

'Then go ahead and use him.'

I stare into Jaime's certainty.

'You need to know the truth, Beth. You have a right to know. Front him out. Let him realise it's not all on his terms now. Your knowledge is your power.' He holds out his hand and I take it. He guides me back down the stairs. *I know what I'm about to do.* I feel the tension in my neck jag and pulse.

'And this Melanie girl? You think you can trust what she's told you?'

'That girl was terrified for her life, Jaime. She's out of her depth already. She's a kid knowing she's going to die.'

I push away the image of Joe's beaten, bloodied face.

'She came to me because I'm her last chance.'

'If you're sure.'

I nod.

'So, call Drew.'

I slowly pull out my phone, my fingers finding the number. It all feels alien; even the thought of seeing him again is alien.

I don't think he's going to answer, but then, 'Drew. Hi. It's me...'

'You got my note,' he says tentatively.

'Yes. Yes, I did. Can we talk?'

The line goes quiet for a moment. I find I am holding my breath.

'Sure. We can talk... I'd love to talk,' he says guardedly. 'When are you free?'

'Any time. You choose.'

'I'm on lates. I can meet you in half an hour if you like? I've got a couple of things to do. I'll text you, yeah?'

'Great. Perfect.' I glance up at Jaime, who nods his approval. I hear Drew take a breath.

'Hey, Beth? Umm… Are you okay?'

I bite my lip. 'I'm fine. See you soon.'

I end the call, aware of Jaime watching my every move as I look around for my car keys.

'Will you tell me everything he says?'

I pick up my jacket. 'Of course.'

But the fact is, I'm dreading what 'everything' might be.

By the time I get in the car, Drew had already sent a message. The sight of the café name fills me with sadness: it's the same one where Sarah and I used to meet. That life feels like a million years ago.

Finding a parking space, I walk quickly to the café entrance. It's quite busy with mums and babies now. The serving staff are bustling about. I sit in a seat facing the door, glancing up nervously every time it shunts wide. There's music going on in the background and the rise and fall of chattering laughter.

The waitress comes over. 'Did you need a few more minutes?'

'I think we're good, actually.' Drew appears in front of me, pulling out the chair. 'Two cappuccinos then?' He looks in playful query, dropping his phone and his keys onto the table.

'Thanks.' I glance up at the waitress. It's clear if he thinks this is a game, I'm really not playing.

I can tell by his body language, he's nervous. He sits, clasping his hands on the table and then unclasps them.

'Thanks for calling me. I can't lie, I've been checking my phone like crazy.' He absent-mindedly turns his phone over. Is he expecting a call?

He glances away and back to me.

'You need to know I would never cheat on you, Beth. Whatever you think you saw that night, you've got it all wrong.'

The bald audacity of the statement knocks the air out of me.

He opens his palms in a helpless gesture. 'How can I prove it to you?'

I swallow my fury down. *Prove it?*

'I want some information, Drew. I want to know everything that's gone on.'

His eyes flicker, but he looks at me calmly. He checks the tables next to us to see who could be listening.

'About Joe. I want to know about Joe.'

'Joe?' He hesitates. The two coffees appear, and we wait until the waitress moves away. 'Why? What's happened? Haven't you heard from him...? Is he okay?'

I'm deciphering every muscle movement, every tic.

He gives me a cautious sideways look. 'What's going on, Beth?'

Can I detect—? He doesn't appear to know. Is he that good a liar?

'Joe's disappeared.'

'What?' His body stops.

If the surprise is fake, then he's a better actor than I thought.

'The death of that boy Leo in the hospital and Joe disappearing. I want to know what you know.'

'I don't understand the connection, Beth... Joe's gone missing? What are you talking about? Why didn't you tell me?'

I'm desperately trying to read his face.

He glances a little to either side before leaning forward. 'Why are you asking me about the boy that died? And Joe? What's going on?'

I'm looking for 'tells'. I push it.

'The girl I saw you with.'

The corner of his mouth moves infinitesimally. It's enough.

'It's not what you think.'

'Then tell me what it is.'

'I can't.'

I lean in slightly. 'Drew. It's time.'

His eyes flit minutely, but he holds my gaze. I can feel it: he's teetering.

'What do you know about Tom Johnson?'

Suddenly I have his full attention.

'I have information on that little subject.' I drop the bomb. 'My question is: do you want it? Or would you like me to give it to someone else?'

The bomb explodes.

'Johnson? Joe? Suicides? What the hell is this, Beth?'

We had a marriage – or so I thought. We were meant to be a family. I smile grimly. I stare down into my coffee cup, not wanting him to see the tears that have gathered, stinging my eyes.

He goes to touch my hand, but I snatch it away. 'Don't.'

He withdraws but I can feel the steady pressure of his gaze.

'Beth, I'm being serious. You've got to tell me what you know. I'm not playing games here.'

Games. Oh my God.

I lean forward. 'Will you tell me the truth for once, Drew? No one's here, no one can hear us, you can deny the whole conversation. All I want is for you to be completely straight with me. From the beginning: Joe. Tell me.'

He looks at me, slightly panicked. 'I don't know what you're asking, Beth! I texted him. He hasn't replied to my messages – I thought he was just pissed off at the way I've treated you. I didn't know what you'd told him.'

I look up at him. 'And how have you treated me, Drew?' I bite my lip. 'You might as well give me the whole sorry story. I suspect I already know, but it would be good to hear you say the words. I think you owe me that much.'

The raking fingers stop. 'Right.' He settles himself, staring into the tabletop. 'I'm telling you this because whatever's been going on isn't going on now, right? I'm no longer involved. I'm burned already, okay?'

He drops his voice and I nod silently. 'From the beginning then: I'd been told there was a Special Ops up for grabs. We weren't told what it was. Hand on heart, I didn't know the detail. I thought it could be analysing some of the paedo chatroom intel, or crap like that.'

'But it wasn't, was it?' I look at him, unflinching.

'No. No it wasn't.'

'Go on. All of it.'

His lips work agitatedly. 'They wanted me to pose as a punter to infiltrate a trafficking gang. I said I wouldn't do it. Like, I nearly came and told you straight out, there and then – but once I heard there were young girls involved, I couldn't walk away. If I'd told you what they were asking me to do, what would you have said?'

I don't answer.

'Exactly.'

'I knew of all the guys on the team; I was the best person for the job. I knew, given a break, I could crack it.'

I drop my eyes to the handle of my cup.

'I got them to sell a girl to me.'

'Who sold her to you?' My heart is in the back of my throat.

'You don't deal with actual people. They're too smart for that. The transactions are made and you never know with who.'

I don't move my head. 'And did you have sex with her?'

'I did not.' His voice is flat and unemotional.

My gaze tracks across the table to where his elbow is resting. The queasy sensation in my stomach turns to a churning wash. I swallow it down.

'And you didn't think they would find that weird?'

Drew looks away. 'I had a cover identity for them to check

what I was "into".' He gives me a look and then pushes his hair back as he leans away. 'This makes me feel ill just telling you!'

But I'm not letting him off. 'You had a cover identity,' I press.

'The cover ID was a man that just wants to talk.' He twitches. 'At first.'

My blood turns icy.

'But she wasn't sold to me as "exclusive". I wanted a girl who would lead me to others who were involved. I found out she was going to that party at a house where there would be other "interested individuals". I was scared what might happen to her. I went along to find out who she was set up to talk to *and* to protect her.'

'Protect your asset.'

He puts his head on one side. 'If you want to see it like that, then yeah.'

'You saw Joe there?'

'*Joe?*' His neck jerks back in alarm.

I look up and stare him straight in the eye. 'Did you involve my son in this?'

He instantly recoils. 'Beth!' He's aghast. 'No, I did not. I definitely did not! Joe was at that party? Are you sure?'

'He was in the street with some young guys. I saw him.'

Drew leans in. 'You have to believe me, Beth, if I'd even got a suspicion of Joe being part of this, I would have come to you. Even if I thought you hated my guts, I would have found a way. You've got to believe that, even if you never trust another word I say.'

I fight my anger down, holding it tight.

'So you say you got burned? They discovered you. How – what happened?'

His face changes, withdrawing a little. 'Beth, I can't—'

'I need to know. No matter how awful, I want to hear it.

What do you know about that house where they're trafficking the girls?'

It's a test, but the test pays off. He blanches. 'You know about the house?'

'I've been there.'

'*What?*' His face goes from shock to fright. 'You've *been* there?' He begins to stumble. 'But you can't have! We'd know – I'd know.'

'Clearly you didn't. Or if you did, you're lying.'

He ignores the barb. 'We got a lead from a trafficker chatroom. Some bright spark discovered a link to a girl who'd disappeared. She'd been victim of abuse, not once but three times, by different people. The only way that could happen is if the offenders themselves were sharing information. Hence us coming into the prison.'

I regard him, puzzled. 'But you interviewed Leo Hargreaves?'

'Amongst others, yes.' He nods.

'But Leo wasn't a sex offender.'

'But we knew his girlfriend was a victim.'

I find myself staring at him, my brain scrambling.

'She was our way in. Hence me posing as a punter. Hence us finding the place where the girls were being kept, and hence the surveillance team. And how we know – or at least I *thought* we knew' – he gives me a look – 'all the people who came and went.'

'So you must've seen Joe? You must have!' I urge. 'Someone must've seen me. I was there!'

But Drew only frowns, shaking his head, but I see his jaw tighten. 'Things in the police are never that straightforward, particularly when it involves vice and money and that includes surveillance footage. The truth is, I have no idea who is taking a backhander and who isn't.' He looks away angrily. 'You have to trust the people you work with not to "lose" videotapes. But when you find things mysteriously get mislaid and you mention it to your superior...' He hesitates. 'You suddenly find there is no viable case now with the excuse that you've been "burned" and the powers-that-be can't make it stick.'

'And Melanie?' I can't keep the note of bitterness and disgust from my voice. 'What did you offer her after you'd done all your "courting"?'

'Zero,' he says dully. 'She gave us zero, so we gave her zero in return. The powers that be said that I'd been sussed, and I was being played.'

Clever girl. I feel a tremble of relief. Melanie's given nothing to either side.

'The whole thing is like a knotted ball of wool, Beth. It's all there, but no one can find the end to unravel it.' I find him studying me. 'But Joe. Tell me what's going on with Joe.'

I take a breath. 'He met Melanie in a bar – don't ask me if it was by accident or on purpose, because I have no idea. He spun her some story about setting up music gigs and parties. She thought it would be exciting.'

'And then?'

'And then you know the rest. She was supposed to bring in the girls who are easy targets, but when she discovered what was really going on, she tried to pull out. That was the incident you got on CCTV of the van on the motorway.'

Drew looks incredulous. 'That was Joe? That was Melanie?'

'They threatened her – Joe threatened her. That's how she ended up being sold. She was supposed to find out what you know, but now she's failed at that as well. The girl is in serious danger.'

Drew sits back in his seat and folds his arms. I can see his brain working.

'So, there's your thread.' I regard him coolly.

He looks up at me.

'It's right there under your nose. The end of your thread is

Melanie.'

'What?'

'She's the hook to get you into the knot.'

'I don't understand.' He looks at me quizzically. 'Melanie wouldn't give me anything, we've already established that.'

'But she'll give it to me.' I play him to see his reaction.

I can see he knows something else is coming.

'However, I want three things in return.'

'Go on.' He almost looks bemused.

'I want a safehouse for Melanie in the short term, and the price of a ticket far away from here. I want her to have a new life.'

'But what has she got really? What can she give me as proof of anything?'

'Her testimony,' I say boldly. I have no idea if this is true. 'She knows the names of the girls in that house, she knows how the names were obtained, you can cross-reference them to the files in the prison. She'll tell you about the drugs and about Leo Hargreaves. You can use me too.' I immediately think of Jaime. *Would he be prepared to talk?*

Drew's eyes are on me. 'Some bit of a girl like Melanie and a bunch of douchebags from convict college are going to pit themselves against the force of a whole police sting? You think?'

I let seconds pass before I drop the real bombshell. 'A bit of a girl and some douchebags – as you call them – plus the investigative journalist I called.'

I watch the momentary flicker of alarm on Drew's face as he debates whether to believe me. My gaze remains steady. I need him to think this is the truth.

'You said three things.' His face is expressionless. I inwardly relax.

'When you make your arrests, you keep Joe out of it.'

Drew chews his cheek. 'I thought you said Joe threatened Melanie?'

I swallow. 'He did and I want him punished for it.'

'And you think he's involved in procuring those girls?'

'I do, and I want him to pay the price for all the things he's done, but Drew, look at me. You know what happens to kids like Joe who end up inside. He's not a strong enough personality to survive it. He'll come out battered by the system, or maybe he won't even survive.' The thought nearly takes the breath from my body.

'You know this, Drew, you've seen it, we both have. Prison reinforces all that brutality and misogyny he's exhibiting.' My voice crumples at the thought that I'm talking about my own child. 'And challenges none of it. I *want* Joe confronted. I *want* Joe to own it. I don't want him thinking he's got away with exploiting people. You'll have contacts on the Youth Offending Team, Drew. There are other options – I don't know, specialised units, therapeutic environments... Something, anything, other than him mixing with people like Johnson, like Childs, who'll feed his contempt for other human beings.'

'I can't promise you anything, Beth, but I'll do my very best. I promise.'

'We'll see then.'

Drew takes a breath. 'So now what? Now you know the whole truth; now you know I wasn't cheating on you...' He hesitates again. 'What about getting what we need out of Melanie?'

I think about the note he left. How easily his words have been forgotten.

'I need to see the proof that you'll keep your end of the bargain first.'

'Proof? How can I prove it?'

'You said it, Drew, "everyone's playing someone". I just want to see if you really care enough about those girls to do the right thing now. I mean *care*, not in here—' My finger taps my temple. 'But in here' – I put my hand on my heart – 'where it actually counts. So go to your bosses, go to the newspapers.

Don't think about the personal cost to you. Do the right thing and find a way to expose this atrocity.'

I know what he wants to say. He wants to give me the police officer's spiel about *this is the way the world works. You'll never stop it. Take this lot of filth off the street and another lot will just take their place.* But he doesn't.

'But what about us?'

My eyes flit across his face.

I see it. I see it all. I see what he's doing.

'Is this you making another kind of deal, Drew?' I ask stonily.

The veil of scales has fallen from my eyes. I feel as though I've been sleepwalking and I've suddenly woken up.

'I let you come back home, and in return you'll expose Johnson and protect Joe from prison. Is that it now?'

His expression is unreadable. I hold his gaze.

'Is that the kind of man you always were, and I just couldn't see it? Or is this the man you've become?'

He doesn't answer.

'You come back to me after you've spoken to your superiors about a deal for Melanie, and I'll give you everything, and everyone you need.' I speak clearly: very concise, and very deliberate.

Drew picks up his cup and swallows the contents in two gulps, shoving his hand into his pocket and chucking the money for the drinks onto the table. I watch him as I would watch a stranger.

'Thank you for your time,' he says, scraping his chair back and standing. 'It was very useful.'

He swings his jacket up over his shoulder. There's a blast of cold air from the door as he bats it wide. He walks quickly past the window and crosses the road.

Was that it then? Is that the end of a marriage?

'Leaving so soon?'

My eyes snatch round.

'I was passing and saw you.' Sarah is standing there. Nate is hunched furtively behind, not knowing where to put himself. 'Was that Drew storming out? I have to say, he didn't look very happy.'

'No. No, he's not.'

'I've left messages.' She pulls out a chair, forcing me to sit back down.

'Have you?'

'I guess you've been a bit preoccupied.' She gestures a chair to Nate. 'I might as well tell you, I called at your house about twenty minutes ago. It was a bit of a shock when your new friend answered the door.'

My stomach plummets.

'I didn't stay long as Nate was waiting in the car.' She looks at him. If the boy could make himself smaller, he'd be folded in two.

'Your friend's chatty, isn't he?' She puts her head on one side. 'It looks as though things have got a bit complicated – with Drew, I mean.'

'Sarah...' I glance at Nate. His eyes are glued to the table.

'There's no need.'

I think she's about to give me a hard time, but then her face changes.

'Fact is, in spite of it all, whatever "it all" is... Let's face it, Beth, nothing in your life has ever been straightforward, has it?' The ghost of a smile plays in the corner of her lips. 'The truth is, I've missed you.'

My throat instantly closes. I can't afford to cry. I don't have the capacity right now; if I start crying, I might never stop.

'I need a friend, Sarah.' I bite my top lip. I glance at Nate. 'I could really do with you on my side, but I need to be blatantly open with you.' My eyes glide over Nate and back to Sarah. *Will he come clean about him and Joe?*

'I should have told you the truth from the get-go, Sarah. But I panicked.'

'I get that.' She pauses. 'That's what I came round to say, really. I think the three of us need to have a conversation, don't you?'

Nate clearly isn't prepared to look at either of us. Sarah gives him an encouraging smile and I ready myself.

'Nate.' I stretch a tentative hand forward on the table. 'I can't tell you how good it is to see you.'

He stares resolutely down.

'This is the first time he's agreed to leave the house.' Sarah catches my eye. 'He's been too frightened.'

'But not now?'

I look at her, but she only offers a pointed shrug.

'Have you heard from Joe, Nate?'

'I'm not sure he wants to,' Sarah puts in sharply.

Nate won't lift his head. His mouth is set in a childish pout. *I know he knows.*

'No, no, I understand that.' I'm trying to keep my voice level. 'But *whatever* has gone on, Nate, and whatever you're worried about, it must be better that we know where Joe is – for everyone's sake.'

I deliberately keep my voice low and unchallenging. 'I know what Joe was involved in.' His eye twitches. 'I know what's been going on.' Nate shifts awkwardly in his seat but still won't raise his head.

'You're not in trouble, Nate. You walked away,' soothes Sarah. 'Thank God.'

I swallow the implied criticism.

'I've been talking to some of the people involved, Nate. And I've been talking to Drew – you know he's in the police, yeah?'

Nate's shoulders flinch.

'So, I'm asking if you'd help me, Nate. If you know anything, *anything* that could tell me Joe's whereabouts, I'd be grateful, so grateful that I wouldn't mention your name at all in connection with any of it – not the holiday, not the airport, not *anything*.'

Sarah snaps a look at me, frowning. 'He would, I'm sure he would, if he could tell you, Beth, then he'd—'

'He's moving them.'

We both stop in shock.

'What do you mean, moving them? Moving who?' Sarah pounces immediately, but I hold up a pacifying hand.

'Do you mean the girls, Nate? You say he's moving them, yes? From the place he's got them?'

'What the hell are you talking about?' Sarah's eyes widen in horror. 'What girls? What's he talking about?' Sarah looks at me, then at her son. 'You told me Joe was dealing! You said *dealing*, Nate. *You* said...' She can't find the words.

Nate shrinks further and further down until his head is practically touching the table.

'It's not like I... I didn't... We didn't... It was only s'posed to be a laugh!' he stutters.

I can see Sarah's face going from white to pink. Her mouth works with anger.

I catch her eye, shaking my head. 'Sarah,' I murmur in quiet warning. 'Sarah.'

Her spine is ramrod straight as the waitress moves in to clear the table.

'Any more drinks here? Tea, coffee?'

'I need a real drink, that's what I need,' Sarah mutters viciously. The waitress scuttles away.

'Nate,' I whisper as gently as possible. 'This is really, really important. I need to ask you this – and this isn't me doubting one word of what you're saying. How do you know what Joe's doing?'

'Yes! Exactly! How—' Sarah interjects but I widen my eyes dramatically.

Nate can barely get the words out. 'He... He keeps wanting me to help him.'

There's an instant chill.

'Help him?'

'He messed up.' He shoots Sarah a glance. 'Not long ago. Like, big time. He thought they were going to kill him. He's scared it's going to happen again.'

I'm aware of Sarah's white face in my peripheral vision.

'What did he do, Nate?' I keep my tone measured and steady.

'One of the girls tried to leave. Joe was supposed to stop her.'

'They? Who's they? And leaving? Leaving what?' Sarah interrupts.

'But she got away and then he was really in trouble. He said they got hold of him, and...'

I don't want to imagine what he's been through. The image of Joe's swollen bloody face comes back to me. 'They beat him up,' I say slowly. 'Badly.'

Nate nods quickly. 'I think so, yeah.'

'There's a gang, a group. They're working young girls,' I explain. Sarah's shocked face rounds on Nate, but I put a quietening hand on her arm.

'Did Joe... Does Joe want out, Nate?' I ask gently. 'Is that what he was wanting? He contacted you because he wanted somewhere safe to go?'

For the first time, Nate manages a glance at his mother. 'I said I couldn't. I said I couldn't help him.'

Sarah looks at him and then at me, absolutely appalled. 'If I'd known, Beth! If Nate had come to me, I would've done something to help Joe. I really, honestly would. I'd've told you!'

'You said you'd go to straight to the cops about Joe if he contacted me again.' Nate scowls. 'That's what you kept banging on about!'

Sarah colours but I quickly shake my head. 'None of that matters now. Nothing matters. All I want is to get Joe out of there and I want to help those girls.'

'Help? They don't want your help,' Nate says gruffly. 'They don't want help from no one. They're doin' alright.'

Sarah and I both stare at him.

'It's Joe who's in trouble. He knows the cops are going in there. They're gonna do a raid. He's got to get the girls out tonight before it all kicks off.'

My look of disbelief pulls back. 'Tonight? The police are going in tonight? How does he know that?'

But Nate only shifts uncomfortably. I'm guessing he knows more than he's letting on, but he's not going to tell me.

Sarah looks at me in dumb horror, but all I can feel is gratitude.

'Thank you. Both of you.' I look from one to the other. 'I can't tell you what this means.' I push my chair back.

'What are you going to do?' Nate's head jerks back in alarm. He's clearly beyond terrified. 'Please don't drop me in it! I don't think you get who these people are.'

'Don't worry, Nate. I said I'll keep you out of it and I will.'

'The police, though. You're not—?'

'I'm not going to do anything that leads anyone back to you.' I put a reassuring hand on his shoulder. 'You've got my word for that.'

I bend to pick up my bag. 'Sarah, you and me, yes? We'll go out somewhere, soon. When this madness is over.'

She lifts her face, but it's full of terror. 'Please, Beth. Tell me what's happening? I'm scared for you – and Joe. Let us know he's alright.'

I take her outstretched hand, feeling the warmth, and give it a squeeze.

'He's going to be alright. It's all going to be alright. I'm going to make sure of it.'

NINETEEN

'What did Drew say?'

Jaime is waiting for me as I step into the hallway.

'Does he know anything? What did he tell you?'

He follows me around the house as I move from one room to another. I'm completely distracted; I don't know where to put myself. I go from the living room to the kitchen and back again.

'It's not just what he said. I've been trying to get hold of Robyn all the way home, but it just goes to voicemail. I don't know what the hell she's—'

'Can you stop walking around, Beth? Just stop and tell me what was said.'

'It's not just Drew, it's who else turned up. Sarah. My friend Sarah.' I slump on the arm of the sofa. 'The woman who came here. The one you spoke to.'

'Ah.' He frowns.

'She brought her son Nate with her. Joe's mate.'

Jaime sinks slowly onto the chair opposite. 'Go on.'

I wave tiredly. 'Drew and his lot have known all along about the girls in that house. They've had a surveillance operation in progress the whole time.' I can't quite get my head around it. 'But they've decided to shut down the operation. So basically, Melanie was telling the truth: she's given them nothing. Drew absolutely swears he hasn't seen Joe coming or going from that house and he isn't on any of the footage.'

'And do you believe him?'

I lift my head. 'Yes, I do actually. I've told him I'll do a deal. I'm sure I can persuade Melanie to talk. I've told Drew he has to guarantee her safety if she agrees to give evidence.'

'Wow!' Jaime pulls a wry face. 'You *have* been busy!'

'He still tried to manipulate me though. Can you believe that? He still tried to hint that he'd protect Joe if I agree to get back together with him.'

Jaime goes very still.

'And guess what else? Drew had no clue I had been in that house. He says he can't trust his police colleagues. The footage from the surveillance could have been doctored.'

'And so they turn off the cameras.' Jaime breathes out, exasperated. 'Of course they do. If they're taking a bung, why wouldn't they?'

'But here's the thing.' I lean forward. 'It was Sarah's son Nate who gave me the best news. Joe has been in contact with him. Joe's clearly in trouble and wants out, only Nate said he couldn't help him. Joe is terrified. He needs to get the girls moved because he's had a tip-off that the police are going to do a raid on the place.'

'Jeez! When?'

'Tonight.'

'Tonight?'

'Although what's weird is if the surveillance op has been withdrawn, why would the cops be talking about organising a raid? It doesn't make sense.'

'That's true... do you think Nate could be lying?'

'He could be. Or Joe's been fed misinformation, or got it

wrong, or is plain panicking. There's no real way to find out.'
My brain is running riot. 'Hang on. Wait there.'

Jaime's eyes are on me as I dash from the room. 'Where are you going?'

But I'm already halfway up the stairs.

'Beth?'

'Melanie...'

'What?'

'Give me a hand, will you?'

Jaime is stumbling up the stairs behind me as I push open Joe's bedroom door.

'Here, you're taller than me, save me getting a stool.' I point to the top of the door. 'Feel along there until you come to a gap in the wood.'

Jaime looks at me, puzzled, running his fingers along the edge. 'What am I looking for?'

'A secret phone. It's Drew's. This is where he keeps it, though I don't know if he put it back. It's how I found out about Melanie in the first place. Only when I threw all his stuff out, I sort of forgot to throw it out too.' I give him a wry smile.

'Hang on, there is something here.'

'Brilliant! Brilliant!' I take the phone and, finding Melanie's number, I message:

> So whose side are you on tonight, Melanie?

'She'll think this is from Drew,' I say to Jaime. 'How she responds will be very telling: does she know about the raid? What's he told her? Let's see, shall we?'

I press 'Send' and look at Jaime just as my own phone suddenly jangles into ringing.

'*Melanie,*' I mouth to Jaime.

'Hi, Melanie, how—' But that's as far as I get as her voice breaks into a frightened sobbing.

'Who have you been talking to?' she hisses.

'What?'

'Someone's grassed me!' she shrieks. 'You said you'd help me! You promised!'

'Melanie. Slow down. What's happened?'

But she's really starting to cry now. 'You bitch! You bitch! I knew I couldn't trust you. You've talked to Drew, haven't you? I told you what they'd do to me! *Oh God!*'

'Melanie!' I nearly shout. 'Melanie, stop! It was me!'

The sobbing falters. 'What was you?'

'You got a text, didn't you?'

There's a silence.

'You just got a text from Drew. But it wasn't Drew, it was me. I sent it. Melanie? Are you still there?'

'Yeah.'

Relief runs through me. 'I was told that the girls are being moved because of a police raid. Is that right? I've spoken to Drew – he told me the police presence has been pulled, but then I get information that there's going to be a raid. It didn't add up.'

'Yeah, I made that up,' she says in a tiny voice. 'I told Joe there was a raid. I have to get out of there; I needed a cover. I needed him distracted to give me a chance to get away. That was all I could think of. If he's concentrating on shifting the girls, he's not watching me.'

'Right. Right. Okay.' I shoot Jaime a look. 'Let me think, Melanie. Let me think about how I can use this to our advantage. So, no one else knows about this "raid", yes? Just you and Joe? He hasn't told anyone?'

'I told him they want him to handle it on his own. Show how capable he is.'

'What time have you said it's happening?'

'One – one o' clock in the morning.'

'So, I'm getting you out of there at midnight.'

'Wha—?'

'I'm getting you out.' I'm avoiding Jaime's eyes. 'I'll be there. There's an alleyway at the side of the house. So I'll be waiting for you at midnight, yes? You've told me you can't trust anyone, but you can trust me, Melanie. I'm offering you your one chance to get out for good. Take it.'

She goes quiet.

'Okay?' I insist.

'Okay?' she says finally. 'You have to show up, Beth. You can't let me down.'

'I won't.'

Jaime stares at me as I end the call.

'Jaime, I need you to do something, too. I need you to organise a vehicle.'

His face says it all. 'I can't believe you're doing this.'

'Jaime...' I warn.

'What kind of vehicle?'

'One that will take five girls in the back.'

'What! You're actually serious about this?'

'Absolutely.' I have never felt more serious in my life.

'You've done it then,' he says simply. 'You've rolled the dice.'

'Only I'm loading the dice in my favour.' I start down the stairs. 'Can you get transport organised for me?'

'You think you're doing this thing by yourself?'

I stop and turn. 'Look, I understand you're scared for me, but you have to think this thing through too. You're only days out of prison, you're on parole, and you've done so much already. There is absolutely no way you can afford to get involved in something that might go wrong.'

'And that's precisely the reason why I'm not letting you walk into this thing alone. This isn't up for discussion, Beth.' He regards me steadily. 'It really isn't.' Now is not the time to start arguing.

'I need to get hold of Robyn.'

'If you give me your credit card, I'll sort out the vehicle.'

I fish it from my bag, handing it over. He goes to take it.

'You will take care, won't you?' His worried eyes search mine. 'You've got such a fire in your belly.' He falters. 'I want you to know it was your fire and belief in me that changed my life. Everything altered that day you walked into that prison. That talk you gave. You said, "Whatever you're facing, I'm here to face it with you." It spoke to something in me. A bit I thought had died. The one remaining good bit.'

'Honestly, Jaime—'

But he stops me with a gentle touch on the back of my hand. 'So now it's my turn to say it.' I can't meet the tenderness in his eyes. 'Believe me, Beth, whatever you're facing right now, I'm here to face it with you.'

TWENTY

I drive all the way to the prison in a kind of mute daze.

I know what's just happened, and I also know I can't let it. I've kept focussed and I've kept myself guarded. I try to block the memory.

Stop this.

The only thing that matters is Joe.

I've come so far. I've changed so much.

Robyn was right: faith and belief are a kind of salvation. Somehow, my faith and belief in Jaime have taken his anger and hatred for the world and transformed them for the good. I couldn't help Joe's father, Simon, but I've helped Jaime. And now I'll do the same to help my son.

The world beyond this car's bubble looks ordinary, but in that ordinariness lurks a darkness that I don't want to peer into. Terrible thoughts keep hovering like wraiths in the corner of my mind.

I imagine him on the bank of that motorway with his hands around a girl's throat.

Did he really do that? Did my son actually do that?

He did, he did, he did.

I hold on to anger: the absolute molten rage. He was a sad kid looking for a father; he was a boy wanting to be a man. If he's become this person, then someone led him there.

Walking quickly through the main doors of the prison, I book in at the front desk.

'Oh hiya! How's it going?' An officer coming out of the gatehouse is smiling at me, and I realise it's the same guy who saw me bursting into tears.

'Need to hitch a ride?' He thumbs over to the main prison block.

'If you're going towards the chapel?'

'Sure.' He nods to the gate staff, unlocking the gate for me to go through.

'I promise not to blub all over you.' I try to keep my voice light. I snatch a glance around. *The thought of bumping into Johnson...*

'Look, we all have those kinds of days sometimes.' He rolls his eyes. 'I'm having one today, actually.'

'Right. Right.' We skirt the perimeter fence.

'Yeah, some days you get the feeling everyone's heading blindly straight into a great pile of crap – no matter how much you tell them politely that maybe they should take their blindfolds off, nobody wants to.'

But I'm barely listening. All I need is to see Robyn. I'm going to have to explain what's happening tonight. She's going to try and talk me out of it. She'll be right: I have absolutely no idea what I'm doing. I know I'm walking into something I have no control over. It's madness. If it goes wrong, then—

The sound of voices in the distance catches my attention.

'Ohh! What was I just saying?' the officer sing-songs, exasperated. 'And there we have it: all in real 4K resolution.'

I see a group of prisoners being escorted along the walkway. My eyes scan the movement of them; there's a visceral tremor of something that my eyes notice before my brain catches up and makes the connection.

Michael Childs.

In that same split-second, I see another face I recognise.

The charity worker, Madeleine.

We pause to let them go on ahead.

'I blame your chaplain friend, frankly.'

We watch as they head towards the chapel.

'Look at that lot! Happy little ducklings, aren't they?' the officer sneers sarcastically. 'Off to some cosy meeting to be royally duped by Childs.'

Madeleine lifts a hand in greeting as she spots me and then Childs says something to her that I can't hear, and she laughs at his joke.

'Where's Childs going?'

'That woman's from a charity, isn't she? Someone said she's to do with safeguarding girls. Lord!' The officer blows his cheeks out. 'If she really wanted to safeguard kids, she'd keep the hell away from him!'

'Who's organised it? You're saying it was Robyn?' But the officer only shrugs.

'Who knows? Probably another of these fantastic la-la-land initiatives from the governor. You know what he's like: thinks it would be brilliant if Childs and others like him are "confronted" with the real-life consequences of their offences – so he's asked this woman in to talk to them so they can all pretend like they've had some "seen the light" moment.' The officer closes his eyes wearily. 'Anyway, you wanted the chapel too, didn't you? Are you sure you want to be in there with that lot?'

I'm like a rabbit caught in a snare.

'Sor-Sorry!' I stumble. 'No. Actually, there's someone... somewhere I need to go first... Thanks... Thanks.' And I turn towards the admin block, hurrying towards the governor's office.

The governor's secretary, Zoe, is standing with a whole lot of files poised in her hand.

'I don't see you for ages and now you're here all the time!' She laughs.

'Is he in?' I'm breathless and she gives me a concerned look.

'You okay?' She frowns. 'Has something happened?'

'I just need to speak to Geoff – the governor,' I add hastily. 'It's kind of urgent.'

She drops the files onto the desk. 'Hang on.' She squeezes my arm as she passes. 'He was just on a call, but let me see.'

She taps his door, pushing it open and poking her head into the gap. She says something I don't hear and stands back, nodding at me to go in.

'Beth! What a surprise.' The governor is standing by the window with his phone in his hand. He waves me towards the sofa, but I hesitate.

'It's Childs,' I blurt.

'Ah... Oh yes! What about him?'

'I've made a terrible mistake.'

The governor looks bemused. 'What kind of mistake? Are you sure you won't sit down?'

'Childs should not be on normal location! I should never have suggested it. He should not be having visitors from professional organisations – particularly ones to do with young girls. I've got it all wrong!'

His expression turns to thinly disguised amusement. 'No... please, Beth, don't worry yourself. He's doing really well – and it's true, that's mostly down to your compelling persuasion.'

'You need to stop his access to everything.'

'Although, I have to say, I was a tad nervous at first!' he says as though I haven't spoken. 'But I'm so glad I agreed. I was just this second talking to the area manager about this very subject. The fact is, it's opened up a whole new range of initiatives with the more –shall we say – problematic high-profile offenders.' He wrinkles his nose. 'It's so difficult balancing public perceptions of sex offenders and rehabilitation programmes. But I'm really hoping that Madeleine Grainger coming in to speak with him will smooth that for us.'

'You need to know what's really going on, Geoff,' I say forcefully. 'I have evidence that one of your principal officers is using all these charitable organisations as a cover.'

'A cover?' He nearly laughs.

'Please, take this seriously.'

He attempts to straighten his face. 'A cover for what, Beth? Who are we talking about here?'

'Tom Johnson.' I know I'm trembling. I can't stop myself. 'Tom Johnson is coercing vulnerable prisoners to have drugs brought in. He's using young girls as drug mules. The girls are specifically targeted: chosen from sex offender files. It makes them more malleable. They're easier to groom because of what they've been subjected to.'

But the governor stops me with both palms held aloft and purses his lips. He's clearly not amused now. 'Look, I'm sorry, Beth. I really am sorry, but I'm going to have to call a halt to all this. I don't know what you've heard or who you've been talking to.' He twitches in irritation. 'These are pretty serious accusations to bandy about, and I think we need to be really careful about what we're saying here. These kinds of things can spiral, and people can end up losing their jobs if we're not really, really careful.'

'You've got charity workers talking to the sex offenders. That charity has access to millions of vulnerable young women —' I start.

'And?' he queries. 'What are we saying here? That their staff aren't capable of handling delicate situations? These are *professionals*, Beth!' he impresses sternly. 'Not a bunch of part-time volunteers.' The message is loud and clear. 'It's a brilliant initiative. Prisoners who have committed sexual offences are confronted with the impact of their offending. It's absolutely groundbreaking for the rehabilitation process!'

'But Tom Johnson is *grooming* the charity's staff to get information!' I can hear my voice: it sounds shrill and over-the-top. 'Those sex offenders are *grooming* Madeleine Grainger *right now!*'

But the governor only gives me a sideways look. 'Tom Johnson? Tom knows all about how sex offenders operate, believe you me. He's been instrumental in guiding all the rehabilitation programmes throughout the prison. He's very well informed, you know. You are aware he was awarded Prison Officer of the Year last year?'

'I can *prove* it. I can *prove* what he's doing.'

But the governor has taken a step towards me. His open hand is gesturing towards the door.

'Gosh, I'm so sorry, Beth, I've got another really important call from Area Office booked.' He glances at his watch. 'I've heard your concerns, and thank you so much for bringing them to my attention. It's great that you feel so relaxed that you can come to me with this kind of stuff. Demonstrates that my management style is working. Very useful. Very useful indeed.'

I'm aware that I'm being corralled towards the door.

'Robyn will back me up,' I say defensively.

'That's great. That's really great – but I think you'll find it's Robyn who's been mentoring Tom in the rehab work.' He flickers a smile.

'*Was*. She *was* mentoring—'

'Thanks, Beth.' The governor reaches for the door handle. 'Thanks so much for popping in. See you soon.'

And with that I find myself standing back in the corridor.

'Everything okay?' Zoe peers up at me over her computer screen. 'All sorted?' She smiles as her desk phone bursts into a violent trilling. She holds up a finger as she answers it and then her eyes flit wide in surprise.

'Oh yes! Yes, she is actually! Hang on.' She flashes me a concerned look. 'It's the Comms Room. They've been trying to find you. It's Robyn.'

'Oh?' I take the receiver, my heart feeling slightly anxious. 'Hello?'

'It's me.' Robyn sounds like she's been running. 'Can you get yourself down to the gate?'

'What? Why?'

'It's Jaime. He's outside the prison.' She sounds scared. I've never heard Robyn sound scared before. 'He's been trying to get hold of you. He says there's a problem.'

'What kind of problem?'

'I don't know. His phone signal kept breaking up because of the jammers.'

'What's he told you?'

'Nothing. He said you'd explain. I'll come and meet you. What's going on, Beth?'

Without a second glance, I hurry back through Admin, finding Robyn on the lower concourse waiting for me. She ushers me into the gatehouse.

'Is it about Joe?' I pant. 'Has something happened? Is it to do with the girls?' I can feel myself spiralling.

'What the hell is going on?' She stands looking perplexed as the security doors swish open.

'I haven't got time to tell you. I'll call you, yes?' I desperately scan the car park. 'Look, there he is, over there.' A set of head-lights flash on and off.

'Wait!' Robyn grabs my arm. 'Should I come with you? I don't want to leave you like this. Something tells me something bad is going to happen.'

'No, no, honestly thanks, Robyn. For everything.'

She hasn't let go of my arm. She grips me suddenly, pulling me forward and I'm wrapped in the warmth of a bearhug.

'You look after yourself. And you call me, right?' she says sternly. 'Promise?'

'Yes, promise. Promise.'

'Okay, go on then, you'd better go.' She releases me, raising a hand to Jaime.

It's getting dark and has started to rain. Running across the tarmac, I see a large people carrier parked up. Its lights blind me, the rain slanting in long needles as I clamber into the passenger side. Jaime is behind the wheel looking anxious.

I don't get a chance to speak before he's hauling the wheel round, slamming through the gears and we begin to pick up speed.

'What's going on? Is it Joe?'

His face is greeny-grey in the weird light.

'He's been attacked.'

'*Attacked!* What? By whom? Wh-What do you mean? Is he hurt?'

But Jaime only shakes his head. 'That's it. That's all I know. Seriously. I don't know who or how, or the circumstances.' He stares into the road ahead. 'I didn't wait to ask questions. I thought we should just get there.'

'Oh my God!' I fumble for my phone. 'I need to call Melanie.'

'Don't!' His eyes flash in the grey light. 'You don't know who's behind it; you might make the situation worse. Let's find out first.'

The phone trembles in my hand. I don't know what speed we're doing but the vehicle swings violently as we make corners far too fast, slewing from lane to lane.

'Hold on, we'll be there in minutes. Literally minutes.'

I glance up. The street comes into view. Craning forward in my seat, I desperately look for the house, scouring it wildly for commotion: shouting, or lights, or signs of any disturbance. But it's all quiet.

'This is it. This is this one.' I point fearfully, but Jaime has already driven past the house and has pulled up at the end of the alleyway. He dips his head, peering up at the houses opposite. 'If there's still police around, they'll be watching. Here – get out this side.' He opens the driver's door. 'We're really close to the wall here; no one will see us.'

I climb over the seats to where the darkness pools thickly onto the pavement and slip quietly into the shadows. We slide into the alley; Jaime leads the way. It's so black I can barely see his outline, his feet treading quickly to where the backs of the houses begin.

The yard lies silent. The same gauzy light glows from behind the dirty curtains. Jaime looks back questioningly and I give a quick nod. He creeps softly towards the door, gently turning the door handle. The gap eases wide. There, standing in the filthy kitchen, is Melanie. She looks tiny and lost amidst the broken furniture. Her face is a white moon framed by a matted tangle of bloodied hair.

I push past Jaime. 'Melanie!' I grab her. 'Melanie! What's happened? Are you hurt? Where's Joe?'

She looks at me as though she's been drugged. Her hand clutches at my arm and in shock I see it's covered with blood. 'Where... where?' My hands check her over frantically, but she only stands, swaying a little, her head moving slowly, her eyes slipping sideways towards the door to the open hallway.

Joe.

Charging into the passage, I desperately cast left and right into the gloomy rooms, but they're empty.

'*Joe!*' I shout hysterically. '*Joe?*' But only silence comes back.

Pausing on the threshold of the last room, I peer inside. The darkness is too dark to see much; I can barely make anything out. I reach for my phone, flicking on the torch and swinging the beam into the shadows. The stench is appalling. Tattered filthy curtains hang limply at the window. My beam picks up small, hunched shapes, quiet figures huddled together. They're still here.

'Oh my God!' I whisper. 'Oh my God! Shh... you're okay, you're okay.' They're shrinking away from me as I crouch, inching forward, my hand outstretched.

'*Here!*' I call out. '*Jaime!*'

I kneel, shuffling forward. 'We've come to get you,' I soothe. 'You're going to be fine. Everything's going to be fine. You're going to be out of here really, really soon.'

I glance briefly over my shoulder; I need Jaime.

'A few more minutes, that's all,' I say to the girls with more confidence than I actually feel. 'We're taking you somewhere safe.'

There's a sound behind me. I look back. Melanie is standing in the doorway.

'Where's Jaime?' I demand. 'We need to move these girls and I need to find Joe. Where is he?'

She blinks blindly as though coming round from a deep sleep. I see she's shaking – her whole body is jittering. Jaime appears, putting his hands on her shoulders, turning her to face him.

'I know you're scared, but we're here now. Can you tell us what happened?' He's looking into her eyes, but she's only shivering and shaking her head.

'I... I'm sorry,' she mumbles. 'I'm so sorry... I tried...' Her gaze tracks fearfully and I scramble to my feet.

'Don't be sorry. We just need to get you and these girls to the car. Can you take care of them? I just need to find Joe. Can you tell me anything, Melanie? Anything at all?'

But Jaime is staring at the staircase. 'Have you seen this?' His eyes flinch towards me uneasily, and I feel a sick lurch.

'Blood.' He swallows. 'There's blood all up the stairs.'

'Look after the girls!' I pant. I can't get past him fast enough, my feet falling over themselves as I grab on to the banister. My phone light swings violently, my panic skyrocketing as I see the sprays of blood arcing from the steps, spattering high up the wall. The moonlit angles of shadows loom frighteningly from the long stair window.

'Joe!' I call out. 'Joe!... *Joe!* Are you here?'

But there's nothing. I fall clumsily onto a tiny square of landing with a long passageway leading off to my right. The open door to a dirty bathroom is lying straight in front.

'Joe... *Joe...*' I whisper, my voice breaking with terror at what I might find.

And then I hear a noise.

'Joe?'

Pushing open the bathroom door, the torch light bounces around the horror of the scene that unfolds before me. There on the floor amongst all the trash is Joe, his sweatshirt thick and sticky with blood, his hands grimed with it, his face a deathly grey.

'*No, no, no, no, no!*'

I drop to my knees in the wet and the filth, groaning as I reach out to touch him. All I want to do is hold him, my hands digging pathetically, dragging the trash away. Something skitters across the floor. The blade of it glints in the torchlight. It's a knife.

'*Jaime!*' I scream into the quiet. '*Jaime!* He's here. Joe's here! Help me!'

With only the light from my phone to guide me, I shuffle round to cradle his head as best I can, stroking his poor, cold face. 'Joe,' I croak. 'Joe... my boy... my boy!' My bloodied fingers slip and slide on the phone pad as I feverishly dial for an ambulance.

There's no connection.

Oh my God.

'Can you hear me? Joe? Open your eyes! Can you hear me?' My eyes snap frantically to the door. '*Jaime!*' I yell. '*Jaime!*'

Where is he?

I stare at the screen.

No service.

No. This isn't happening. This isn't. It isn't.

'Hold on, Joe... Hold on... I'm going to get someone. You stay with me, you hear me?' Pulling off my jacket, I bundle it up and place it gently beneath his head and then crawl frantically to the doorway.

'Jaime! *Melanie?!*' I shout. But there's no reply.

Floundering frantically down the stairs, I stop abruptly at the bottom, sensing a difference. The room where the girls were is empty. No Jaime. No Melanie. The dread labours high in my chest, knifing and twisting, strangling the air as something terrible, impossible, dawns.

'Jaime?' I whisper.

Grabbing at the front door, the wind from the street sweeps past my face and I blink into the space where the vehicle was parked. It's empty. I nearly drop my phone in my haste, bursting to see those tiny little bars lighting up.

'*A-Ambulance* please,' I stutter, giving the address. 'Hurry... Please hurry! I think... I think my son is... dying.'

As soon as the words are out of my mouth, the reality of what I've said hits me, punching the breath from my lungs and sending me crawling on all fours back up the stairs. Gathering him to me, I stroke the hair from his face, covering his arms with mine, trying to keep him warm.

'My love. My boy,' I murmur, kissing his forehead, his cheek, letting my tears run down his face and then wiping them away with shaking fingers. 'You can't leave me... You just can't. You're mine, you're my baby.'

Whatever he's done, whoever he is, the people he's hurt, is all here lying dying, in my arms. I gaze into the blurred whiteness of his face; I see the boy he was; I see the man he was becoming. So, so young. There was time to change: time for him to be different. It didn't have to be this way. There's a deep ticking silence that goes on forever.

There's nothing left to give. There's only a pain that squeezes in a vicious band around my heart.

'Joe. Joe...' I whisper, my lips hovering over his eyelids as a shiver, a tiny, tiny movement, tickles my skin.

I jerk back. His eyelashes flutter, almost imperceptible.

'Joe?'

A surge of joy grips me.

'Joe?'

A whirl of blue strobe light fills the stairwell and there's the tinny clatter of radios as a paramedic appears at the top of the stairs. He crouches down beside me, offering me words of kindness that make me cry and cry. He takes me gently by the arm and leads me out onto the landing while a rustling crowd of uniforms gather in a circle.

I press my spine into the wall, feeling the dig of resistance between my shoulder blades. Without the person holding me upright, I'd crumble. I'm helpless. More than helpless.

'He'll be okay?' I feverishly gaze into the face of the officer. 'He will, won't he...? Just tell me – just say he'll be okay.'

'Beth?'

Drew is standing on the top step.

'Beth! What the hell?'

A blur of bodies jostles past. He looks into the room at Joe. He glances at an officer who is dropping the knife into an evidence bag. The only thing I am aware of is the warmth and strength of the person holding me upright. Without him, my knees would buckle. The officer's expression is kind; I could collapse and weep right there and then.

'Thank you,' I say to him, but in that split second, I see Drew look to that evidence bag again and the question that passes momentarily between them.

'You can't honestly think...' I look manically from one to the other. 'You can't for one second believe...?'

'Beth... Beth, calm down!' Drew has his hand on me. 'You know how it is. You know we have to ask the difficult questions.'

My head snaps around to the doorway. All I can see are Joe's splayed sneakers between the kneeling paramedics either side.

'Let me go!' I struggle from the officer's grasp. 'Joe! Let me go to him!'

But Drew's grip tightens. 'Beth, listen! Beth. They're the professionals; let them do their job. Beth, you know the score. We have to work out what's gone on here. You have to give us your statement.'

Drew's hand on my arm moves firmly to my back as I find myself being propelled awkwardly down the stairs. The front door is open. There's a myriad of swirling lights and police radios. An officer is standing there holding a car door open as Drew bundles me towards it, dipping my head to push me inside. The door shuts with a slam and there's the clunk of the lock. He gets into the front passenger seat, swivelling around to look at me, but glancing at the officers milling about outside. I can see by his eyes what's being considered.

'Drew! This is me! You know I wouldn't hurt Joe. You know that!'

But he only scans quickly over his shoulder before speaking.

'Look, you're going to have to tell me right now what you were doing in that house.' He sounds urgent and stressed. 'I shouldn't even be having this conversation right now. The moment my colleague gets in this car, it's out of my hands, you get that? Now, tell me. What happened?'

An officer is walking towards the car. He pauses to speak to someone.

'Joe had been attacked – that's all I know,' I say quickly. 'We planned to get the girls. We found Melanie in a state of shock.

She had blood on her clothes; she kept saying she was sorry. I ran past her upstairs and found Joe. I tried to call for help, but my phone wouldn't work. When I came down, they'd gone. They'd all vanished.'

Drew looks quickly at the officer outside. 'You keep saying "*they*" and "*we*". Who's we?'

'Jaime. I came with Jaime.'

'Jaime?' Drew's face snaps in shock. 'Jaime who?'

'Lee. Jaime Lee.'

The air goes very still.

'You know Jaime Lee?' In the interior light, his face looks like a ghost.

'From the prison. He's a Listener. He's someone I trained. He got released recently—'

'What the hell are you saying, Beth? *Jaime Lee?* You're not serious?' He rubs a hand across his face. 'Tell me... *tell me* you haven't had anything to do with Lee. Tell me that you're not involved with him in any way at all.'

'Involved? What do you mean involved?' I retort hotly. 'You think that just because he's out of prison, he's—'

'*That's* who you came here with?' He skews further in his seat. 'I don't believe this. I don't believe this is happening right now.'

'But I don't get it, Drew. I don't understand what you're saying!'

'You. Don't. Understand?' He's shouting now. 'You really don't, do you? You really, honestly, don't!'

He twists viciously up in his seat, his hands coming over the headrest. His clenched fists rise and fall in frustration as though he'd like to punch me.

'You know who Jaime Lee is, *yes?* You *do* know, Beth?'

My head is shaking violently. I can't think, can't get any words out. I just want this to stop.

'*Jaime Lee. Sex offender. Trafficker.* Did ten years. Would have been a lot longer if he hadn't messed up the girls he got hold of.'

'No, Drew – you have that *all* wrong. You have that completely wrong. He was doing a sentence for murder – or, or manslaughter, I don't know. It was his *father*. He told me all of it, Drew. You have the wrong person. Totally the wrong person.'

All the time I am talking, I can feel his eyes on my face, the frown of his brow deepening. He's totally mistaken. I *know* it; I absolutely *know* it.

'Can you hear yourself?'

I hate his tone; I hate the patronising accusation of stupidity behind every syllable. I want to strike him; I want to reach out and smack that supercilious sneer from his mouth.

'We were on to Jaime Lee as soon as he was released,' he says slowly. 'But he instantly disappeared. He knew we'd be watching him. He's highly manipulative. A master at grooming. He persuaded some of his victims to give evidence in his defence – can you believe that? They were so deep into it, they thought he was caring and looking after them. That's why we knew we couldn't make anything stick. The drugs charge was the only way to get him in prison, so that's what we went for.'

No, this isn't right.

'We saw her tonight: Melanie, loading the girls into the car, but she was acting alone as far as we could see. Jaime Lee definitely wasn't with her then.'

The memory of how he parked so that we couldn't be seen in the darkness.

No, my head says. *Don't listen to this.*

'Did he ever divulge where he was staying when he was released? Did he ever tell you?'

I feel my mouth opening and closing, my brain falling over itself, but no words come out.

The officer outside shouts his goodbyes, putting his hand on the door handle. Drew glances at me, begging me to speak.

'*Beth?*' he says urgently.

The officer yanks the door wide and the car judders.

'He blinded them, Beth.'

'What?' The words have no meaning.

'Jaime Lee. Blinded some of the girls before he took them, so that they couldn't testify against him later.'

The car bounces as the officer drops into the driver's seat. 'Who's interviewing her?' He glances at Drew, reaching for the ignition.

A whole cacophony of horrifying images flash in front of my eyes. I am beyond sickness. Beyond fear.

Jaime.

Joe.

Those girls.

The images buck and sway in front of my eyes.

'I'll give you everything,' I say. 'I'll tell you anything you want to know.'

Drew and the officer share another look.

'I'll come to the station. Here—' I fumble in my pocket and pull out my keys. 'I'll need a change of clothes – you'll want the ones I'm wearing, won't you?' I can barely believe I'm saying these words. It's like a nightmare I've walked into.

We drive. I see the shopfronts moving, all lit up in the darkness; it's as though I'm in some kind of trance.

I don't ask anything. Drew doesn't speak to me again. At the station, I answer all their questions.

'Where is he? Where's Jaime Lee?' they keep asking.

'I don't know,' I answer. 'I don't know. I don't know. I don't know.'

They let me go. For now, I'm told.

It's almost dawn when I stumble blearily out onto the pavement. My head is full of whirling images: of that bathroom, the blood. Joe's white face.

Fumbling for my phone, I search for the one person I need right now.

'Robyn,' I whisper. 'It's me.' Something breaks inside. It's as though I've suddenly woken up to... *pain*. I'm choking with it. 'Something terrible – something awful... I don't... *Oh God.*' I can't get my breath.

'Beth! Thank the Lord. I've been so worried.' Her voice sounds loud in the silent street.

'Robyn, you have to help me. It's Joe.' I gulp. 'The police... Drew... Told me about Jaime. What he is. What he's done.'

'Jaime?' I hear the alarm.

'Please come and get me, Robyn, please!'

'*Shh!* Of *course*. Of course. Shh!'

'You have to come! I need to go see Joe! He's been stabbed!'

'Stabbed...?' She falters in shock. 'Joe?'

'They think I did it, Robyn. The police think I did it!'

'They can't!'

'And... And Jaime...' I can't get my thoughts together; my throat constricts. 'He's in it, Robyn. He's been in it all along.' My voice breaks. 'He's taken the girls. He's in it with Melanie. I can't believe how I've...' I start to cry harder now, trying to smother the sound.

'Okay. Okay.' Her voice is soft. 'Don't you worry now. I'm just pulling on some clothes. Hang on. Hang on in there... Keys, keys. Right. Where are you?'

'I'm outside the police station.'

'You've told them everything?'

'All of it.'

'I can't believe this,' I hear her muttering and the slam of a car door. 'Jaime, Jaime, what have you done? You must be so scared, Beth!'

I feel suddenly vulnerable and exposed standing here as though he might appear at any moment.

'Please,' I urge her. 'Can you hurry?'

'I'm literally pulling onto the main road now,' she says breathlessly. 'Just stay where you are. I'll be with you in minutes.'

I furtively glance up and down the street, pacing a little, scared that at any second I'm going to see a van, a car, with Jaime behind the wheel.

'I'm nearly there, just round the corner, Beth. I know you're frightened. Just hold on. He's not going to get you – I am.'

I scan the streets again and again, checking behind me, terrified. There's a car turning into the road up ahead, and my heart soars as I see it's her. I've got my hand on the passenger door even before she comes to a standstill, launching myself into the passenger seat and immediately shrinking down.

'Can we just get out of here?'

'Wow! Wow!' she breathes. 'You honestly don't know how good it is to see you, Beth! My goodness, when you told me about Joe! And Jaime.'

The engine whines, picking up speed. I can't even begin to articulate what's in my head.

'You'll help me, Robyn, won't you? We can go to the hospital. I need to find out what's happened to Joe!'

'Hush... Shush... Of course I'm going to help you. We'll go there now, yes? I'll go in – you can't, it might not be safe.' She glances across. 'Look at the state of you! I'll ask all the right questions, don't worry about that. I'll do everything I can, Beth. I promise you.'

The warmth of her hand clutching mine makes me want to cry. I can't stop shaking. She touches the blood that's dried on my knuckles: Joe's blood. I start to cry again.

'Here.' She pulls a packet of tissues from the centre console.

'There should be a bottle of water in the door pocket. Do the best you can.'

The water sloshes over my trembling hands. 'Who *is* Jaime, Robyn? Why didn't we know? Drew can't be right about him, can he?' I moan. 'What a mess!'

'None of that matters right this minute. None of that's important.' She looks at me sternly. 'Let's find out about Joe first. He's our priority.' Her expression softens. 'Look, Beth, I'm here now. I'll sort everything... Just look at you!' She tuts. 'You're on the point of collapse. Get some of that water down you and lie back. Close your eyes if you need to.' She looks at me with pity and disbelief. 'What you've been through, Beth. It's too much. It really is, too, too much.'

I inch my neck back, trying to ease the kinks. I can't stop myself envisioning Joe lying in that hospital without me. I gaze through the windshield at the road ribboning out. The square lines of houses loom up on either side like ghostly sentinels; their zigzagging roofs pattern out against the stark yellow flare of the passing streetlamps in the almost light. All thoughts of my son sends a tight feeling into the pit of my stomach as the fear flutters higher.

'Right, we're coming up to a main road here, Beth. Stay down, will you? If Jaime's looking for you, he'll know this will be the first place to start.'

I slide down in the seat.

'I'll just park up around the back in a side street just in case he knows my car. You wait here. It'll be safer. Okay?'

She parks up and reaches round to unclip the seatbelt.

'Remember, just stay hidden.'

She clambers out, pausing to stoop with one hand on the door.

'Hold tight. I'll be back before you know it. Joe's going to be fine, you'll see. Soon as I know anything, I'll call you.'

I peer up tentatively as she crosses in front of the bonnet. I can't make out where we are. It's a street of poor-looking terraced houses. My head is buzzing as I ease myself lower in the seat. On either side, some of the windows are boarded up. A lone streetlight flickers and goes out but the day has barely dawned. I shiver, pressing myself further into the dim interior.

'*Come on, come on, come on,*' I whisper into the quiet, my fingers fiddling with my phone. But the phone and the street stay silent. My heart feels weird: fluttery, and I have a sudden wash of vertigo where the road wavers queasily. I blink down at my phone again. There's barely a signal. Moving it around, I open the car door, tilting it this way and that, waiting for the tiny bars to move.

This is pointless, my head says. *I'm going to have to get out and walk. I can't just sit here, and...*

I stop.

I know this street.

I know where I am.

I've been here before.

This is nowhere near the hospital.

I whirl round at a sound behind me. Out of the gauzy dawn I'm aware of two figures moving in on either side. I start to back away.

Johnson.

He's found me.

I try to break into a run, but my legs feel like they are encased in lead. A weird fizzing sensation pounds in my ears and the road in front of me undulates like molten tar. The two shapes bear down, growing larger. I'm wading through treacle. My arms flounder uselessly. Their faces fade in and out as though they are made from rubber.

Then I focus.

'Robyn.'

I hear my own voice as though it's very far away. Her features slide into one another like a jigsaw puzzle. I blink at the sight of the dried blood on the front of her shirt. It crinkles in furrows in the folds of her neck.

'Blood,' I say dully.

'There you are!' another voice chimes in. 'We thought we'd lost you.'

The face comes closer: wavering in and out of focus, bobbing like a pale balloon.

'Good to see you again, Beth.'

Jaime.

His broad smile seems to cut his whole face in two.

'I told you, Beth,' Robyn chimes in, 'you don't need to worry anymore. We're going to sort it. We're going to sort everything.'

Her voice fades in and out of my consciousness.

The bottle of water, a voice in my head says. *The water.*

I try to fight it, I try to stay in the here and now, but the darkness closes in fast. It zooms in on all sides, squeezing the light out, narrowing me down to a tunnel of nothing that sends me hurtling through it at lightning speed – arms flailing, legs trailing behind, the wind stinging past my face at a rate of knots, down and down I go.

Straight into the black.

TWENTY-ONE

A shallow stream runs past me. I am aware of it chuckling over its stony bed, bubbling downstream in a never-ending wash of water.

I think I must be lying on a riverbank, the moss cushioning my hip, the sunlight warming the side of my face as I attempt to open eyes that are sticky and heavy with sleep. The glare is too bright, the lumpy dig of the moss damp and uncomfortable, the sound of the water, not chuckling, but gurgling, and behind it...

Everything begins to adjust painfully.

Behind it is the sound of someone singing.

My webbed eyes peel open.

There is no riverbank. I am not outside.

I am in a room with a single grubby window. From here, there's the line of rooftops and chimneys silhouetted against a lightening cloudy sky. I am lying on my side on a filthy mattress on the floor. The bare floorboards span away from me in dirty stripes. Right in my sightline is a single wooden chair with a box crate in front of it. Beyond that is a doorway with the door slightly ajar, the sound of water coming from the other side.

I attempt to move, but my hands are bound with a band of

plastic that digs in, raw and smarting. Lifting my head and easing my shoulder, I manage to prop myself up.

'You need to lie down and keep still.' A harsh whisper hisses from somewhere behind my head. By craning backwards, I see a huddled figure of a girl I instantly recognise as the girl from the room. She's tiny. Her eyes look huge in the heart-shaped face.

'Pretend to be asleep. Close your eyes. It's better that way.' I hear the fear.

'Where are we?' I whisper back.

But her head only moves back and forth, silently.

'What's your name?' I try again. 'I'm Beth.'

Her mouth opens, her eyes flickering pointedly to the doorway where the drum of the water is punctuated by the out-of-tune singing.

'Kate... I'm Katie,' she manages, swallowing hard. 'You... You're the one who said you'd come to rescue us, aren't you?' She glances again at the door.

'Where are the others, Katie? Are they in there?'

But she only shakes her head again, tight-lipped. The sound of the water stops, and she eases herself further into the wall. I lie down quickly, feigning sleep, burying my face in the filthy ticking, letting my hair fall over my eyes. Through half-closed lids, I watch the doorway. There's the muted sound of someone talking; the voice is female, but I can't make out what she's saying. Suddenly, Melanie appears with a dark-haired girl, no more than fifteen, following her. The girl is wrapped in a dressing gown, with a towel, turban-style, covering her head. Her skin is so white it's almost translucent.

'What's mine like, then?'

Melanie ignores the question, guiding her to the chair and pushing her to sit before picking up a wide-toothed comb.

'Nice.' She begins to untangle the locks of wet hair. 'They're all nice,' she adds.

'You met him?'

'No.'

'You seen him then?'

Melanie pretends she hasn't heard.

'Is he handsome? Is he lush?' The girl smirks in the mirror and begins to giggle.

'There might be a whole lot of them in the room when you go in,' Melanie says carefully. 'They're all lush.'

'What? I get to choose the one I like the most?' The girl swivels round in the chair and Melanie has to push her to face the mirror again.

'Yeah, you'll get to choose,' she says steadily. 'Remember, you're in charge.' She reaches down to the floor where a hairdryer is lying, switching it on, and begins to dry the girl's hair.

I watch, keeping completely still. Melanie looks lost in some world of her own as she combs and combs the girl's hair, transforming it into a long, black, shimmering tide.

'Look at me, Libby,' Melanie says. She puts her fingers under the girl's chin and lifts her face, pushing the strands of hair away from her forehead. 'You're strong and sexy, yeah?' She smiles. 'You're going to have them all wrapped round your little finger.'

Libby smiles happily back at her. 'Am I having lashes?'

'Yeah, you're having lashes.'

Melanie sounds like a mother talking to a little child. She walks around to the crate and pulls out a bag of makeup, tipping it into Libby's lap, and picking up a bottle of foundation and a palette of blusher. Within minutes, the pale cheeks are transformed into a doll's face, the lips slicked and painted into a huge cupid's bow, and the eyes spiked black with cow-like lashes. She's no longer a child, but a parody of a woman. An ache yawns in my gut.

'You're done.' Melanie stands back to admire her handiwork. 'I'll take you through to get changed. You'll see a coat hanger with your name on it. Just put the stuff on and then put your dressing gown over the top 'cos you'll freeze. Okay?'

Libby smiles excitedly, the slash of red like a violent abuse.

'Am I prettier than the other girls?'

'What?' Melanie scowls.

'Have you made me prettier than the others? Am I worth more?' Libby's eyes are big and pleading.

'Yeah, you're the prettiest,' Melanie says offhandedly, packing the makeup back into the bag.

'So, has mine got money? Will he take me on holiday?'

'What?'

'Will he buy me stuff?'

Melanie shakes her head, irritated. 'Not if you keep talking so much.' The girl widens her eyes. 'Men don't like girls who talk a lot.' She takes her to a door over in the corner and glances back at me. I don't move.

'I won't be a minute,' she says to Katie. 'It's your turn next.' She opens it. Beyond I can make out a shadowy landing space and the top of a stairwell.

The door clicks closed behind them, and I snap a look up.

'The girls are told they have to make themselves pretty or they won't get a man to like them,' Katie whispers. 'They've all been told that. They all believe it.'

I stare at her in horror.

'You said about rescue; they don't want to be rescued. They think that these men are going to give them a good life and treat them nice.'

'*Katie,*' I hiss in disbelief. 'They can't believe that, surely?'

'Oh they do.' She nods, dumbly. 'Have you seen their lives? Any way out and they'll take it.'

'But you don't think the same?' I whisper.

'Lib and I were in care together.' She sniffs. 'We sneaked off to go to an afterparty she knew about.'

My heart and stomach collide.

'I got talking to this lad.'

My gut tumbles.

'I thought he was gonna be my boyfriend. He said he ran all these gigs in Ibiza, and he picked out girls to do promotional stuff.'

Katie, no.

'He said I could do any kind of modelling because I was pretty. He introduced me to this agent fella, Tom.'

'Tom?' My lips articulate the name. 'Tom Johnson?'

She nods quickly. 'I thought it was safe when I met the promoter 'cos she was a woman. A woman wouldn't let bad things happen, would she? Only this one, Robyn... she would.'

The room swirls. I can't wake up.

'The girls won't believe what's happening, even if you tell them. They've been told stories of living in big houses, or becoming a dancer, or a singer – so that's what they think.'

'And the guy, the guy you said was your boyfriend...' My heart shivers. 'What happened to him?'

'He started off being nice, but then got more and more nasty. Robyn had him doing all sorts to the girls – the ones they decided to punish for being mouthy.' She turns her face away. 'Only one day he went too far, and the girl tried to run away.' She looks towards the door. 'Only they...'

'Only they what?'

'They caught her.'

She looks at me with massive, frightened eyes.

'They hanged her.'

There's no oxygen in the room.

'Who did?'

'Robyn hanged her to show the girls what happens. And they sliced the boy as punishment for being too soft. Robyn sliced Joe up.' She nods again.

Robyn.

I stare at her. My mouth opens. The scream has stuck in my throat.

'But they're not taking me this time.' She shocks me back. I realise her gaze has locked onto mine. 'They're not touching me again.' She wraps her arms protectively around her thin body. 'You have to take that bit of yourself, and lock it away somewhere safe. They think they've got you, but it's only the bit on the outside. You have to find a way to disappear inside yourself where they can't find you.'

'This time, Katie, you really are going to disappear,' I say, quiet and forceful. 'I'm going to make sure of it.'

But her eyes don't move. Only her hand comes up to rest on her knee. 'You don't need to help me. I have this.'

Between her fingers there's something tiny and silver.

It's a blade.

She turns her wrist over, showing me the whiteness of her skin with the glassy pale blue veins in rivulets just beneath the surface.

'You cut this way.' She runs the tip of her finger from the elbow crease down towards her palm. 'If you're serious.'

'Katie—'

'And I'm serious.'

There's the sound of voices on the other side of the door and Melanie appears.

'Come on.' She beckons to Katie. 'All you've got to do is get changed. They don't want you made-up. We'll just put a brush through that birds' nest,' she jokes.

Katie wobbles into a crouch and then stands, shakily. She's dressed in a man's shirt. There's deep purple bruising up her thigh that's turning to yellow, and a reddened criss-cross of cuts around both knees. The band of pain around my heart tightens.

She shuffles stiffly forward as though she hasn't used her legs in a long time. I glance at her hand and see the glint of the razor hidden between her fingers.

She staggers a little and winces as Melanie grabs her arm. As she does so, my eyes catch a tiny flicker of silver that skims the hem of her shirt and tinkles unnoticed to the floor. My eyes snap up to Melanie.

'You don't make life easy for yourself, do you?' she admonishes. 'All you have to do is go along with things. That's not so hard, is it?'

Katie glances back at me. Her look is hard and piercing.

'Bye,' she says in a tiny voice.

I know my voice will fail me if I try to speak as I watch her being guided away.

Quickly levering myself up, I shuffle forward to where the sliver of razor glitters on the bare wood. Easing my foot out of one sneaker, I tread down the band of my sock until the material wrinkles and sags, letting me wriggle it off. Inching my bare foot across the floor, I feel for the cold metal under my toes. Taking a breath, I pray that I don't slice myself to pieces as I slide it forward, gently inching it into a gap between the boards. I rub the plastic tie on my wrists back and forth on the blade, praying desperately.

There's a quiet click – and the plastic gives. My heart misses a beat. *A couple more... just a couple more,* I beg, and suddenly my hands spring apart. I'm so shocked, I can't move for a second, but then grab for my sneaker, fishing for the blade and slipping it into the cuff of my sleeve.

The sound of a shower drowns out the creak of my footsteps as I tiptoe towards the door. Easing it open, I peer out, cautiously. It's a long, bare landing space. There's another door across the way, slightly ajar, and the sound of girls laughing. Through the gap there are the shadows of movement: more laughter, and the clatter of hangers on a rail. A waft of sweet perfume filters along the passage and more giggling. *Girls playing dress-up.* The tread of footsteps on the wooden stairs jerks me back.

It's Jaime.

'Oh well done you!' he's saying. 'What a bombshell you were. You did brilliantly!'

'Do you think they liked me?' Libby's voice rings out. 'I hope they did!'

'Of course they did. They loved you. I mean, who wouldn't?' He's holding her hand as he guides her forward towards the door.

'A real princess!' he declares, pushing it wide.

There are squeals of excitement as the rest of them gather around her, squawking, begging to know how she got on.

'All the details!' I hear one of them saying. 'Right from the beginning!'

Jaime pauses to lean in the open doorway, arms crossed, pleased with himself as he surveys the girls' shouts of delight. There are five in total, including Katie, who doesn't move. She's crouched against the far wall, her arms wrapped tightly around her knees. Jaime's head moves slowly around like a searchlight.

'You, Trouble,' he says pointing to her. 'You're next.'

Katie struggles up, trying to walk in shoes that are much too high.

'Bare feet,' Jaime orders. 'You'll look younger.'

I press myself back into the doorway as he guides her down the stairs. She's wearing a simple white shift dress. His voice booms into the hallway, and I tip forward a little to crane over the banister.

I hear a door opening: I think it must be under the stairs. From here a dim yellow light pools out across the hallway. There's the scuff of feet on the tiled floor.

'There's no point doing all that again!' Jaime barks. 'Do you wanna go down there and say hello to your friend again?'

'I'm not scared of you. I'm past being scared.' Katie's voice rings out, bold now. 'I see what you are. I know what you're doing.'

A door squeals open, and from between the banisters I glimpse a long red carpet with a divan bed covered with cushions. There are lights set up on either side and three cameras. A laptop is sitting on a table. Robyn walks forward.

'Are we ready?'

She guides Katie to the bed before drawing out a chair in front of the laptop. There's a Skype dialling code and then I see Robyn break into a broad grin as the multi-screen shots fill with men's faces.

'Hello there and welcome!' she says brightly. 'Finally! Sorry about the delay, we've had a few technical issues, but it's all sorted now. Thanks so much for registering your interest. Wow! There's a lot of you!' She laughs. 'I can tell you this next one is the best of this particular bunch, and that's why we're asking for sealed bids. We think it's only fair. We'll go through all her particulars—'

I hear the twitter of one of the clients asking a question.

'Yes. Oh yes... she's been broken in. We wouldn't be passing them on if they hadn't.' The sound of Robyn's voice fades to a low murmur as Jaime closes the door.

I need to act, and act now. Glancing round, I creep down the first two stairs. Snapping a look behind and down the hallway, I edge my way down to the front door. It's old and solid, with a fanlight window letting in a semi-circle of half-light. My fingers pat over the wooden panel, feeling for the catch – it turns, but the door holds fast. Frantically combing the door, I find a deadlock. The bolt squeals in protest as I attempt to draw it back, when the sound of Jaime's voice sends me whirling round.

'Humiliate me, would you?' he's screaming. 'I warned you, bitch! You wanna screw me over? I'll show you what screwing over means!'

The cellar door is sitting open and I dive inside, crouching into the shadows. Peering through the gap, I see Jaime savagely dragging Katie by the arm along the hallway, closely followed by Robyn.

There's a sudden loud crack. I wince at the sound, sure that it's a bone snapping in two. Katie cries out: a shrill, keening scream. Jaime is shrieking obscenities as I hear the blows raining down: I can almost feel the fists whistling through the air.

Her screams stop.

There's only deathly quiet.

I screw my eyes tight shut, burying my head deeper into my wrapped arms, steeling myself, holding on, tighter than tight.

I'm aware of voices. A sudden shock of brilliant light pours over me and I startle a look up.

'Ohhh!' Jaime says almost cheerfully. 'Aren't you the clever girl?'

I can't move. My spine has frozen. My eyes flit into the hallway. Katie's bloodied body, like a broken puppet, is lying at the bottom of the stairs. Melanie is cowering on the step above her. The rest of the girls have gathered behind, silent and wide-eyed.

Robyn holds on to the banister for balance as she toes Katie's hip.

'This is what happens—' She prods her a little more. 'To mouthy girls.'

There isn't a sound.

'I know you're not all like this silly girl here! I know some of you are really clever and can see the opportunities available. Let's sort out the cream from the crowd, shall we? Which of you are the real businesswomen and want to make some serious cash?'

A couple of eyes flicker downwards.

'Come on, you lot! Didn't you hear what I said? Come on! One of you must have something about you. Where's your drive and ambition? Don't sell yourselves cheap – there's a whole lot of guys just desperate to spend their money!' Robyn catches Jaime's eye and they share the private joke.

'I will!' Libby stands up on the top step. 'I'll have a go.'

'Good girl!' Robyn beams.

'*No!*' I suddenly jerk into life. '*No! Stop!* Don't you see what they're doing? They're *selling* you! Don't you get that?'

Libby stands there, staring down, uncertain for a second, then she shakes her hair back in some appalling parody of a photoshoot.

'"'Cos we're worth it",' she parrots, giggling. 'Isn't that right, Robyn?'

'You're all worth every penny!' She chuckles, winking at me. 'See, Beth? You come in here on your progressive women's white charger, thinking you're going to save everyone.' Her palm sweeps grandly over the girls. 'And what do you find? You find no one wants to be saved. They're all sensible, that's why: strong, intelligent girls, all capable of deciding what they do and don't want for themselves.'

'They're *kids*,' I spit back. '*No more than children.*'

'Some women are children too, you're right.' She smiles down at me. 'Gullible. Desperate to believe anything a man says to them. Always selling themselves short and then whinging when they get a raw deal. At least these ones have their heads screwed on. They know what the market is offering; they know the precious service they can deliver. This is true free market forces in action – I mean, watch this!'

Robyn marches along the hallway and reaches for the bolt. 'Now. Observe closely.'

She stands back, opening the door wide; the cool air gushes in.

'Anyone that wants to leave, can.' She gestures out of the door. 'Go on, no one is stopping any of you. Look... I'll stand right back over here. No pressure.'

No one moves.

'See?' She looks at me with a casual tilt of the head. 'No bars or bolts required. That's the thing with girls.' She narrows her eyes. 'It's all about hearts and minds. Once you've firmly captured a girl in here, and in here—' Her hand goes to her heart and then to her temple. 'They're yours. Probably for the rest of their lives. And you haven't had to do a thing. You're all career women, aren't you?' She loudly addresses the mute, pale faces before turning to me. 'They all know their worth, just like Libby says.'

'Unlike you, Beth,' Jaime says quietly.

The sound of him saying my name makes me flinch.

'All that running around trying to save your son, trying to save me – rescuing people to make them "better", when what you're really trying to do is to fill that great black empty hole of nothingness inside yourself. You know it, I suspect Drew knew it and I think your son definitely did.' He bends and puts his face close to mine, forcing me to look at him.

'The problem is, Beth, people can smell it on you.' He breathes in, deeply. 'That stink of desperation, the need to be loved. They shy away from it. The fact is, you suffocate people and so they can't stand it. They can't stand *you*.'

I'm crying now: with fear, with grief.

You're going to die, the certainty inside me says. *You can't save anyone; you can't even save yourself.*

'You're twisted; you're depraved. You killed Leo,' I whisper. 'You hurt my son. You did that.'

'Oh, for God's sake! Leo killed himself,' Robyn retorts. 'Pure stupidity, *that's* what killed Leo, and please don't bring up your boring son. Him!' Robyn rolls her eyes heavenward. 'I cut him from gizzard to craw.' She smilingly traces a line up to her neck.

'And so you plan to murder me too, do you?' I counter shakily. 'And you think it's that easy? I'm not a child like Joe. I'm not a poor kid, like these girls, with no one and nothing—'

'I'm bored now!' Jaime interjects. 'Let's get these girls back upstairs. Melanie, get to it will you? I've got one body to cut down and one to string up.' He laughs. 'Come on, you – move.'

His knee pushes hard into my shoulder, shoving me down the cellar step. I glance back at Melanie. She has her arm around one of the girls who's crying. They look like thin, shivering ghosts.

'Come on! Get a move on!' Jaime boots me again, my feet slithering beneath me on the wooden steps. I grope at the empty darkness, my hands scrabbling against the brickwork. A sudden metallic ping of a light switch, and the steps beneath me illuminate. An electric bulb swings the walls into weirdly bobbing shadows. There's a gust: a stench rising up in waves as his hand reaches, grabbing me roughly round the back of the neck, and dragging me down to the bottom.

I flail blindly as the stench gains momentum: billowing up in thick reeking clouds as I retch and retch again.

Feet.

My sight suddenly fixes: bare blue toes suspended in mid-air. I see the grey-tinged skin, the mottled network of red tramlines on grey shins. I gag.

'You've never seen a suicide then? Not close up.' Jaime's feet stutter in front of me; his grip tightens on the nape of my neck. 'That's about right for your sort. You don't have a clue, do you? Talk about it all the time, yada yada yada. It'll be good for you to have some first-hand experience.' I hear the crackle of paper and his hand dips to wave something in front of my face. 'Here.'

My eyes blur and focus. I see the handwriting; it's mine, but I can't make out the words.

'As soon as I saw it, I thought it would come in useful for something – only at the time I didn't know what.'

The haze of words becomes sharp.

I don't think I can forgive myself. I've driven everyone away. I can't see any way out of this mess. I'm completely alone.

The paper swings in front of me. Jaime's vice-like grip loosens and I manage to lift my head. Something inside me plummets. The body bobs and sways. Her hair, bedraggled and matted, hangs over the bloated mess of her face. Her tongue protrudes, monstrous and purpled from between her swollen lips. There, hanging right alongside her, is a second noose.

My arms thrash in panic, instinctively lurching to try to make it back to the bottom step, but Jaime grabs my ankles, hauling me back. I fight, kicking out, yelling and screaming, but he snatches me with such force, my jaw hits the concrete and for a moment all I can see are stars.

The room spins; the shadows and the light dance as I feel my legs immobilised in some iron grip. I try to fight, but all the energy drains from me. His hands are everywhere, constricting my movements, pinning me down, holding me fast. I can't wrestle free as he expertly flips me upright and I feel the thick, knotty coarseness of a rope being slipped around my neck. The revolving room comes back in a rush of certainty of what's about to happen – and suddenly I am on my feet, the slack of the rope heavy on my shoulder before I feel its bite.

I can't breathe.

I gasp. As he hauls me higher, my hands come up, clawing as I choke. *Air, air.* My lungs burn.

Jaime's face looms in front of me, panting. 'There's a chair here.'

I hear the squeal and drag of wood.

'Climb it; it'll loosen the pressure.'

My windpipe is collapsing, there's a pounding of blood in my ears and my eyes bulge and pop, stinging with my own heartbeat, but I shake my head furiously.

'No. Won't—' My voice comes out thin and strangulated. 'They'll know... that I didn't do this to myself...' I hiss, but Jaime only smiles and increases the tension.

My jawbone creaks in a shriek of bone; my teeth squeal and

grind, clamped so hard I think they might shatter. A strange noise begins to gargle from between my lips. But even as my head is screaming, my feet are clambering wildly, looking for the chair edge. My knees jerk and dance and Jaime moves the chair closer. In that split second, I'm up and on it, the breath thundering into my lungs as I gulp and gulp, knowing the sadistic game – and I'm playing right into it.

He reaches again for the rope – high up this time, his shirt-sleeves falling back, his gleaming teeth bubbling with spittle at his delight, giggling as his fingers close around the rope and the blood in my ears begins to sing again.

But his expression stalls. I know his eye sees it before he feels it.

There's the sudden spring of brilliant deep red. The spray is vertical, a raining shower of red heat that patters against my cheek. Jaime turns his head in shock, as there's another spurt that jets in an arc from his neck across the ceiling. His mouth opens in sheer surprise, the blood staining the white of his bared teeth, as fear flares up in his eyes.

He lets go, falling backwards, and I fall too, gasping and coughing, sucking at the air: dear sweet, glorious air, slipping clean and cold into my lungs.

The tiny blade flickers from between my fingers; it tinkles prettily onto the concrete as I crawl choking towards the stairs, not pausing to look back, only hearing the gargling groan of Jaime's death rattle echoing behind me.

Each stair edge is agony, but I reach up for the door bolt, my hands slipping on the handle as I wrench it, scrabbling out into the hallway.

Katie's body is lying there, her bare feet, so small, so innocent. I pause to touch the hem of her dress, pulling it straight – and her cheek: so soft, so young, once so full of life. So full of fighting spirit.

They did this.

They.

They did this to all of us: Joe, Leo, me. All these girls.

I am galvanised by a fury. A lava-hot, blazing rage as I charge up the stairs, bursting into the room, the anger in my heart so huge, I could tear down walls with the force of its blast.

Robyn wheels round. There's a girl in front of her pirouetting, half-naked and smiling, her shoulder so tiny under the weight of Robyn's controlling hand.

Shock is written all over her face as I barrel into her, knocking her sideways, screaming for Melanie as she hits the floor.

'Melanie!' I scream at the top of my lungs. 'Fight back! For once in your life, fight back!' I'm yelling her name over and over. 'Don't let them do this to you...! Fight!'

I almost can't believe it when Melanie's dark hair flies in front of me as she barges me out of the way. She's like something possessed. The room shimmers with heat: pure, raging fury as she claws and punches, teeth snapping, a frenzied punching and kicking, ripping at any bit of Robyn she can get hold of.

Robyn's screams rend the air, a high-pitched gibberish, as Libby comes out of nowhere, pouncing like a cat, throwing herself into the melee, tearing at her clothes, biting and kicking and stamping wherever she can. Robyn manages to turn on her side, curling into a ball for protection, her hands coming up to shield her head as suddenly the other girls join in, picking up anything they can find, stabbing and beating, the howls for mercy stifled amidst the shrill hysteria as they unleash every ounce of revenge on her soft flesh.

I pull back a little, panting. Robyn senses my movement; a sudden leap and a roar and she's up off the floor, clamouring for a way out. With a frantic shriek, she makes a run at the window, crashing through the glass in a blaze of blood and shards as she disappears into a whiteness of sky.

There's silence.

It's as though we've all been turned off by a switch. The only sound is our laboured breathing. No one moves; we don't look at each other.

I stare at Libby, crouched there, fingertips poised, staring at the floor as though she's just woken from a kind of dream.

The cool morning air gusts through the broken window, bringing with it the moaning of sirens. The sound barely breaks through my consciousness.

I have no sense of my body: no arms or legs or head. I am a thing made of stone, the blood drying on my skin as it tightens like a glove.

Somewhere, behind me, there's the thunder of feet on the stairs and the panicked shrill of voices calling for assistance. I am frozen here: trapped in this space, unable to move or speak, as though I'm only aware of what's going on around me through a thick plate of glass. People are talking, asking, explaining – but it has no meaning. They're all muffled and very far away.

'Beth.'

Someone is saying my name. I could be dreaming; I'm not sure.

'Do you want to know?'

My eyes shift dully. Drew is standing at my side. His hand is outstretched. I follow it and realise it's touching my arm. He's talking to me: asking me to do things – trying to get me to speak. There are no words.

'Do you want to know about Joe?'

My neck creaks round to look at him; his eyes are kind, concerned. I see something there that I haven't seen in a very long time.

Drew's grip tightens and releases.

'I went to see him. I went to see Joe.'

I'm fully awake.

'It's okay. He's okay. He's pulled through. He unconscious, but he's holding his own.'

I let his words flood over me.

'The hospital gave me his phone. He was tracking you, remember? I wanted to make sure you were okay. I followed you and found yours smashed in the street outside.'

He's telling me things, asking me questions. I have a blanket around my shoulders, but I don't know how it got there. My eyes shift to the girls. There are three officers, tending them, stooping in turn, talking gently to them in hushed tones. They're wrapping them in blankets too; I see their endless gestures of reassurance and hear their kind words. The girls watch them, dazed, as though they've just woken from a coma.

'You're very brave,' a police officer is saying to one of them. 'How old are you, my love?'

'Almost fifteen,' the girl whispers, her eyes batting slowly. 'Tomorrow's my birthday.'

'Well, happy birthday for tomorrow,' the officer says, smiling, glancing over and catching my eye. I see a whole raft of emotion in the look: disguised disbelief, horror, shock, anger at what these girls have been through. Oh yes, anger: I know that emotion. I've held on to it for so long. It gave me the strength do what I've done; it gave me the fury to never give in.

'You're okay, my sweet,' says the officer, helping one of the girls up. 'We found you. We've got you now.' She catches my eye again, holding out her hand for me too. 'It's a good job you found each other.'

There's something about the way she says those words that sends a great wash of overwhelming grief from the base of my stomach to the back of my throat. I can't stop it; it's like a tide I can't hold back. I see the shock on Drew's face as I grab hold of the woman's hand, hanging on for dear life, and let the tears come.

TWENTY-TWO

They let me sit at Joe's bedside.

He's a mass of tubes and bandages. There are scans and charts and nurses and doctors telling me how lucky he is to still be here. I know I'm the lucky one because despite my own injuries, I still have a son.

I listen to the bleeps of the machines that tell me he's doing okay while he's sedated. I hold his hand and stroke his face and tell him that I love him, no matter what.

I haven't been back to my house.

I've had to ask Sarah to go and get some of my things because I can't set foot in the place. I've given Nate my car. I don't want that either. Everything in my life feels tainted right now: a reminder of the person I no longer am, or actually want to be.

'You alright, Beth, love? Want a cuppa?'

A nurse rustles past me, hooking the chart onto the bottom of Joe's bed. 'Marion will be round with the trolley in a bit. I've asked her to bring some sandwiches in.' She winks. 'You look like you could do with feeding up.'

'Thank you.' I smile. 'That'd be nice.'

'You only got discharged a couple of days ago, didn't you? Have you been home yet? You should, you know. We'll look after Sonny-Jim here, don't you worry.'

'I know. I just prefer to stay.'

'Okay.' She smiles.

I watch her as she checks the tubes and bags and monitors attached to my son.

'Beth', as she was, doesn't exist anymore. I stand up straighter, look people clearly in the eye. I say what I want and what I don't want. I don't apologise for how I feel. There is no Drew, no marriage, no recriminations, no talking, no arguing. Nothing. I am my own person. I will take responsibility for me. I have a son who is nearly an adult, and as an adult, he too will take responsibility for what he's done.

When Joe comes round, he'll be interviewed. He'll know all the things I've told the police. He'll find out that both Jaime and Robyn are dead and there's just him and Tom Johnson left carrying the can. He will be charged; I'll make sure of that. He will also make reparations to the girls he's abused; I'll make sure of that too.

'Oh! Looks like there's a visitor for you!'

I follow the nurse's gaze. Melanie is standing in the doorway.

'Alright, darlin'?' the nurse says.

'Is it okay?' She gestures.

She looks different: she's cut her hair. Somehow it makes her look even younger. I stand up to welcome her. She seems awkward and uncomfortable as though I couldn't possibly want to see her.

'Don't be silly,' I say. 'Come in.'

She drags a chair over, wincing at the sound and glancing at Joe.

'They're going to bring him out of sedation soon.'

She doesn't answer.

'Melanie...' I start.

'How is he?' She looks nervously at his still form.

'He's okay. He's doing well... Physically,' I add.

'Then the police will want to talk to him?' Her eyes lock onto mine.

'Melanie. What he did to you—'

'No, what *I* did,' she interjects. 'What I went along with.' She shakes her head in disgust. 'Nadia said I should come and see you. I mean, I wanted to anyway, but—'

'Nadia?' And then the name registers. 'Ohh, from Victim Support, Nadia. You've seen her then?'

'We all have.' Melanie nods enthusiastically. 'All the girls. She's been great. Really great.' Her cheeks turn pink. 'And that's why—' She pauses. 'I came to say I'm sorry. I need you to know.'

I hold my hand out to her. She glances at my palm before tentatively taking it.

'Melanie, look at me.'

Her eyes manage a cautious sweep upward.

'You are not to blame. You are not to blame for anything that happened.'

'That's what Nadia says, but I am. I let things happen, things I knew weren't right... Things that made me feel sick, but I pushed those feelings away. I did that. I did it.'

'You weren't the one in control. You were being groomed and manoeuvred. You thought you met Joe by accident. You didn't. You were coerced.'

Her eyes dart. I'm nodding to reassure her. 'Tom Johnson, the officer, already knew he could pull your strings because of Leo. They primed you. They primed Joe. There were no coincidences. They used me to legitimise and cover up what they were doing. If it helps you to hear, I pushed for one of the worst child sex offenders to be moved back onto the wing. He would have given them all his victim contacts. I did that, Melanie. *Me.* No one else.' I look away at the memory. 'I even helped an officer carry a load of prisoner files. The files were for Johnson. I carried the names and horrific details of the crimes and handed them over to a monster.'

'But you couldn't've known!' She looks at me, shocked. 'That officer couldn't've known!'

'Exactly. And neither could you. And that's precisely what Nadia is getting at.'

Her eyes widen with quiet realisation.

'Your evidence against Johnson is vital, Melanie. You're the one person who links this whole thing. All you have to do is tell them what happened to you.'

'But I helped Joe,' she interrupts. 'I encouraged those girls to get involved, so what does that make me?' She looks across at Joe lying in the bed and nods her head firmly. 'I'll have to take what's coming, but...'

'What?'

'Will they do you and me for murder though?'

The baldness of the statement shocks me. I almost can't believe what took place in that room, in that house. It feels like some nightmare that never really happened.

'We were in fear for our lives,' I say, parroting Drew. 'We'd been drugged and abused and kidnapped. We were acting in self-defence.'

She says nothing for a moment then quickly pushes her chair back and stands.

'Thank you for seeing me. Thank you for being nice to me.'

My eyes scan her face. 'Keep in contact, won't you, Melanie? I want to know how you are.'

She nods briefly, stooping to plant a tiny kiss on my cheek. There's a moment of warmth from her breath and then I'm left alone with the bleeps and the clicks.

Suddenly, and for no reason, I need to breathe real air. I need to get out. I meet a surprised-looking woman in the corridor with a cup of tea in one hand and a plate of sandwiches in the other.

'I'm just popping out for a while. I'll be back soon,' I tell her, hurrying down the ward towards the lifts.

The main hospital doors swish open and I greedily gulp down the cold that hits my face. The world feels alien: unfamiliar, as though I've never set foot in it before. Stepping off the kerb, I begin to walk towards the exit, not knowing where I'm going.

'Taxi, love?'

There's a chap leaning against the side of his cab, smoking a cigarette.

'I'll do you a deal wherever you wanna go.' He grins at me toothily.

'Okay,' I say automatically.

'All yours,' he says, opening the rear door.

I slide into the potpourri perfumed interior.

'Where we off to, then?' He glances at me in the rear-view mirror.

In that moment I know exactly where I want to go.

My mother's house looks just as it always has. The front lawn is shorn to scorched earth, and the plants in the circular bed have precisely six inches of completely weed-free soil between each one. I smile as the cab draws up to the driveway, but my smile fades to something else that wobbles dangerously in the back of my throat.

I pay the driver, pausing to stand and gaze at the house for a moment as he wheels round and drives away. The birds sound the same. The clouds look the same. The front door sits there, just as always. I take hesitant steps towards it, feeling as though this is the first time I have been here. I raise my hand to knock, but I don't need to as the door opens under my knuckles and my mother's worried face appears in the gap. I find myself doing something I have never done before, not in my whole life, and certainly something I could never imagine: I collapse into her arms and I let her hold me while I cry.

A LETTER FROM THE AUTHOR

Dear reader,

Huge thanks for reading *The Son* – I hope you were hooked on Beth and Joe's journey. If you want to join other readers in hearing all about my new releases and bonus content, you can sign up for my newsletter.

www.stormpublishing.co/elena-wilkes

If you enjoyed this book and could spare a few moments to leave a review, that would be hugely appreciated. Even a short review can make all the difference in encouraging a reader to discover my books for the first time. Thank you so much!

The Son came about after having eavesdropped on a conversation between a mother and her seventeen-year-old son.

I have to say it was a rather shocking exchange: the boy was severely berating his mother, telling her that she had repeatedly 'failed' various petty duties, and he felt that he was 'owed' an explanation. The whole time she remained calm and pleasant, while attempting to reason with him.

It was in equal measures appalling but also a fascinating instance of pure misogyny. I remember thinking that if the seventeen-year-old had been her partner and not her son, then the exchange would be instantly recognisable as an abusive, coercive, controlling relationship and one (you would hope) she found the strength to walk away from.

However, this was her son. There would be no question of leaving and she could never just 'walk away'. The best she could probably hope for, I suppose, was that he would 'grow out of it', somehow, and realise his behaviour was unacceptable.

But what if he didn't? What would happen if his behaviour became much, much worse?

That was the central question: how far would Beth go to save her son?

Thanks again for being part of this amazing journey with me and I hope you'll stay in touch – I have so many more stories and ideas to entertain you with!

ELENA WILKES

facebook.com/elenawilkesthrillers
twitter.com/elenathrillers

ACKNOWLEDGMENTS

Writing is such a rollercoaster of a business.

The difference between a manuscript sitting in a file some-where and gathering virtual dust and actually being out there in the world are the people who make that happen. So, firstly, thank you to Kathryn Taussig at Storm Publishing for taking on *The Son*. These are very unpredictable times, so to have your work recognised right now is massive. I really can't say thank you enough.

Again, a huge thank you to Kathryn and also to Sara Jafari for their super, spot-on editorial. Your comments and observa-tions were very astute and exactly right. I hope I've done them justice.

Thank you to the Storm team. Wow! You have been amaz-ing! The cover design is stunning, and the marketing and publicity people are totally on-the-ball. Storm really are that breath of fresh air in the publishing world.

Thank you, of course, to my three bestest writing buddies: Amy Beashel, Tess James-Mackey, and Ko Richardson. Your support, encouragement, Prosecco and crisps at 5 p.m. actually do mean the world. Love you lots.

Thank you too to Jenny Blackhurst and her terrifyingly sharp interrogation on plot points. There's a woman who can scare me into writing the story I need to be writing.

And thank you to my husband, Ian, for putting up with me when I'm writing (and every other time) and who manages to survive the 'death stare' when I'm furiously typing and all he's said is, 'Would you like a cup of tea?' I really couldn't do any of it without you.

Made in the USA
Columbia, SC
16 October 2023

24513407R00193